The Black Widow Clique

The Black Widow Clique

Genesis Woods

www.urbanbooks.net

Urban Books, LLC
300 Farmingdale Road, NY-Route 109
Farmingdale, NY 11735

The Black Widow Clique

Copyright © 2018 Genesis Woods

All rights reserved. No part of this book may be reproduced in any form or by any means without prior consent of the Publisher, except brief quotes used in reviews.

ISBN 13: 978-1-945855-67-2
ISBN 10: 1-945855-67-3

First Mass Market Printing December 2018
First Trade Paperback Printing May 2018
Printed in the United States of America

10 9 8 7 6 5 4 3 2 1

This is a work of fiction. Any references or similarities to actual events, real people, living or dead, or to real locales are intended to give the novel a sense of reality. Any similarity in other names, characters, places, and incidents is entirely coincidental.

Distributed by Kensington Publishing Corp.
Submit Orders to:
Customer Service
400 Hahn Road
Westminster, MD 21157-4627
Phone: 1-800-733-3000
Fax: 1-800-659-2436

Melonee

"Happy anniversary, honey."

The word floated through the air and pulled me from my train of thought. I was sitting in front of my vanity, brushing my hair and thinking about my life, when my husband of two years walked up behind me and slipped his arms around my waist and kissed my neck.

"Happy anniversary to you too, love," I said and smiled as I looked at him through the mirror. "I'll be ready to leave in ten minutes."

"No need to rush." He released me and stepped back. "As a matter of fact, I was hoping you still wanted to stay in tonight. I'll have Lupe prepare us a romantic dinner, and then we can just enjoy each other for the rest of our evening."

I turned around to face him. "I wish you would've said something earlier, babe. I already sent Lupe and everyone else home for the night. I didn't want any interruptions after we came back from dinner, when I changed into the little surprise I picked up for you from Frederick's today."

He bit his thin bottom lip, then lifted my hand up to his mouth and kissed the back of it, trailing a path of light pecks all the way up to my collar. After he inhaled the scent of the Chloe Love Story perfume he had given to me earlier, I felt the moan that escaped from his throat vibrate against my neck.

"Hmmm. You know I love the way that fragrance smells on your skin. What are you trying to do to me, woman?"

I stood up from my stool and wrapped my arms around his neck. Looking into his forest-green eyes, I saw the same sparkle he always had whenever he was trying to sample a taste of my goodies. I brushed my fingers across his tanned olive skin, admiring how smooth and wrinkle free it was. No one would ever know my husband's true age just by looking at him, since he looked as young as a colt but was as old as a mule. If this were some other point in time, I probably would've enjoyed being married to Mr. Douglas Wayne Evans III. He wasn't my type physically or skin color wise, but he took care of me and treated me like a queen. Far better than anyone of my race had.

I remember the day that we *accidentally* ran into each other at his car dealership. I knew that once he saw my thick and stacked five-foot-nine frame, my smooth coffee-bean skin, my granite-colored eyes, and my gorgeous Rembrandt smile, he'd be putty in my hands.

It took only a couple of days for him to ask me out, a couple of weeks for him to say that he loved me, and a few months for him to ask me to marry him. Of course, his daughter from one of his previous marriages had objected to our short courtship, but once he'd added my name to his will and insurance policy, I didn't really give a fuck about how she felt.

Douglas was the perfect example of why when it was my turn to get hitched, I chose to go for the type who was more seasoned, was quick to fall in love, and had already had multiple marriages. It was so easy to get them to fall totally head over heels for you and change, or add your name to, any document, entitling you to half or, in some cases, all their fortune. Sometimes you did meet one who was smart enough to make you sign a prenup; however, as long as my name was on the insurance policies, I didn't care. My being a great actress in the bedroom was what would really seal the deal. The age factor wasn't a huge issue for me, but I did prefer my future husband to have a certain maturity, as it worked in my favor. With Douglas being thirty years my senior, he got a kick out of his associates and friends praising him for pulling in a young and beautiful trophy wife like me.

"Frederick's, huh?" he asked as he caressed my cheek with the back of his hand. "How about we skip dinner and everything else and you go change into my surprise while I get yours?"

I jumped up and down in his arms, pecked him on his lips, then ran off to the luxury two-story walk-in closet he had made especially for me in our master bedroom.

God, I'm really going to miss all of this, I said to myself as I entered my clothing sanctuary. Any designer you could think of hung from the hangers on the racks. The custom built-in vanity and the dressing area were every girl's dream. The bag and shoe storage sections could hold over a thousand purses and heels each. I had thought about just keeping the house so I wouldn't have to part with my closet, since my name had already been added to the deed, but that was against the rules.

"Honey, I'm ready for my surprise now!" I heard Doug call out, so I grabbed the Frederick's of Hollywood bag I had tucked in the bottom of my lingerie drawer and dumped the contents onto the closet island. Since I had just gotten out of the shower and lotioned up a few minutes before Doug came into the room, I didn't have to freshen up. I dropped the robe I had on to the floor, exposing my naked body, and slipped into the red-bow front-open teddy. Once I had secured my feet in the six-inch caged booties and fluffed my hair a bit, I walked back into the master suite.

The look on my husband's face told me that he approved of his gift.

"Fuck. I can't wait to unwrap you, Mel. Can I unwrap you, baby?" he said as he started to stroke his miniature dick. I didn't say a word as I walked over to him and took over the back-and-forth rhythm he had going on his penis, which he seemed to be enjoying.

Sucking in a sharp breath, he let his head fall back and his eyes roll to the back of his head. The big vein in the side of his neck started to pulse noticeably, so I knew he was on the verge of cumming.

I stopped stroking his dick when the sound of glass shattering caught my attention.

"Did you hear that?" I whispered.

"Did I hear what, Mel?" he asked as he placed his hand on mine, willing me to continue with my knuckle shuffle.

I heard the sound of more glass shattering.

"There it is again! Did you hear it?"

This time he opened his eyes, then stood there for a minute, trying to see if he could hear any noise. "Baby, I don't hear anything, and I don't know why you're so paranoid. I set the security system before I came up here, so if there's an intruder, don't you think the alarm would have gone off already?" He sat down on the edge of the bed and pulled me onto his lap. "If it will make you feel any better, I can go check."

I nodded my head, and he lifted me up out of his lap and left the room.

I sat on the bed, waiting, for what seemed like ten minutes before he returned.

"I told you it was nothing," he said. "No broken glass, no unlawful entry. Maybe Lupe or Juan came back to get something they left, got it, then left right back out. I mean, they are the only other people with the security codes beside me, you, and my daughter, so it's plausible." He put his hand under my chin, brought his face to mine, and gently kissed my lips. "Now, back to me unwrapping my gift."

"You not about to unwrap a damn thing, muthafucka!" a masked gunman said as he burst into our room.

I screamed at the same time that Douglas yelled, "What the fuck!"

Two more gunmen rushed into the room, black masks adorning their faces and their weapons aimed at us. Douglas took in the scene and realized that we were outnumbered and unarmed, so he pushed my body behind his and tried to reason with the intruders.

"Look, fellas, you can take anything you want. If you need cash, I got a few thousand in the safe. If you want cars, the keys are on the key rings in the kitchen, and if you want some shit to pawn, there's some jewelry in the closet. You can have it all. Just don't harm me or my wife."

"Nigga, shut the fuck up! We don't need you to tell us shit. As a matter of fact, since you opened your mouth, we're going to take everything you just offered *and* your wife," gunman number two said.

"Hell yeah. I'll unwrap the shit out of her and make her swallow all my babies," the third gunman added.

I looked at the first gunman, who was standing in the corner, looking mad as fuck. I couldn't tell if he was upset with his partners for wasting time or for looking at me the way they were.

Douglas cleared his throat, then tried to reason with the masked men again. He even offered to write them a check and not report their crimes if they let us go.

"Dude, shut the fuck up. You must think we stupid or something, huh? We don't want no fucking check. Like my boy said, we're going to take everything you offered in the beginning, plus your sexy-ass wife as a bonus," said the gunman number one.

Pushing me farther behind his back, Douglas cleared his throat once again, pushed out his chest, then said, "Over my dead body."

"Well, have it your way," gunman number one responded with a sinister smirk.

The gunshots went off so fast, I never had time to react. All I remembered was hearing four loud-ass pops before Douglas's body jerked and his head snapped back. Blood splattered all over my face and body before I finally felt my throat getting sore from screaming so loud.

When Douglas's frame hit the floor like a large sack of potatoes, I dropped down and started to crawl over to him, intent on stopping his bleeding. His blood had already stained his clothes and the carpet. As I crawled over to him, the sound of a hammer being cocked back on a gun caused me to freeze in my tracks. Two seconds later, a pair of gemstone-green eyes I knew all too well leered at me before total darkness took over.

Fiona

Two years later . . .

"Okay, Mel, so you'll start that stripping gig at Club Decadence tomorrow night."

"Stripping? What happened to me bartending?"

I had to close my eyes and count to ten real quick. Although Melonee was my best friend, I couldn't stand her ass sometimes. "Mel, did you even read the file I gave you last week?" I asked as I went into my kitchen and grabbed a Corona out of the fridge. The fact that she didn't answer my question and continued to flip through the television channels led me to believe that she had not. "Come on, Melonee. How many times do I have to tell you that you need to read any and every file I give you on our new marks? You see how you almost fucked up that Doug Evans hustle in the beginning!"

"I didn't mess up shit. If memory serves me right, it was my not knowing about his allergy to nuts that got me in the door to begin with."

I sat down beside her on the couch and looked at her as if she was crazy. "Please explain this to me."

She snatched my beer out of my hand, took a swig, then gave it back. "I don't know how or why you drink that nasty shit and go as far as adding lime and salt to it, like that helps the taste." She shook her head and stuck out her tongue. "I tell you about you hood bitches."

She went on. "Anyways, back to Doug. That day I started working at his dealership, the dumb-ass secretary that he was humping before I got there brought him a salad that had walnuts in it. When his throat started to close up, the dumb girl just stood there like she didn't know what to do. After I heard someone scream that he kept his Epi Pens in the top drawer of his desk, I hopped up from my seat, grabbed one of those things, and stabbed him in his thigh. After he was able to start breathing and shit again, he thanked me for saving his life after knowing him for only five minutes. Told me that he could tell what type of heart I had just by what I'd done. Then you know what happened next. I took ole girl's job and her spot as his bed buddy. My dearly departed husband didn't know what he was getting into by messing with a girl like me."

"And neither will the rest of these rich fuckers who fall into our web of deceit."

"You got that right."

We high-fived each other and just continued to talk about the old scams we used to pull together when we were teenagers and the ones we'd been getting into ever since we'd grown up. For as long as I could remember, Melonee and I had always been about our money. If we weren't boosting shit from the mall and reselling it to the people in our neighborhood, we were doing car accident scams with Melonee's baby daddy, Proof, also known as Jaylen, and his crew, or we were doing the fake check hustle. At one point we were even doing the "slip and fall" scam at the grocery stores, but once they caught on to what we had going down, we hurried up and shut that shit down. Just thinking about those days had me dying in my head.

Melonee and I had actually met through my dad and her mom. They dated for a few years back in the day. At first, we really didn't like each other much, but after our parents kept forcing us to go on these family outings, we had no choice but to get along. By the time our parents broke up, we were already best friends and thick as thieves. It was weird for a minute after their separation, because whenever we would have a sleepover at one another's house, either Melonee's granny would have to drop her off at my house or my older brother, Max, whom we call Cowboy because of his love of those old Western movies, would have to take me over there.

I didn't know what caused our parents to split up, but whatever it was had them damn near clawing each other's eyes out whenever they were in each other's presence. Even after Melonee's mom turned around and married her new boyfriend, they still had some type of animosity between them. Whenever I'd ask my dad what had happened, he'd tell me to stay out of grown folks' business and tend to whatever it was that teenagers were supposed to do. Never understood that statement, but, hey, I made it do what it do.

When we were about fifteen, both Mel's life and mine changed for the worse. The dude that her mother had married ended up beating her ass to death one night because he swore up and down that she and my father were sleeping with each other behind his back. I swear, when Melonee called my phone, crying and going hysterical, I didn't know what to do. My father, who was sitting next to me, grabbed my phone from me and calmly spoke to her. Once she was finally able to get out what had happened, I swear, the look on my father's face sent a chill down my spine. It was as if his soul had left his body and some psycho had completely taken over. He went upstairs and changed out of the sweats and the wife beater he had on and into a black T-shirt, black jeans, and some black tennis shoes.

When he came back downstairs and headed to the door, I asked him where was he going. He simply told me, "To handle some business." After getting a couple of things out of his safe behind the entertainment center in the den, he gave me a hug, kissed me on my forehead, and left.

Although I witnessed my father's arrest, I didn't hear from him until a few days later, when he called collect from the Los Angeles men's detention center. Turned out that my dad and Melonee's mom had still been messing around, even though they both had moved on to other people. So when Melonee had called and told my dad that her stepdad had killed her mom, my father had gone and killed him that very same day, right in front of Melonee, the police, and whoever else was out there. He ended up getting sentenced to thirty years in prison. My life, as well as Melonee's life, went from sugar to shit in a matter of ten seconds. She moved in with her granny, who was on a fixed income, and my brother went crazy and basically blew through the little money that my dad had left us, so Melonee and I ended up doing what we had to do and needed to do to get by.

"Uh, earth to Fiona," Melonee said, snapping her fingers and bringing me out of my thoughts.

"Yeah? What's up?"

She looked at me funny. "Are you okay?" Her gray eyes got a little darker, something that happened whenever she was in her feelings.

"I'm good, girl. Just thinking about this new hustle."

"Speaking of this new hustle, what's the prey's name again?"

I rolled my eyes. Not only had she not read the file, but also she hadn't even look at it to at least see what his name was. I got up from my comfortable couch and grabbed the manila folder that was sitting on my dining-room table.

"His name is Roman Black. Here!" I said, giving her the *Forbes* list I had printed out.

"Okay . . . Roman Black. Net worth, seventy-four-point-nine million. Source of wealth, RTD. What's RTD?"

"Real Time Delivery. It's the company that's buying out UPS and is thinking about taking over FedEx. You haven't heard of them before?"

She shook her head.

"Well, now you know."

"But seventy-five million? It's going to be hard to get next to him, Fee. We're used to thousandaires and shit, not no multimillionaires. You see how I had to fight Doug's daughter for almost a year in court, trying to get the little money I got from him. That little bitch was contesting damn near everything, talking about foul play."

"And whose fault was that? I told you to make sure you knew where all the cameras were before the shit went down. But no, you only thought about checking the inside of the house. Good thing Cowboy was able to get ahold of the tape that showed your dingy ass talking to Proof on the patio an hour before the home invasion. What the hell was he doing there so early, and what were y'all arguing about, anyway?"

She got up and went to fix herself a drink at the bar next to my kitchen. The white tights and tank top she had on clung to her body like a second skin. Every dip and curve in the right place, without a hint of fat anywhere. The mismatched ankle socks she had on threw me off a bit, but she always wore her socks like that.

"Some dumb bullshit, as always. He thinks we're still in a relationship even after I've told him a million times that we're not. Just because we have a daughter together doesn't mean shit.

He was on my head, talking about I better not give that nigga Doug another shot of pussy before he dies." She laughed and took a sip of her drink. "Do you know that the whole time I was married to Doug, Proof would text me every day, talking about NPT?"

"What's NPT?"

"No pussy tonight."

We burst out laughing, because I could see Proof's sprung ass sending some text like that. She swallowed that first shot down whole, then took another.

"Girl, even with the dude before Doug, he would do the same thing. We should've never brought him on," she said.

I could see where she was coming from. Things had gone a lot smoother when Proof didn't know fully what we were doing. But after the incident we had had when it was time to kill my then husband, Kenneth, we both decided that having some muscle would be better than getting caught up with a murder charge and spending the rest of our lives in jail.

Melonee

"Bitch, make sure you read that file as soon as you get home. My inside source at his company said that he's scheduled to have a business meeting with some potential investors in a couple of days at Decadence," Fiona said.

"What does that have to do with me? From what you just told me, he doesn't even like strippers," I responded.

"He doesn't, but I need you to keep your eyes and ears open. Maybe one of your new coworkers knows something we don't about him that will help me to get closer."

I shook my head. *That* was her problem: she was always overthinking shit. I told her all the time to just let things flow. Men could tell when you were trying too hard to get their attention. That was why I never read any of those files. My natural charm and wit were what attracted them to me. My looks and my body were just added bonuses.

"All right. I gotcha," I said as I backed out of her driveway. Then I headed toward the freeway.

Fiona had said that she got a job as a waitress in the VIP section of Club Decadence, the strip club, so we'd sometimes be working together. I wondered why she got to keep her clothes on but I had to take mine off. It wasn't like she was slacking in the body department. I mean, her breasts weren't as big as mine, but she had some wide hips and a nice-shaped ass. Her stomach was flat but not toned, so sometimes when she wore crop tops, you could see faint signs of a small pudge. A true fan of the thirty-inch Brazilian weave craze, Fiona had had some purple and violet bundles of different lengths sewn into her head. The color didn't really compliment her light brown skin, but after she thinned out her eyebrows and put her makeup on, I liked the look a little more.

After getting off the freeway at my exit, I stopped by McDonald's for something to eat. I pulled into the drive-through and ordered a Chicken McNuggets Happy Meal for the munchkin and a Filet-O-Fish combo for me. I thought about getting my granny something too, but I decided not to, knowing she already had a big pot of black-eyed peas on the stove and some bacon-grease corn bread in the oven.

"Good afternoon, ma'am. Your total's going to be ten dollars and thirty-seven cents."

"Can you add three oatmeal-raisin cookies and three sugar cookies?" I asked the drive-through chick politely as I handed her a crisp new twenty.

"Sure. No problem." She took my money with one hand, then put her other over the mouth-piece of her microphone. "And by the way, I love your car. I can't wait until I start making some real money so that I can get me one just like it."

I smiled as I glanced at the peanut-butter interior of my Jaguar C-X17. I didn't know her financial status or anything, and I'd never intentionally knock the next person's hustle, but working at McDonald's part-time was not going to pay for a car like this. Instead of saying what was actually on my mind, I opted for some words of encouragement instead.

"At least you're starting somewhere. Just keep working hard, and you'll get it one day."

"Is that how you got yours?"

I hesitated for a second. I'd never actually had a real job in my life, so I didn't really know how to answer that. If you could call baiting, marrying, and killing men for money a job, then I guessed that was what it was, but I wasn't about to tell her that.

"Yep. Doing a job that I didn't necessarily love, saving up, and working hard allowed me to buy this pretty little bitch as well as a few other things."

The way her eyes lit up with excitement over what the other things could be made me laugh. I remembered a time when I used to get all excited about material things. That same drive and hustle that I could feel radiating off of her was what had got me to where I was today. Although I loved being able to go into any store that I wanted to without worrying about checking price tags, I felt I was missing something deep down inside me. Everything I'd ever dreamed of having when I was younger was in the palms of my hands, yet if I was being real honest, I wasn't 100 percent happy. I mean, I was caked up like crazy, had racks on racks on racks, even for a rainy day, and was the mother to the cutest little six-year-old in the world, and yet I wasn't content.

"Excuse me, ma'am. Your order!" broke me from my train of thought. It was either that or the loud blaring of horns from the cars behind me. I was so zoned out that I had to look around for a second to remember where I was. When I looked up at the drive-through chick, she had a weird expression on her face as she handed me my food.

"Uh, are you okay? It seemed like you checked out for a minute," she said.

I smiled, slightly embarrassed. "I'm sorry about that. With your questions, you just had me thinking about the way I grew up." I checked to make sure my order was correct. "Thank you for my food, and I'll see you around."

She nodded her head, then started talking to the ratchet-ass person who I could hear hollering through her headset. With music blasting, babies making all kinds of noise, it was a wonder she could hear anything the girl was saying. I shook my head as I pulled off; I didn't think I could ever do her job. I'd be cursing the majority of the people who came to my window, ordering out food.

Pulling into my granny's driveway, I couldn't help but smile at the old lady as she crouched on her knees in her green khakis, yellow button-down shirt, sunflower apron, and gardening gloves, tending to the begonias and dwarf irises she had planted a couple of weeks ago.

I climbed out of my car and walked up to her. "Granny, what did I tell you about being on your knees on that hard-ass ground like that? The reason why I bought you that expensive-ass kneeling pad was so that you would be comfortable when you were out here working on your garden."

She waved me off. "My mommy didn't use one, and neither did my grandmother, so I'm not about to break with tradition because you young people don't wanna do any hard work nowadays. I'll never understand how y'all want everything to be done so easy but to come out looking like twenty years' worth of work." With the help of my arm, she rose up off the ground. "If you don't remember anything I've ever taught you, please remember this one thing, Melonee. Nothing worth having comes easy. You have to work hard for what you want, in life and in love."

"I know, Granny," I said, then kissed her on her nutmeg-colored cheek. She'd been saying that to me ever since I could remember. "Where's the munchkin at? She never misses the chance to help do the flowers with her Memaw."

"She's in the house, already eating."

"Already eating? Granny, you know I bring her McDonald's every Thursday. Why would you sit her down to eat them black-eyed peas and corn bread?"

"I didn't feed her anything. Even though the homemade food I cook would be way better than that processed mess you like to bring her." She gathered up all her little shovels and pruning tools. "Her daddy came about twenty minutes ago with some pizza and chicken wings from that place she likes so much."

I rolled my eyes. This was the shit that got on my nerves about this muthafucka Proof. Whenever I would ignore this nigga's phone calls or unexpected drive-bys, he would always bring his dumb ass over here and try to catch me slipping with that "spend time with my baby" bullshit. I wanted to hop back into my car and go straight home, but I knew my baby girl would be heartbroken since she looked forward to my Thursday visits. Looking at my granny with pleading eyes, I silently asked if she could go kick Proof's ass out, because that was the only way he would leave, but when she started to slowly shake her head, I knew that request was a no go.

"Don't look at me like that, Ms. Thing. I told your hot ass not to mess with the little nigga when he first started to sniff around you," my granny fussed as she started walking to the front of her house. "To keep it quite honest, though, Mel, you might need to take a few lessons from him about certain things."

"A few lessons like what?"

"Hard work being one. That boy worked his ass off to get you to finally give in to his advances. And look what happened when you did."

When we walked into the house, Proof and Madison were sitting in the middle of the living room, having a princess tea party with her little friend from down the street and a few of her favorite stuffed animals. Yellow feather boas, tiaras, and pink bubble gum lip gloss were the attire for the event, and each one of the guests was in uniform, including Proof's ass. As much I couldn't stand my ex outside of our co-parenting of Madison, I couldn't help but smile at the scene before me. Seeing this six-foot-four, 245-pound, athletically built man with a walnut complexion abandon his hard-core street persona mask and change into one of his daughter's fashionably dressed, pinkie-pointing tea party guests, complete with clip-on earrings, did something to my heart.

Times like this were when I wished things between Proof and me had turned out better than they had. But after five years of being the main chick with side-chick benefits, I finally gave up on whatever it was you could say we had. Even with him looking like the exact replica of that model Don Benjamin, I couldn't do it. Granny often told me that I had given up on my family too fast. I would always shake my head when she said that. If she knew how many *other* families this nigga had tried to start while we were together, she'd probably feel a lot differently.

"Mommy!" Madison screamed, grabbing my attention as she ran toward me, the clear beads at the end of her neatly braided hair hitting against each other and making that loud bead noise.

After kneeling down, I scooped my little munchkin into my arms and gave her a big hug. Because I was still dealing with some things related to Doug's estate and business dealings in Florida, I hadn't seen my baby girl in almost two weeks. Proof and I had both agreed some time ago that Granny should take care of Madison full-time. With the business that we were in, we didn't feel that it was safe for either of us to keep her in the homes that we lived in. None of our marks knew about our real personal lives, but that didn't mean that they couldn't find out, especially if they dug deep enough.

After kissing her all over her face and making her laugh, I placed her back on the floor.

"Mommy, come play tea party with me and Daddy. We just finished eating our desserts, so now it's time for a spot of tea." My baby tried to say that with a fake English accent. I laughed because it sounded horrible, yet it was so cute.

I looked at Proof, who was still sitting on the pink bedsheet, with a cup of tea in his hand and one of Madison's Mad Hatter hats from

Disneyland on his head. When I was on my way to see my baby today, I hadn't expected to be spending time with her father as well, but if this was what was going to make my little munchkin happy, then I was going to have to be okay with it.

I allowed Madison to pull me over to the sheet and sit me down on the floor, next to her stuffed rabbit and Minion dolls.

"Okay, Mommy. This is for you," Madison said as she handed me a small teacup on a saucer and then poured what I assumed was some Lipton Brisk Tea into my cup. "Now, hold the handle with your right hand, stick your pinkie up in the air, and take a sip."

After listening to my daughter's directions, I did as she said and took a sip of the cold tea.

"Is it good, Mommy?"

"Yes, it's very good, baby. Did you make it?"

She laughed. "Yes and no. Daddy sort of helped me make it. He poured the water in the cup, and I scooped the brown powder stuff in and stirred it around. I took some out to Memaw to try, and she said it was too sweet, so me and Daddy had to put some more water in it."

My eyes connected with Proof's, which were already on me. "How long you been over here?"

He shrugged his shoulders. "For a few hours now."

"Why?"

He looked at Madison, who was in her own world, playing with her stuffed animals and her little friend, then back at me. "Because I wanted to see my baby . . . and talk to you about something."

"Talk to me about what?" I tried to stop the eye roll that followed my question, but I couldn't. If Proof wanted to talk to me about *something*, that meant that he knew about our next job and what my part would be in all of this. I could bet my last dollar that he wasn't too happy with what my new occupation was going to be and that I was going to have to hear his mouth about it.

He looked at Madison again. "Maddy, I think Memaw wants a cup of tea. Why don't you and your friend pour her a cup and take it out to her? You never let her taste the new batch we made."

"Okay, Daddy," Madison said as she picked up her teakettle and another cup to take outside to my grandmother. Her friend stood up after her and followed her out. As soon as the sound of the screen door closing echoed through the house, Proof went right to the point.

"So you're okay with being a stripper now? What part of the game is that? Did you even tell Fiona to try to find you another job? Or are you going to be okay with taking off all your clothes for all the world to see?"

I stood up and walked into the kitchen. If I was going to have this conversation with Proof, I needed a shot of my granny's Jack Daniel's, which she kept in the cabinet above the stove. Proof followed me into the kitchen.

I took out a shot glass and the bottle of Jack Daniel's, then filled the glass to the rim. "Jaylen, you know as well as I do that this is only a front. Once Fee gets in good with the target, I won't have to do it anymore," I said.

"You shouldn't be doing it in the first place. What do I look like being okay with letting my girl take off her clothes for niggas I know and don't know?"

I emptied the shot glass, then poured myself another drink. "First off, I'm not your girl. Haven't been for some years now. Secondly, if you're going to keep tripping over the jobs I have to do, or the men I have to marry, and what goes on in all of that, I don't think you should be a part of the clique anymore. I told Fiona when she first brought up bringing you on that this was a bad idea, especially since you still have feelings for me."

"And you don't have them for me!" he yelled at the top of his lungs. "If I'm not mistaken, it was you who came to my house to get this dick whenever that old fuck Douglas was out of town! It was you who was screaming about how much you missed me, missed us, and what we used to have. It's only been a year since we stopped fucking, Mel. Even then, that didn't stop your ass from sending me those late-night 'What you doing?' and 'Are you busy?' texts. We both know what time it is when people send out shit like that after midnight. Come on now! I meant what I said to you the day after we killed ole boy. If we can't be back together as a couple and as a family, then I ain't fucking with you, regardless of how much I love you."

"Then why are we having this conversation about me stripping? Obviously, I don't want to go down that road with you again, or we'd be together now."

Proof wiped his hand over his face and mumbled something under his breath. Yeah, I knew I was sending mixed signals when I allowed him to dick me down while I was married to Doug, but shit, could you blame me? I was used to that wild, rough, and thuggish sex. Doug had always wanted to make love to me and be gentle, and I didn't want that, especially when I wasn't in love with him.

"Look, Jaylen, we should've never started messing around again. That was my bad. I'm also sorry for leading you on in any kind of way. It was never my intention to make it seem like we were getting back together or anything. All I want is for us to be great parents to Madison, and that's it. If ever we talk or have a conversation, it should pertain only to things about our child. Other than that, don't question me or say anything to me about what I have going on or what I do outside of her. We are coworkers and parents, and we are not a couple anymore, so we have to find some kind of balance between the two."

Proof licked his lips, then folded them into his mouth. Those gemstone-green eyes that I used to love so much stared at me so intently that I began to feel a little uncomfortable.

"Are you all right in here?" my granny asked as she slowly walked into the kitchen. Her gray eyes, which mirrored mine, looked from me to Proof, then back at me. I could see Madison's small hands resting on her hip as she stood behind my granny, as if she was scared to look at me or her dad.

"Yeah, we good, Granny. Proof . . . that is, Jaylen and I were just having a little conversation," I said.

Granny sighed. "Well, your *little* conversation could be heard all the way at the back of the house. It scared away Madison's friend. Now I'm going to go on upstairs and take my little baby up to my bedroom so we can find some more things to wear for her tea party. I expect the both of you to have whatever it is you were arguing . . . *talking* about hashed out and over with by the time we get back downstairs, you understand?"

"Yes, ma'am," I replied.

When Proof didn't answer her, my eyes traveled over to where he was standing behind the island in the middle of the kitchen. His fingers were interlaced and his hands sat on top of his head as he looked up at the ceiling and swayed back and forth.

"Uh, Jaylen, I know you heard my granny talking to you," I said.

His gaze traveled from the ceiling to Granny. "Ms. Regina, I heard everything you said, and I apologize for disrespecting your house and yelling."

"It's okay. Just make sure you don't do it again," Granny said. "And for the record, I totally agree with what you were saying." She side eyed me. "I told Melonee that too. Either piss in the pot or get up. You can't do both." She turned her attention back to Proof. "And you, Jaylen, you have to be okay with whatever choice Melonee makes. If she decides to get up, you can't do nothing but respect it and let her go, because trying to hold her in place when she really doesn't want to be there isn't going to do nothing but push her farther away. Let her go. If she comes back, then you know it was meant to be. If not, you gotta move on, just like she did."

My granny looked at me one last time, gave a quick head nod, then turned around and headed upstairs, with Madison following right behind her.

"Look, Jay—"

He cut me off. "Naw, your Granny is right. Maybe it is time for me to let you go. It's clear that what we used to have is in the past, with no signs of it ever coming back."

"Jaylen—" I began, but he cut me off again.

"We good, Mel. My bad for even coming at you like that about the stripping thing. From now on, our conversations outside of work will be strictly about Madison and whatever it is that she needs. I won't question you about any of your jobs or what you're doing behind closed doors with future targets. Because you're my child's mother, though, I will always have your back, so if you need me, call me. Other than that, you won't have to worry about any heat coming from over this way."

I nodded my head. "Thanks, Jaylen. And I promise not to hit you with any of those late-night 'What you doing?' and 'Are you busy?' texts again."

We shared a laughed before he walked around the island to where I stood and hugged me.

"I'm about to get up out of here to meet with the rest of the crew. Cowboy has some information for us about dude's security and shit. Be careful at the club, and don't go getting your ass beat by some Ronnie- and Trix-looking bitches because you wouldn't let them get a taste of that goodness between your thighs."

I pushed Proof off me and socked him in his rib cage. "Boy, you already know how I get down. I'ma be Diamond Jr. in that bitch if any of those hoes try to test me."

"That's what I'm talking about. I'm about to go say bye to my baby. Before I head out, you need anything?"

I watched as Proof's eyes scanned my body lustfully; then he licked his lips.

"Naw, Madison is good. *She* doesn't need anything."

He nodded his head, smirked, then went upstairs to say bye to our daughter. After washing the few dishes in the sink, locking the door when Proof left, and making another pitcher of raspberry iced tea for the tea party, I joined my granny and Madison on the pink bedsheet in the middle of the living room and spent time with my two favorite girls. I was going to enjoy this little time I was spending with my baby as much as I could, because come next week, I'd be on another one of my extended vacations from them both, and I didn't know when I'd be back.

Fiona

"Okay, so tonight you'll be waitressing in the VIP section up top. The redhead who normally works it called out again. Something about a stomach virus or something of that nature," said Raul, the owner of Club Decadence, as his dark eyes stayed focused on my little bit of cleavage that was barely visible, thanks to the black tank top I had on. "You think you'll be okay up there?"

I nodded my head. "Yeah, I think so. I shadowed Molly for a few hours last week, and I think I seen enough."

He squinted his eyes a little, then placed the stub of cigar he'd been holding between his middle and index finger back in his mouth. "VIP guests are top priority." He raised one of his perfectly arched eyebrows. "They don't pay the big bucks for all that privacy to have to wait on anything." He narrowed his eyes and blew out a thick cloud of smoke. "And when I say *anything*, you do know I mean anything, right?"

I said nothing in reply.

He licked his lips as his eyes slowly scanned my body up and down for a few seconds before he let out a hearty laugh. "You know, Fiona, I like you. Doesn't seem like you scare too easy."

"When you've seen half the things I've seen in my life, it's kind of hard for anything or anyone to scare you."

Which in some ways was true. Watching my father get damn near beaten to death by the police before they threw him in the back of that police car for killing Shaunie's ex-boyfriend was the most frightening thing I had ever seen. I had sat on the edge of the sidewalk, crying my eyes out, afraid of what my father going to jail would mean for me and my brother. I'd been so distraught, I started to hyperventilate, and the EMTs had to give me an oxygen mask. I lay there for almost ten minutes, the oxygen mask on my face, terrified about my and Cowboy's future. But when my eyes connected with my father's in the back of that cruiser and he smiled, then motioned for me to keep my head up, something inside me changed at that moment. If he wasn't afraid to kill for the woman he loved, or to spend the rest of his life behind bars for making sure the person who killed her wouldn't see the light of another day, what could possibly scare me?

I ran through in my mind everything that had the potential to be scary. *Does love scare me?* I wondered. Shit, that emotion had left me the day my mama left us. *Being broke?* I had more than enough money saved up, thanks to my ex-husbands. *Death?* It sucked, but we all had to die someday. *Going to jail?* If Pops could do it with a straight face, so could I. Like I said, wasn't too much out here that could scare me, not even doing whatever was necessary to get the attention of our next mark in the VIP section.

Yep, Roman Black and a few of his colleagues were scheduled to be here tonight for a little deal-closing celebration. One of the strippers Melonee had become close to in the past two weeks had given her the heads-up. Candy had worked at Decadence for the past five years and had designated herself the welcoming party for any new stripper who came into the fold. The chick was a bona fide cokehead, and everyone knew it. You got her to sniff a few lines, and she was giving up the goods on everyone's business, including that of this sick bastard who owned the club.

Raul thought his Rico Suave–wannabe ass was God's gift to women. Yeah, he had a little flavor, but his pockets weren't fat enough for me. He didn't even have a health-care package for his employees, so I doubted he had any type of personal insurance policies with big payouts. Although the club was a nice spot, it wouldn't do a thing for me if he met an untimely death.

As he continued with his lame speech and literally blew smoke in my face, I nodded my head and smiled every few seconds so it looked as if I was listening to him. Every so often my eyes would scan the entrance to the club to see if Roman and his entourage had arrived. According to Candy, whenever Roman did come to hang out, he would do so with his brother, Benjamin Black, and his best friend, Marques King.

According to the info I had pulled up online, Benjamin was Roman's stepbrother and the vice president of Real Time Delivery, and he didn't make quite as much money as Roman did, but he wasn't slacking in the money department, either. I thought about switching the target from Roman over to Benjamin, but I nixed the idea when I saw how much Benjamin's ass was in the tabloids.

Benjamin had to be photographed any and everywhere: from designer stores on Rodeo Drive to drive-throughs at Starbucks and McDonald's. The media loved him, which was a good thing if you were part of a company that needed to stay relevant, but it was bad if you were planning to kill his ass. Paparazzi camped outside his homes, waiting to take pictures of the plethora of female vixens doing the walk of shame or of him sunbathing in the nude around the pool.

Now, as for Roman's best friend, Marques, he was almost as bad as Benjamin, with his philandering ways. There were a few pictures floating around of his sexy ass with different socialites and celebrities too.

A trust-fund baby living off of his family fortune, made from the luxurious King Palace Resorts and King Palace Hotels all over the world, he would have been a great target as well, except for the fact that he came from a family with many members who were still living, and such men were even harder to swindle. They always had that one family member who would question the "new girlfriend's" intentions, especially if you didn't come from money like they did. We didn't need anyone who had a lot of time on his or her hands to start digging into our backgrounds. I mean, if someone did look, there wasn't really too much to find, but if somebody took the time to look *carefully*, he or she would be able to see a few patterns in our time line.

The light dimming in the room grabbed my attention. The loud thumping sound of some slow heavy-metal group vibrated through the speakers. A slim white leg with a seven-inch stiletto heel came from behind the curtain and bounced slowly to the beat.

"Shit!" I heard Raul hiss as he snuffed the rest of the cigar out and stood up straight, abandoning his lax posture against the bar. "I told her ass to cool it on the lines tonight. She knows we have the Blacks coming in at any moment."

I looked at Raul for a moment, then turned my head back to the stage and almost pissed on myself. The way Candy's high ass was stumbling to the pole had me laughing my ass off. Her long platinum-blonde wig with the Chinese bangs had shifted a little too much to the right, causing the left side of her face to be covered, while the smeared eye shadow and blush on the right side of her face could be seen clear as day. The big smile she had on her face as she twirled around the pole like a happy fairy told me that the shit I had given her a few minutes before she hit the stage was some straight fiyah. I made a mental note to thank Proof for the Tony Montana I had bought on the low from him earlier. I didn't know where he had got it from, but whoever's product it was had to be selling that shit like hotcakes. Especially if it had you feeling as good as Candy looked.

My phone buzzed in my apron pocket. I pulled it out and saw that I had a text from Melonee.

Bestie: Do you see this shit? LOL

Me: Cocaine is a hell of a drug.

Bestie: LOL! U stupid. Did they get here yet?

Me: Naw. But be ready.

I slipped my phone back into my apron pocket, then turned to get my tray ready for my first round in VIP. Because the high rollers were the only ones in there, we had to walk through the door with a bottle of this expensive-ass cognac that was exclusively made for Club Decadence, along with a few shot glasses to whet the big spenders' taste buds. Whenever we explained that the small particles floating around in the brown liquor were actually pieces of four-teen-karat gold, the big spenders declared that this warranted a taste of the signature drink. Once they got a taste of the smooth cognac with a hint of sweet honey, they would request a whole bottle. At ten thousand dollars a pop, the cognac was seriously overrated, but with me earning a smooth 25 percent on every bottle I sold, you know I was pushing the shit like crazy.

"Molly called out again, huh?" Lupe, the spit-fire bartender, asked as she handed me a bottle of the cognac, which was called Decadence Gold.

"Yeah. Raul said she has a stomach flu or something."

"The bitch better not be pregnant," I heard her mumble under her breath as she turned to wipe the counter down.

I silently laughed to myself, because she and Molly killed me. Both of their dumb asses had fallen for Raul's weak-ass game and were fucking him at the same time. A couple of nights ago, I had had to break up a fight between the two women, because Raul had slapped Molly on her ass and in return she had grabbed a handful of his dick. Instead of swatting her hand away, like I assumed he would've, he had just let her massage his small bulge through his pants, until Lupe had had enough of the visual and had charged into Molly headfirst.

Luckily, the club wasn't opened yet and only a few employees saw the little catfight between the two of them. Molly actually got the best of Lupe's ass, until I stepped in. Raul grabbed Lupe and took her to the back of the club to have a few words, while I took Molly into the kitchen to try to calm her down. It was then that I offered to pour her a glass of something to drink. Once she nodded her head, I went back out to the bar and fixed her a glass of Diet Coke with a couple of shots of rum and brought it back to her, but not before pouring some crushed laxatives in it to give her the runs. I needed her to be gone for a few days so that I had my chance to get close to Roman. I knew that if she was working, her ass wasn't going to trade shifts with me and work my areas for shit.

I had gathered up my things and was just about to turn around and head up to the VIP section when the most alluring smell entered my nose. The hairs on the back of my neck stood straight up, and my pussy began to tingle. After slowly turning around, I came face-to-face with one of the most gorgeous men I had ever seen.

Damn. Them few pictures online do not do him no kind of justice, I thought as Roman Black and his entourage made their way through the club. Even Benjamin and Marques had this aura about them that said, "We have money—and lots of it."

I watched as the three tall, sexy men led the way into the VIP room, followed by six short Japanese men dressed in expensive, sharp business suits.

"There's a lot of money in that room tonight," Lupe said from behind me. "I know Candy's going to be mad she missed this."

I looked back up at the stage and didn't see Candy anywhere in sight. Raul had hurried up and got her stumbling, high ass down off the stage. I knew it was more than likely that he was going to send her home or make her sit her ass down until the high passed.

"I wonder who Raul's going to have take her spot in VIP," Lupe mused. "You know those Japanese men love their American Barbies with blond hair."

"That may be true, but if you ask me, a little chocolate ain't never hurt nobody," I said as I texted Melonee to let her know that Roman was here and that she should get her ass to VIP ASAP.

This was the first time in the two months that we'd been here that Roman had finally made an appearance at Club Decadence. If everything went according to plan, we'd be millions of dollars richer before the end of the year, much thanks to my new soon-to-be dearly departed husband, Roman Black.

Melonee

I watched Raul drag Candy's ass off the stage, literally kicking and screaming. Whatever she was high on had her tripping way more than normal tonight.

"So it's just fuck me tonight, huh, Candy?" Raul questioned her with his thick Spanish accent.

"What'd I do, Daddy? I was just trying to have a little fun. You know Candy only has eyes for her Latin lover." Her words were a bit slurred, but I knew Raul had heard everything she said.

Candy wobbled down the dark, narrow hallway until she landed on the couch in the dressing room with a loud plop. After pulling the platinum-blond wig off her head and throwing it across the room, she unhooked the clip holding up her natural brunette-colored hair and shook it out.

"I don't even know why you wear that fake shit, when you got a head full of beautiful hair already," Raul mumbled as he paced back and forth in front of the couch. Every time he would look down at Candy, he'd stop for a quick second and shake his head.

The black linen suit he had on hung loosely from his body but could not hide that huge python print going down the side of his leg. Fiona always said that he padded himself, but the shit looked real to me. The way he would have Candy screaming in his office every other night, before he closed up, told me he was working with a little something down there.

Now the shadow of his five-foot, eleven-inch frame covered Candy's body completely for a second before he started to pace back and forth again.

"Can you please stop walking so much! You're making me blow my high," Candy said, grabbing the bridge of her nose and laughing hysterically.

Raul's gaze went around the dressing room a few times before it finally landed back on Candy. You could tell he was thinking about slapping some sense into her but didn't want a room full of strippers to see him do it. I could read the look he had on his face from anywhere. It was the same look my mother's ex-boyfriend Dezmond would have on his face before he started to whip my mama's ass.

"Everybody out!" Raul shouted, but nobody moved. Some of the strippers who had already been here for most of the day were sitting down and counting their tips, while the other ones were huddled up in their little cliques, doing drugs, licking on each other's pussies, or gossiping about someone in the room.

When Raul saw that no one was trying to move an inch, he pulled out the small 9mm he had on his waist and cocked the hammer back. "You bitches must be hard of hearing or something. Get the fuck out, or get shot the fuck down!"

The sound of the metal clacking must've got everyone's attention, because the room cleared out in twenty seconds flat.

I turned around in my chair and continued to apply my makeup to my face. Fee had just hit me, telling me that our target was in the building and that I needed to get ready. Because Roman Black didn't have a thing for strippers, my job was to mesmerize everyone in his entourage who did. While their eyes were on me, Fiona's job was to try to get in good with Roman so that the two of them would eventually exchange numbers and start from there.

"Lucky, that includes your ass too." Raul's voice pulled me from my train of thought. "You need to get up to the VIP section, anyways, so that you can take this dumb-ass bitch's spot," he said, looking at Candy.

I didn't know how Fiona had known that Raul would have me take Candy's spot tonight in the VIP section, but it worked. I didn't even have to use the little speech I had come up with in case he decided to send someone else.

"I just need five more minutes, Raul, baby, and then I'ma be out of your way."

Raul wiped his hand over his face, then rolled his eyes. "Five minutes, Luck. You better be glad I have to go use the bathroom before I put my foot in her ass."

Candy started laughing again. "I'd rather have your dick, but I guess I'll be cool with your foot."

I couldn't help the chuckle that escaped from between my perfectly glossed lips. Although I didn't agree with Candy's drug habit, she was a cool and funny girl, nonetheless. If it weren't for her, I wouldn't know half the moneymaking tricks to get this money. Between her tips, the YouTube videos I'd watched, and the pole-dancing classes I had taken on the weekend, I had easily become the top-paid stripper at Decadence in a matter of weeks. If marrying for money ever stopped working for me, I knew I'd be all right if I came back and did this gig full-time.

"My girl Lucky Charms!"

I turned my attention to Candy's high ass when she called out my stage name.

"You make Mama proud out there tonight, okay? And you tell Fiona that I stuck to my end of the deal, so I will be expecting my package before I leave tonight." She ran her thin fingers through her dark hair, then turned her glassy gaze toward me.

"What deal are you referring to, and what package are you talking about?" I asked, sliding my feet into the rainbow-rhinestone, fringe thigh-high boots I had bought especially for tonight. Once I fastened the buckles behind my legs, I walked over to the full-length mirror and looked at myself.

"The deal where I put that bug in Raul's ear to have you take my spot in VIP, and the package of that good-ass blow she promised to get me again for my help."

I shook my head. Leave it to Fiona's ass to already have shit in motion so that we could get this money.

I admired the way my thick chocolate frame and curvy body looked in the pink slingshot bikini that I had on. My ass swallowed the G-string whole, and my titties sat up just right for the thin piece of fabric that covered the nipples of my perky triple D breasts. The four-leaf clovers tattoo I had over my back and right hip had been brought to life on my dark skin by the baby oil I had rubbed all over my body. I made a mental note to have a few more clovers added to cover up the stretch marks that were slowly coming in on my waist.

"You know them tattoos is the reason why I gave you the name Lucky Charms. That and your body looks magically delicious in anything your wear."

"Shut your high ass up, Candy. How do I look, though? You think they will like it up there?" I pointed in the direction of VIP.

Her eyes roamed over my body. "They'll love you. Just put your hair up."

I screwed up my face. "Put my hair up? Why? I just got it done," I said, looking at the new jet-black weave I had sewn into my head earlier. "You don't think they will love my curls?"

Candy tried to stand up but fell back onto the couch and started laughing at herself again. Once she got over her laughing fit, she was able to stand up and then slowly walked over to me with one heel on and one heel off. Her makeup was smeared all over her face, and her eyes were red as hell. The little white boy shorts she had on now looked like panties since the back was so far up her ass. Because her breast implants were so big on her small frame, you could see every vein on her titties. Her chest reminded me of a road map, with all those blue lines.

Candy stepped up behind me and put her hand on my shoulder. With these stiletto boots on, I was about a foot taller than her, so she had to poke her head out to the side to talk to me in the mirror.

"You have to wear your hair up because it will bring more attention to your face. With your dark skin and those beautiful eyes, those men will have a complete playground to look at. From your gorgeous face down to that sexy, thick, fully nude body. The more things they enjoy looking at, the more money they will be willing to throw."

Fully nude?

Now, I wasn't aware that I would have to get completely nude in the VIP section. The reason why I always wore my hair down and over my shoulders was that I still kinda felt covered up after I removed my top. My hair would lie against my breasts kind of like a blanket.

Downstairs we had to remove only our tops, and I had assumed it was the same way in VIP. I didn't mind wearing a thong and showing a little ass sometimes, but I now had to show the cookies too. I didn't know if I was totally okay with that. I mean, there were some things I felt weren't for the world or strange eyes to see, and my insides were at the top of that list. You had to have a little mystery to you.

Candy's loud laugh broke me from my thoughts again.

"You didn't know, huh? That's one of the reasons why this club is so popular. We have full nudity and alcohol. Those other clubs that offer full nudity don't serve an ounce of liquor, but Club Decadence does."

Candy slapped me on the ass, then headed back to the couch. "My high is seriously coming down. I need to find Fiona."

"I . . . I . . . don't think I can do that," I finally said, thinking of the spread-eagle trick I did on the pole. I didn't feel comfortable being that open.

Candy waved me off. "Girl, you can and you will. That's the other reason you should wear your hair up. Bring attention to your face and upper body, instead of that sexy thing below your waist."

Raul walked in. The fire he had had in his eyes before he left earlier was gone, and a satisfied smirk was across his lips.

"Time's up, Lucky. Sunshine's about to go on, and you're up after her. Plus, I need to finish talking to Candy in private," he said, licking his lips and eyeing my body lustfully. "We have some high rollers up there tonight who requested to see some dark meat, and I don't want to keep them waiting. Remember, house gets ten percent, and you have to tip the DJ before you leave," he added, taking his eyes off me and focusing on Candy.

I looked at myself in the mirror one last time before I went and grabbed my tip purse and a rubber band for my hair. As much as I hated to mess up my curls, I would take Candy's advice if that got the men to look more at my face than down below.

Think of the money . . . think of the money, I chanted to myself as I slowly walked down the dark hallway and up the spiral staircase. Even though the music was loud and thumping, all I could hear were the gulps of air I kept breathing in and the rattling of the fringe on my boots every time I took a step.

Once I reached the VIP section, I peeked at the stage from behind the curtain and scanned the crowd for Fiona. When my eyes finally landed on her, she was in the middle of the room, where a large party of men sat. Japanese men in expensive suits were on one side of the table, while a few American men with equally expensive suits sat on the other. It wasn't until Fiona moved to the left a bit that my eyes landed on one of the finest men I'd ever seen.

Even in the dark room, I could see his smooth olive-colored skin. The caramel-blond hair that formed a five o'clock shadow along the edge of his face trailed up to the top of his head in a low cut. His dark eyes were cast down at the phone in his hand, and a look of pure boredom was etched across his face.

Maybe he's, like, a bodyguard or something, I thought as I took in his attire. Unlike his sophisticatedly dressed company, this fine specimen had on a red T-shirt, a pair of khaki shorts, and some green Chuck Taylor high-tops. One of his well-toned legs was covered in ink, just like one of his muscle-toting arms.

"Damn," I said breathlessly when a small smirk played on his lips after the fine dude sitting next to him whispered something in his ear.

I watched Fiona walk around to each man and take his order. When she got in front of the sexy suit sitting next to the guy in the red T-shirt, her smile became even bigger.

That must be Roman, I thought as I took in dude's dark features. He was another sexy white boy with dark hair—I'd give him that—but he was not as sexy as his bodyguard.

"We have a sweet treat for you fellas tonight here at Decadence. A new addition to the VIP lineup," Sunshine announced. "This sexy lady has been here for only a couple of months and has already left a lot of these fellas broke and waiting for more. Make sure when you dig in them pockets tonight, you dig deep enough to show my girl some love, because she's definitely about to give you a show. I know when God made her, he had to have them damn hearts, stars, horseshoes, clovers, blue moons, hourglasses, rainbows, and tasty red balloons in mind, because her whole body is magically delicious. You guys, give it up for Decadence's own Lucky Charms!"

Oh shit. Oh shit. Oh shit.

I was so caught up in Red T-shirt that I hadn't heard Sunshine's set end. Hearing the beginning of DJ Drama's song "Wishing," featuring Chris Brown, Skeme, and Lyquin, come on, I realized there was no way I could turn back now. Placing my purse next to the DJ's bag, I said a silent prayer, took a deep breath, then did my snake walk onto the stage. The spotlight was so bright that I couldn't see a face in the crowd. That was a good thing; however, I didn't want to miss the edge of the stage and fall on my ass. Reaching my hand out, I grabbed ahold of the pole and spun around a few times, signaling in a low-key way for the light dude to raise the lights on the rest of the stage.

As soon as he did that, I could see every pair of eyes in that room on me. It wasn't until I lowered myself to the floor in a split that the hairs on the back of my neck started to stand up. My stomach, which had been just fine, started fluttering like crazy, and even my palms began to sweat. I kept a straight face and closed my eyes, as I didn't want to give off the vibe that something was going on. It wasn't until the fluttering got stronger that I decided to open my eyes and look out at the crowd. As soon as my gaze connected with a pair of the sexiest green eyes, I almost lost my breath. Those eyes belonged to Red T-shirt. The look on his face wasn't one of disgust, but it wasn't one of lust, either. It seemed as if there was a mixture of pity and incomprehension in his expression. When he shook his head slightly, then started playing with his phone again, something inside me switched.

Was degrading myself like this actually worth getting this money? I felt a little ashamed at myself.

My eyes scanned the rest of the men's facial expressions in the VIP section, and there was no doubt that they were enjoying the show. Even the mixed dude who had a curly man bun on the top of his head and was dressed similarly to Red T-shirt couldn't take his eyes off me.

For some reason, though, I started to feel even more ashamed. And I started to feel undesirable. I started to feel some type of way. Red T-shirt still hadn't looked up at me, and I started to feel like I wanted to cry.

That was why when the DJ started to slowly fade out of DJ Drama's song and move on to the next number, I acted as if I was walking back only as far as the curtain, but instead of turning around when I reached the curtain, I kept going and walked out. Covering my bare breasts with one arm, I picked my purse up off the floor and headed back to the dressing room.

I wasn't worried about finishing my set. Wasn't worried about picking up my tips or about what Raul was going to say. All I knew was that I needed to get out of here, and all it had taken was a look from the sexy guy in the red T-shirt to make me feel that way.

Roman

My eyes drifted back up to the stage, where the most beautiful woman I'd ever seen was willingly about to degrade herself for a few lousy bucks. I hadn't been paying attention to anything going on in this club until my eyes caught sight of a smooth chocolate leg coming from behind the beaded curtain. When the rest of her body came out, I couldn't stop staring. Her curvy frame did something to me that no other woman had ever been able to do just by her physical appearance alone—make me hard.

The way her hips, waist, breasts, and ass filled out the small bikini she had on had my dick so hard that I had to cross my leg over my knee and place one of the sequin pillows from the chair over my lap to adjust myself. As if that wasn't enough, when my eyes finally roamed up to her face, my heart started to skip every single beat imaginable. Her almond-shaped eyes were a misty granite gray and contrasted with her smooth dark brown skin. High cheekbones, a strong jawline, and a fine nose gave her that high-fashion supermodel look. Then there were those full, pouty lips that had a light pink gloss adorning them.

I bet those lips are as soft as pillows, I thought to myself.

But then ole girl just ran off the stage.

"Aye, man. What was all that about? You know ole girl or something?"

I didn't hear a word.

"*Hello*! Earth to Roman!" I heard Marques say, while snapping his fingers in my face. "Dude, where the hell did you just go? One minute you were about to say something, and then the next minute you completely zoned out. You okay?"

I looked at my best friend since childhood and nodded my head to let him know I was fine. The look he gave me told me that he didn't believe me, but he left it alone for the time being and grabbed a drink off the waitress's tray. I was sure he'd ask me about what I'd been thinking about sometime tomorrow, when we weren't among company, which happened to include my brother, Benjamin. Marques knew that I wasn't too keen about the fact that Benji was now a part of my professional life, let alone my personal life. I had to nip the bud somewhere before the two crossed.

My father, who was actually Benji's stepfather, had insisted that I give Benji a spot underneath me once I was appointed CEO of our family company, Real Time Delivery. We were a huge parcel service that was taking over and not really giving a fuck. FedEx, DHL, and UPS were just a few of the companies that we were trying to and going to shut down, especially with me at the forefront now. I'd been the CEO for only the past two years, but so far, I had everyone talking about RTD, and I wanted to keep it that way.

Benjamin, on the other hand, had everyone talking about other things. The types of things that didn't have anything to do with our family business and how good we'd been doing for the past twenty years. Although my father's blood wasn't running through his veins, Benjamin was treated as if it was. In fact, the title of chief executive officer could have been his, had he learned how to be more discreet with his personal life. He was indeed next in line to take over everything my father had built while we were away at school and getting that real-world experience. However, one too many public scandals swirling around Benjamin was enough for my father to pass the CEO title along to me, the more responsible, reclusive, and private son, rather than to the wild, "loved to party and flaunt beautiful women," and "never on time to a meeting, because he was trying to sober up from a hangover" son.

I watched as Benjamin talked to the potential investors from Japan, whom we were trying to get to invest in the new RTD international company we wanted to have open by this time next year on their side of the Pacific Ocean. Benji was a natural when it came to negotiating these business deals, as he just couldn't stay out of the limelight.

Given his careless ways, you'd never think that he was fluent in six languages, had graduated at the top of his class from Columbia, and was already a millionaire by the age of nineteen, after he invented a swizzle stick that changed colors in your drink if the date rape drug Rohypnol was present. My brother was smart; he just always made stupid decisions. Before he could make any more improvements to the swizzle stick, a major company approached him and offered him a boatload of money for his idea. With him being of age and not needing a parent to be present, he signed over his rights to the swizzle stick and was given a check for two million dollars.

He was happy and living on top of the world after depositing that check into his bank account, and the money allowed him to move out of our family home, buy more than a few cars, and party his life away. He ran through those two million dollars before he even flipped the calendar to age twenty-one, and was left broke, homeless, and with a few DUI charges under his belt. Then, to make matters worse, after perfecting the design of the swizzle stick that Benji had come up with, the company who bought the idea from him for two million dollars sold it to an even bigger company for a billion.

That ball-busting blow, mixed with the drugs and the wild life he continued to live while back under our parents' roof, only contributed to the overdose scare he had a few years later. However, ever since doing a short stint in rehab and reconnecting with his biological father, Benji had been on the straight and narrow path. However, his previous shenanigans played a big role in his position in the family business.

When my father made the announcement that he was passing the torch on to me and crowning me head of the company, everyone was happy about his choice, including Benji. But even though he was happy for me, it seemed at times that Benji was still competing against me for my father's accolades. This explained why he had crashed the meeting I had today with the Japanese investors. Ten minutes before we were to end our presentation, there he was, waltzing into the conference room like he owned the place, then charming these uptight assholes with his fluent Japanese and suggesting we come to this strip club to celebrate the start of a beautiful business deal. As much as I hated how he'd popped up at the meeting at the last minute, I was kind of glad he had. I didn't think the translator I'd hired to translate at the meeting had done a good job in the two hours we spent going back and forth with negotiations. It had taken Benji only five minutes to come in and seal the deal, and now he had us at this upscale strip club, enjoying drinks and looking at all these scantily clad women. Well, at least they were.

"So you will have all the paperwork done by when, Roman?" Benji asked, breaking me from my thoughts.

When I looked up, all eyes were on me, including Marques's. "What did you say?"

"Dude, you zoned out again," Marques whispered in my ear.

Benji smirked and said something to the investors in Japanese that made them laugh.

"Yew like stwip club, hey?" one of the investors asked me in his broken English.

"No, not really. But if you like it, I love it," I replied.

All six heads turned to Benji for a translation. After he finished speaking to them, they all laughed again, then summoned the waitress over for more drinks.

"Can we get two more bottles of the Decadence Gold, the assorted sushi platter, some of those filet mignon sliders, and a side of those crispy onion rings?" Benji told the waitress after our clients had ordered. "And make sure you put it all on the boss man's tab here," he added, patting me on my chest and shaking my shoulders.

The waitress turned to me. "And what about for you, handsome?" she asked. She was a nice-looking girl, no doubt about it, but I wasn't checking for her at all. Given the different shades of purple in her hair, the tons of makeup on her face, and her eagerness to get me to notice her, I had already decided she was more Benji's speed than mine.

The whole night she'd been over here in our section, and she'd been trying to get my attention, which I was used to, but I wasn't about to bite. I didn't like a pushy woman or the type of woman who came on to a man before he came on to her. *Let me make eye contact with you first to let you know I'm semi interested, and then let me take it from there*, I had kept thinking. Girls like her were the ones my uncle Kazimir had always told me to watch out for. "If a woman has the balls to approach a man for sex, she will use those same balls to kill him," he would say in his thick Russian accent.

In answer to her question, I told her I was just fine, and then I continued to go through the e-mails on my phone as she seductively licked her lips and eyed me up and down.

"If there's anything else that you do need, Mr. Black, please know that I won't have a problem making sure you get it," she said and twisted her hip so that a small bit of her ass was poking out in my direction. "Anything you need, I'm here to make it happen."

Ignoring her, I continued to mess around on my phone until she finally got the picture and walked away.

Marques stared at me. "Man, if you don't want her, I'll sho' take her."

Benji leaned over. "You or my *little* brother wouldn't know what to do with a girl like that," he said as we all looked in the direction in which the waitress had gone.

"Yo, Roman can take her down, just like the both of us could. Right, Ro?" Marques said, looking at me.

I shrugged. "You already know she's not even my type."

"But shawty's bad, though. You gotta give her that," Marques noted.

"Shawty?" Benji asked. "I see you've been watching *Sunset Park* again." He laughed.

"Man . . . fuck you, Benji," Marques growled. "You know the majority of my family is from New York. So it's only natural that I pick up on some of their lingo."

"Lingo?" Benji shook his head. "Marques, make up your mind, bruh. You're either from the East Coast or the West Coast. Stop mixing the two."

I had to laugh at that, because Marques did switch up the way he talked a lot. I noticed it all the time. But I was so used to it now, that it didn't bother me at all. I guessed he could feel the same way about me as well, seeing as I could switch from English to Russian in a heartbeat whenever my mother's side of the family came round. Well, more specifically, my uncle Kazi.

"Up for a little friendly competition, fellas?" Benji asked after he finished explaining something to the investors.

"What kind of competition?" Marques asked.

Benji smiled and looked at Marques, then over at me. "Let's see who can get the waitress's number before we leave, and get her into his bed before the end of the night."

"Awww, man, that ain't no friendly competition," Marques replied, waving Benji off. "We already know she wants Roman's ass. I bet she gives him her number and address written on her panties before we leave for the night, without him even asking."

Benji looked back at the waitress, who was looking back at us, and rubbed his hands together, fire blazing in his eyes and a small smirk on his face. "Five hundred dollars says I'll get her number and have her on the front page of every gossip blog tomorrow morning, when she leaves my house in the same thing she has on right now," Benji offered.

Marques thought about the bet for a minute before he looked at me, then back at Benji. "I can't get with that. But I say five hundred dollars you *don't* get her number at all and she disses you for Roman."

Benji stuck his hand out and shook Marques's hand. "That's a bet. Now watch me work my magic. Oh, and your ass better have my money in the morning. I know you just got access to all that trust-fund money, so you're good for it."

I shook my head as the two of them continued to go back and forth with this silly bet. Needless to say, by the end of the night, Marques was five hundred dollars richer and Benji had to settle for taking one of the strippers home instead.

The waitress, whom I now knew as Fiona, did slip her number to me before we left, but I crumpled up the napkin she had written it on and threw it right in the trash. Like I said before, she wasn't my type at all, which was kind of weird in a way, because the stripper who had run off the stage earlier wasn't my type, either, but for some reason, I couldn't shake her from my thoughts. Those gray eyes and full, plump lips were the last thing I saw that night before I finally made it home and fell asleep.

Melonee

Lying in my bed, I closed my eyes and prayed that whoever was knocking at my door would leave at any second. Unfortunately for me, my prayers weren't going to be answered anytime today. For the past fifteen minutes, someone had been banging on my door as if they were the police, and I had yet to get up and see who it was.

The reason for that was that I already knew who was crazy enough to be knocking on my door at six in the morning. Only one person would try to piss me off to the highest degree because I did something she didn't like.

The loud buzzing of my phone told me that my unwelcome guest had switched to calling my cell phone back-to-back since I wasn't answering the door at all. I reluctantly answered the phone.

"Melonee! I know you hear me out here! If you don't want me to wake the rest of your building up, you better come open up this damn door!" she screamed in my ear.

Shit! I silently cursed. Fiona knew that these assholes around here would have no problem calling a residents' meeting and fining me for the loud disturbance or, better yet, voting to put me out. Yet here her loud-ass mouth was.

The residents had never had a problem out of me until I had a few shouting matches with Proof a few months back, and that had ended with me paying a nice amount of change for the home-owners' rule violation and receiving a warning letter signed by the HOA and informing me that if I broke one of the rules again, I would be asked to leave. Well, if they asked me to move out, it wouldn't really matter one way or the other. I still had my three-bedroom, two-and-a-half-bathroom home in Baldwin Park, which I stayed at in between jobs, as well as my granny's house, which I had paid off a couple of years ago. Of course she didn't know that. The check she sent to her mortgage company went right back into an account I had set up for her when I got my first big insurance payout. She had a debit card for it and everything. I had told her that it was my account and that I wanted her to have access to it just in case the munchkin needed anything while I was away for all those months. Every now and then she used her card, but other than that, the money was just sitting there, gaining interest.

The house phone I had installed only for security reasons began to ring, which told me that someone from the HOA and or the management was calling. Instead of dealing with them this early, I sluggishly got up from my bed and walked to the front of my townhome. As soon as I swung the door open, I was met by a very pissed-off Fiona and a smirking Cowboy.

"I knew your ass would get up if I called that landline," Fiona said, walking into my house uninvited. "Thanks for getting me that number, bro."

I didn't even look at Cowboy as he followed behind his sister and made himself comfortable on my couch. I should've known his ass had my unlisted number somewhere.

Normally, I would go and slip on some shorts or something, seeing as I had on only a white wife beater—with no bra—panties, and my yellow Tweety Bird socks, and I had a male guest, but I knew that Cowboy wasn't checking for me. For as long as I'd known him, he had never brought a girl around, which had led me to believe that he liked playing with dick rather than pussy. So seeing a little of my skin wouldn't do anything to him.

"Fee, what I tell you about coming around here with all that loud shit? You already know what went down the last time with Proof's ass. Do you want me to get kicked out or something?" I said as I sat on my lounge chair across from Cowboy.

Being that I wasn't 100 percent sure of his sexual preference, I did pick up one of my big decorative pillows and place it on my lap so that it covered my nipples, which were starting to poke through my shirt, and any view of my sweet peach he could possibly get by sitting across from me.

"Bitch, please! It's been over a week since your ass ran off the stage like Flo Jo, and you've been MIA ever since. I've called, Proof has called, hell, even Granny has called a few times, but you haven't picked up for anyone. What if something was wrong with Madison?"

I rolled my eyes. Her ass could be so dramatic sometimes. Fiona knew damn well that if something was wrong with my daughter, Proof's ass would've busted this door down to get to me or would've blown my phone up to tell me something like that. Shit, my granny had the house phone number but had never called it once, so I'd figured that whatever it was that they wanted wasn't that important. Besides, I knew that Fiona, Proof, and the rest of the clique who had been hitting me up only wanted to know what had happened that night I left the club.

Fiona shook her head. "Do you see this shit, Cowboy? The bitch doesn't even have anything to say. The only reason I knew her ass wasn't dead was that she been watching movies and TV shows from my Netflix and Hulu accounts."

I looked over at Cowboy, who was sitting there on the couch, laughing his ass off. He had always been a little silly, but the boy was smart as hell, especially when it came to that computer shit. I didn't know the gist of everything he could do, but I did know that the boy could find out any and everything about you, from your professional life to your personal stuff, in a matter of minutes. He was the person from whom we used to get those crazy personal details about our marks, details that they had secretly thought no one knew about. Like, for instance, no one ever knew that my deceased husband, Douglas, had a real big fetish for feet. All I had had to do was get my toes done with red nail polish and he'd give me anything I wanted, including adding me to all his insurance policies after only a month of dating. Cowboy had found his profile, which was under a different name, on one of those freaky fetish Web sites, and we had used that against him.

I looked at the time on my phone. "So is this why you came to my house at seven o'clock in the morning, banging on my door like you were the police and yelling at the top of your lungs like a crazy woman? You wanted to bitch about me watching movies and TV shows on your Netflix and Hulu accounts?"

"Mel, if you don't stop acting stupid, I'm going to really beat your ass, on top of the ass whipping I already owe you for that little stunt you pulled. By the way, Raul said if you ever want to strip again, you need to have your ass back to work by tomorrow night, or he's going to let you go."

I gave her the stinkiest look I could muster. "Tell Raul he can kiss my natural black ass. I'm never going back to that club again. We will just have to find some other way to get at Roman Black."

Cowboy and Fiona shared a look, then turned their attention back to me.

"And why, may I ask, don't you want to go back?" Fiona asked as she turned on the bar stool she was sitting on and shook her head. "Melonee, this could be one of our biggest scores. We could all actually stop doin' this shit if everything goes according to plan, and you can finally find that fairy-tale love you've always talked about having. Why do you wanna fuck it all up? Because your conscience decided to kick in on the night we been planning for, for the past three months?" She stood up from her seat, walked over to where I was sitting, and sat on the arm of the lounge chair. "If the money isn't enough motivation for you anymore, just think about that 'happily ever after' life fit for a princess you've been promising Madison."

It was just like Fiona to bring up the one thing she knew I'd always wanted, in an effort to entice me into getting back on board with this whole thing. I mean, I understood everything she had just said. We could all finally start living our own lives and doing whatever it was that we all had dreamed of doing, but for some reason, I didn't want to go through with this anymore. I didn't know if it had something to do with the way the guy in the red T-shirt, the one I thought was a bodyguard, had looked at me that night, but something just didn't feel right about it anymore. The look he gave me with those piercing green eyes had made me want to straighten my life out and do better. His aura had made my whole body freeze up and relax at the same time, and then the disappointing look on his face when I was about to remove my top had made me feel like shit. I had felt all these different emotions in the presence of a man whom I didn't know from Adam and who had probably already forgotten about the ho-ass stripper who ran off the stage in the middle of her set.

"Look, Fee, to keep it one hundred, I didn't want to be a stripper in the first place. I agreed to it only because I wanted to be a team player and do my part. Yeah, the money was good, and I enjoyed meeting some of the girls that I met, but I can't get with that again. I'm down to doing anything else so we can get this money and finally be done with this shit, but if stripping is my only option, then y'all can count me out." I shrugged my shoulders. "Sorry."

A look of annoyance flashed across Fiona's face before it was replaced with a small smile, and then she nodded her head.

"Lucky for you, Cowboy was able to get access to Roman's schedule for the next few weeks. It just so happens that he's scheduled to attend some kind of charity function on Friday night, and as of yesterday, you and I will be in atten-dance."

"Why do we have to attend the charity thing? You didn't get his number that night at the club?" I asked.

She licked her lips, then smoothed her hand over her purple-hued hair, which was in a slick ponytail. The black one-piece jumpsuit she had on hugged every small curve of her body. Fiona was a bad chick and would probably make any man she met and fell in love with happy, but her mind had always been and would always be on money. Those green pieces of paper came before any and everything, including her heart.

"Roman was a bit occupied with the Japanese men he was entertaining, so I never got the chance to talk to him or slide him my number. However, his brother, Benjamin" —she smiled and shook her head—"that boy is something else. He kept flirting with me the whole night and wouldn't leave me alone about getting my number before he left."

I thought about Roman and how he had looked in that French-cut designer suit he had on. Yeah, with his dark hair, dark eyes, and sexy chiseled face, he'd looked fine as he talked to those Japanese men, but he was no match for his . . . *Wait*, I thought. I hoped the dude in the red T-shirt wasn't Roman's brother, Benjamin. I needed to take a look at that file again. Maybe I could find out who that dude really was, figure out if he was a Black.

"Um, Mel, I know that look on your face," Fiona said as she looked from me to Cowboy, then back to me. "Is there something you need to tell us? Do you not want to strip anymore because you met somebody? The way you were just looking is the same way you used to look whenever Proof's dumb ass would come around. All love struck and shit."

Just then Cowboy cleared his throat and sat up straight in his seat, which caused me to turn my attention to him. When our eyes connected, he smirked. Cowboy and Proof weren't the best of friends, but they had hung out together a lot when we were younger. However, the minute Proof and I became a couple, Cowboy had kind of distanced himself from us. It wasn't until Fiona and I had thought of putting together the Black Widow Clique that he started coming around more. When we'd found out he was a whiz kid with the computer, we knew we needed someone with his talents on the team.

I opened my mouth to say something, then closed it. Only to do the exact same thing two more times. I didn't think I was in love with Red T-shirt, but was I? How could I be? There was no such thing as love at first sight, correct? I mean, it would probably be totally one sided on my part, but still, there was no such thing, right?

I laughed to break the little awkward moment I had just had. "For your information, no, I haven't met anyone. Besides, when would I have had the time? Between dancing at the club all night and sleeping during the day, I really haven't had much of a social life."

Cowboy opened his mouth to say something, but I held my hand up and stopped him before he could utter a word.

I went on. "And before you even say it, no, I haven't talked to any of the customers or my regulars. I would just dance for them, and that was it. I made it very clear that I wasn't interested in a relationship, and they all respected that. Especially if they wanted to continue getting lap dances from me."

Cowboy looked at me through squinted eyes, then pushed his big square glasses up on his face before he stood up to his full height of six feet two. My eyes scanned his body from head to toe, and I couldn't do anything but shake my head. All that sexy milk chocolate cuteness had gone to waste. When he finally decided to come out of the closet, he was going to break a lot of hearts.

"Well, Mel, Fee and I have to get going," he announced in his smooth baritone. "We're about to go visit Pop's for a few hours. The charity party is this Friday, at eight. Both of y'all's names are on the list as guests. If there's some kind of auction, Fee and I figured that she should make a huge bid to try to get Roman's attention. Maybe outbid him on something he really wants, to get some sort of flirty dialogue going, and then Fiona can handle everything from there. Your job will be to entertain his brother Benjamin if he tries to step to Fiona again. You know how it all works after that."

Cowboy walked toward the door, then stopped and turned around. "Oh, and next time you have a male guest in your home, Mel, put on some damn clothes. There's only so much I can take before my thoughts start to turn nasty. You and I both know that Proof would try to kill me if I took down his baby mama."

Oh shit. I guessed my gaydar was off. Cowboy's ass had been checking me out. I pulled my wife beater down and crossed my arms over my breasts.

"All righty then," I said. "You guys be safe, and tell your dad I said hello. And next time, I'll make sure to put on something more appropriate."

Cowboy winked at me and nodded his head, then turned back around and walked to my door. Fiona was right behind him.

"Fiona!" I called, and she turned around as Cowboy walked out the door. "What are we going to do about our outfits for this party? I'm pretty sure this is going to be a black-tie affair, so we will need one of those fancy joints, right?"

Being the drama queen that she was, Fiona rolled her eyes and smacked her lips. "I'm still mad at your ass for ignoring my calls, bitch, but since you know I love to shop, I guess we can meet up on Wednesday or Thursday and hit the Beverly Center to see if we can find something to wear."

"It's a date," I replied. Then I smacked her hard on the ass, nudged her out the door, and closed the door in her face before she could curse me out.

After kicking my door for good measure and calling me a bitch at the top of her lungs, Fiona finally left.

As I went back into my bedroom, my mind drifted back to those beautiful green eyes and that caramel-blond hair. I knew my job was to distract Benjamin at the charity event, but if red T-shirt guy was there, I didn't know if I'd be able to stick to the script again.

Fiona

After being on the road for a little over three and a half hours, we finally made it to Chuckawalla Valley State Prison in the desert town of Blythe. For over ten years, my brother and I had been making this trip once a month to visit our old man, and the shit never got old. Because of my father's current living situation, he missed out on a lot of my and Cowboy's lives, and our one day a month was the time we all had to catch up on things.

We checked in the car and then ourselves and waited in the lobby to be called back. I looked around at all the women, men, and children who were here to spend some time with their loved ones, and shook my head. It seemed that every year since my father had arrived here, the number of visitors had gotten higher. Some of the people sitting in here had been coming for as long as I had, while others were just now starting this ride.

"Do you know her?" I whispered in Cowboy's ear as I leaned over. Some chick I hadn't seen up here before kept looking at my brother as if she was trying to place his face.

Cowboy looked up from whatever he was doing on his Apple watch, stared at the girl for a quick second, then looked back down. He was silent.

"Well?" I said.

"She looks familiar, but I doubt it. If anything, she's probably seen me in passing or knows someone who looks like me," was his response.

"Dude, she's staring a hole into the middle of your forehead. I know you feel her staring at you."

He glanced over in her direction again, then blew out a frustrated breath. "Fee, I told you I don't know her. And if I do, I surely don't remember her, so she can continue to stare all she wants. I'm not checking for her or any other female right now."

"Except Melonee," I wanted to say, but I kept that little comment to myself. Cowboy's infatuation with my best friend was weird to me. I was pretty sure Mel knew how he felt, because he did everything a love-struck fool did whenever he was around her, and I did remember him hinting to her a few times that he'd be a better man for her than Proof, but she never took the bait. Melonee looked at Cowboy the same way I did, as a brother, and he couldn't seem to understand that.

"Man, what's taking so long? We're normally in the back by now," Cowboy stated, watching a few people get called up to the receptionist desk to check in.

"Do you see all these people in here today? I told you we should've left earlier."

"You're the one that wanted to stop by Melonee's place, because she wasn't answering her phone."

"Like you didn't want to go," I said, smacking my lips.

Cowboy brushed his hands down the front of his dark-wash jeans, then picked at the imaginary lint on the button-down white shirt he had on under his black blazer. He picked his foot up off the floor and rested his ankle on his other leg. My big brother was looking kind of spiffy. I thought that until I looked down at the *Star Wars* socks he had on with his suede loafers, and rolled my eyes. This boy was such a nerd.

Thirty more minutes passed before we were finally allowed to go to the back and join the rest of the people in the visitation area, which looked like a lunchroom. After finding a spot all the way in the back of the room, Cowboy and I sat down and waited patiently for our father to enter. When he finally did, the biggest smile spread across my face, and I jumped out of my seat and into his open arms.

"Daddy!" I screamed, damn near causing us both to fall down on the floor.

"Baby doll, you act like you didn't see me just last month," my dad said with a chuckle.

"I know, Daddy, but I miss you like crazy. I can't wait until you're out of here." I grabbed both sides of my father's face and kissed each cheek. Looking at him, you couldn't even deny that I was his child. I was the spitting image of him. Cowboy, on the other hand, looked like our ho-ass mama.

"What's up, Junior?" Daddy asked Cowboy, calling him by his government.

Cowboy stood up and gave my father a hand slap, then a one-sided hug. "Nothing much, Pops. How you feeling?"

"Better . . . now that I get to spend some time with my offspring. What's been going on? How are y'all? How is Mel? And how is my grand-baby?" my father asked, referring to Madison. Because he considered himself the father figure in Mel's life, it was only right for him to claim her daughter as his grandchild.

"We're all fine. Just trying to make it. Madison's little butt is growing every day. She's almost as tall as me," I stated, picturing my godbaby's cute little face.

"You act like that's a surprise, with your short ass. Everyone is taller than you," Cowboy quipped, and I punched him in his arm, causing my father to shake his head and laugh.

We sat there for about two hours, catching up and reminiscing about old times. It felt so good to see my father smiling, laughing, and just shooting the shit, like we used to do in our living room back in the day. Sometimes I forgot that these prison walls and guards were surrounding us, as it felt so much like old times. Then there was the fact that my father kept up his appearance, the same way he had when he was on the streets. He still had that smooth, blemish-free caramel-colored skin that he was known for. His curly hair was thicker than ever and cut low, and his facial hair was trimmed to perfection. He looked as if he'd just stepped out of a magazine shoot. The only thing that brought me back to reality was the green scrubs-like jumpsuit my father had on every time I came to see him. Every inmate in here walked around with that prison uniform on, I guessed to tell them apart from the visitors.

Cowboy and our father had just started to play a hand of spades when I figured now was the right time to ask my dad for that information I needed.

"So, Daddy, have you talked to Uncle Dro lately?" I asked sweetly, trying to butter him up.

He ignored my question, like always, and continued to play their game.

"Daddy, I know you just heard what I asked you."

"I did, but I don't know why you keep asking me about your uncle. You know me and that nigga never really got along when I was out, and we damn sho' don't get along now."

Which was true. My father and his younger brother were like night and day. While my father liked to work for everything he got, my uncle Dro was the type to get it by any means necessary. The last time we saw my uncle was when my father was arrested for this murder charge. Uncle Dro came by the house, trying to see if my father had left any money behind or anything that he could use to try to make some money, but after he came up empty handed, he left, and we never saw or heard from him again.

"I know that, Daddy, but I need to talk to him about something."

I could see my father's eyebrow rise on his handsome face, but he never responded. Cowboy, on the other hand, stopped playing the game altogether and turned toward me.

"What the fuck you need to talk to him about? And why don't I know anything about this?" he barked.

"Look, I just want to reach out to him and see how he's doing. I can't be a concerned niece? I mean, he is the only family we have left." I turned toward my father. "If anything happens to you, Uncle Dro will be the only living relative that we have. Don't you think we should at least have each other's numbers?"

Cowboy and my father looked at each other for a minute, then continued to play their card game as if I hadn't just said something. We sat in silence for what felt like forever, as they played a few more hands, before my father finally spoke again.

"I don't know what you're up to, Fiona, but I hope for your sake that you don't plan on including your uncle in anything you have going on. He may be fam, but the nigga will kill you and anything else standing in his way if there is some money involved."

"It's nothing like that, Daddy, I swear," I said, with my legs crossed underneath the table.

"Yeah, it better not be." He gave me a pointed look, then turned back to his game. "So what's going on with school? Shouldn't you be graduating soon?"

I looked at Cowboy, who just shook his head and smirked.

"Yeah, Daddy, I have a few more semesters, and then I'll be done." My father didn't know anything about the BWC, the Black Widow Clique, and didn't need to know. He had questioned me about the packages and the money that I put on his books faithfully every month without me having a job, but I had told him that I had sugar daddies who gave me whatever I wanted, including money. Which, in actuality, was true. I had just left out the part about marrying them, then killing them for even more money.

"And what about you, Junior? You still doing that computer stuff for that big technology company?"

Cowboy nodded his head but didn't look my father in the eye, which was a sure giveaway that he was lying, but if my father noticed it, he sure didn't say anything. He just continued to ask us about our professional life, which then somehow turned into questioning us about our personal lives.

"What about you and Mel, Junior? You guys should be together now that she doesn't mess with that no-good nigga she got pregnant by, right?" my father asked Cowboy, with a smile on his face.

"Man . . . ," Cowboy replied as he wiped his hand down his face and blew out a breath. "Melonee ain't fucking with me like that. I've told her a few times that she should be with me, but she just laughs it off like I'm telling some kind of joke."

"Do you laugh with her?" my father asked.

Cowboy shrugged his shoulders. "I did the first couple of times I told her, but this last time I stepped to her, I was serious, and she just waved me off."

"Maybe you should show her. It might be better than telling her."

"I do—" Cowboy said, but he stopped talking when I nudged his knee under the table. Our father didn't need to know that he was the reason Mel always found out about the girls Proof was cheating with.

When I said my brother was a beast with this computer shit, I meant it. If e-mails, text messages, pictures, Snapchats, whatever were deleted, he could dig them up, bring them back to life, and send them straight to you as if they came from another person's phone.

"Just give her a little more time. She's probably still hung up on my grandbaby's daddy. Just keep on doing you and being there for her, and she'll eventually come around. That's what happened between me and her mama," my dad said with the biggest smile on his face. Anytime he talked about Melonee's mom, he would always get that love-struck look in his eye and have a smile on his face that went from ear to ear. Mel's mom was his first and only true love, and no one would ever change that. Even after her death, he still had all this love in his heart for her.

We spent a few more hours with our father before visitation was finally over. After saying our good-byes and giving each other hugs, Cowboy and I headed back to his car. Before we hit the road for another three-and-a-half-hour drive back to L.A., he warned me about Uncle Dro, and then, against my father's wishes, he wrote down the last number he had for our uncle on a piece of paper. He told me to keep any contact with our uncle to a minimum, and then he pulled out of the prison parking lot.

"So what do you really need that nigga Pedro's number for?" Cowboy asked as soon as we got on the freeway.

I looked at my brother for a minute, trying to determine if I really wanted to tell him what

I needed Dro's number for. I knew he'd be down with the money part of the plan, but the other part, he might be in his feelings about. But because he was my right-hand, and I had never kept a secret from him, I decided to tell him, anyway.

"What I'm about to tell you may have you feeling some type of way, but in the long run, we'll be set for life if everything goes right," I said.

He raised his eyebrows at me, then looked back at the road. "You already know I'm down for whatever and I'm going to always have your back. We all we got."

I nodded my head at my older brother and turned down the volume on the radio. If we were going to do this, I needed his undivided attention when I gave him the rundown on this plan.

Roman

"So I take it that the meeting with Osamu Takahiro and his colleagues went according to plan?" my father asked as he sat at the head of the dining-room table for our Sunday brunch.

"Yeah, everything went smoothly. I had my assistant send over all the paperwork this morning. Now we just wait for them to sign on the dotted line, and then everything's a go."

"What do you think made them agree to everything? Don't get me wrong, son. I know you can run this company just as well as I did, but you almost lost their backing the first time you met with those investors."

I thought about my father's question for a minute. The first time I met with Mr. Takahiro and his team, the meeting ended with neither party coming to an agreement on a return on investment they would derive if they invested their money in this new RTD international company. We could easily finance everything ourselves, but a smart business never used its own money, especially when expanding overseas.

After I talked with our lawyers and our accountants, I was reassured that I had done the right thing by declining their offer to invest a majority of the money in the company if they could be guaranteed a 45 percent return on investment, regardless of whether the company made a profit or not. I actually started to look into other sources as far as investment went, but a week after my meeting with Mr. Takahiro, I received a phone call requesting that we have another sit-down. There was no doubt in my mind that my father was behind it. Though he had been retired for two years, he still found ways to get involved in company business.

I shrugged. "Um, honestly, Dad, it was . . ."

"Me, of course," Benji said, announcing himself as he entered the room.

Every Sunday it was the same thing with him. Brunch was always served at twelve o'clock, and he always came waltzing in at two o'clock, with whatever sorry girl he had talked into his bed following close behind him. This morning, his tail was some blond girl with the weirdest-shaped nose I'd ever seen. Then, if that wasn't enough, her eyes were big and popped out, as if she had a scared look permanently attached to her face.

She pulled a few strands of her hair behind her ear, then sheepishly waved to everyone sitting at the table before taking a seat. Her tall, superthin frame told me that she had to be some kind of model, the type of girl Benji normally went for. I just hoped that messing with him didn't end her career before it actually started.

"Benjamin, dear, who is your guest this week?" asked Benji's mom, Julia, who was also my step-mother. Sitting regally in her chair across from my father, and looking like Cindy Crawford, she scooped up a tiny bit of eggs on her fork and placed it in her mouth. She hadn't even look up from her plate as she asked the question. That was just how repetitive Benji's actions were every week.

"This is Stacy."

"Sammy," the young woman said, correcting.

"I mean Sammy. We met a couple of days ago at the opening of the new Waldorf Astoria Hotel in downtown L.A." I watched as Benji placed big spoonfuls of eggs, fruit, sausage, and home fries on his plate. Not once did he offer his guest any of the food, let alone a plate to put some on.

Benji started to stuff his face as he continued to give himself praise. "Yeah, Dad, if it wasn't for me coming in to save the day, Roman here would've had another failed meeting."

My father wiped his mouth with his napkin and gave all his attention to Benji. "How so?"

"Well . . ." Benji stuffed a whole sausage link into his mouth and chewed a few times. "Osamu and his guys had already told the translator that they would agree to twenty percent of the company, but I guess the translator either didn't really understand too well or wanted to take matters into his own hands. When I walked in, he was trying to get Osamu to agree to ten percent, while Roman here was sitting at the table, playing *Toy Blast* or *Words with Friends*."

My father turned to me. "Is that true, son?" he asked. He looked at me with a hint of concern in his dark eyes.

I shook my head. "First of all, I wasn't playing no *Toy Blast* or *Words with Friends*."

Benji laughed and stuffed another sausage into his mouth.

I went on. "Secondly, I had no idea that the translator was trying to get them to agree to a lower percentage. Honestly, I'm not mad at him for doing it. Had he gotten them to agree to ten percent, I would've promoted him to your job, Benjamin. At least he was trying to negotiate on behalf of the company. You, however, were just ready to party, as always."

Benji pointed his knife at me and nodded his head.

"I take it you all went out to celebrate after Benji showed up and closed the deal?" Julia asked.

"Contrary to what you may believe, Ma, Osamu and his guys asked me what place was a good place to go celebrate," Benji explained. "Just so happens that I was in the mood to see some titties and ass, so I told them about Decadence."

"Benjamin!" Julia snapped. Her cheeks turned a few shades of red as she held the linen napkin over her mouth. "Where are your manners? You know we don't talk like that at the breakfast table. It's enough that you bring these *guests* that we've never met before every Sunday." Julia looked over at Sammy. "Sorry, beautiful," she said, then nodded her head and went back to eating.

"Now, back to this celebration. Do you think taking them to Decadence is what really sealed the deal?" my father asked with eager eyes. He always liked hearing stories about closing deals.

"I think so. That and a little friendly wager," Benji replied, winking at me.

"Friendly wager? This could be interesting," my father mused. "Do tell about this wager."

"Well, there was this waitress in our section who kept trying to get Roman's attention, but again, he was on one of his *Toy Blast* and *Word with Friends* binges," Benji said. "Anyways,

Marques bet me five hundred dollars that I couldn't get her number by the end of the night. While we were making the bet, I told Osamu and his people about it. They, too, had noticed the way the waitress had been ogling Roman, so they got in on the action as well."

Benji finally turned to his guest, who had been sitting there quietly and taking in our family conversation. "You want a plate or something? There is plenty of food for you to eat."

She shook her head. "No thank you. I have a show later on tonight, and I don't want to look fat."

We all gave each other quick glances, more than likely thinking the same thing. After a few seconds of awkward silence, all eyes went back to my "will sleep with anything with two legs" stepbrother. Only Benji would bring someone to a brunch who didn't want to put another pound on her one-hundred-pound body.

"Well . . ." My father cleared his throat. "What happened with the bet?"

Benji chewed some more of the food in his mouth, then took a big swallow of his orange juice. "I came home thirty-five hundred dollars richer." A slick smirk spread across his face.

"You didn't get her number," I interjected. I distinctly remembered the waitress with the purple hair sliding her number to me and me throwing it away.

"I did to get her number," Benji countered. "As soon as you threw it away in the trash can, I retrieved it and showed them my evidence."

"You cheating bastard . . . ," I snarled.

"Roman!" Julia snapped at me this time. "What did I just tell your brother about language at the table?"

I hated when she tried to talk to us as if we were teenagers. My father had married her when I was only three years old, and she had never treated me any different than she had her own son, Benji, but that hadn't stopped me from missing my real mother. Sometimes I wondered what our life would be like if she were still alive. Would my father be as happy as he was now with Julia. Would I have been the pawn in a bitter divorce?

From what my father and my uncle Kazi had told me, my mother had one of the most beautiful souls they'd ever seen. Her heart was as pure as gold, and she loved me more than anything in the world. It was that love that she had for me that had her sacrifice her own life when a home-invasion robbery took place at our house the day after my father left to go out of town for business. Four men entered our home, looking for money, jewelry, and anything else that they could get their hands on.

Instead of being satisfied with what my mother gave them, they wanted more, and when she couldn't produce any more, they threatened to kill me. When one of the gunmen pointed his gun at me, my mother covered me with her body, and when he pulled the trigger twice, she took both bullets that were fired from the chamber. She died while lying on top of me that night, right after she smiled, kissed me on my forehead, and closed her eyes for the last time. All I remembered was her long blond hair, which smelled like roses, and those emerald-green eyes, which resembled mine.

My mother's death rocked my whole family to the core. My grandfather, who was in Russia at the time, flew out with my uncle Kazi and a few other family members and tried to take me from my father. They felt that I'd be better off with my Russian side of the family as opposed to with my workaholic single white father. That and they wanted the only connection to my mother close to them. My father, however, wasn't having it. He told my grandfather and my uncle Kazi that he loved my mother just as much as they did and that he needed me with him, or he'd go insane. He couldn't bear the thought of losing the love of his life and his son all in the same year.

Needless to say, my Russian family left me out here with my father and returned to Russia, with an agreement to get me every summer. A year after my mother died, my father met and married Julia after only a two-month courtship. A lot of people, including my uncle Kazi, didn't agree with their union, because it happened so fast, but twenty-seven years later, Julia and my father were still together, with no signs of leaving each other.

I longed for the type of love my father had shared with my mother when they were together and was now sharing with Julia. I had come close, but I had never got that gut feeling my father had always told me I'd get when I found *the one*. Well, that was until I laid eyes on an ebony beauty with the most amazing gray eyes I'd ever seen. The moment my eyes connected with hers, I felt as if the wind had been knocked out of me. Like I had just got socked in the stomach and couldn't catch my breath for anything. Had it not been for my phone going off, I would have never taken my eyes off her. I mean, what she was doing wasn't the ideal job I'd want for my future wife, but as demeaning as being a stripper was, I understood that some people had to do whatever it took to make it in life.

A piece of pineapple hitting me on the side of my face brought me back to whatever discussion I'd been missing as I sat there, daydreaming about the girl from the club.

"See? This is what I was just talking about. Roman's mind is always on other things, rather than being on closing these deals." Benji laughed, wiping his hands on the linen napkin. "But that's okay. What else are big brothers for? When little brother isn't handling his business right, who better to swoop in and save the day than me?"

"And the way you dress could help a little as well, Roman," Julia added. "I can't believe you wore a red T-shirt, some tan shorts, and a green pair of Converse sneakers to a business meeting. What were you thinking, honey? Your father and I didn't pay all that money for a personal stylist when you were promoted for you not to take full advantage of what they have to offer. You are the head of the company now, so you need to dress like it. Maybe then you won't need your big brother over here to come in and help with closing those deals," she said, nodding her head at me, then looking over at Benji, who was now texting on his phone and completely ignoring his guest.

"How I dress shouldn't mean anything. I never see Bill Gates in a three-piece suit or, hell, even Mark Zuckerberg. Why does the way I dress have to determine the outcome of a deal?"

"Because, son, when people see you dressed like you own the place, they will treat you as such," my dad interjected. "What businessman dressed to the nines will respect another businessman who comes to a meeting about money in an outfit that probably cost no more than fifty bucks?"

The question was rhetorical, but I answered it, anyway. "The same businessman who does the research on the company he's going to potentially invest in and make a shitload of money with. I have dressed this way for the past two years and have brought more money to the business than you did your first two years, Dad. Granted Benji has helped with the Japanese investors, but that shouldn't take away from the other deals I've closed all by myself—dressed in some Chucks, shorts, and a T-shirt."

My father shifted in his seat, then turned toward me. His features were similar to mine. He was a large man like me, with hooded eyes, tan skin, a strong chin, and a chiseled jawline. The only difference between us two was his dark hair and my blond hair.

"Look, Roman, if you can't wear a suit every day, like a normal CEO should, could you at least wear them to business meetings? Appease your old man, will you?" my dad pleaded.

I doubted that it would happen anytime soon, but I did nod my head in agreement.

My dad sighed. "That's my boy."

"Oh, and while we're on the subject of suits . . . ," Julia interjected. "Can you please wear one to the

Gold Hearts Foundation Charity event on Friday? There will be a lot of important people there whose pockets we want to dig deep in for your foundation. We raised a little over half a million last year. I'm sure we can double that if the founder of Gold Hearts and CEO of RTD comes dressed to the nines. You know all those rich people will have no problem donating those big bucks as long as you look like you would be able to donate to their charities the same amount they do to yours."

Again, I nodded my head. Maybe I did need to start dressing the part if I wanted people to start taking me seriously. I'd just hit up Marques later on today to see if he could get us an appointment scheduled at his cousin's tuxedo shop. If I was going to step out in a suit, I at least wanted it to be designed to my liking and to fit my style.

I looked over at Benji to gauge his opinion about what my father, Julia, and I had just talked about, but he was too busy whispering in his one-night stand's ear and making her giggle like a little schoolgirl. The thought of bringing a date to the charity event crossed my mind but left just as fast. I didn't want to be bothered with any of the girls I could call, especially since they didn't have those mesmerizing gray eyes.

Melonee

I walked around the Beverly Center all by myself, trying to find an evening gown that caught my eye, thanks to my no-good best friend. Fiona's ass had stood me up, and she hadn't even had the decency to call or text and say why. I had called her phone all morning long and then an hour before we were scheduled to meet, and each call I made went straight to voice mail, which was odd. But I figured she was still upset with me for not answering the door the other morning. I knew when she finally checked her messages, she was going to be a little upset, because I had cussed her ass out something terrible on a few.

It was her idea to go shopping and her idea for us to crash this dumb charity event, which I wasn't so keen on going to. If it wasn't for the fact that I hoped to see red T-shirt guy again, I probably would ditch this shindig and do something else, like go to see Madison. I was starting to miss spending time with my munchkin, and to be quite honest, I'd rather be spending time with her, sipping tea and eating cookies with her stuffed animals, than with the stuck-up bougie people that I knew would be at this event.

When I'd talked to my granny today, she told me that Proof had stopped by earlier and had brought Madison a few things, saying that they were from me. As much as those gifts probably lit up my baby's face, they really didn't do anything for me. I would rather have been the one giving those toys to her and seeing that beautiful smile on her face, as opposed to her dad. Everything had better go according to plan Friday night, because if not, my decision to just bow out and leave the Black Widow Clique to Fiona and the rest of the crew would be that much easier.

I window-shopped for a few more minutes before I spotted this cute pair of tan ankle-strap heels in the display window at L. K. Bennett. Maybe if I picked my shoes out first, it would be easier to find a nice dress. Just before I walked into the overpriced store, my cell phone, which was in the back pocket of the jeans I had on, vibrated. I took out my phone, and a huge smile spread across my lips when my aunt Bree's face lit up my screen.

"Auntie?" I said sternly when I answered the call.

"Niece?" she replied, her voice just as stern as mine.

After what felt like ten minutes of awkward silence, we both laughed.

"Bitch, what you up to?" Aunt Bree finally asked after we stopped laughing.

With my aunt being only five years older than me, she and I were more like sisters rather than auntie and niece. After my mother was killed, my aunt Bree had tried to step up to fill in the void that I endured, but with her being away at college, getting her PhD, and then working full-time as a chief scientist for MedStar Health Research Institute, it had been hard for her to juggle her life and mine at the same time. Especially when she already had her home and career set up in Maryland.

With my phone glued to my ear, I walked into the store and picked up the shoes I had my eyes on. "Nothing really. Just looking for something to wear to this charity event I have to go to tomorrow night."

"Charity event? Tomorrow night? Did we meet someone new? Perhaps someone you would actually fall in love with and marry for the right reasons?"

Aunt Bree knew everything about the BWC and what it was all about. Although she had been against it from the start, and had lectured Fiona and me countless times about karma and what would happen if something ever went wrong, she was still low-key okay with what we were doing.

"Naw, nothing like that. Just another job," I replied as I motioned to the saleswoman to assist me. "Do you have these in a size nine?"

The saleswoman nodded her head, then headed to the back of the store.

Aunt Bree sighed. "Another job, huh? Mel, when are you going to stop gambling with your life and do something productive with it? And where does Madison fit into all of this? You're a great mother, don't get me wrong, but how long do you think she's going to accept you leaving for these long periods of time and not feel some type of way about it? I know she has Proof and Granny there, but you gave birth to a young princess. You have to teach her how to be a queen."

"I know, Auntie. But how can I teach her how to be a queen when I've never been treated like one?"

The saleswoman returned with a couple of shoe boxes and placed them in front of me after I took a seat. "I brought you a nine and a half as well, because these particular shoes happen to run a little snug."

I mouthed the words *thank you*, then tried on the shoes as I continued to speak with my aunt.

"Look, Mel, I know you're probably tired of me preaching this to you, but I love you, and I only want what's best for you. What ever happened to you opening up that little bakery you and your mom used to always talk about?"

I smiled at the memory of one of my mother's dreams for us. Because she and I both had had a love for the cartoon character Strawberry Shortcake, we had always talked about opening our own bakery just like her, with all the cakes, cookies, pies, and tarts you could imagine. We'd also sell different-flavored coffees and teas, but our specialty would be the baked goods. My mother had even wanted to make sure you could smell fresh strawberries whenever you walked through the door. Strawberries were one of her favorite scents. I hadn't known how that would be possible with all the other goodies being made in the store, but my mother had insisted on having that smell.

A single tear escaped from my eye and ran down my cheek. I didn't even know that I was crying until the saleswoman walked back up to me and handed me a tissue.

"I'm still going to open Berry Tasty," I said, mentioning the name my mother and I had come up with for the shop. "I just have to do this one last job, and then Fiona can have it all."

My aunt smacked her lips, and I could just see her honey-brown eyes rolling to the back of her head. She had never cared for Fiona very much but would never tell me why. Whenever she came to visit, she would mainly steer clear of Fee, or else a shouting match between them would always start up. I'd asked both of them at different times what all the beef was about, but every time I'd asked, they both just waved their hands and said, "I don't fuck with her."

"You already know how I feel about your little friend, so I'm not going to even get into that. All I'm going to say is, watch her, because she's a sneaky bitch, and I wouldn't put anything past her."

After trying on both pairs of shoes, I went with the half size and walked to the register to pay for my selection.

"I hear you, Auntie, although I doubt I have to watch anything about Fiona. That girl is an open book and has been my best friend for years. She and I are cut from the same cloth, so if she was thinking about stabbing me in the back, I'd know before she even tried to do it." I paid for my shoes, grabbed my receipt and bag, then headed out of the store. "Enough of this 'watch your back' talk. To what do I owe the pleasure of this phone call?"

Aunt Bree laughed. "Leave it to you to change the subject whenever someone talks about your precious Fee. Anyways, I was calling to let you know that I requested a week or two off from work and will be out there in a couple of months. Make sure you clear your schedule for a few days so that me, you, and Madison can do our spa weekend, okay?"

I nodded my head, as if she could see me, because my throat had suddenly become dry. I tried to swallow, but the lump in my throat was not going anywhere. My palms began to sweat, and the butterflies in my stomach began to go insane. Taking a deep breath, I tried to stop whatever was happening to me, but that didn't seem to help, as whatever it was intensified. The last time I felt like this was when I was . . .

My eyes scanned the somewhat crowded mall, in search of the only person who had ever made my body feel this way. Red T-shirt guy was somewhere near, but I had no idea where. I heard Aunt Bree's voice on the other end of the phone, calling my name, but my attention was being pulled elsewhere. I almost thought that I was going crazy, standing still in the middle of the mall, with my cell phone on my cheek instead of my ear, franticly looking around. That was until my eyes connected with those sexy green orbs that had been invading my dreams since the last time I saw them.

I took a sharp breath, then slowly released it as he held my gaze. I could tell by the way he was looking at me that he recognized my face but couldn't place where he knew me from. As his eyes raked over my entire body, a tingle shot from my heart right to my clit, causing me to squeeze my thighs together. The jeans I had on were skintight, so the friction increased the thumping of my shit. Good thing I had chosen to wear a blue blazer over my white tank top, or else my hard nipples would be on full display right now.

I watched him watch me for what felt like hours, before the same curly-haired mixed dude he was sitting next to at the club walked up to his side and began to look at me too. I watched as his friend's eyes scanned my body first, then opened wide with recognition when he finally looked at my face. Red T-shirt guy, who was still staring at me, didn't move a muscle. Even when his friend pulled him over and said something in his ear, his gaze never faltered. It was pretty evident that whatever his friend had said made him remember where he knew me from. His eyes, which just a second ago had been full of lust, now were filled with that same disappointment I'd seen that night at the club. My heart sank to the bottom of my stomach and killed all those butterflies fluttering around. My breathing came back to normal, and my legs began to get some type of feeling in them again. With one last look, I decided that I would just pull something from my closet to wear to the charity event, and then I turned and walked away.

"Melonee, are you okay? What's the matter? Mel! Say something, damn it! Do I need to call Proof?" I heard Aunt Bree screaming as I put the phone back up to my ear.

"No. I'm . . . I'm good, Auntie. I just . . . I just . . . I gotta go. I'll call you later on tonight or tomorrow, okay?"

"But, Mel, wait . . . ," was the last thing I heard Aunt Bree say before I ended the call and put my phone back in my pants pocket.

Me running into this guy a second time and getting this feeling had to mean something; I just didn't know what that something was. I'd never felt this way about anybody, so it was crazy that this complete stranger seemed to drive my mind, heart, body, and soul crazy, and I didn't even know his name. Hopefully, he'd be at this charity event in a couple of days and I could find out what this feeling was all about . . . and whether it was good or bad.

Fiona

Rays from the morning sun were bursting through my blinds and damn near slapping me awake. Three hours of sleep just wasn't enough for me, but I had to get up and get my day started. I grabbed my phone, which was on the nightstand next to me, and looked at the time. A soft groan escaped from my throat, because it was too early for me to be getting up.

"What time is it?" a rough, deep voice asked as I sat staring at the ceiling. When I didn't answer, his arm snaked around my waist and pulled me deeper into his side. My nipples instantly became hard when I got a whiff of his subtle yet masculine scent. Remnants of his Clive Christian cologne filled my nose and caused a slight shiver to go down my body.

"It's a little after nine. Why? Are you ready to leave me already?" I asked, hoping his answer would be no. I could feel his lips curl up into a smile against the back of my neck.

"You would think that after a night like what we just had, you'd be up serving me breakfast in bed . . . naked," he replied.

I licked my lips and smiled. He wasn't ready to go yet. "Maybe I didn't enjoy it as much as you assume I did," I told him.

The devilishly handsome man lying next to me opened one of his eyes and turned his head toward me. The small rays of sun coming through the blinds cast a light glow over his tawny-colored skin. My eyes skimmed over his very masculine and impeccably fit body. This man's whole aura screamed, "Bad boy," but I didn't care. I was grown and could most definitely handle anything he threw my way. That sexy smirk I couldn't get enough of was plastered across his face, with a hint of naughtiness behind it.

"With the way you were screaming my name last night and scratching up my back, I highly doubt you didn't enjoy my sex," he countered.

He was right. I did enjoy the hell out of his sex, but I'd never tell him that. I needed something from this man, and before things became too complicated, I had to make sure I'd be all right on my end.

Instead of responding to what he'd said, I pulled my burgundy silk sheets off my naked body and got up from my bed.

"I like my eggs over easy and my toast lightly toasted," my guest said, with a hint of humor in his voice.

Because I didn't turn around to acknowledge his request, I knew he didn't see my light eye roll and the big-ass smile on my face. He'd get that breakfast this time, but the next time we hooked up, I bet that it would be him bringing me breakfast in bed.

"Oh, and before you go, you might want to get that," I heard him say to my back, and I instantly stopped in my tracks.

"Get what?"

"Your phone." He pointed to my dresser. "It's been going off all morning."

I waved him off. "It's no one important."

"No one important, huh?" He laughed and ran his hand over the five o'clock shadow forming on his face. "If that's your boyfriend, I can leave and get up with you some other time."

I turned back around to face him, with my hands on my hips. Walking closer to the bed, I made sure he got an eyeful of every inch of my naked body. "If that's your way of trying to ask me if I'm in a relationship, then the answer is no. I enjoy the company of men who understand that I don't want a relationship or situationship right now. All I want is some good sex when I call, and maybe a few meals in between."

He nodded his head after lustfully eyeing my body one last time, then laid his head back down on my pillow and closed his eyes. Obviously satisfied with the response I had just given him.

I left my cell where it was at and proceeded down the hall to my kitchen. I didn't have to look at my phone to know that it was Melonee calling me again. We were supposed to go to the mall this morning and shop for dresses. I knew she was going to kill me for standing her up, but I didn't care. Although it was my idea for us to go, I couldn't let this opportunity I had right now pass me by. My mind was always on the money, and it would always stay that way.

Roman

"Roman, you should just go after her."

"Go after who?" I said, trying to play it off.

Marques stopped looking at the overpriced shirt in his hand and gave me a pointed look. "Ole girl from the strip club you were just having a stare down with," he said as he nodded his head in the direction she had just taken off in.

"How did you know . . . ?"

"Bruh, I'd remember that body and those eyes anywhere. Shawty's shape is superbad. Ass, titties, small waist, smooth chocolate skin, not a scratch or scrape anywhere, and those thick, full, juicy lips. Woo . . . If you weren't my dude, I would've gone after her myself." He shook his head. "Just promise me this one thing," he said, placing the shirt back on the rack. "Hook a brotha up with someone she is related to or is good friends with, please. You know birds of a feather flock together, so someone in her circle is bound to be as fine as she is. And you know

I don't discriminate, either. That body and those looks ain't come from just anywhere. Either her mama is hot or her grandma is shutting shit down. I'll take either one if they even look a third as good as she does."

I smiled and shook my head at Marques's crazy ass. Only he would put a bid in for some-one's mother, aunt, or grandma and really mean it. No woman was off-limits to him. Big, tall, small, skinny, young, old. As long as you were a woman and looked good to him, he had no problem hooking up with you.

A lot of people were turned off by his realness, while some never took him too seriously because of his family heritage. When you were the heir to a multimillion-dollar luxury hotel chain, some people tended to think that you were stuck up and snotty, like most heirs were. Marques, however, was totally different and had been that way since we were little kids.

Being 100 percent black, as he would say, with a little bit of Spanish blood mixed in to explain his head full of curly black hair, Marques had no problem getting any woman he wanted. His light skin, light brown eyes, over six-foot frame, and basketball-player build did play a part in driving the women crazy, but that wild curly mess on the top of his head and around his face got 'em every time. If his family business was not worth well over nine figures, if Marques were a struggling actor who worked at Starbucks part-time, he'd still have no problem picking up women.

"Aye, man, she's getting away. You better hurry up and try to get at her before one of these other cats that's staring at her does," Marques said.

I didn't know why Marques mentioning other men starting at Gray Eyes got under my skin, but, for some reason, it did. Even when he had just talked about how sexy she was, I felt some type of way about that. It felt like she belonged to me already, and I didn't even know who she really was. Our eyes connected as she turned to look at me one last time before she disappeared completely into the crowd.

I felt Marques's hand touch my shoulder. "See? I told you to go after her. What if you don't see her any more after this?"

That was a good question, one that I really couldn't answer. What if this *was* the last time I saw her? I mean, I had gone back up to Decadence a week after the first time I saw her, hoping that she had returned to work, but when I'd asked the flirty redhead in VIP if my mystery girl was coming in that night, the redhead had informed me that Lucky Charms had quit working there and that she didn't have any way to contact her. After I tipped the waitress with a hundred-dollar bill, she'd managed to remember my mystery girl's real name. Melonee.

I had left there empty handed that night and had thinking and dreaming about Melonee's beautiful face and sexy gray eyes ever since. It was so bad that I would get distracted at work with thoughts of seeing her again. So much so that Benji's ass was picking up on some of the slack I was putting out.

Something was pulling me to her, and I had no doubt that I'd run into her again. When that moment came, I was going to make sure she didn't get away that time.

For a couple more hours, Marques and I shopped in his cousin's overpriced store for nice suits to wear to the charity event. Finally, we both decided on going with some custom Hugo Boss three-piece suits. His a dark navy blue, and mine a smoky gray. After Percy took our measurements and promised to have the suits done and ready to wear by tomorrow evening, we went and had lunch at a restaurant up the street.

While we waited for our beers and appetizers, I went through work-related e-mails on my phone, and Marques cupcaked with some girl he'd met a few days ago on his. Finally, the waiter came back with our order and placed the hot food on the table. Just when I was about to dig into the blackened salmon meal and enjoy one of my favorite things to eat, my phone rang. As expected, Benji had finally decided to return my call after ignoring my calls all last night and this morning.

"Hello," I answered, but I was met with silence.

I popped a piece of grilled asparagus in my mouth and chewed for a few seconds before I said hello for the second time. When I was met with silence again, I pressed the phone closer to my ear and tried to make out what was going on in the background. The faint sound of Benji's phone being tossed around could be heard, followed by a nasal, high-pitched laugh.

"Aye. You okay?" Marques asked. "Because your facial expression just changed drastically."

I nodded my head and pointed to my phone. "Benji sex dialed me again."

Marques wiped his hand on the linen napkin and laughed. "Aye, I'm starting to think he does that shit on purpose, just to rub it in your face that he's getting some pussy, while you're using your left hand to pleasure yourself."

The nasal laughter in the background suddenly turned into a series of moans and loud screams, which had me hanging up the phone.

"Benji's dick will eventually fall off from the numerous infections he's going to get from fucking all these random women, while I'll be balls deep in my wife's pussy and popping all kinds of babies inside her every nine months," I said.

Marques shook his head and stuffed a piece of his steak in his mouth. "I still don't understand why you're doing this celibacy thing, but I can respect it. Men should be selective with their dicks, just like some of these women are selective with who they giving it up to."

About a year ago, I had made the decision to become celibate after having meaningless sex with countless women and not getting any kind of satisfaction or mind stimulation, or having any genuine interest in whoever the woman was that I was dealing with. I would get completely turned off either after the sex or after going on a few dates.

I'd never been the relationship kind of guy, anyway, since my father took up the majority of my free time when I was in college, grooming me to step into the CEO role as soon as I graduated. I didn't have any time to enjoy being a young man while going after my bachelor's degree in finance. If it weren't for the parties my frat house had on campus during my college years or the travels Marques and I enjoyed during summer breaks, I probably would've never had any type of social life. All my father had ever believed in was work, work, and more work.

Thinking back, I may have had one serious relationship when I was younger. During my high school days, I did date the captain of the cheerleading squad for a few years. Shelly Richfield. I thought she and I would get married and everything, being high school sweethearts and all. But that shit changed when I caught her in the football team's locker room, having sex with Marques's older brother, Siah, right before our senior year. I never looked at women or relationships the same way after that. That was, until I laid eyes on Melonee. Maybe she would be the woman to change my whole outlook on women and being in a committed relationship. Then again, it could be my body reacting to not having the feeling of some tight, wet, sweet pussy wrapped around my dick for the past twelve months. I didn't know what Melonee was working with, but I had every intention to find out.

"Aye, man, while you were sitting here, obviously daydreaming about sexy chocolate, I had the waitress wrap our food to go," Marques said, breaking me from my nasty thoughts. "Just got a call from Miss Porsche. She's in town for a few, and you know she had to hit your boy up." Marques stood up from the table, with a huge smile on his face.

He started texting on his phone with one hand while holding our to-go boxes with the other.

I remained seated at the table and waited for Marques to finish texting.

"Yo, Porsche just texted me and said Tina's out here with her too and was asking about you," he informed me a minute later.

Tina. I hadn't heard that name in a while. The Tiffani Amber Thiessen look-alike was a pretty girl, but her sexual prowess and personality were on another scale. That was why I never gave her my contact info after that night we had sex. The only way for her to relay a message to me was through Porsche and Marques.

I stood up from the table, ignoring what Marques had just said, and put on my leather jacket. It was a beautiful day outside, so I had decided to ride my bike and handle my business for the day. I touched a back pocket of my khaki shorts to make sure my wallet was still there, grabbed my keys from a front pocket, then placed my phone in a side pocket.

"Thanks for lunch, man," I told Marques. "Text me if Percy needs any more measurements from me or if he has a problem with getting those suits done by tomorrow evening. I don't want to have to borrow one of Benji's tight-ass suits, Q, so tell your cousin to get on that shit."

Marques laughed. "Man, Benji's suits wouldn't even fit your ass. You see how tight they are on him. His package shows through his pants. I'm, like, bruh, come on."

"The girls seem to love it." I shrugged my shoulders.

"Then maybe I need to get me a few pair of those nut huggers, if that's the case. I thought I was bad with the hitting and quitting these chicks. Benji's ass takes the cake, though. Instead of trying to take your job from you, he needs to open up a brothel or one of those sex rings."

My eyebrows furrowed as Marques and I gave each other a brotherly hug before we parted ways. What he had said sorta struck a chord with me. For the past couple of years, I'd had the feeling that Benji wasn't happy with his position in the company and was looking for ways to move up to my spot. The way he'd been crashing my business meetings and taking the reins, checking over things, and overseeing projects that weren't part of his job description were signs that he was eyeing the CEO post.

I loved my brother to death, but I swore to God that he'd have another thing coming if he ever tried to cross me.

Melonee

"Yo, Mel. Let me holla at you for a second."

I turned around and looked at Proof as he jogged down the small flight of steps right outside the door to Cowboy's house and caught up with me. It was the night of the charity event that Roman Black was throwing, and Fiona thought that a BWC meeting needed to take place. Because this was the last night that Roman Black was going to be in the city before he went out of town for a couple of weeks, we needed everything to go according to plan tonight, with no interference like last time.

One of Cowboy's hacker friends had managed to hack into the hotel's computer system and add two of our crew members to the list of outsourced employees who were working at the charity event tonight. Their jobs were to keep an eye on Roman Black and to report whenever he ducked off to the private office or a private bathroom. Once we were notified about that, it was then Fiona's responsibility to follow him wherever he went, strike up a conversation with him, and get him to fall into her web of seduction. Because Fee had the gift of gab and had already met Roman before tonight, we figured it would be easy for her to get closer to him than anyone else could.

A little while earlier, I had looked at the way the black, floor-length evening gown she had on hugged every curve of her backside. The strapless water bra she had picked up from Victoria's Secret made her normal B cup breasts plump up to perky-looking Cs, allowing her hourglass shape to be more defined. Her freshly coiffed auburn-streaked hair, which was pinned up on the top of her head in a weird bun, with long spiral curls hanging down in the back, gave her the elegant look that we were aiming for.

Cowboy's suggestion for her to change the purple hair and tone it down to a more natural color would probably cause Roman to notice her this time, as opposed to when she was waitressing at the club.

Proof looked me up and down and bit his bottom lip when he finally made it over to me. "Before you go, I just want you to know that you look real pretty tonight. You almost make a nigga wanna throw on a tux and escort the mother of his child during a night out on the town."

I blushed. "Thank you, Jaylen, but we both know that about an hour in, we'd be going at each other's throats."

He shook his head. "Naw. I don't think so. We never had a problem getting along. It was . . ."

"The plethora of bitches you couldn't leave alone?" I said, finishing his statement for him. "I should've known you'd do the same thing to me that you did to Remi. As the saying goes, 'The same way you get them is the same way you end up losing them.'"

Proof looked at me for a minute, then stepped farther into my personal space. He took his finger and brushed it along my jawline, then lightly trailed his fingers down the side of my body. The purple mermaid evening gown with the sweetheart neckline that I had on clung to my curves just as much as Fiona's gown hugged hers, except I filled out my dress perfectly, and I didn't need to share any of my secrets with Victoria to get that perfect hourglass shape.

"Regardless of what or who I did outside of you, just know that you are the only one who's ever had my heart. Shit, to be honest, that mutha-fucka still belongs to you. Why do you think I tried so hard to get you pregnant? Out of all the women you've seen me with, why do you think none of them ever gave birth to my babies? You are the only one who was blessed with that gift."

I opened my mouth to say something, but he kept talking and didn't let me say a word.

"I strapped up with every single one of those bitches. But you, you had me so gone that I didn't care if I fattened you up with three or four babies back-to-back." He laughed, but when he noticed that I hadn't joined in, his face became somber. "Look, I know I should've stepped to you when that whole Remi thing was officially over, and I probably should've never fucked around on you while we were together, but please believe me when I say that you are the only girl I've ever loved and probably ever will love."

I could tell by the look in Proof's eyes that he meant every word he'd just said. Were this a few years ago, I would've been ready to take him back and see if we could be the couple and family I had always dreamed we'd be. However, the pain of him breaking my heart as many times as he did, and my experience of finally being treated the way I knew I deserved to be treated—even if it was by a mark—had made me realize that my time with Jaylen had come and gone. We would always be bonded because of Madison, but other than that, we were better apart than we were together.

We stood in front of each other—just steps from the SUV that would take Fiona and me to the charity event—lost in our own thoughts, for what felt like hours. The only thing that broke me from mine was feeling Proof's hand cup my cheek as he tried to lean in for a kiss.

"What the fuck are you doing?" I asked, stepping back from his touch and bumping into the door of the tinted-out black SUV that Fee and I would be riding in.

"I'm sorry, Mel. I just thought . . ."

I shook my head. "Whatever it is, you thought wrong. Did you forget about our argument in my granny's kitchen? I thought we were cool on this!" I pointed between us.

He wiped his hands over his head and blew out a long breath. "I . . . look, Mel . . . see . . ." Proof was at a loss for words, which was rare, seeing as he always had something to say.

"You two lovebirds through, or do you need another minute?" Fiona laughed as she walked up to us.

"First of all, you can cut the lovebird shit." I looked at Proof. "Secondly, we're good, right?"

Those green eyes went to Fiona, who was smirking, then back to me. He nodded his head. "Yeah, we good." He looked at Fiona again. "I was just telling Mel to be safe."

"Safe? Or were you telling her not to fuck Roman's fine-ass brother if he happens to game

her up tonight? I'd be all over that sexy hunk of
man if I wasn't trying to get his brother to give
me a chance," Fiona said.

I rolled my eyes at Fiona and hopped into the
back of the truck once the driver opened the door.
I was over that awkward moment with Proof,
and I was over listening to Fiona go on about
Benjamin Black. She'd been trying to push him
on me ever since we started this job. If you asked
me, she seemed more infatuated with him than
she was with Roman. The way her eyes would
light up whenever she brought him up, you'd
think she . . . I shook my head. Naw. Fiona would
never jeopardize our getting this money. Then
again, would *I* be willing to? Especially if I ran
into the Blacks' bodyguard again?

My mind drifted to that day at the mall when
those piercing green eyes visually raped every
single part of my body. If I saw him tonight,
would I run, like I did last time? I wanted to
figure out what this pull was that we were expe-
riencing. I needed to put my big girl panties
on and woman up. Yeah, I knew my mind was
supposed to be on keeping an eye on Roman and
causing a distraction if Fiona got the chance to
be alone with him, but my heart wanted to be on
something else. If I was lucky, that something
else would give me the life I'd always dreamed of.

***

"Who has your ass over there smiling like that?" I asked Fiona as we pulled up to the venue. She'd been snickering and giggling the whole hour we'd been on the road. Texting whoever it was back and forth.

"Oh, just some dude I met at the club. He and I kicked it a few times. One time being the day you and I were supposed to go to the mall. He had my ass up cooking breakfast and shit after giving me the dick down of my life."

"At the strip club?" I asked as we got out of the truck.

She nodded her head.

"Is he a regular?"

"Something like that." She smirked, texting again.

"Do I know him?"

She shook her head. "I don't think so. I met him when I shadowed ole girl in VIP when we first started working there."

I just nodded my head and stopped with the questions. Fiona was the type who was close-mouthed when it came to the men she dealt with on a personal level. Because she wasn't the "relationship type," she had said numerous times that there was no need to give out any info on a man she'd probably fuck for a few months, then drop to be with the next one.

Her phone chimed again, and she went into another giggling fit.

"Well, can I at least know the name of the dude who's got you acting like a little schoolgirl just from a text alone?" I said.

She looked at me as if she was thinking about something, then gazed back down at her phone. "His name is Meyers, and no, it's nothing serious. You know if it ain't about money, I don't take it seriously."

I didn't say anything else as we walked into the lobby of the Beverly Hills Hotel.

"What in the hell?" I heard Fiona say under her breath. "This, this, this is . . ."

"Beautiful," I said.

I walked into the lobby of the five-star hotel and looked around in amazement. The person hired to put this charity event together had done the damn thing for St. Jude Children Research Hospital. They had gone all out with this Heaven's Little Angels theme and had me looking at the beautifully decorated venue in amazement.

"I think we need to sign in over there," Fiona whispered in my ear, grabbing my attention. "I doubt Roman is here right now, so let's make a few rounds, stop at the bar, then find our seats. Cowboy said we will be at the table directly to the right of his." She gazed around the lobby.

"If I'm looking as good as I feel, this night might end way sooner than expected," she added, with a lift of her perfectly arched brows.

I nodded my head and walked in the direction of the sign-in table. Once we were each given a program and a seat number, we entered the main room, parted ways, and walked around a bit. When we met up at the bar, we both ordered drinks and talked for a minute, then parted ways again. While Fiona went to work one side of the room, I kind of nursed my Coke and rum not too far from the bar. I was so over people complimenting my smooth dark skin and then, in the same breath, asking if my eye color was real or contacts. Like people of color didn't have blue, green, gray, or even hazel eyes. Yeah, it was rare, but it did happen. And if one more person asked me if I was related to Stacey Dash, because of my eye color, I was going to scream.

I walked toward the back of the room and tried to blend in with the rest of the expensively dressed partygoers, who, like me, didn't really want to be here. I looked down at my wrist for the time and remembered that I'd taken my watch off to wear a gold cuff instead. I went to look inside the clutch I thought was tucked snugly under my arm, and got the shock of my life when I reached for it and it wasn't there. I almost started to panic, but then I remembered that the last place I had it was on my lap in the truck. But then I recalled that when I'd refresh my lips with another coat of gloss, I'd placed my clutch on the seat. I must have left it there.

My eyes scanned the room for Fiona, but I couldn't find her anywhere.

"Hey, Mel, girl. I was just looking for you," Fiona said, coming up behind me from out of nowhere.

"Where are you coming from? I just looked for you around this whole building and couldn't find you anywhere."

Fiona waved me off. "Girl, you know what I was doing." She ran her tongue over her lips, then winked at me. "I'm always looking for our next victim."

I shook my head and didn't say a word. Just like the rest of the members of the BWC, Fiona knew that this was the last web of lies for me. After this last score with Roman Black, I was going on to live that "happily ever after" life with my baby girl and whomever the Lord decided to bless me with.

"Where did the driver say he would be with the truck?" I asked, changing the subject.

Fiona stopped gazing at the partygoers on the dance floor and turned to me. "Why? You trying to leave or something?" Her voice was laced with a little attitude, but none that others would take notice of unless they were standing right next to us.

"I need to go get my clutch. I left it on the backseat, and my phone is in there."

"Damn it, Mel. You're supposed to be my second pair of eyes. What if Roman Black walks into the room before I can spot him and one of these Bible-toting, charity-crying, 'we are the world' hoes get to him first?" she whispered. "What's going on with you? It's not like you to not have your head in the game. Are you okay?"

I rolled my eyes. Sometimes Fiona's ass could work my nerves like no other, but she was my best friend, and I had promised to always have her back. Yeah, those sexy green eyes and the thought of maybe seeing them tonight had constantly run through my mind the whole ride here, and that was more than likely the reason why I had forgotten my clutch on the backseat, but she didn't need to know that.

"Look, you already know I got your back. But I also need my phone, just in case the munchkin hits me for our 'I love you and good night' call. If I miss it, you know she'll be devastated, and so will I. It's the only thing that keeps me sane right about now."

Fiona looked at me, then shook her head. "You better be glad my goddaughter's happiness is a priority for me." She gave me a pointed look. "The driver said he'd be parked out in front somewhere. Just look for the red TCP number on the right side of the bumper. He said that's how we'll know it's him."

Without another word, I turned and headed for the exit. Hopefully, the tinted-out SUV wouldn't be too hard to find. I was halfway through the lobby when I heard a familiar voice and a body stepped into my path.

"Well, well, well, if it isn't the gold-digging ho of a stepmother who killed my father," she snarled.

I looked around the crowded lobby to see if anyone was paying attention to her little outburst. It seemed as if everyone was in their own little world and was not paying too much attention to us, but I would have to hurry up and check this little bitch and be on my way before she caused a scene.

"Riana," I said, acknowledging the fact that I saw her but communicating that I really didn't want to talk. I tried to step around her, but she stepped into my path again.

"You really think you could get away with what you did, huh?" she growled.

I shrugged my shoulders. "I haven't the slightest idea of what you're talking about."

Her blue eyes turned into slits, and her cheeks flushed a light pink. "You won't get away with it.

As we speak, I have someone looking into who you really are, and once we find that out, all that money that was rightfully mine that you took when my father died will be emptied out of your little bank account and thrown into mine."

"For someone so concerned about her father's death, you sure do threaten me about his money a lot."

"You'll pay for what you did."

Tears started to slide down her cheeks, and I almost felt sorry for her ass, but when I thought about the court cases she had put me through and all the extra money I had had to spend on lawyers' fees to get ahold of Douglas's money, I didn't give a fuck.

"Maybe you need to take another Valium or two. You're starting to be that uptight, delusional bitch that I never cared too much for. If it wasn't for my late, great departed husband, your grown, spoiled ass would've been cut off the minute I said, 'I do.'" I walked up closer to her so that only she could hear what I was about to say. "You know, you should be thanking me, really. Had I not signed off on that trust fund, your ass wouldn't have gotten shit."

"I fucking hate you!" she yelled at the top of her lungs. "You killed my father, and you will not get away with it!"

By now, all eyes were slowly starting to focus on us, and I had a feeling that things were going to get a lot worse. Once Riana noticed that a crowd was starting to form around us, she decided to kick things up another notch.

"To all the rich bachelors in the room," she yelled, "please steer clear of this . . . this . . . this . . . gold-digging ho right here." She pointed at me. "Not only will she take you for everything you got, but her murdering ass will also try to make sure your families don't get to touch a dime of your money. This conniving bitch lured my father in with her web of lies, then killed him for the insurance money and everything else my father had to his name." She started to sob. "Don't end up like my father . . . thinking this bitch is the one for you, just to end up buried six feet down not too long after the ink has dried on all those insurance policy papers."

I could hear the guests surrounding us chattering among themselves and trying to figure out if anything Riana had said was true. I looked around and noticed that all eyes had shifted toward me as everyone began to digest what this stupid bitch had said.

"Don't try to run now," she slurred as I began to walk toward the exits again.

About a minute later, I could hear the water from the large fountain in front of the hotel falling into the layered pools. The smell of water hitting concrete started to waft by my nose, which let me know that I was almost out of the lobby and away from all the prying eyes and thoughts.

"Soon you'll get what's coming to you, and everyone will know how you're nothing more than a lying, conniving, and manipulative little slut bucket who marries men—"

Her words were cut short by the sliding doors that closed behind me after I walked out of the lobby and into the cool night air. On instinct, I wrapped my arms around myself because it was a tad bit windy. Those Santa Ana winds were already starting to pick up, and it was only the beginning of September.

I looked back at the scene I'd just left and could see a couple of the hotel's security guards trying to get Riana to calm down. By the way her arms were flailing around and her mascara was running down her face from crying hysterically, I could tell that she was still in her feelings about seeing me and about what had just gone down. I almost felt sorry for her, because I was the reason why she was now fatherless. Technically, it wasn't I who had killed Doug, but I had had a hand in it. She'd never be able to prove it, though, and neither would anyone else, so I didn't take her little threats seriously.

I stood there watching how everyone's attention was now turned to her. Those same prying eyes were now focused on her instead of me. When a bystander started pointing in my direction after one of the security guards asked Riana a question, I quickly turned my head and started walking down the winding walkway that led to the parking lot, trying to get as far away as I could from the commotion and Riana's crazy ass.

I scanned the crowded parking lot, in search of the SUV we had arrived in, with so many thoughts running through my mind. I made a mental note to tell Fee about the little confrontation Riana and I had just had in the middle of the hotel lobby. I had a feeling that Riana would be a problem in the future if we didn't get Proof and his crew to handle her ASAP.

The cool night air caused me to shiver a bit. I wrapped my arms around myself again and sniffed the nippy breeze as it passed me by. After scanning the parking lot, I walked in circles for about twenty minutes before finally spotting the car that Fiona and I had ridden in. The driver was leaning against the driver's door, smoking a cigarette and playing on his phone, when he noticed me walk up. He stood up straight and went to put his cigarette out, but I stopped him by shaking my head before he had the chance to throw it on the ground.

"I just need to get my purse out of the back," I said and held my hand up.

He gave me a friendly smile and nodded his head, then opened the rear door for me. After grabbing my clutch from the backseat and checking to make sure all my things were still in it, I headed back to the party, though I did not really feeling like going back.

I'd just stepped off the curb near the hotel entrance when a blacked-out Tahoe swiftly passed me by, causing me to stumble back in the process. The driver slammed on the brakes, causing a crimson hue to light the space in front of me. When I lowered my eyes to read the license plate number and memorize it so that I could have Cowboy hack into the DMV's system and suspend the license of the asshole who was driving the Tahoe, I noticed the truck slowly backing toward me.

My guard immediately went up, but it came right back down when a thought crossed my mind. *Maybe this is a sign from God, telling me not to go back into the event.* I mean, from where I was standing, I could clearly see the hotel entrance and the lobby beyond it. The little scene Riana had caused was now cleared up, and everyone was back to mingling. Something in my gut kept telling me that I needed to skip the festivities and head home, so that was what I decided to do. Even if this wasn't my driver, I was willing to pay whoever was behind the wheel anything he wanted to get me out of here.

The car stopped in front of me, and without a second thought, I walked up to the back door, opened it up, and hopped inside.

"Can you please drop me off in Woodland Hills, off Broadway and Abagail? I'm willing to pay you whatever the charge is if you can do this for me," I said.

Knowing that money talked, I didn't even wait for a response from him before I leaned my body against the door, looked out the window for a brief moment, and then closed my eyes. My body was still covered in goose bumps, and I didn't know why. That little mishap from earlier had scared me, but not that much. I had sat in silence for a few moments, wondering why the driver hadn't begun to drive, when my stomach started to flip around wildly. The fine hairs on the back of my arms and neck began to rise, and my heart started to skip a few beats. An intoxicating fragrance I hadn't noticed when I first got into the truck took over my senses and caused a low moan to slide from my lips.

I clenched my thighs together to slow the light thumping of my clit and to prevent my arousal from seeping out. What was really going on? The last time my body reacted like this was when I was near . . .

My eyes popped open, and I immediately sat up straight. I tried to calm my breathing and my thoughts, but nothing I did seemed to help. My first instinct was to run, but then I could sence a presence I hadn't noticed before all over the back of this truck. I reached for the door handle, but a soft, warm hand lightly grabbed my wrist and pulled my hand back.

When I raised my head and looked into the rearview mirror, my gaze connected with a pair of eyes that I knew all too well and that had often invaded my thoughts of late.

With a dry throat and a trembling voice, I managed to say only one thing.

"You."

Roman

I didn't know if someone was playing a cruel joke on me or if God was really looking out for me. The minute she opened the door and slid into the backseat of the truck, my dick had strained to get out of these dress pants so that it could enveloped by her wet mouth or by the warmth I could feel radiating from her sweet core the minute her body reacted to mine.

My driver, Mike, and I had just pulled up to the charity event when I decided to ditch the whole thing altogether at the last minute. Surely, my father and my stepmother would have something to say about my absence, but I'd be willing to take a thousand tongue-lashings if it meant that I'd be in *her* presence again.

Those gray eyes stared into mine through the rearview mirror and almost took my breath away. The light makeup she had around her eyes only made the green specks in her eyes pop out even more, pulling me deeper into this hold she already seemed to have on me. When she licked her lips, I damn near came on myself just from that gesture alone.

The way her smooth chocolate skin felt on my fingertips only made me want to explore her body even more.

She opened her mouth to try to say something again, but she was still struggling to speak.

I cleared my throat. "If you need a ride home, I'll be more than happy to have my driver drop you off."

She dropped her gaze from the rearview mirror to her wrist, which I was still holding, then looked back up at my face.

"I'm . . . I'm so sorry. I thought . . . I thought that this was my car." She tried to turn and open the car door again, but my grip on her wrist tightened, causing her to stop.

"The offer to drop you off still stands. I don't mind," I said.

"I'm pretty sure you need to be inside the party, guarding your employer. I don't want you to get fired because of me." She looked me up and down with lustful eyes. "By the way, you must have some outstanding perks. Your suit looks like it cost a grip."

My eyebrows furrowed. "Guarding my employer? Perks?"

"I'm assuming this must be the car that just dropped Roman Black off at his charity event, since you're in here," she said. "You are his bodyguard, aren't you?"

Because I had decided to skip the party, I'd already removed my tuxedo jacket and thrown it in the back. The bow tie had been next to go, after I'd rolled up the sleeves of my white dress shirt and unbuttoned the top three buttons. I looked more like I was on my way to happy hour with some coworkers than to some fancy shindig. Had I had on some loafers instead of the patent-leather wing-tipped Dolce & Gabbana dress shoes, I would've assumed that I was an office worker. But a bodyguard? I couldn't help the laugh that escaped from my lips.

"What's funny?" she asked, pulling her arm from my grasp. I could tell by the look on her face that she was already missing my touch, but she tried to quickly cover it up with a deep but cute scowl.

"No disrespect, but I highly doubt Roman Black firing me would ever happen. I mean, unless I decided to fire myself."

She reared that beautiful head back, with a confused look on her face. "What?"

After turning my body toward her some more, I reached out my hand and officially introduced myself. "Roman Black."

"Roman Black? Stop lying!"

"Last I checked, that was the name I was given at birth." I still had my hand out, hoping she'd place hers in mine. I was missing her touch too, and I needed it now.

"Wait one minute." She shook her head. "You can't be Roman Black. I don't remember the picture in the fi . . . ," she said, trailing off.

"The picture where?" I asked, with one eyebrow raised.

She bit her bottom lip and looked out the window. "I don't remember you having blond hair in that picture in *Finance Daily*." She turned and looked at the top of my head. "Do you dye your hair or something? I thought you had dark hair."

I felt the rumbling in my belly this time as I laughed. "To answer your question, no, I've never dyed my hair in my life. Always been blond and always will be, thanks to my green-eyed and blond-haired Russian mother. Now, who you might have me confused with is my brother, Benjamin. He's the other half of the Black brothers, but with dark hair. He was also featured in that same magazine, but a month later."

I could tell by the look on her face that she was thinking about something. Even when her lips started moving as she talked silently to herself, she was inwardly battling something, and I was curious to know what it was. However, that thought had to take a backseat right now and get brought up at some other time. I was more interested in getting to know her right now and seeing if she too felt this connection that we shared. The girl who had haunted my every thought since I first laid eyes on her was sitting right beside me, and I wasn't about to let this chance slip away from me again.

"By the way, you look beautiful tonight, Mel."

Her eyes snapped to mine. "How do you know my name?"

As I poured myself a shot of the scotch Benji had given to me as a congratulations gift this morning for the deal I had closed with another overseas investor, I told Melonee how I had come to know her name.

"So why didn't you say something to me that day in the mall?" she asked as she accepted the shot I had poured for her. By the way she downed it in one gulp, I could tell that she was still nervous to be in front of me.

"Honestly, I was feeling the same way you were," I said as I poured her another shot.

She tipped back the crystal tumbler and held the second shot of scotch in her mouth for a second, then swallowed hard. "What do you mean?"

I placed my crystal tumbler back on the bar and looked at her. "Does your stomach do somersaults whenever you're near me?"

She slowly nodded her head.

"Does your throat get dry, your palms start to sweat, and the hairs on your arms begin to rise whenever we're close to one another?"

Melonee nodded again, then poured herself another drink. "Arm hair *and* neck hair," she noted before she downed her third shot.

I scooted closer to her, closing the small gap between us. "If I wanted to kiss you right now, would you stop me?"

"I don't think—"

Before she could object to my request, I grabbed the back of her neck and pulled her face toward mine. When Melonee tried to say something again, I crashed my lips into hers and felt a jolt of electricity shoot through my body. I knew she felt it too, because the second it happened, her eyes opened wide, before resuming their sexy gaze.

Her lips were as soft as pillows and tasted so sweet to me. I couldn't get enough. I deepened the kiss, then stopped when I felt her open palm run across my chest, then start to push me back. At that moment I knew that what could be the best kiss of my life was about to end, and after sampling those luscious lips one last time with a quick peck, I finally returned to my side of the seat and just stared at her.

I watched as Melonee touched her lips, then looked at her fingers, as if she could lick something off them to savor the taste of our kiss.

"Why . . . why did you do that?" she asked, still in sort of a daze. Those gray eyes remained focused on her fingers, but I could see the hairs on her smooth dark arms rise, right along with some tiny goose bumps.

"Honestly?" I shrugged my shoulders, then shook my head. What I was about to say sounded weird even to me, but I hoped she wouldn't freak out too much. "Because from the moment I saw you, I've felt this pull or connection to you, and it's only gotten stronger. I'm not sure what it is, so please don't ask me why," I said as I reached out and gripped her exposed thigh.

Sometime during that kiss, the hem of her dress had got hiked up, and I didn't know if it was by my hand or hers. Either way, I didn't care. I dragged my finger up and down her thigh and then continued on with what I was saying. "There's something about you that I can't get out of my body. In all my years, I've never felt anything for someone I hadn't even spoken one single word to. It's weird, but weird in a good way. Like something deep inside me is trying to tell me that you are the one designed for me."

She locked eyes with me for a second, then looked down at my lips. I was far from a mind reader, but I had a pretty good idea of what she was thinking about. Subconsciously, I ran my tongue over my lips and regretted it the moment I did. Melonee's taste still lingered there, which caused my dick to swell two times bigger than its normal size. The combination of the resistance of my pants and the indention of the zipper was starting to become too much. I needed to free my man or get out of Melonee's presence. I didn't want to freak her out any more than I might have already, so I decided that the latter would probably be best.

"If you still need that ride to your home, Juan will be more than willing to drop you off," I said.

"José," said the Rico Suave–looking driver, correcting me, after clearing his throat and shaking his head at me through the rearview mirror.

"Well, *José* can still drop you off. Where did you need to go again?"

For five minutes, we sat in complete silence, waiting for Melonee to say something to let us know what she wanted to do. If she chose to go home, I would have no other choice but to respect her wishes and make sure she made it there safely. If she decided to hop out of the car and go back into the charity event, I'd probably follow right behind her and endure the endless hand-shakes, pictures, and meaningless conversations with the other guests in attendance if that meant I could spend some more time with her during the night. I wanted to see what this connection we had was all about, and I refused to let her slip away from me again.

"Excuse me, Señor Black. I'm not rushing or anything, but has the lady made a choice?" José asked.

We both looked at Melonee, he through the rearview mirror and I from my seat beside her, and waited on an answer.

"Well? Have you decided on what you—" I began, but I stopped when those full, sumptuous, and delectable lips ascended to mine.

"I want to go wherever you want to go," she said between kisses. When her tongue snaked into my mouth and wrapped around my own tongue, I lost all train of thought and any notion of whatever else was going on in the world.

However, I did feel the truck start to move and head out of the parking lot of the hotel. I was pretty sure José knew where to go, seeing as neither one of us was going to be coming up for air anytime soon. My loft was only twenty minutes away, and it was the only address he had for right now.

Roman and Melonee

I quickly scanned my text messages.

Q: Where are you, man? Everyone's looking for you.

Benji: If you need me to step in for you, bro, you know I don't have a problem with saving your ass again. Just say the word. . . .

Dad: Do not embarrass me or the family like this, Roman.

Dad: Where are you, boy?

Dad: Maybe I should've appointed Benjamin as CEO, since you obviously have better things to do.

Benji: Don't worry about anything, bro. As always, I saved the day at your charity event. Enjoy that hot piece of ass. I know I would if it were me. LOL

My eyebrows furrowed at Benji's last text message. How did he know I was with someone? A female, at that? Trying to forget about everything going on outside this car, I tucked my phone back into my pocket after sending

Marques a quick text and turned my full attention back to Melonee. My lips were missing the
touch of hers, and I wanted to kiss her again, but
she was going on about whatever it was she was
talking about as my eyes drank up her beautiful
features.

"I don't know why I told you any of that," she
said, looking at me and smiling. Those alluring
eyes pulling me deeper into her. "But there's
something about you that makes me feel so
comfortable. And that kiss . . . that kiss . . ."
She touched her lips. Those gray orbs, which
were starting to become my favorite part of her,
sparkled in the dimness of the car.

"I don't want to be the one to brag or anything,
but I tend to have that effect on people sometimes."

She smirked at my response. "I bet you do."

We silently stared into each other's eyes as
José drove down the coast, heading to my beach
house in Malibu. I had decided to take her to my
second home, away from the city, thus avoiding
any chance of running into anyone who could
interrupt this night, like Benji or my parents.
Surprisingly, Melonee had gone along with the
change in plans. At first, she'd just wanted to
go home, but after we'd kissed, then talked for
a while and realized that we did not want our

night to end until we tried to figure out what this connection between us was, she accepted my offer to have a late dinner at the beach house.

I'd already called ahead and informed my staff about my arrival within the next forty-five minutes. They had strict orders to get everything prepared for us, then to leave the house for the rest of the night. I wanted to continue to enjoy Melonee all by myself, without any interruptions from anyone.

Her phone going off again caused my gaze to shift down to her soft manicured hands. Images of her fingers tracing the thick veins on my dick and her thumb lightly brushing the tip of my mushroom head before she placed it in her sexy-ass mouth had me repositioning myself in my seat. My pants were already on the verge of busting at the seams. I needed to get my thoughts in order before I exposed her to something more than she needed to see right now.

As Melonee looked at her phone's screen, I could tell by the look on her face that whoever it was who was texting her was someone she didn't want to be bothered with at the moment.

"Boyfriend?" I asked, hoping her answer would be no. A small pang of jealousy surged through my body and settled in my chest at the thought of her belonging to someone else.

Ignoring my question, Melonee began to text feverishly on her phone, a frown etched across her beautiful face. Even though she looked mad, her beauty still turned me on and again had my dick twitching against my leg.

I kept my eyes trained on her as she went back and forth with whomever she was texting. A frown remained on her face, and every now and then her eyebrows would rise and then her eyes would roll. When she bit her bottom lip and smiled at something on her screen, that same pang of jealousy shot through my body again and had me reacting before my mind could catch up with what I was doing. I reached across the seat, snatched her phone from those delicate fingers, and powered it off, but not before seeing the name Proof flash across the screen and a picture of him and some little girl who looked like a mix of him and Melonee light up in the background. I wanted to ask her who the man and the little girl were, but I opted to save that question for later on.

"You won't be needing this for the rest of the evening," I said as I tucked her phone in one of my pockets and poured myself another drink. "I don't want anyone messing up what we have going on."

She turned in her seat and leaned back against the door, eyes ablaze and arms folded across her chest. My eyes traveled down to the sweetheart neckline of the purple gown she had on. It hugged the roundness of her melon-size breasts just right. A flashback of the night I first laid eyes on her at Club Decadence shot through my mind. Whether Melonee wore a string bikini or was totally clothed in an evening gown, her curves were enough to make any sane man go crazy.

She cleared her throat. "My eyes are up here." I shifted my gaze from her breasts to her face. A sexy smirk played on her lips. "Now that we have that established, may I please have my phone back?"

My lips formed into a sly smile. "Please? I never pegged you for the type to beg."

She drew her bottom lip into her mouth, and I swear, my dick grew a few inches longer. I could tell by the way her eyes grew when she looked down at my lap that she'd seen my growth. It was my turn to smirk when she began to cough and grab her chest, trying to control her breathing.

I took a sip of my drink and offered her my glass. With her eyes still on me, she snatched the tumbler out of my hand and downed the remaining alcohol in one gulp. A small laugh escaped my lips when she held the glass out for another shot. Obliging her request, I filled the tumbler up with another double of the brown liquor and watched her gulp that down too.

"I get the sense that you're nervous about something," I said.

She shook her head from side to side and then flipped the glass up to her mouth again, making sure she consumed every last drop. "I'm . . . I'm not nervous. Just a little curious." She swayed a little and grabbed her head.

"Are you okay?" I asked and gently grasped her arm, concern evident all over my face.

She lightly patted my hand that was on her arm, and nodded her head. "I'm good. I just became a little dizzy, that's all." Melonee blew out a small breath and looked at the half-empty bottle of alcohol. "That's some strong stuff. Where did you get it from again?"

After picking the bottle up from the bar, I handed it to her. "My brother, Benji, gave it to me as a congratulations gift today. I closed a deal we've been trying to get for some time now."

Melonee placed the bottle back in my hand after examining the labels on the front and back. "That's some good shit. My best friend would love it. It's got me over here stuck and ready to go to bed." When she laughed, something inside my chest fluttered.

"Don't go to sleep on me yet. We still have so much to do." I gently grabbed her wrist and pulled her hand into mine, interlacing our fingers in the process. Something about our connection felt so right, and I knew she felt what I did the minute our hands touched. "Did you feel that?"

Melonee observed our joined hands, then looked out the window. Although lit streetlights lined both sides of the street, you couldn't see anything but utter darkness beyond them. We were passing the large sand dune in Malibu, which meant that we were almost at my home.

"Have you ever regretted something you've done in your life, and wished that you could take it all back?" she asked all of a sudden.

Her question threw me for a loop for a few seconds, because it was totally off the subject I was trying to be on. But when Melonee looked back at me with glossy eyes, my instincts had me pulling her into me and holding her in my protective embrace, forgetting all about what was going on between us. Something was weighing heavily on her heart, and everything inside me wanted to make it better for her. I kissed her on top of her head.

"Honestly, I can't say that I have. My life's been pretty much planned out for me since the day that I was born. After my mother died, it was like my father started grooming me to be the man he wanted me to be. He knew that one day I'd take over his company, and he wanted to make sure that I was capable of doing so. I never really had much of a childhood and never really experienced life as a teenager. It wasn't until I went away to college that I got to enjoy life a little bit. If it wasn't for my best friend, Marques, dragging me to some of the campus parties or us spending summer vacation in Russia with my uncle Kazi, I'd probably be a thirty-one-year-old virgin with no type of game whatsoever."

Melonee laughed at my little joke, and again, something in my chest began to flutter. I could listen to the sound of her laughter for the rest of my life and never get tired of it. After the laughter died down between us, we remained in a comfortable silence, locked in one another's arms, until we arrived at my house. José pulled into the circular driveway and stopped right at my front door. He jumped out and opened both back doors of the SUV. Melonee and I climbed out.

"Wow, Roman. This place is beautiful," Melonee said, complimenting me on my four-bedroom, three-bathroom beach home as we walked up the small flight of steps to the front door.

After I pressed my thumb on the security pad and then quickly entered a four-digit code, the door unlocked, and with little effort, I pushed it open, then allowed Melonee to enter before me.

"Oh my God," were the first three words to leave her lips after her eyes landed on the surprise I had had my staff set up for her.

I looked around in amazement at the setup before me. Candles of different shapes and sizes were lit up all over the place, giving the room a romantic glow. The inside of Roman's beach house was even more beautiful than I could ever have imagined. The ocean-blue, coral, and tan color scheme flowed perfectly throughout the house. Whoever had decorated this place was going for that Jamaican resort feel and had executed it very well. Pictures of ocean views and seashells lined the walls, while tropical ceiling fans with blades that looked like palm leaves spun above us.

From where I was standing, you could see the waves of the ocean crashing along the beach, thanks to the fact that the walls in the back of the house were made of nothing but glass. Anyone passing by would be able to see right in here, but that million-dollar view of the Pacific at your doorstep was so worth any gapers. I was still looking around Roman's beautiful home in amazement when his strong arms wrapped around my waist from behind and he pulled me into his hard chest. I didn't know what it was about this man, but something inside me felt so at peace with him.

None of the bad things I'd done in my past, or even the screaming match I had just had with Douglas's daughter, Riana, seemed to matter at all when I was with Roman. Being in his arms just felt so right. These feelings I had for Roman kind of scared me in a sense, because I'd never been this comfortable with anybody, not even Proof. His ass had chased after me for some months before I even let him kiss me. Roman, all he had to do was touch any part of my body, and I was putty in his hands. I shook my head. Yeah, I didn't know what all this meant, but I was going to live in and enjoy this moment for as long as I could, just in case it never happened again.

"What's on your mind, beautiful?" Roman whispered in my ear. I smiled at the goose bumps that had begun to tickle my skin. His voice alone was turning me on, and it wasn't the alcohol that had me feeling this way.

"I was just looking at your home and noticing how beautiful it is. I've always wanted to own a beach house, and looking at yours makes me want one even more."

Roman kissed me on my shoulder, walked from behind me, and then grabbed my hand. Those lips and kisses were going to be the death of me. "C'mon. Let's go out to the patio. I had my chef prepare us something to eat, since we haven't eaten yet."

Roman led the way to the patio, where a romantic dinner for two had been set up. The sound of the waves hitting the sand was the first thing I heard as soon as I stepped through the double-paned sliding doors. I hiked my dress up a little and kicked off my shoes, not caring about the coolness of the wooden deck under my feet. The smell of the purple hydrangeas in the centerpiece on the table mixed with the smell of the ocean and created a soothing scent that calmed my senses. The orange flames of the white dinner candles surrounding the floral centerpiece leaned to the left and flickered every time the wind kicked up. Roman pulled out my seat, and after I sat, he scooted me toward the linen-draped table.

"I didn't know if you prefer red or white, so I had my staff supply us with both." He filled one wineglass with ruby-colored Merlot and the other with a sparkling Moscato. He placed both glasses before me.

"Which do you prefer?" I asked as I picked up the glass of Merlot.

"Neither really. That's why I went back out to the car and got this." He held up the bottle of brown liquor his brother had given him.

I downed the red wine in my glass and then held the glass out to him. A slow smile spread across his face as he opened the half-empty bottle in his hand and poured me a shot.

"I think you like this drink a little more than I do," he said.

"I'm surprised you like it at all," I countered.

He squinted his eyes. "Why would you say that?"

I took a sip of my drink and placed the glass back on the table. I used the teal linen napkin to pat the corners of my mouth dry before I replied. "Because on the ride here, I think you said something about a Russian uncle in Russia, which leads me to believe that you have some kind of Russian in you."

He took a seat across from me, poured him a drink, and sat back in the chair, shoulders squared, his low gaze on me. I could tell by the way his knee was touching mine under the table that his legs were stretched out and slightly open. Thinking about the size of the dick print I had seen earlier, while in the car, I realized that sitting with his legs open might be what worked best for Roman. There was no way in this world that he could sit with his legs completely closed, working with a thing like that.

His voice was low when he spoke. "My father has Irish roots, and my mother is Russian. But what does that have to do with what I like to drink?"

I shrugged my shoulders. "I thought Russians like drinking only vodka."

The sexiest laugh escaped his throat after he finished off the drink he had poured himself. Roman licked his lips and kept his predator-like gaze trained on me. I shrugged my shoulders again and took another sip of my drink, trying to hide the way my cheeks were heating up from the blush I could feel coming on.

"Vodka is the official drink of the country, but that isn't the only thing Russians drink. Saying that is basically like saying all black people drink malt liquor."

I nodded my head and raised my glass to him. "Touché."

After staring at me for a few more minutes with that same sexy-ass hunting look, Roman removed the silver tops from our plates, and my mouth immediately began to water.

"Let's eat," he said.

Roman didn't have to tell me twice. I picked up my fork and knife and dug into the delicious surf and turf dinner before me. Steak cooked medium, a lobster tail as big as my whole hand, asparagus tips sautéed in garlic and butter, and some of the creamiest mashed potatoes I'd ever had in my life. And to top that all off, everything was still piping hot, as if the chef had just finished making the food in the kitchen. I had just put the last piece of the perfectly seasoned and tender steak in my mouth when I finally came up for air.

"You like?" Roman asked, chewing the piece of lobster he had just dipped in butter.

"More than like. I love." My eyes connected with his as soon as the words left my mouth. Roman's jaw slowed down its chewing and then stopped as something unsaid passed between us.

"Melonee . . ."

"Roman . . ."

We said each other's name at the same time, smiles immediately gracing our faces. I waved my hand for him to continue, but he nodded his head to me, as if to say, "Ladies first."

I cleared my throat, then took a sip of my white wine. I needed a little bit more of this liquid courage to get through what I was about to say. After clearing my throat again, I gathered the little bit of nerve I had left and opened my mouth to speak.

"Roman . . ." I shook my head. "There's something I need to tell you, and I don't know how you're going to take this. Obviously, there's something between us. I feel it, and I know you feel it as well. For the past couple of years, I've been feeling like there was something missing in my life. I mean, I've had a couple of relationships in my time, but they've never made me feel . . ." I wrung my hands, trying to find the word to say.

"Whole," he said, finishing my sentence for me.

"Yeah, whole." I nodded my head and smiled. "I've been telling my best friend this for the past few months, and all she ever does is laugh at me whenever I bring it up. Fee doesn't believe in love or being in love, for that matter, so I knew she'd never understand the way that I felt. But you . . . It's like you get it . . . like you get me, and we don't really fully know each other yet."

Roman grabbed my hand in his and kissed the back of it. That gesture was so small, yet meant so much to me. My eyes became misty.

I went on. "I don't know what this is that's going on between us. Maybe it's fate or the biggest mistake we will ever make."

He smiled, and my heart fluttered.

"Whatever it is, though, however we decide to figure this out, I don't want there to be any secrets between us." I took a huge breath, then picked up my glass of liquor and drank the rest of it. If I was about to tell him that I actually knew who he was, and if I was going to reveal why I knew this, I wanted to be past drunk, since I figured he would kick me out of his house, leaving me stranded and brokenhearted. I took another deep breath, then focused my eyes back on his. "Okay, so you know earlier, when I told you that I didn't know—" I began, but I was cut off by the ringing of his cell phone.

"I'm sorry. I thought I turned mine off the same time I did yours."

I watched as Roman patted his pockets down until he found his ringing phone. When the loud noise stopped, he looked up at me and smiled. Only to frown when the phone began to ring again.

"I apologize, Mel. Let me take this right quick, and I swear we won't be interrupted again."

I nodded my head, relieved, since I needed some time to think about what I was about to tell him. Roman stood from the table and walked to the edge of the dark patio.

"What?" he barked into the phone, with his back turned to me.

I couldn't hear everything he was saying, but I could make out bits and pieces.

"Tell him I'll see him and Mom on Sunday for brunch. . . . I don't care, man. Why is that any of your business? Do not come to the beach house." He looked at me over his shoulder, and I smiled. Whatever the person on the other end of the phone had said must've pissed him off, because at that moment he turned back around, another frown etched across his sexy face, and lowered his voice. "Tell her I said hello. . . . No . . . because she's nothing but a gold-digging bitch, and you know I despise women like that. . . . All right . . . I'll get with you later. . . . I'm not being rude. . . . Yeah. . . bye."

I watched as Roman's back expanded when he flexed his muscles. Even with the white dress shirt he had on, I could still tell that his body was ripped with muscle underneath. When he turned back to me, he had a smile on his handsome face again. He turned off the cell phone in his hand.

"Sorry about that," he said, reclaiming his seat. "We shouldn't have any more interruptions. Now, what were you saying?"

Romans words about despising gold diggers kept ringing in my mind. Even if I explained to him what the Black Widow Clique was all about, I had no doubt that he would still see me as the one thing he hated the most. My palms began to sweat, and my heart began to beat at a faster pace. Did I tell him everything and hope for the best? Or did I go ahead with the change of plans Fiona had texted me about earlier, before Roman snatched my phone away and turned it off. I thought back to the texts Fiona and I had exchanged.

Fee: WYA? Did you find the car?

Me: Yes and no.

Fee: ???

Me: I found a car, but it didn't have my purse in it.

Fee: Okay. So what was in the car you found?

I hesitated for a second, trying to decide if I wanted to tell her the truth or not, but Fiona and I had never kept secrets from each other, so I told her what I had found.

Me: Roman Black.

It took her a few minutes to respond.

Fee: WYA? Is he coming in?

Me: Sitting next to him. And IDK. I don't think so.

A few more minutes passed by before she responded again

Fee: Okay. Change of plans. If he makes a move on you, go for it. You keep saying you want out. Well, this is your chance to make it happen. One last mate and bait, and then you can make your exit from the BWC with your cut of whatever you can get your name on and nothing else.

Fee: Text the address to wherever he takes you so that we can know that you're safe. We'll meet up at my house tomorrow, okay?

Before I could hit her back, Roman snatched my phone out of my hand, turned it off, and tucked it in his pocket. My mind went back to the two times it took Fiona forever to respond to my text after I told her that I was with Roman. She must've been telling Proof and everyone else about the changes in the plan in other texts, because I didn't think it was a coincidence that Proof's name flashed across my screen the minute I told Fiona where I was.

Roman's chair scraping across the wooden deck caught my attention and pulled me from my thoughts. A look of concern was on his face as he kneeled beside me and took my hand. His light cologne mixed with the ocean scent. His tattooed arm rested in my lap and had my insides slowly coming to life. The dark blond hair that lined his face and the top of his head was perfectly arranged. Those piercing green eyes bored into mine, conveying so many emotions.

"Are you okay, Melonee? I've been trying to get your attention for the past five minutes. It's like you totally zoned out and went somewhere else. Am I boring you that much?" He smiled, and I could feel the moistness between my thighs.

I opened my mouth to say something but instead crashed my lips against his. It didn't take Roman any time to oblige my tongue's request to enter his mouth. The moment our tongues found each other, a moan escaped from his throat and traveled all the way down to my pussy, causing my clit to tingle and thump like crazy. When Roman broke our kiss, it felt as if a piece of my soul had left my body.

"Wha-wha-what's wrong?" I whispered against his lips. Then my tongue tried to seek refuge in its new home again.

"What did you want to tell me earlier?" Roman asked breathlessly, his low eyes searching my face for an answer.

I didn't want to lie, yet I didn't want to tell the truth, either. However, I did want to feel him inside me, and if I were to say what I really wanted to tell him, my chances of having his dick buried deep in my love might evaporate.

Another dizzy spell, just like the one earlier, hit me, a little harder this time, and caused my head to fall back. Luckily, Roman didn't notice the pained expression on my face and began to place small kisses down the length of my neck. I moaned in response to his touch and pulled him closer to me. I heard the sounds of my beautiful ball gown ripping at the seams. Another spell hit me, and I ignored it again, while making a mental note never to drink that much in one night again.

"Tell me what you wanted me to know," he said in between kisses. "It sounded important."

"I—I—I just wanted you to know, uh, that I, um, don't have a boyfriend." *Damn.* It wasn't entirely what I wanted to say, but he didn't have to know that. I could feel Roman's smile against my sensitive skin.

"So that means . . ." He kissed my shoulder. "Your heart . . ." He kissed the spot above my right titty. "Your body . . ." He kissed my neck. "Your pussy . . ." He leaned down and kissed the part of my gown that covered my juice box. "And your soul belong to me now?"

I grabbed his face on both sides and kissed his soft lips. "Only if you promise to never hurt me, them, or it." I knew that what I had just agreed to let him claim would never go any further than what we did tonight, but I didn't give a fuck.

Roman found the zipper at the back of my dress and began to slowly pull it down. "You will never have to worry about me hurting you, Melonee, or any part of you. If I break your heart, honestly, I'd be breaking mine too."

We stared intently into each other's eyes for what felt like forever. The connection we both felt was growing stronger and stronger with every touch, kiss, and look. After grabbing my hands, Roman, stood up and then pulled me up from my seat. As soon as I stood up straight, the gown, which had hugged every curve of my frame, fell to the floor, leaving my body on full display.

Roman looked at me from head to toe with an appreciative expression on his face. He bit his bottom lip and mumbled something in Russian, which I didn't understand. The lustful glint in his eye told me that whatever he had just said was a good thing and that he really liked the black lace bra and matching thong set that I had on. Not taking his eyes off me, Roman slowly unbuttoned every button on his shirt until his chest was in view and the sexy cut of his abs, pecs, and arms was on full display. He grabbed my hand after looking my body over one more time, then headed back into the house. By the time we reached his bedroom door, Roman had left a trail of his clothes as well as mine on the floor.

Now that he was completely naked in front of me, I couldn't help the way my eyes assaulted his body, from his broad shoulders to his muscled chest, to the eight-pack abs and the deep V cut that led to what could only be described as a third leg. Even his thighs and calves had me licking my lips in anticipation of our bodies being tangled together.

"After you," he offered after pushing open the bamboo double doors to his bedroom, with their contemporary waterfall glass. There was a predatory look on his face again, as if he was ready to eat me alive.

I stepped into his bedroom, and my feet were greeted by the softest carpet I'd ever felt. The only description for the way my feet and toes felt as they sank into the lushness of his carpet was *walking on clouds*. That was exactly what it felt like, and I didn't ever want to come down.

Roman's bedroom was everything I expected it to be. A glass wall like the other ones in the house gave you a breathtaking view of the beach and the boats that bobbed in the distance. A Villa Valencia king-size canopy bed with marble columns for posts and linen drapes sat on a platform in the middle of the room. Expensive bedding and decorative pillows covered most of the top of the bed. A bookcase stacked with all sorts of books lined the wall on the other side of the room, and antique pieces of bedroom furniture were arranged throughout. Huge plants had been strategically placed around the room, giving it a sort of tropical rain forest feel. I was so in awe of everything in the room that I didn't notice Roman walk up behind me. He pushed me gently onto the soft bed.

"You can see the rest of the room in the morning," he said as he nestled his hard and sexy body between my open legs. "I have to be inside you right now. I need to feel your walls suffocating the life out of me." The tip of his dick brushed against my clit, and my whole body went crazy. I could feel my juices running down the slit in my ass and making a puddle beneath me.

"Please . . . Roman," I damn near begged. My clit and his dick were rubbing together and causing a friction between us that needed to be tended to. I opened my legs up wider, welcoming him into his new haven of pleasure. Taking his lips to mine, Roman placed his dick at my entrance and slowly began to slide into me.

"Fuck!" we both moaned in pure bliss the second our bodies became one.

The farther he pushed into me, the wetter and tighter I became. I sucked him deeper into my being.

"I don't ever want to not know what if feels like to be inside you, Melonee. I don't think I could go a day without it," he whispered in my ear as his slow strokes gave way to a faster pace. "Whatever you really had to tell me doesn't even matter anymore, as long as it ends with you becoming mine."

I arched my back at his words and allowed him deeper access into me. My pussy was so wet now that his dick easily glided in and out of me. The slow burn that started in my toes slowly made its way up my legs and thighs and into my belly. I knew I was about to cum, and Roman did too.

"Give me my shit, Mel," he growled into my neck. His hips moved from side to side and worked my insides like crazy. "Don't make me take it from you. . . . Shit." Sweat started to roll down his face and drip onto mine, but I didn't care. A few drops landed in my mouth, and surprisingly, I savored the masculine taste.

"Fuck," I moaned as my breathing changed and my hips started rocking into his.

"Give what now belongs to me and only me, Melonee. I'm not going to ask again," he said, his left hand circling my neck. My eyes rolled to the back of my head but popped back open when Roman began to lightly squeeze my neck. The slight cutoff of air to my body mixed with the way Roman was fucking me almost had me there. It wasn't until those green eyes looked into mine, mirroring the same love I had for him, that I finally let loose and became all the way undone.

Roman repeating the word *mine* over and over in my ear was the last thing I heard before my eyes rolled to the back of my head, my body flatlined, and I totally blacked out.

Roman

The annoying sound of the seagulls cawing constantly woke me from my sleep. I was confused about why I was even able to hear seagulls this early in the morning in the city. I rubbed my hand over my face and tried to focus my eyes on anything other than the back of my eyelids, but I was having a hard time doing so.

What the hell did I have to drink last night? I thought to myself as I sat up on the side of my bed. I tried to remember anything that had happened between the time I left to go the charity event and now, but I kept coming up with a blank. I remembered hopping in the back of the car that José drove and riding to the hotel hosting the yearly event, and even I remembered sitting in the car and debating whether or not I wanted to go into the hotel. Anything after that . . .

Placing my hands at my sides, I pushed up from the bed, with the intent of heading into the bathroom, but I fell back down on the bed the second I stood up. My body felt weird, nothing like it usually did when I woke up to take my morning piss. For some reason, I felt like I'd been hit by a Mack truck, and couldn't move or feel a muscle in my body to save my life.

"What the hell is going on?" I was feeling around the bed for my phone to check the time when my hand hit what felt like a stiff object on the opposite side of the bed. When I tried to focus my eyes on the body that was obviously lying next to me, I had to blink a few times before I could make out a curvy frame lying underneath the turquoise sheets.

Who the hell did I bring home last night? I thought to myself as my eyes began to wander around the bedroom I was in. *And why am I at the beach house?*

My vision was still kind of blurry, but I could make out some of the antique furniture pieces that the decorator I hired when I bought this place some years ago had placed in this room. I shook my head, trying to get my vision together, but all that did was make me dizzier and push the vomit sitting in my stomach up to my throat. It sprayed out of my mouth all over the plush carpet. My eyes watered as I gagged a few times on nothing but air. Remnants of whatever I had eaten and drunk last night turned the light beige carpet at my feet red.

After grabbing the bottled water off the nightstand, I poured some in my mouth, swished it around, and spit it right back into the bottle. I could feel the bile rising from the bottom of my stomach again and decided to try to make it to the bathroom this time around. When I placed my hands at my sides and pushed up again, this time I was able to stand up and stay on my feet, though I swayed from side to side. It felt like I was drunk off my ass and was having the worst hangover ever. Stepping over my "masterpiece" on the floor, I slowly walked to the en suite bathroom and dropped to my knees in front of the porcelain toilet, just in time to catch another round of vomit. After finishing, I managed to crawl to the sink and rinse out my mouth with mouthwash and wash my face with a few splashes of water. Although the splashing did help me to wake up a little more, the pounding pain going on in my head had me squinting my eyes, trying to feel some type of relief.

Ding-dong!

I heard the doorbell ring, followed by what sounded like thunder hitting the door. Not only was the noise annoyingly loud, but it had my head aching way more than it had been a minute ago. Using the walls for support, I walked out of the bathroom in search of some shorts or something else to put on to answer the door. The banging continued as I slowly moved around the room, forgetting what I was looking for. I sat down on the edge of the bed, and then I looked back at the body lying in my bed and tried to remember anything that had happened last night. I squinted my eyes a little more than before, trying to get a glimpse of her face, but her dark hair was sprawled out over the pillow and was covering her face. I shook her foot to try to wake her up, but she didn't budge at all. After moving my hand to her thigh, I lightly squeezed it a few times, but she still didn't wake up.

I rose to my feet and, without the aid of my hands, walked around to the side of the bed on which the unknown woman lying and stood in front of her. I moved her hair from her face a little and was greeted with some of the fullest, most beautiful lips I'd ever seen before. My dick instantly began to twitch as flashes of those sexy lips wrapped around my dick sometime last night flashed in my mind. With my vision still a little blurry, I took in her smooth dark skin, and another memory hit me. I looked in the direction of the glass window. Now light from the rising sun was coming in the room. I remembered the way the moon lit up the room last night and illuminated her dark skin, making it look like the smoothest velvet. Sexy expressions on her face and mine began to play like a gag reel in my head. The sound of her moaning my name and asking me to fuck her harder and deeper started to float around in my mind as well. I went to pull the covers off her but stopped when the banging on the door started up again, this time way louder than it was the first time.

"Roman Black, this is the Los Angeles Police Department. Open the door now!"

Los Angeles Police Department? I said silently. *What are the police doing at my house?* My eyes shifted to the woman lying in my bed. *I know this don't have anything to do with you. I don't pay for pussy, and I never will, so you can't be a prostitute.*

Looking around the room, I tried to find something to slip into so that I could answer the door and address whatever was going on with the police. Not seeing my pants or shorts on the floor, I walked back over to my side of the bed and started to feel underneath the covers. I could feel wet spot after wet spot as my hand glided over and under the sheets and comforter, but there was no sign of any of the clothes I had had on last night. After opting to grab some gray sweats and a T-shirt out of the dresser adjacent to the bed, I made my way to the bedroom door and opened it. As soon as I stepped out into the hallway, I could see a trail of clothes scattered over the floor, leading to the sliding glass doors. As I followed the trail and picked up clothes along the way, images of last night started to flash in my mind again.

"Mr. Black. We have reason to believe that a very serious crime was committed here last night. Please open up the door so that we can rectify this situation if it's a mistake," a voice called through the front door.

Very serious crime? Rectify this situation? What in the hell is he talking about? I thought. I dropped the clothes I had gathered outside my bedroom, pulled on the T-shirt and the gray sweats I had found in the dresser, and headed for the front door. Wiping my hand over my face, I braced myself for whatever was about to happen once I opened that door. And then I opened it.

"There has to be some sort of mistake . . ." My words trailed off when the clicking sound of multiple guns being cocked hit my ears. I held my hands up, sobriety coming back instantly. I looked through the open front door, and my eyes scanned the front of my home. Dozens of police cars were on my lawn, along with various news outlets and paparazzi. The minute those vultures saw that it was me who had answered the door, the flashes on their cameras started going off.

"Mr. Black. Mr. Black . . . Is it true? Did you kidnap, beat, and brutally rape a Ms. Melonee Reid? Where is the body, Mr. Black? Is it still in there?" a news anchor shouted from her spot on my lawn.

"Mr. Black," said the balding officer who was standing directly in front of me, with his gun aimed at my chest. I could tell he was nervous by the way his hands, clasped around the butt of the gun, moved rapidly from side to side. Sweat beads were forming on the top of his head and the side of his face. "I'm going to need you to slowly step out of the house, with your hands on your head."

I put my hands on my head. "I don't understand what's going on here. Why are you all on my property at the crack of dawn, with guns drawn and the media all over my lawn?" I narrowed my eyes at the one I assumed was in charge of this circus. His eyes darted from mine to those of an officer who was standing by his side. I turned my attention to this other officer to try to get some answers.

"Mr. Black, we need you to step out of the house so that we can make sure the claims that you abducted and raped a Ms. Melonee Reid are false," said the balding officer.

I looked at him with squinted eyes, letting what he'd said run through my mind. *Melonee Reid? Melonee? Melonee? Oh shit!* My eyes bucked, and I turned my head in the direction of my bedroom. *Melonee's in my bed. That's whose sexy fuck faces keep flashing in my head*, I thought to myself, and I could feel my dick getting hard when I remembered how wet and tight her pussy was and how that muthafucka came when I told it to. But rape . . . kidnapping? Where was all this coming from? Melonee and I had skipped the charity event as two consenting adults so that we could try to figure out what this connection between us was. Where did they get this 'kidnap, rape and beat up' thing from?

I turned my attention back to the police and the media and began to smile. A deep, low rumbling started at the bottom of my stomach and turned into a full-blown laugh by the time it reached my mouth. I put my hands down. "Okay . . . okay. Who put you guys up to this?" I shook my head. "Was it Q's crazy ass? Nah, it couldn't be him. This has Benji's name all over it." I clapped my hands and laughed again.

"Nice try, everyone. But the shit isn't going to work anymore. You all can get the hell off my property now."

The balding officer spoke again. "Mr. Black, this is not a joke. Now, please, lace your hands behind your head and step outside."

I did as he had instructed. Camera lights started to flash again, and I could hear the reporters talking to each other in hushed tones. I looked at the officer standing next to the balding one and noticed that there wasn't an ounce of humor on his face.

"You guys are serious?" I asked, my nerves starting to work a little. "I assure you that no crime was committed here. Where would you even get an idea like that?"

"We received a frantic phone call from one of your neighbors, claiming they heard a woman screaming for her life a couple of hours ago," the balding officer informed me.

"I assure you her screaming for her life a couple of hours ago had nothing to do with any harm coming to her. If you want to go check, Melonee is in my bed right now, sleeping soundly. As a matter of fact, I'll go wake her up so that you can see for yourself."

The balding officer tried to stop me from walking back into my home, but by the time he started to scream out his demand for me to stay put, I was already walking down the hallway. When I reached my bedroom, I knocked a few times and announced through the closed door that the police were coming back to check on her. I knew by now she should be up, considering the loud commotion going on in front of the house.

But Melonee said nothing.

"Melonee," I called through the door, "Melonee, the police want to have a word with you."

When she still didn't respond, I walked into my bedroom and looked around. The place was a complete mess, and stuff was everywhere. Wet burgundy spots were all over the carpet, and soil from overturned plants lay in piles around the room. All the things that were wrong in my room, things that I didn't notice when I woke up this morning with a hangover, were staring me right in my face. My eyes went over to the side of the bed that Melonee was on. Even after all the screaming and my calling out to her, she was still knocked out. I walked over to her side of the bed and began to shake her and call her name, but she still didn't awaken.

After I moved her hair away from her beautiful face was when I noticed the big bruise covering her cheek and most of her chin. Her beautiful lips were swollen to the size of golf balls and were busted down the middle. I swallowed the lump in my throat and shook my head. This couldn't be right. All we did last night was have the best sex of our lives, making love to each other until we couldn't take it anymore. Where had all these bruises come from? What the fuck happened after I blacked out last night?

"Mr. Black, please step away from Ms. Reid," the balding officer said as he came through my bedroom door, the gun still in his hand.

"You need to call an ambulance. Call an ambulance now! Something's wrong!" I shouted. "She . . . she . . . wasn't like this last night."

"Mr. Black, please step back, or I will be forced to make you step back."

Ignoring his threat, I kneeled down on the side of the bed and tried to make her wake up. "Mel, it's me, Roman. Please wake up. What happened to you? Come on, baby. Get up."

Her lifeless body remained still on my bed, and I could literally feel myself about to go crazy. I was so into trying to get Melonee to wake up that I didn't see the other officers file into the room, until they tackled me down to the floor and handcuffed me. As I kicked my feet in the air as they held me down, the sheet that covered Melonee's frame caught on my leg and slid off her body.

As the police began to drag me out of the room, one of the officers turned his head and took a look at Melonee. "Oh my God," he said.

When I looked over at the bed, I saw that Melonee's perfect body was covered in bumps, bruises, and fresh cuts. Blood was splattered all over her smooth dark skin and the bed. My soul literally left my body the second my eyes landed on her. When I first woke up, I couldn't remember everything that had happened last night, but with the arrival of the police, I had sobered up completely, and everything we did and said had come back to me.

"Mel," I cried, trying to get back to her and cover her up, but the officers dragging me out of the room tightened their grip and I couldn't move.

"Someone call the bus. She's still breathing, but she's barely hanging on," the balding officer shouted as he stood next to Melonee. "Make sure the media is out of the way when they get here so we can get Ms. Reid to the hospital as soon as possible," he told one of the officers who was just standing around. He turned to me. "As for you, Mr. Black, you are under arrest for the rape and brutal beating of Ms. Melonee Reid. Anything you say can and will be used against you in the court of law. If you cannot afford an attorney . . ."

I heard my Miranda rights being read to me, but all I could concentrate on was Melonee. A lawyer was the furthest thing from my mind. I wanted—no, I needed—to make sure she survived this. I needed her to know that I would never hurt her in any way. Like I had told her last night, all I wanted was a chance to have her heart, which she willingly gave to me. If she came out of this alive and I was able to prove my innocence, I was going to make this up to her for the rest of my life.

Fiona

The second I pushed open the heavy wooden doors of the ballroom in order to exit, the rapid flutter of camera flashes going off blinded me. Keeping my arm raised to block my face, I walked around the large crowd of paparazzi and pushed past a few guests as I tried to make it out of the place unnoticed.

I'd almost made it past the big water fountain in the center of the lobby when someone grabbed my arm and I was pulled behind the large backdrop that had the name of Roman's charity for orphaned kids stamped all over it. The fact that I recognized who had grabbed me had my mind at ease, but he still knew that us possibly being seen together in public was too risky. Regardless of how good a hiding space this was.

"Meyers! What the fuck?" I hissed through gritted teeth. "You know better than to grab me like that. In public too."

My body instantly betrayed me by melting into his the second he pulled me to his hard chest. Memories of our fuck fest a couple of nights ago began to flash through my mind, and I couldn't help how wet my thighs were becoming underneath my dress.

"You know I can smell that, right?" he said.

He kissed my neck, then lightly brushed his nose across my bare shoulder. I looked up at him with questioning eyes and watched how his lips formed into a lazy smile as he returned my heated stare. Those sexy dark features of his handsome face turned me on even more. His hands traveled down the length of my body until they settled comfortably on my ass. He bent down and attached his lips to mine, squeezing two handfuls of what he deemed his favorite play area on my body.

"I'm not saying you smell bad or anything," he said against my lips. "The scent I'm talking about is that sweet smell coming from between your legs." He paused. "We," he said, referring to his dick and his face, "spend so much time down there that I can practically smell you in a room full of people with my eyes closed. So delectable . . . so intoxicating . . . so alluring."

Meyers peppered my jawline with kisses and stopped at my neck. A soft moan escaped my lips and oddly snapped me out of the trance he had me in. I placed my hands on his chest and tried to push myself away from him. But his grip on my ass tightened, and he pulled me closer to his frame. I could feel his rock-hard dick on my belly and almost gave in.

"Meyers," I hissed again, averting my eyes from his. "We cannot do this here. What if we get caught or someone sees us? All of this would be for nothing."

"You worry too much," was his response as he began to hike up the expensive ball gown that covered my body. "Stop tripping so much and let me have a sample of that sweetness between your thighs."

"Meyers," I said again, this time my tone a little less harsh. His fingers on my exposed hips caused the little bit of concern I had about being caught to evaporate. I tried to wiggle out of his hold, but I stopped when he pushed two fingers deep inside me.

Wrapping my arms tightly around his neck, I buried my face in his chest and moaned as my body shook from the pleasure. "Can . . . can we go somewhere else and . . . and do this? Ummm, like that bathroom, ooh, down the . . . the hall or in a place with less eyes and . . . people?" I tried to get out. Meyers's fingers were working the fuck out of my G-spot, and I knew it would be only a matter of time before I came.

His breathing was choppy and short, which told me that he was on the verge of coming as well. He knew that I hated when this happened without my mouth or my pussy being wrapped around his dick. I threw my head back the second his lips attached to my neck, and began to rock my hips faster on his fingers. I could hear people walking by, in their own world, or stopping to take pictures in front of the backdrop, oblivious to what was going on behind it. The boisterous cheers and laughter of other guests and the loud elevator music playing in the background probably played a part in them not being able to hear us, but I knew that would all change the second I reached my climax.

My throat went dry, and my body began to shake. The knee that was helping Meyers support my body weight went out, causing him to push me up against the wall for a little more support. I could feel his phone vibrating in his pocket, and mine vibrating between our chests. My heart rate started to pick up, and the burning that had just been in my stomach was now centered in my core, where Meyers's finger was.

"You better hold that shit until I can get my dick into you," Meyers whispered into my ear, pressing all his body weight against me. Even with all the loud noise going on around us, I still heard his belt buckle clanked after being released. "I want to feel you cum on my dick, and you better hold that shit, Fiona."

I closed my eyes tight, trying to fulfill his request, but my body had a mind of its own. Arching my back, I prepared myself for the wave of pleasure I was about to experience. Just before I hit my peak, Meyers pushed his swollen head into my pussy and began to fuck the orgasm right out of me. With one hand wrapped around my waist and the other one clamped over my mouth, suppressing the loud scream I felt was about to escape my throat, Meyers buried his face in the crook of my neck and continued to viciously pump into me until both of our juices coated his dick and the inside of my pussy. His body shook a couple of times and twitched for a few seconds. I could tell by the muffled sound of his moans that his bottom lip was tucked into his mouth and his teeth were biting down on the soft flesh a little hard as he tried to suppress his own cry of pleasure.

We stayed against the wall and connected to each other until the feeling in both of our legs came back. Meyers slowly let me go, kissing me on my lips. I lowered my eyes to his meaty dick and watched as he stuffed it back into his pants and fastened them back up. After making sure his clothes and his look were intact, he kissed me on my lips again and helped me pull my dress back down.

"I'll be at your house after I leave here, so don't go to sleep," he whispered in my ear, causing my nipples to harden.

I shook my head. "I don't think I can go another round."

He ducked his head, then looked back up to me with that sexy boyish grin, his chestnut eyes sparkling with mischief. "You can, and you will." He tapped my hip. "Text me when you make it home, and I'll be there an hour after that."

I closed my eyes for a second to try to get my mind right. When I opened them back up, Meyers had vanished, leaving the scent of his musky cologne in his wake. The constant flashing of the paparazzi cameras started up again, but now it was my cue to get up out of there. After making sure I looked decent enough to be back in public, I slid from behind the backdrop and then shimmied behind a large ficus plant that was next to it. Pretending that I had dropped my purse and its contents, I bent down to pick up my things, then walked through the rest of the hotel lobby and out the sliding doors.

"Where the hell have you been, Fiona? We've been sitting here for thirty minutes, waiting on you," Cowboy fussed as I slid into the back of the Mercedes Sprinter. Proof, EB, Wiz, and Mouse were already in their seats, all eyes focused on me.

I ran my hand over my hair and rolled my eyes.

EB smirked. "If I didn't know any better, I'd say she just got through getting that ass tossed. I know that look on her face." He nodded his head knowingly. "That's what took you so long, huh, Fee?"

"Nigga, you would know," Wiz commented. "I mean, y'all did fuck around for a couple of months back in the day." He looked me up and down and then smiled. "Yeah, bro, I'd have to agree with you. She looks a little different from earlier. Cheeks all rosy and shit."

EB nodded. "Uh-huh."

"I think she's glowing. And look. Her cheeks are turning red," Wiz said.

I could feel the blush go through my body on the inside, and I tried my hardest not to let them see how red my cheeks actually were. I turned my head away from them and looked out the tinted window.

"Fuck all that shit y'all talking about," Proof interrupted. "What the hell happened tonight, and where in the fuck is Mel?" I could feel his eyes burning a hole in the side of my head, but I continued to look out the window.

He went on: "One minute we're all in place, waiting for this mark-ass muthafucka to show up, and the next we're getting text messages from this nigga." He pointed at Cowboy. "Talking about it was time to head out." Proof focused his eyes back on me. "Did that nigga Roman ever show up? Did you get up with him? And for the last fucking time, where the hell is Mel?"

The whole car became quiet at the sound of Proof's voice rising. We all knew that he could be a hothead at times, but he was even crazier when it came to Mel's ass. As much as he preached that "We're just friends" bullshit, we all knew he still wanted to be with her.

"Fiona." He called my name with so much authority, I kind of jumped at his tone.

All eyes were trained on me again, and everyone's smile was gone, as they waited on me to respond.

Proof blew out an exaggerated breath and mumbled something to himself. Then he said, "Fiona, I know you hear me talking to you. Where the fuck is Mel, and why isn't she in the car with us?"

Ignoring him yet again, I took my small compact out of my purse, opened it, and looked at myself in the mirror. After applying a fresh coat of lip gloss on my lips, I puckered them together, blew myself a kiss, and smiled. I did look different, but I wouldn't call it a glow. Only dummies who were in love had that type of shit, and that wasn't me. Then it dawned on me why I looked different. Who wouldn't look different when they knew it was only a matter of time before they came up on a shitload of money? If everything went according to plan, Roman Black's money would be mine, and I wouldn't even have to go through the whole ordeal of getting married and trying to get him to add my name to the insurance paperwork. Oh no, if shit went how it was supposed to go, the Black Widow Clique would be sitting on millions soon.

After closing my compact, I placed it back in my purse, then pulled out my phone and sent out a couple of texts. When I looked back up, all eyes were still on me, and I knew I needed to say something before all hell actually broke loose.

"Mel is where she needs to be," was all I said.

Proof opened his mouth to say something, but I stopped him before he could utter a word.

"She's good, trust me," I said. "If we don't hear from her in a few hours, Cowboy can just trace her phone, and we'll go get her. Until then, let her work her magic so that we can get this money."

Proof closed his eyes and pinched his nose, trying to control his temper. When he finally looked at me, I could tell that he wasn't satisfied with my answer or wasn't feeling it.

"Look, Fee, you, of all people, know that I'm all about getting money, so on that tip, we're cool," he said. "But that doesn't have anything to do with telling me where Mel is. Regardless of what she does in the BWC, she's still my baby moms, and I need to know that wherever she's at, she's okay. Not just for the crew's sake, but for Madison's as well."

I thought about what Proof had said, and I understood where he was coming from. If anything bad ever happened to Mel, it would tear my heart up to see my godbaby crying for her mother. I turned to look back out the window, contemplating whether or not I should tell them the truth. I knew they'd probably all hate me when it did come out, but I was betting that their cut of the money we were about to get would soften the blow of my lie a little.

Out of the corner of my eye, I noticed Cowboy fidgeting with his laptop, which told me he was already trying to figure out Mel's whereabouts.

So to ease their minds and to stop Proof from messing up the plans, I decided to tell them where she was.

"Mel's not in this car, because she managed to get in the car with someone else," I said.

"Someone else? Like who?" EB asked before Proof got a chance.

I looked each one of them in the eye, smiled, then looked back out the window and told them what they wanted to know. "She's with Roman Black." I turned my head to catch the expressions on their faces.

The looks on their faces made me laugh, and I prepared myself for the myriad of questions I knew they were about to ask.

My phone had been going off all night, and I had yet to answer it. I was so hung over from partying with Cowboy, Proof, and the rest of them niggas that I had lost track of time. After rolling over in my bed to block the sun from hitting my face, I closed my eyes and tried to get a few more hours of sleep before it was time to meet up with my brother to discuss some business. I'd just slipped into a comfortable slumber when my phone rang for the thousandth time.

I wanted to ignore it again, but something told me to at least look at the screen to see whose face popped up. When I looked down and saw my bae's sexy smile gracing my screen, I slid the phone button to the right and said hello.

"You sound like you had a long night last night," his smooth voice said through the phone.

I blushed because he knew that he was part of the reason why my night had been so long. After shooting pool for a few hours with the clique and drinking more than I should have, I had decided that it was time for me to head home. I had grabbed my things and was heading up to Cowboy's guest room when I saw the notification button on my cell blinking. Besides the Google alerts I had set up for potential marks, I had a few missed calls and text messages from Lover Boy. I bit my bottom lip and moaned at the dick pics he'd sent me. It had been a few hours since his ass pulled me behind that backdrop at the charity event, and my hot ass was ready for more. As I looked at the pics, my mouth watered and my pussy thumped, just thinking about feeling him inside both holes.

When I tried to call him back, I became a little upset when he didn't pick up the phone and sent me straight to voice mail. I was two seconds away from cussing him out when I received a text from him telling me to come outside. I was so excited when I read that message that I practically ran out of Cowboy's spot.

As soon as I walked out the front door and across the lawn, a black stretch limo pulled up in front of me and the back door swung open. Not only was I greeted by one of the sexiest men I'd ever seen—still wearing his custom fitted tuxedo and smelling like all kinds of new money—but also the smell of that good Cali Kush was in the air, and I was so ready to hit the blunt a few times and go back to his place. Safe to say, we never made it to his spot. We fucked in the back of the limo while we rode around the city for hours. Dawn was slowly creeping up when he dropped me back off at Cowboy's house and I hopped in my car to go home.

"I did have a long night. I probably would've been in my bed at a reasonable time had someone not wanted to fuck the shit out of me in the back of the limo."

I could hear him smiling through the phone. "Hey, I wanted to take you to my house, but I couldn't resist. I told you your smell is alluring and intoxicating to me." He laughed. "I am kind of bummed we never made it back to my place, though. I really wanted to christen a few rooms there since we've already christened every inch of your place."

"Because when we just meet up at my house, it doesn't complicate things. Well, at least not for me."

He yawned into the phone. "What do you mean?"

"Well, you know that I'm not the relationship type of girl. To me, when you start spending the night at each other's houses, those nights start to turn into days, then into weeks at a time. That shit starts to mean something other than just fucking after a while. You're starting to want to spend time with that person in their element to see how they live. You start to study people's patterns and begin to adapt to their ways. When we just stick to coming to my house, we only see one way . . . and that's mine. We drink, we smoke, we fuck, and then you go on your way. Now, a couple of times I have slipped up and let you stay the night, even cooked your ass breakfast a time or two, but it won't happen again."

He laughed. "It won't?"

"Hell naw. Why do you think after the limo dropped me back off at my car, I didn't follow you home, like you wanted? I was not about to spend the whole night with you, and I was not about to start up this whole ritual of cooking you breakfast in the morning," I said, laughing when my line beeped. I looked at my phone screen to see who was calling me on my other line. When a number I didn't recognize popped up, I kept on with my conversation.

"What if I want you to make me some breakfast right now?" he asked.

"Your ass would be out of luck."

"Really? You wouldn't feed me anything?"

I thought about it for a second and was just about to answer when there was a knock on my door.

"Hold on one minute. Someone's at my door," I said into the phone.

Not waiting for his response, I placed my phone on my dresser, then went to my door. I looked through the peephole and couldn't see anything, because the person who was on the other side of the door had their finger covering it. There was only one person who did that. Melonee's ass. What the hell was she doing here if she was supposed to be dealing with Roman? I swung the door open, expecting to see her gray eyes grilling the hell out of me, but was surprised by someone else instead.

"What the fuck—"

He cut me off as he marched past me into the living room. "I told you I was hungry. You was gone let me starve?"

"See, this that shit I was just talking about. Only people in relationships pop up at some-one's house like this."

Lover Boy pulled me to him and cradled his nose in my neck. I could feel the long breaths he was taking as he inhaled my scent.

"Damn, you smell so good."

"I always do, according to you. Now, what do you want?" I said, pushing him off me, but not really wanting to be out of his grasp.

"I told you that I was hungry, and damn it, I'm about to eat." He licked his lips as he looked my body up and down. The small T-shirt I had on left nothing to the imagination, and my pantyless ass was on full display.

"Meyers, if you don't go somewhere else . . . You just fucked the shit out of me a few hours ago. You should be tired or at least on E right now," I said, looking down at his semi-hard dick.

"Who said anything about fucking you? I said I was hungry. Now, feed me willingly, or I will be forced to take it."

I wanted to say something smart, but I stopped when my phone started going off. I could tell by the *Star Wars* ringtone that it was Cowboy.

"Unless you want them to hear you scream-ing my name, I advise you not to answer that,"

Meyers said as he backed me into my bedroom and over to the bed, where I fell on top of my orthopedic mattress.

As soon as my ass hit the sheets, my legs parted, giving him all the access he needed to dive right into his breakfast and eat it up.

"Fuck!" I moaned when his lips latched onto my pearl and began to suck as if his life depended on it.

I came so hard and so fast, I almost blacked out from the impact. I knew his face had to be covered in my juices with the way that orgasm just hit me. I was looking down to watch him handle his business when our eyes connected. There was something about that penetrating gaze that had me ready to forget about being all about my money and to give this love thing a chance. Maybe what Melonee had said about quitting after this job and getting into a real relationship for a change could be a good thing.

Naw. Who am I kidding? Dick and a hurricane tongue will never have me breaking my rules. However, I can bend them for the time being, I thought.

I started to roll my hips as he continued to dine on this fine cuisine. The feeling of another orgasm hitting started to build in my stomach, but it was knocked back when my phone rang again. Cowboy was calling for the fifth time now, and I needed to answer the call, because it had to be important.

"Baby . . . ," I called out, but my utterance fell on deaf ears. It was like Lover Boy was in a trance and wasn't trying to hear shit I was saying.

I tried to scoot back a little to get his attention, but I only got pulled back down to his open mouth and his arms put my thighs in a choke hold.

"Baby . . . ," I said, moaning this time, because the figure eights he was doing with his tongue had my heart rate picking up.

"I already told you, whoever that is will hear you calling my name if you answer," he said in one breath before he buried his face back in my pussy.

I came for the second time but quickly got over the high when Cowboy called my phone again.

"This better be important," I said between gritted teeth as I answered the phone.

"Fee, whatever it is you're doing, you need to get to the hospital ASAP," Cowboy said quickly.

"Hospital?" I said, trying to sit up, only to get knocked back down. "Fuck," I mouthed to myself as I came again.

"It's Mel. She . . . Man, it's all bad. Just get your ass to Cedars-Sinai and call me when you're downstairs," Cowboy rushed to say before hanging the phone up in my face.

Hospital? What the fuck?

I managed to hop up this time and liberate myself from Lover Boy's grasp. I headed to the bathroom.

"What are you doing? I wasn't finished with my meal," Meyers protested.

Ignoring him, I entered the bathroom, turned on the shower, and hopped in. The water was cold as hell, but I needed something to calm my hot ass down. Had Cowboy not called to say that Mel was in the hospital, I probably would be riding Lover Boy's dick right now.

"I have to get to the hospital," I said after I hopped out of the shower, dried off, and started pulling something to wear out of my drawers.

"Is everything okay?" he asked, grabbing my shaking hands and pulling me into his embrace.

"I don't know. My brother just called and said that my best friend is in the hospital and I need to get there."

"Did he say if she was okay?" he asked as I put on some clothes.

"I don't know what's going on. I hope she's okay. I should've fucking called her last night, like I told myself to. If anything serious is wrong with her, I'll never forgive myself," I said as I walked to the front of my house in search of my keys and purse.

"Maybe you should let me drive you," he said as he followed behind me.

I looked at him like he was crazy. "We are not in a relationship. That right there is something people in a relationship would offer to do. I can drive myself, thank you," I said. I opened the front door and held it open for him to walk out.

"So when am I going to see you again?" he said as he walked out the door.

I walked past him and headed straight for my car. "You know where to find me, so we will see," I called over my shoulder.

I got in my car and didn't even wait to see if he had made it to his before I pulled off and headed toward the hospital. I said a silent prayer and prayed that nothing really bad had happened to my best friend. I didn't think I could stand seeing Madison or Granny dealing with this if it was bad.

"Damn it. I should've listened to my dad," I said aloud to myself as I sped down the freeway.

Melonee

Three months later . . .

Blinking my eyes a few times, I tried to raise my arm to block the bright lights that were shining in my face, but I stopped when a sharp pain shot through my entire body.

"Don't move, baby. Let me go get the doctor," I heard my granny say, but I couldn't quite focus my eyes on her face.

With blurry vision, I scanned the room but still couldn't quite make out where I was. I tried to speak but wasn't able to due to the tube that was lodged in my throat. Fear instantly gripped my body, and I started to move around wildly.

"Mel, be still, baby," a familiar voice said to me as the person to whom it belonged firmly planted his hands on my shoulders to stop me from moving so much. "You're only going to make it worse if you keep twisting around so much. I know you're scared right now because you don't know where you are, but try to be still until Granny comes back with the doctor so that he can check you out."

I could feel the water start to build up in my eyes as my vision became clearer. When my eyes focused on Proof's face, tears seemed to continuously roll down the side of my face and into my ear.

I tried to speak again but couldn't. Proof handed me a dry-erase board and a marker so I would have some way to communicate.

Seeing him here and hearing my granny's voice had so many thoughts running through my head. I could tell now that I was in some hospital, but I hadn't the faintest idea why. I turned my head to the side and could see all sorts of flower bouquets and "Get well soon" balloons spread throughout the room. Some you could tell had been here for days or weeks, while others looked like they had just been brought in. The TV, which was muted, was on *The Wendy Williams Show*, which told me that Fiona was somewhere in the vicinity.

When I focused my eyes back on Proof, I couldn't really read the expression on his face, nor could I stop looking at his wild facial hair.

I pressed the marker against the dry-erase board and managed to write one word, although it hurt like hell to write it.

Madison?

Proof squinted his eyes, then mouthed what I had written. "She's with my parents right now." He looked down at his phone to see the time. "I actually gotta go pick her up in about thirty minutes. Then I'm going to bring her back up here to see you."

A feeling of relief washed over me. I didn't know why I was here, but at least my baby was all right.

Where am I? I wrote underneath Madison's name.

"You're at the hospital. Well, you've been in the hospital for a little while now. Do you remember why you're here?"

As I erased the board with the sheet that was lying over my legs, I tried to remember what I had done last night, but I couldn't remember anything. I could feel Proof's eyes watching me carefully as I began to write on the board again.

What happened?

The way Proof looked at me, then wiped his hand over his face as he shook his head, told me that whatever the story was, it wasn't going to be good.

"Why don't you wait until Granny and the doctor get back to ask that question?" he said. "It might be better if you hear it from one of them."

Hear it from one of them? I said to myself. What could have possibly happened to me that was so bad that he didn't want to tell me himself? Maybe hearing it from my granny or the doctor was a good thing, so I pushed that question to the back of my head and decided to ask another one. Hopefully, he would be able to answer this one and wouldn't need someone else to.

How long have I been here?

Proof was just about to open his mouth when my granny walked back into the room, followed by a nice-looking Indian man who reminded me of the dude who played Suresh on that TV show *Heroes*.

"We'll take it from here, Jaylen. You need to go pick up my other baby and bring her back up here so that she can spend some time with her mother now that she's awake," my granny said. Then she placed her hand on Proof's shoulder and whispered something in his ear. He looked at me with sorrow in his eyes, then turned around and left the room.

The Indian dude, who I was assuming was my doctor, checked my vitals, then wrote some things down on my charts. After checking my eyes and reflexes, he sat on the edge of my bed, then looked down and read what I had written on the dry-erase board.

"Nice to finally see you awake, Ms. Reid. You had us scared for a minute when you first got here," he told me.

I looked down at the board on my lap, and he followed my line of sight.

"Do you remember anything that happened to you?" he asked.

I shook my head no.

"Do you remember the last thing you ate?"

I thought about it, then shook my head no again.

"What about the last person you were sexually active with?" he said.

My eyes opened wide, then darted to my granny. She stood at the foot of my bed, with tears in her eyes and her hands covering her mouth. I could see that she was tightly gripping the white handkerchief she always carried in her purse.

I shook my head, and I could tell that the doctor was confused about this by the way his eyebrows furrowed.

"Are you saying you don't remember or . . . ," he said.

I lifted the dry-erase board and wrote on it.

Over a year since sex.

The doctor and my granny exchanged a look, then turned their attention back to me.

"So you haven't had sex with anyone in the past three months that you can remember?" the doctor asked.

I pointed to the last thing I had written on the dry-erase board and looked at this doctor like he was dumb. I knew who I had slept with last, but for some reason, it felt like this doctor knew something I didn't.

My eyes traveled back to my granny before I wrote another question. This one was directed to her, and I hoped she would just answer it.

What's going on?

I didn't know what was wrong about what I had written, but as soon as my granny read my question, she broke down in tears. Her sobbing was so loud and heart wrenching that I started to cry myself. All the monitors that were hooked up to me started to go crazy, which caused a few nurses to run into the room.

"We're fine," the doctor said. "I'm in here. If we need anything, or should Ms. Reid slip back into a coma, I'll call you."

The nurses nodded their heads, then walked right back out.

Coma? Did he just say, "Slip back into"? I wondered. I could hear that my granny was still crying, but I now needed answers. How long was I in a coma, and how in the hell did I get into one?

"I can tell by the different expressions on your face that you have a lot of questions running through your mind. Before I begin to answer those questions for you, though, let me remove the tube from your mouth and get you some water, because your throat is going to be really dry." The doctor rose up from my bed and paged one of the nurses. "Now, this may hurt for a second or two, but everything will be fine. Take a deep breath on the count of three, okay? One . . . two . . . three."

I wanted to scream when he pulled that long-ass tube out of my throat, but I couldn't. After coughing for what felt like two hours, I drank a few sips of water from a cup with a straw, which the blond nurse who had come back in to assist held for me. Then I laid my head back down on the pillow. My throat was a little sore; however, my comfort level was better. My voice came out a little hoarse when I spoke, but the doctor told me that in a day or two, it would be back to normal.

"Now, Ms. Reid, to answer some of your questions. You've been in a coma for the past ninety days. The morning you were brought in, we didn't know if you were going to make it or not. You suffered extensive internal bleeding as well as head injuries."

Internal bleeding? Head injuries? Was I in a car accident and don't remember? Since my throat was so sore, I hurriedly picked up the marker and began to write on the dry-erase board.

Was I in an accident?

The doctor looked back at my granny, who looked at me, then back at him, and nodded her head. I didn't know if she was saying yes to my question or telling the doctor to continue.

"Ms. Reid . . . May I call you Melonee?" the doctor asked as he sat down at the foot of my bed.

I slowly nodded my head, never taking my eyes off my granny.

This was the first time I had noticed just how stressed out she actually looked. Her eyes were red, and she looked really tired. The peach blouse she was wearing and the black dress pants she had on were slightly wrinkled, which was so unlike my granny. She started her mornings off with ironing her clothes for the day, and then she would go downstairs to make breakfast for herself and Madison. I took in her pecan-colored skin and didn't like how pale she looked. It was as if she hadn't been in the sunlight for days.

"Melonee, as I said, for the past three months, you've been in a coma." I tried to say something, but he held his hand up to stop me. "Don't try to talk right now. Just listen." When I rested my head back on my pillow, he continued. "The morning you were brought in, you were in real bad shape. Someone had really done a number to you. You were severely beaten, and you were so bloody that initially, the police thought you had been shot. You suffered some blunt trauma around your rib and chest area, which caused internal bleeding."

He went on. "During surgery, we were able to stop the bleeding and also make sure that none of your vital organs were affected. This person or persons that attacked you were really trying to kill you or to make sure you didn't remember anything about what happened, because the blows to your head were enough to actually kill you. For a second there, we thought we had lost you, but something inside you kept fighting. A CT scan was performed after your surgery, and thankfully, you suffered only limited swelling to your brain."

"Baby, do you remember anything about the person who did this to you?" my granny asked, but for the life of me, I couldn't remember anything.

"She probably won't remember anything right now, because she's suffering from short-term memory loss," the doctor noted.

"Short-term memory loss? How do you know that?" My granny walked closer to me. "You know who I am, right, baby?"

I could see the tears start to build up in her eyes again, which caused them to build up in mine.

"Granny," I said, but I could barely get the word out.

"See? She remembers me. Her memory isn't lost."

The doctor shook his head. "She remembers you because, as I said, she is suffering from short-term memory loss. Anything before the night of the attack, she will most likely remember, but everything after that may come back or might not come back at all."

"Well, can she take some sort of medicine to get it back? Now that she's awake, we can finally put that bastard in jail, where he belongs."

I didn't know what my granny was talking about, but I sure was about to try to find out. When I reached for the dry-erase board, which I had placed on my belly, I was shocked by the small bulge, which I didn't remember being there. I pulled the covers down from over my breasts and almost had a heart attack. Good thing I was already in the hospital.

"What's wrong with my stomach?" It hurt like hell for me to say that, but I needed answers.

"Baby, I don't know how to tell you this," my granny said, trying to explain, "but that vicious asshole didn't just stop at beating the living crap out of you. He . . . he . . ." My granny couldn't even finish the sentence before she started sobbing again.

"Melonee, what your grandmother is trying to tell you is that on top of beating you damn near to death, your attacker also raped you."

"Raped me?"

He nodded his head. "The police found you naked in a beach house in Malibu after they received an anonymous call from someone. Your underwear and clothes were ripped off and discarded. We did a rape kit on you and found some vaginal tearing, lacerations, and bruising. There was also the presence of semen, which we collected and gave to the police to test for DNA." He looked at me as if he was trying to say something with his eyes, and I gave him that "Okay . . . and?" look.

He continued. "A pregnancy test was performed a few weeks after your rape to confirm if you were pregnant or not, and the test came back negative. The second test that was done came back with the same results, so we didn't think anything of it. Well, that was until the nurse who was originally assigned to you went on vacation and you were given a new one."

I was tired of him beating around the bush, and the medicine I had just been given in my

IV by the blond nurse was making me sleepy. "What are you not saying?" I asked.

He wiped his hand down his face and looked down at the floor. "Well, the nurse who administered the first two tests had a lapse in judgment due to her pro-life beliefs. A selfish choice was made for you by her, which in turn resulted in her immediate termination from Sacred Hearts."

"Meaning?"

He blew out a frustrated breath. "Meaning that we were unaware that you were with child for a number of weeks. The falsified paperwork completed by the nurse indicated that your tests were both negative. By the time we realized that this was not true, it was too late to terminate the pregnancy, given that you were in a coma and were still healing."

The pain that shot throughout my whole body was unbearable as I sat up in my bed, trying to comprehend what the doctor had just said. "Are . . . are you trying to tell me that I'm pregnant and carrying the baby of the man . . . the man who attacked me?"

I saw the doctor slowly nod his head, but I didn't see or hear anything else after that, because everything around me went black.

Fiona

I sat in the hospital cafeteria, sipping on my cup of coffee, nibbling a cream-cheese Danish, and watching the news. Although Melonee's attack had happened three months ago, they were still reporting on it because of who her attacker was.

"Representatives from the Black family's legal team declined to answer any questions pertaining to the case being built against Mr. Roman Black when asked this morning," said the reporter. "However, a close source to the family has informed us that Mr. Black is still out of the country and will not be back in the States until he is subpoenaed or officially arrested for the assault and brutal rape of twenty-six-year-old Melonee Reid. Sources close to the billionaire bachelor says that Mr. Black still denies these allegations while in Russia and will continue to deny them until his name is cleared. This is Anna Brinks reporting live for KCAL Nine News at noon."

As the reporter started on another story, I took one last bite of my cream-cheese Danish and threw the rest away. Just thinking about one of the biggest paydays since we started the BWC going down the drain had suddenly made me lose my appetite. The doctors weren't sure if Melonee would remember anything once she woke up, but I was planning on making sure I helped her out with that. If we couldn't get to Roman Black's money through his heart, we'd for sure get to it through a rape and attempted murder charge. I just needed to make sure Melonee at least remembered something about her attack that would point fingers at Roman.

I was still sitting in the cafeteria, with thoughts about this money rolling around in my head, when Proof walked in and sat down on the empty seat in front of me.

He wiped his hand down his handsome face and blew out a frustrated breath. I could tell by his red eyes that he had not been sleeping too well. If he wasn't at home taking care of Madison, he was at the hospital, waiting for Melonee to open her eyes.

"You look like shit," I said and laughed. Proof and I had always had this love- hate relationship, but he knew that he was my boy.

"I feel like shit, sis. Between being at the hospital the majority of the day, then going home and taking care of Madison at night, I don't know which way is up."

"What about Granny? Why don't you have her watch Madison for a couple of days?"

He shook his head, then picked up my semi-warm cup of coffee and took a sip. The way his face scrunched up after that first taste, I could tell he wasn't ready for the shitload of sugar I needed to drink this bitter shit.

"Man, Fee, your ass is going to be up in one of these hospital rooms in a minute with diabetes if you keep drinking your coffee like this."

I waved him off, then let my head fall back so that I could gather up my auburn strands into a messy bun on the top of my head. When I brought my face back into Proof's view, I couldn't help but notice the spaced-out look on Proof's face. Although the redness in his tired eyes stood out, you could not miss those hypnotizing green irises of his. For a second, my mind almost went to a place where it shouldn't go while I sat in front of my best friend's baby daddy, but when I saw small tears start to build up in the corners of his eyes, I knew my lustful thoughts needed to be changed to ones of concern.

"What's wrong, Proof?"

I watched as he willed the tears not to fall, but he lost the battle once his eyes connected with mine. "I should've been there, Fee. I'm always there when Mel needs me. And not because I still have love for her, but because she's my daughter's mother. It would kill me if I ever had to tell Madison that her mother was gone and was never coming back. Do you know how bad I felt the night she was brought here, all fucked up and unresponsive? I'm still trying to figure out how she ended up at this fool's loft that night. How did she even run into him? EB, Mouse, and Wiz said that she was in the ballroom with you but left a little after that. She didn't tell you where she was going?" He looked at me, and I could tell that he was expecting an answer.

"She said something about leaving her purse in the car we rode in, and she said she needed it for something. I told her to leave it, but she insisted on retrieving it."

"I should've been there that night. But I just had to take out this new chick I met, trying to convince myself that I was really over Mel." He shook his head as the tears continued to fall. "Three months, Fee! For three months, I have had to keep telling Madison that her mother was just sleeping because she needed some rest." He held the bridge of his nose, then used those same fingers to wipe away the couple of tears that had just run down his cheeks. He cleared his throat. "I don't know how you're going to take this, but fuck it. This is something that has been on my mind ever since Mel said it."

He hesitated for a minute, then spoke. "I think we should shut down the BWC or at least give it a rest for a few years. Shit is starting to go left, and it's only a matter of time before some other shit happens that has all of us either in jail or in the hospital, fighting for our lives. If this wasn't a wake-up call for that ass, I don't know what would be."

I nodded my head, then looked down at the red leggings I had on. My feet, which were in a pair of all-white Ones, began to tap the shiny tiled floor. I pulled at the hoodie strings hanging off my shoulders and started making loose loops. A few times I had thought about the BWC shutting down, but I had changed my mind each time, as Cowboy would show me pictures of potential clients and tell me their estimated net worth. I also thought about all the stuff Mel had said that day I went to her apartment about finding real love and being married for real. Yet again, that money had your girl saying, "Fuck love." Looking at the situation my best friend was in, and recognizing all the hurt that it had caused her and everyone close to her, you would think that my mind would be made up. However, maybe this was the wake-up call she needed to actually disengage from the clique. I mean, we would no doubt always be best friends, but she could easily be replaced, along with his ass and anyone else.

"I hear everything you're saying, bruh, and please believe me when I say that thoughts of shutting down the BWC have crossed my mind on more than one occasion." I was lying, but he didn't have to know that. I grabbed my coffee from him and took a sip. "Everything you just said is the same thing I was just telling Cowboy. Maybe it is time to change up some things. Had Roman Black actually responded to any of my advances, that could easily be me up there in Melonee's hospital room, trying to wake up."

I dropped my head, and the tears I didn't even know were there began to fall. "As far as how she ended up running into him, your guess is as good as mine. We were waiting for his ass to show up all night, but he never did."

"And at Melonee's expense, we know why now." Proof placed his hands in the pockets of the hoodie he had on, then leaned back in the seat. "You don't think somebody has the drop on us and knows what it is the Black Widow Clique does, do you?"

I shook my head. "Naw, I don't think so. Besides, Cowboy makes sure to erase unnecessary shit from our records that could get us caught up."

"That may be true, but there are always ways to find out certain information about people and who they are associated with and what they do. Something just ain't right about this. I'm not a big fan of that muthafucka Roman Black, but I doubt he would need to drug a girl and take advantage of her, damn near risk his whole career and freedom, just to take some pussy, which I'm sure he can get at the drop of a dime."

I looked at him like he was crazy. Whose fucking side was this nigga really on? The only thing that needed to make sense to him was that his baby mama was laid up in the hospital, almost dead, because of Roman Black.

"I don't put nothing past anybody. We weren't in the car that night when he and Mel got together, so we don't know what went on. One thing I do know is that white people are crazy, especially those Russians," I said.

Proof looked at me for a long minute, then looked down at his watch. "All right, Fee. I'm about to be out. I have to go pick up Madison so I can bring her back up here to see her mom. Madison was the first person Mel asked for when she woke up."

I hopped out of my seat, damn near knocking over the table. "Mel is up!"

For the first time in three months, Proof finally smiled. "Yeah, she's been up for a little over twenty minutes. Granny wanted the doctor to tell her about everything that happened to her, including the baby, so I stepped out to give them a minute. They should be finished explaining things to her by now. You need to get your ass on up there. I know she might need her best friend right about now, I mean, that is, until me and Madison get back."

I playfully punched Proof on the arm, then gave him a sideways hug. I didn't even say good-bye or attempt to wait on the slow-ass elevator. I raced up those eight flights of stairs. I wanted to see if any of Melonee's memory was back. If not, I had to make sure she remembered everything I needed her to. Starting with Roman Black's face.

Roman

I stood at the large bay window overlooking the picturesque scene of my uncle's backyard. For a man so deadly and deep rooted in the Russian mafia, you'd never take him to be the landscaping, green-thumb type.

The plate of freshly made *zapekanka*, a breakfast cake, that the maid, Alyona, had just brought into the den filled the air with a tantalizing aroma. My stomach yearned for it, but I hadn't eaten a thing since I made it to Russia, besides a bottle of water and an energy bar every now and then. I hadn't indulged in any of Alyona's homemade dishes that she had brought to me during my stay.

So lost in thought, trying to remember what had happened three months ago, I didn't hear my uncle come in until he spoke to me in his deep Russian voice.

"You not eating isn't a good thing."

I turned at the sound of his voice and looked down at the plate full of breakfast goodies behind me.

"I don't have an appetite, Uncle."

He smacked his lips and continued to look down at the envelopes he was shuffling through. "Your stomach tells a different story, no?"

Without responding, I turned my gaze back to the backyard and smiled. Ever since I was a little boy, my uncle Kazimir had always been able to tell what was bothering me before I said a word. He had said he was always able to do that with my mother, and now that she was gone, he exercised that skill with me.

Memories of the summers I would spend out here while growing up filled my mind, and I couldn't think of a day when my uncle was never there for me. Even when he would leave, unannounced, for a week or two during my summer vacations, when he came back, it was as if he had never left in the first place. Anything I had done in those days when he was gone, he knew about, and he would handle any situation that came up accordingly. I mean, I wasn't an unruly teen who did crazy and dumb things, but with Marques and a few of my Russian cousins egging me on, I did get into a little trouble.

"Every time I see you, you remind me more and more of your mother," Uncle Kazi said as he came and stood next to me at the window. He'd put down the envelopes, and now a crystal glass of chilled vodka was in his hand. He took a sip.

With us standing next to each other, you'd never think that we were related. My uncle didn't share the same blond hair and green eyes I'd inherited from my mother. His dark hair, dark eyes, and statuesque frame were all thanks to my *dedushka*, or grandfather, Vlad. Although twenty years older than me, my uncle Kazi didn't look a day over thirty. Didn't act like it, either. His gym workouts paled in comparison to mine. Whereas I went three times a week to the gym, he worked out twice every day. Russian mafia tattoos decorated both of his arms, and my mother's and grandmother's faces were the centerpiece for the mural on his back.

NO HONOR AMONG THIEVES was written in Russian across the front of his chest, and my mother's and grandmother's middle names were on his rib cage.

With him being the type of guy who wore a three-piece suit, you'd never know he had all that ink on him. Unless, of course, you were in the confines of his home, like I was now, and he was shirtless, which he was as he stood next to me, his colorful body artwork on full display.

"KRASIVO . . . ," I heard him say as he looked out at the view of his backyard.

"Yes, it is a beautiful sight, Uncle. You did a great job."

He nodded his head and took another sip of his vodka. "Your mother always wanted a garden like this. Always talked about the sweet smell of her purple roses, chamomile, peonies, azaleas, and Gerber daisies waking her up in the morning." He smiled. "Every time the first morning wind blows and the fragrant aroma of those flowers fills my bedroom, I know it's her telling me to get up and do something special with my life."

"Something special?" I asked, with one eyebrow raised. I didn't know what could be more special than being an enforcer for the mafia, but, hey.

"Special as in finding love and settling down with someone who would give me my firstborn son and love me the way that I deserved to be loved," Uncle Kazi replied before he sighed and looked at me with sorrow in his eyes. "Natalya is probably rolling over in her grave right now. My life isn't anything like how she wanted it to be." I felt my uncle's hand lightly clamp my shoulder. "This girl you supposedly harmed, you love her, yes?"

See what I was saying? The whole time I'd been here thus far, my uncle had been gone. Yet he already knew what was going on with me. Because I didn't want to seem like an even bigger fool for being in love with the one woman who could potentially put me in jail for the rest of my life, I started to lie, but like always, my uncle already knew what the matter really was.

"There's no need to lie, nephew. I already know. Only a broken heart will make a grown man pass up Alyona's home-cooked meals. Especially her *zapekanka*."

We shared a laugh.

"Is it weird that I'm in love with a girl who thinks I raped her and almost beat her half to death?"

He shrugged his broad shoulders. "I've seen worse."

I turned from the window, grabbed the plate of *zapekanka* Aloyna had left, sat on the red-leather couch, and began to eat.

"I've gotten word from my source in the States that she's awake. Did you know?" my uncle said.

I sat up straight in my seat and sat my plate down. Melonee being awake was news to me. The last time I talked to Marques, he had said that she was still in pretty bad shape.

"I need to go see her," I said, getting up and heading toward the door to the den.

"You will do no such thing!" Uncle Kazi said sternly as he rounded the couch and stood toe to toe with me. "That would not be a smart idea, seeing as you're the number one suspect in her attack." He stepped back and took another sip of vodka. "Besides, only immediate family is allowed to see her right now."

"But—"

"But nothing, Roman!" The sound of his crystal glass being slammed down on his desk echoed throughout the room. "You are not to see or contact her, or even step foot in that hospital, until we clear your name. Do you understand?"

I didn't respond, but he knew I understood.

"And don't think I don't know about all those floral arrangements you've sent her during the past few months. Stop that immediately. Those can be traced back to you, and we don't need to give the police any more ammunition than they have." Uncle Kazi picked his now empty glass up and swirled the ice cubes around. "I have a gut feeling that someone set you up, and until we find out who it is, you need to stay away from that young lady and anyone associated with her, *ponimayesh*?"

This time I nodded my head. "I understand."

My uncle Kazimir's glare stayed on me until
he felt that I truly understood. I'd listen to my
uncle for now and stay away from Melonee, but
eventually, I had to find a way to go see her. My
life depended on it, literally and figuratively.

"Aye, yo! My man's back in town!" Marques
yelled as he gave me a brotherly hug in the
airport's baggage claim area. I had just arrived
back in California, thanks to his family's private
jet. After staying in Russia for another week and
going over things with my uncle, I had felt it was
time for me to get back home and out of hiding.

After everything went down that night with
Mel, the paparazzi and news people had been following my every move, trying to get a statement
or catch me in some incriminating situation.

Because of the high-paid lawyers that I had
on my side, and the fact that Melonee had
been in a coma, I'd been able to stay out of
jail after posting a five-million-dollar bail and
agreeing to inform the authorities of my travel
plans. The fact that I was still CEO of Real
Time Delivery and needed to travel for different
meetings overseas had allowed me to retain
possession of my passport, and so far I'd been
able to handle my company business.

"I'm glad to see you too, man," I said back to Marques as he grabbed one of my bags.

"So how was your homeland? I know you missed this sunny California weather," he said as we headed to his car.

"Bruh, you just don't know. The only things I'm going to miss about being back home are spending time with my uncle Kazimir and Aloyna's cooking."

"Ooh, did she make that *zapayaya* stuff? Dude, please tell me you brought me some back," he said excitedly. I didn't realize he had stopped walking until I got to his car and he wasn't there to open it.

"Come on now, man. What kind of best friend would I be if I didn't?" I called over my shoulder.

"Shit. The kind who would have had to walk his ass home if he hadn't," he replied when he caught up with me.

We stared at each other seriously for a second, then broke out in a fit of laughter.

"I missed you, my guy," Marques said, pulling me into another hug.

"And I you. But enough of the mushy shit." I stepped from his embrace. "What's been going on?"

The look on Marques's face told me that there was about to be some bullshit, but this was something I was already prepared for. "Get in the car first, and then I'll fill you in," he said.

Without another word, we hopped into his brand-new Porsche and sped away from the airport.

It was a little before noon, and traffic on the 105 was a little heavy. We sat lost in our own thoughts for a few minutes as the radio blasted Drake's new CD in the background. From the corner of my eye, I could see Marques look at me every so often, then back at the road. I didn't know what his facial expression meant, but I thought I had a pretty good idea.

"I didn't do it," I said after turning the music down.

He sat back in his seat, with one hand on the steering wheel, while he lit up a cigarette. Eyes still focused on the car in front of us. His wild, curly hair sat high in that man bun he always wore on top of his head, while his equally curly beard was surprisingly trimmed but still covered most of his face.

"Really, Ro?" He blew out a puff of smoke. "I've been knowing you damn near my entire life, and you've never had to take the pussy from any chick. Even before you became Mr. CEO. Do you not remember all the pussy we got in college, or do you need me to break out the spring break pictures?"

I laughed. "Naw, man, please leave those where they're at. I already have this *rape* thing hanging over me. I don't need some girls I won't even remember coming forward and talking about I raped them too."

"Man, please. I may not be a lawyer or care for our judicial system, but I do know that there's such a thing as a statute of limitations."

"You really need to stop partying and watch the news sometimes. Did you not just see what happened to Bill Cosby?"

"And did you not just see how all those charges were dropped?" He smacked his lips. "Them bitches know they were lying, and so did the courts that entertained that foolery."

"I get what you're saying, bruh, but I just don't want to add anything else to my plate right now. Besides, Uncle Kazi told me to lay low and drown myself in my work until he can look into some more things."

Marques shifted in his seat a little, then took a pull from his cigarette. The look on his face now told me that my plate was just starting to tip over.

"What's going on, man? I know I've been laying low for a minute and keeping contact with people to a minimum, but I kind of feel like there's something going on that I'm missing," I said.

Flicking his cigarette butt out the window,
Marques looked over his shoulder and switched
lanes, then ran his hand down his face. "When's
the last time you talked to your parents or Benji?"

It had been a minute since I'd talked to them.
More like two and a half months, to be honest.
A few days after I was arrested and released
from jail, I totally shut out everybody except
for my secretary, who kept me informed about
work-related things and the lawyer whom I'd
hired for this case. I didn't want the company to
be tied to what was going on with my legal issues,
so I had reached out to a college buddy of mine
whose law firm was the best at these types of
high-profile cases.

"I haven't spoken to anyone, really. I was
advised by Chasin and Uncle Kazi to keep to
myself, since I didn't really know who wants
to set me up." Chasin was my lawyer.

When Marques started heading toward my
home and not my office, as I had asked him to,
prior to landing, I wondered what was going
on. I had a few documents that required my
signature, and I wanted to get that out of the way
since I was still technically on my mini vacation
and out of the office.

"Look, man, I know by now you've figured out
that I'm not taking you to your office right now,"
he said.

"I can clearly see that now. My question, however, is, why?"

Marques licked his lips, then looked at me. "You know I've never lied to you, right, and I never will?"

I nodded my head. "I know that, and you know that it's always been the same way with me. So what's up?"

As we sat behind one of those big diesel trucks, waiting for the traffic to start up again, Marques kept his eyes trained on me.

"Ro, man, while you were gone, there was some decision making going on that I don't think you've been informed about, seeing as you're not ready to kill anybody."

"Okay . . . ," I said slowly. I had no idea what he could be hinting about. My secretary had been keeping me posted about things going on at my company, and my uncle had been supplying me with info about the case the DA was trying to build against me. So I was confused.

"I'ma just spit it out, because I can tell by the look on your face that you're still lost." He blew out a breath, as if to say, "Here we go." "The reason I'm not taking you to your company is that I was instructed not to. I was told that if you stepped foot on the premises, the police and the media would be notified about your arrival."

I laughed loudly at what Marques had just said. He must've gotten the wrong information. Last time I checked, I was the only one who could make decisions like that. Last time I checked, my title, CEO, hadn't changed, either. I laughed again and slapped Marques on his shoulder. When I finally noticed that he found nothing humorous, my laughter died down.

I cleared my throat. "You're not serious, are you?"

"Would I play with something like that?" Marques asked as he lit up another cigarette.

The smoke he blew out passed by me and went out the window. I wasn't a smoker, but at that moment, I thought about taking a few pulls of his cigarette to calm my nerves.

"Did you know about the moral clause in the contract you signed when your father appointed you as CEO?" he asked.

"I knew it was there, but I didn't really pay much attention to it."

He took another pull from his cigarette. "Well, you should have. Especially since this thing with ole girl went down. You've been stripped of your CEO title as of last week."

"Stripped of my title? How is that? My father hasn't—"

Marques cut me off. "Your father? He's the one who brought that moral clause bullshit up with the company's lawyers. Chase hasn't said anything to you?"

My lawyer, Chasin, hadn't said anything to me. As a matter of fact, no one had. I had turned my business phone off last week, after some reporter kept harassing me with phone calls. I had wanted to change the number then but had decided to wait until I got back in town. I reached into the duffel bag sitting between my legs and pulled my phone out. Once it was fully powered on, notification alerts started going off back-to-back. When my phone started buzzing in my hand, I looked down at the screen and noticed that Chasin was calling.

"Speak of the devil," I mumbled.

"If I were you, I'd answer that," Marques said with his eyes still on the road.

I looked at my phone screen again before I accepted the call. "Yeah, Chase. what's up?"

"Roman! I've been calling you all week! Where have you been? Never mind that. Where are you at now?"

"I'm in the car, with Marques. We were headed to my office, but I've just been told that I'm not allowed there."

Chasin blew out a long breath. "Man, that's what I've been trying to call you about since the last time we talked. Last week a new person was appointed CEO of RTD and will remain in the post until further notice."

"Yeah, I just heard that," I replied, looking at Marques, who was shaking his head. "But I have yet to hear who it is."

"Well, you don't have to look too far," Chasin noted. "They appointed Benji as the new CEO of Real Time. The board voted on it last week. And because your father still has a controlling vote in the company, he was able to vote in your absence. I'm sorry you had to find out like this, man, but just know that this is only going to be temporary. Once we clear your name, once all these charges against you are dismissed, the board members can call another meeting and do another vote to have you reinstated."

With the news I had just heard, it felt as if the weight of the world had fallen on my chest and I couldn't breathe in much air. Did they really just say that I was no longer CEO of my family's business? Did Chasin really say that my own brother, who wouldn't know how to run a Fortune 500 company if it came with instructions, was now in charge? Why didn't my parents call and say anything? Or my uncle Kazimir, for that matter?

He supposedly knew everything. Where were his sources when that board meeting was going on? Or did he keep the news from me?

I could tell by the silence from Marques in the car and Chasin on the phone that they were waiting for me to say something.

"Aye, Ro. You all right, bruh?" Marques asked, breaking the silence.

"Yeah, I'm good, man. Take me to my parents' house, though, so I can get some answers from them about what I just heard."

"Chasin, thanks for filling me in, We'll talk soon," I said into the phone before I hung up.

I needed to know why nobody had felt the need to call me about this serious matter, and how everyone in the company knew what had happened before I did.

Melonee

The day had finally come for me to leave this hospital, and I couldn't have been happier. My munchkin was here to roll me out in my wheelchair, as well as Proof, Granny, Fiona, and my aunt Bree, who had flown in last week. She said she had wanted to come sooner, but Granny had told her to give me some time to heal and deal with what had happened before she came.

I looked down at my growing belly and rubbed it. Although I despised the way this baby was conceived, I had to get over it and deal with carrying this fetus to full term since it was too late for me to get an abortion. The doctor had advised that if I really wanted to terminate the pregnancy, I could, but in doing so, I would more than likely have to forget about having a baby anytime in the future.

After countless talks with God, my granny, and the hospital's psychologist, I had made the decision to have the baby, then give it up for adoption. I didn't think I could spend the rest of my life looking at the face of a child who resembled the man who had raped me, no matter how much money Fiona kept telling me that he was worth.

I still couldn't remember everything that had happened that night, but bits and pieces flashed in my mind from time to time. Especially when Fiona or Cowboy would show me pictures of the man who everyone was saying had raped me. Those piercing green eyes of his stayed in my head and sent chills through my entire body whenever they would pop up.

"Are you okay, Mel? Madison has been asking you the same question for the past three minutes, but you haven't responded," I heard my granny whisper in my ear.

We were outside the hospital lobby, waiting on Proof to pull the car around, and I was too ready to go. Other than having a few bruises on my face and a couple of bones that were still mending, I was doing pretty good for someone who was almost beaten to death. Even with the few pounds I had gained since I ended up in the hospital, I was doing okay.

I looked down at my baby girl's face and smiled. She was the perfect mixture of her father and me, with her beautiful brown skin, round face, doe eyes, heart-shaped lips, and pretty hair.

Proof and I did good with little Miss Madison. She was my joy, and I would always love him for blessing me with her. For as long as I was in the hospital, Proof had made sure to bring Madison to see me every day, claiming that she wouldn't let him live if he didn't. If you asked me, Proof had been more afraid about me not coming out of that coma than I might have been if I'd known what was happening at the time. He didn't think I'd seen those tears falling from his eyes the day that I woke up, but I had. I turned my attention back to Madison.

"I'm sorry, Munchkin. I didn't hear you. What did you say?" I twirled one of her Shirley Temple curled pigtails with my fingers as her small hands played with the other one.

"I said . . . can I name my little brother or sister whenever she or he comes out of your belly?"

I froze when I heard her question and felt the awkward moment linger in the air. This wasn't Madison's first time asking me this, so I didn't know why it still made me feel funny to give her an answer. Proof had always been there to deflect the question until now, and her ass thought she was slick this time for deciding to ask me while her daddy was gone. I looked up at my granny, who was standing behind me, for some kind of help, but when I saw the expression on her face,

I knew I was going to have to deal with this on my own.

According to my granny, regardless of the way in which the baby was conceived, he or she was still a blessing from God, and I totally agreed, but my psyche wouldn't allow me to see it that way. I looked to Fiona for help, but as always, her face was buried in her phone. When I looked for my aunt Bree, she was nowhere in sight.

"Baby, what did Daddy tell you about asking Mommy that?" I knew you were not supposed to answer a question with a question, but I didn't know what else to do.

"He . . . he said not to ask you that," Madison said with her head down. "But I heard Gammy ask God to help you change your mind, and if Gammy asked God to help, then He will, right, Gammy?"

We both looked over at my granny at the same time. Excitement and curiosity in Madison's eyes, but slight anger in mine.

"Hey, hey, hey . . . Why the sour face? Don't tell me you're not ready to leave?" Aunt Bree asked, breaking the tension. She looked at me, then Granny, and shook her head. "Mama, leave this girl alone already. If her doctor gave her the okay, then she's okay. Stop worrying so much.

She's going to be just fine. I'm here for the next two months to take care of my favorite niece, and please believe that she is going to make it to every appointment on time with bells on. She'll be A-one in no time."

"Yeah, well, you make sure a few of those appointments are to the ob-gyn," Granny retorted.

"What's an od-gn, Gammy?"

"A doctor for your—"

"Well, would you look a here!" Aunt Bree yelled, cutting Granny off. "Jaylen finally found his way to the front of the hospital. I mean, we've only been sitting here for an hour. Pull your ass up into this blue section. We might not have a handicapped placard, but we do have a handicapped person."

"What's a handicap, TT?" Madison asked.

"Girl, stay your little ass out of grown folks' business and get your little tail in the car," Aunt Bree said, then turned in the direction of Fiona. I caught the small eye roll and heard when she sucked her teeth. "If you're riding with us, you need to come on. Ain't nobody about to wait for you."

"You don't have to wait!" Fiona snapped, with attitude equal to Bree's. "My brother's coming to pick me up, anyway, so I'm good."

"Yeah, I bet," Aunt Bree said as she turned her back to Fiona and, with Proof's help, got me in the car, then fastened my seat belt. "I'm telling you, niece, you need to watch that trick. Something is off about her. Always has been."

I waved Aunt Bree off and sat back, getting as comfortable as I could in my seat. Her and Fiona's "no love and hate" relationship had been going for years. Even when my mother was alive, she used to give out those little warnings about Aunt Bree and Fiona. But in all the years I'd known Fiona, she had always had my back and had never done me wrong. When my mother died and Aunt Bree was away at college, it was Fiona who had held me all night while I cried, even though she had sorta lost a parent too. Their little beef was starting to get on my nerves, and with Aunt Bree being out here for the next two months, one of them was going to have to wave that white flag. My sanity depended on it.

"Okay, everybody set and ready to go?" Proof asked as he hopped into the driver's seat and fastened his seat belt.

His cologne surrounded my whole head, and I inhaled the scent deeply. He was back to his regular self now that I was getting better. The fresh low cut and his neatly trimmed beard had his yellow ass looking good as hell, and as enticing as those green eyes were, I remembered that we were only co-parents to Madison now and nothing more.

"Fiona's staying here?" Proof asked when he caught sight of her outside the car.

Aunt Bree sucked her teeth again. "Yes. So can we go now? Damn. Your concern should be on getting your baby mama home, and not on whether or not this trick needs a ride or not."

Proof laughed. "Same ole Bree, I see. Two college degrees, a master's, and a high-paying job could never change your ass."

"You damn right, and just wait until the day I get to stick my foot up her ass. Those degrees and that high-paying job haven't changed the way these hands whip ass, either."

While they continued to laugh and go back and forth about whether or not Aunt Bree could really kick Fiona's ass, I closed my eyes and dozed off for a minute.

Like always, the second I touched down in la-la land, those green eyes of his invaded my dreams. His face was so close to mine that I could literally see through him. Everything he felt inside, I could see dancing within his soul. Nothing about the way he felt or looked at me screamed, "Rapist." Whenever I would try to touch him, he would back away, only to step back in front of me when my hand returned to my side. We would just stand there and stare at each other for what felt like forever before he would inch a little closer to me and brush his lips against mine.

I bit my bottom lip to try to stop the urge to try to touch him again from building inside me. That was of no use, because as soon as I saw the small glint in his eye, I crashed my lips against his and locked my arms around his neck. A blazing fire shot through my body and jolted me out of my sleep.

"What the fuck!" I heard Proof yell as he tried to stop the car from swerving and slammed on the brakes, causing me to bump my head on the frame of the window. The loud squealing sound of the tires screeching still rang in my ear, as the smell of petrol fuel began to rise in the air. "That asshole just crossed over lanes and stopped in front of me. Is everyone all right?"

"No, we're not all right, Proof. You just rear ended the back of someone's car with all of us in here."

"You're saying that as if I did this shit on purpose, Bree."

"You should've been paying better attention is what I'm actually trying to say."

"What's wrong, Mel? Are you okay?" my granny asked, ignoring the bickering between Proof and my Aunt.

"Niece, do you wanna go back to the hospital? Can you tell me how many fingers I'm holding up?" Aunt Bree quizzed. "Proof, you need to try and turn this muthafucka around or something and head back to the hospital!"

"Don't you think that's what I'm trying to do? I knew it was too soon to take her home. She should've stayed another week!" Proof yelled as he hit the steering wheel and pulled out his phone.

It wasn't until I heard Madison's question that I felt the tears coming down my face.

"Mommy, did Daddy hurt you? Why are you crying?"

"Baby girl, are you in any pain right now? Is the baby okay?" Granny asked.

Complete silence fell over the car as everyone waited on me to respond. I didn't know what it was about that dream, but it had triggered something inside me. It had opened up a part of my mind that I had blocked out.

I turned to face my family, then uttered the only words in my mind at that moment.

"I . . . I think I remember what happened."

Fiona

"I swear to God, I can't stand that bitch," I said through gritted teeth as I slipped into the passenger's seat of Cowboy's car.

The cold AC and the cool leather on the seat immediately took my body temperature down a few notches and had me blowing out a frustrated breath. I picked the fast-food cup up out of the cup holder and took a sip of the soda, which I was sure Cowboy had drunk.

I'd been at the hospital every day since Melonee was brought here, and I was so glad she was finally being discharged. I had offered to take care of her for a couple of weeks at my house, but Bree's bitch ass had immediately shut that down the minute she stepped into Mel's hospital room. I thought I had done a good enough job of drilling into Mel's head that Roman Black was the one who did this to her, but you could never be too sure. Even if she never remembered what happened, that baby growing inside her belly would be just the pawn we need to checkmate his ass and get the money, after all.

I shook my head as thoughts of how much I hated Bree continued to run through my mind. "Do you know what the sad part is?" I said.

Cowboy remained silent and continued to pay attention to the road, because he knew that the question was rhetorical.

I went on. "I don't even know why she doesn't like me. I've never done shit to her for her to not like me. Ever since we were younger, Bree has always tried to come between me and Mel, to interfere in our friendship. It wasn't my fault that I was there for Mel after Shaunie died, while she was on the other side of the country, living her life."

Cowboy laughed. "Come on, Fee. You know damn well she wasn't out there just *living her life*. You act as if she didn't come home for her own sister's funeral or stay a few weeks after that."

"Are you my brother or hers?" I asked with an eye roll.

"I'm your brother, but I hate when you put people off like that. Especially people we consider family."

I reared my head back and looked at him with the stinkiest face I could muster. "That bitch is *not* my family." Cowboy's ass was crazy to even imply that shit. "See, that right there is what's wrong with people today. So quick to call someone who doesn't share any of your DNA family. That bitch probably wouldn't even spit on me if I was on fire." I sat up straight in my seat and pulled my ringing phone out of my purse. "The only family I have is you and Daddy. Fuck everyone else."

I could feel Cowboy's eyes on me as we stopped at a red light. "What about Mel? You don't consider her family? I mean, with her being your best friend and all, I assumed you considered her somewhat like family."

I smirked at Meyers's name flashing across the screen of my phone and ignored the call. This dude was making me feel some type of way, and I didn't have time for that right now, especially if what he was calling about didn't have anything to do with getting this money.

"Mel's like my sister, but as far as family goes . . . no, I wouldn't consider her that. Would I lie for her? Yes. Would I steal for her? Of course. Would I kill for her? Hmm . . . as long as some money is involved, yeah. But would I die for her?" I shook my head no. "That's where the difference comes in with calling someone your family or not. I would die for you and Daddy, no questions asked, but for anyone else . . .that'll never happen. If it ever came to me and Mel being in a situation where a gun was trained on her and I was given the opportunity to save myself or push her out of the way and save her instead, Mel would die every time."

I knew what I'd just said was a little harsh, but like I said before, the only family I had was Cowboy and our father. They were the only two I would lie, die, steal, and kill for. One had already been taken away from me behind some bullshit, and I refused to let it happen again.

Cowboy laughed again, drawing me from my thoughts. As he got on the freeway, he said, "Damn, Fee, you a cold piece of work. I bet if you asked Mel those same questions, she'd say yes to all four."

I shrugged my shoulders. "That's because everyone's definition of *family* is different."

We sat in silence for a few minutes, lost in our own thoughts. I didn't know what Cowboy was thinking about, but I couldn't get Bree's smart-ass mouth and voice out of my head. The day that this bitch flew into town and graced us with her annoying presence at the hospital, I had just happened to be in the little bathroom in Mel's hospital room, on my phone, talking to Meyers about some business. Her ass hadn't even been in Mel's hospital room for five minutes before she started talking shit. I'd heard everything from my spot in the bathroom.

"So where's that so-called best friend of yours? I assumed her face would be the first one I seen walking up in here."

Mel coughed. "She was just here a second ago, before I dozed off. When I woke up, she was gone. She's probably on the phone with her new boo. I think she really likes this one. Every time he calls, her face just lights up."

"New boo?" Bree scoffed. "Fiona's face ain't lighting up about anything unless it involves money in some type of way."

"Leave my best friend alone. Not everyone believes in falling in love and riding off into the sunset like me. I think that's why she and I get along so well. We balance each other out. I keep her from going deep into the dark side, and she helps me to take it there when love starts to cloud my judgment," Mel responded with a laugh.

I sat on the toilet, just listening to them talk. I wanted to see if Bree would say why she didn't like me. As if she were reading my mind, the next question out of Melonee's mouth was just that.

"Why don't you like Fiona, Aunt Bree? I don't ever remember a day that you did."

I could hear Bree's sandals slide over the floor as she moved from one side of the room to the other. The cushion on the chair she must've sat in made that low sighing noise cushions made when someone too heavy sat down on them. I felt sorry for that leather and stuffing underneath her ass. Although she wasn't super big like the old Mo'Nique, Bree's curvy, size 18 frame was still packing some meat.

"It's not that I don't like her. I just don't care too much for her."

"Why?"

"Fiona reminds me of one of the girls I used to hang with in high school. When she was in my face, it was always 'I love my best friend' this or 'My best friend is the best' that, but behind closed doors, she felt differently."

"Differently how?"

"I don't know. Before your mom died, your friendship with Fiona seemed genuine to me, but after Shaunie passed and Maxwell went to jail, something seemed different. Then, after you guys started the Black Widow Clique, it got worse. Fiona used to have this bright fire in her eyes, but after everything happened, it's like it went away. And when someone's light goes away, nine times out of ten, they believe someone blew it out. Once they assume who did *it in their head, they start plotting against them on some revenge-type shit."*

What Bree was saying was partially true. I'd give her that. My light did go out the second my father was taken away from me. I lost a parent on that day too, but no one seemed to care other than Cowboy.

"So what are you trying to say, Bree?" I could tell by the strain in Mel's voice that she was trying to move around in her bed. The doctor had told her that it was okay to sit up, but that she should page the nurse to assist her if she wanted to change positions.

"I'm saying what I've always said. Just keep your eyes open with her. People who you consider family that aren't don't always feel the same way as you."

Something else she and I agreed on, but she'd never know that.

Tired of hiding out in the bathroom and ear hustling, I flushed the toilet like I'd just finished using it, turned on the water to wash my hands, then sprayed a few spritzs of air freshener to make it look believable. Holding my stomach with one hand and waving my face with the other, I walked out of the small bathroom.

"Please remind me to never eat that nasty cafeteria food again," I said, all smiles, as

I faced Melonee. I waited five seconds, then turned toward that bitch Bree. "Oh, hey, Aunt Bree. When did you get here? I was just asking Mel if she had talked to you."

Bree smirked, then ran her fingers through her layered bob cut. Her smooth dark skin resembled Mel's, but it had a bronzier tint to it. Her makeup was flawless, as always. Different earth-tone eye shadows accentuated her almond-shaped eyes, while gold-tinted lip gloss adorned her lips. She was dressed simply in some distressed boyfriend jeans, a white tank top, and a green fitted blazer. I had to give it to Bree. She carried her weight well and would give any of those Victoria's Secret Angels a run for their money. She reminded me of that plus-size model Precious Lee and even looked like her a little bit.

Her hazel eyes scanned me from head to toe. I could tell that the white shorts I had on and my pink off-the-shoulder top were a little too hoochie for her, but I didn't give a fuck. I wanted to be comfortable while I was sitting in this hospital damn near all day. Plus, it was hot as hell outside.

"First thing, my name is Brenae. Only friends and close family can call me Bree," she snapped. "Which leads me to the second thing. I have only

one niece and one great-niece. Those are the only two who can call me auntie."

"Bree—"Melonee began, but I cut her off.

"It's okay, Mel. Aunt Bree gives me that little speech every time she comes around. I call her Auntie. She tells me not to, just for me to do it again. You would think after all these years she'd just leave it alone."

One of Bree's perfectly arched eyebrows rose as she stood up from her seat and walked toward me. Her eyes never left mine as she began to talk to Melonee.

"Niece, you just remember what your aunt Bree just told you. Not everyone you call family feels the same way. I've come to learn that the eyes never lie. They have the power to show you exactly who people are, even with blinders on."

I laughed and shook my head. "So now I have some ulterior motive on being Mel's best friend, and you can see this in my eyes?" I turned to Mel and bent over laughing. "See? I told you Aunt Bree is a trip. She ain't that much older than we are, but I think I can learn a thing or two from her, like how to be a delusional bitch."

"I got your delusional bitch, all right," Bree replied as she charged toward me.

"What's going on in here?" Granny asked as she came through the door, with Madison and a wide-eyed Proof behind her. "We could hear you all down the hall. Brenae, when did you get here?" she said, turning her focus from me to Bree.

"I just got here thirty minutes ago, Mama. Where were you?" She gave Granny a hug and a kiss on the cheek, then looked at me and smirked.

"Hey, TT's baby!" Bree said, grabbing Madison. "Who's TT's favorite and only great-niece?"

"Me," Madison managed to say as Bree tickled her.

"What's up, Jaylen?" Bree said. She and Jaylen gave each other a sideways hug, and then Bree handed Madison to him.

A quiet tension filled the room while everyone looked around at each other, trying to see who was going to spill the beans on what had happened before Proof and them walked in Mel's room.

"Well?" Granny said. "Don't all talk at once." She looked from me to Mel, then to Bree.

"Granny, you know how Bree and Fiona are. Arguing like family does over who loves me more." That was Mel's weak attempt to cut some of the tension, but it didn't work.

I looked around the room. "Seeing as we are breaking the 'two visitors at a time' rule, I'm going to go ahead and bounce. I have some things to take care of before the day is over."

"Do any of those things happen to be a certain mystery man your best friend has yet to meet?" Mel asked.

I laughed and headed for the door. "Mel, you already know I only hump, then dump. I don't have time for these men out here, unless he's loaded with some money. If his net worth is right, I might fall in love." I opened the door but turned around. "Then again, who am I kidding? Love don't live here anymore. I might marry him for a few months, then kill him later on down the line for his money."

Mel spit the water she had just drunk out of her mouth, while Proof tried to stifle a laugh, and Granny gasped. When my eyes landed on Bree, she just rolled her eyes.

"I'm just kidding, y'all. I'll find love one day, just not right now. Who knows? Maybe Aunt Bree can hook me up with one of her scientist friends. I hear they make a lot of money," I said.

All eyes went to Bree.

She snorted. "As if any of my colleagues would date a money-hungry ho . . . chick like you," she said, correcting herself.

"Better to be money hungry and getting this bread than dry as a desert and looking for love," I countered.

Bree's wide eyes turned to Mel, who also had a shocked look on her face.

Yeah. Checkmate, bitch, *I thought as I finally left the room.*

"What you over there laughing at?" I heard Cowboy ask, breaking me from my thoughts.

"Nothing. Just thinking about Aunt Bree's . . . oops, I mean Brenae's face when I checked her on some shit a couple of weeks ago."

Cowboy shook his head, then pushed his glasses up on his face. It wasn't until then that I noticed my brother was a little dressed up. I wondered where he was coming from.

"You better stop fucking with Bree. You know she knows about the BWC, and with the connects she has, she's a better ally than enemy."

I waved him off. "I ain't worried about her. She's not going to do or say anything that could get Mel's ass implicated right along with me." I rolled down the window and let the humid breeze hit my face. "Besides, she's not the only one who knows people in high places. Now shut the hell up and let's get this long-ass ride over with. I'm ready to see my daddy."

The Black Widow
Clique 2

Roman

I stood in front of the house that I grew up in, memories of my childhood flooding my mind. My mother's beautiful face and laughter playing repeatedly. Visions of her standing in the kitchen, making breakfast, while keeping a close eye on me as I played outside on the veranda, kept looping around, for some reason. I shook my head. It seemed like after my mother passed, this house, which used to be filled with so much warmth and love, became cold and isolated. The feel of being a family had died a long time ago, when my father brought Julia and Benji into the house. Gone was the smile that seemed to always be on his face whenever my mother was around or gave him some type of affection. Now all he wore was a stoic expression, which I couldn't quite read at times.

After walking up to the front door, I let myself in and followed the aroma of the Sunday brunch spread, which I could smell as soon as I entered my father's home. House staff waved hello and nodded their heads in greeting as I walked past the different rooms they were busy cleaning. Pictures of me and Benji as children decorated the walls. Our college degrees hung on one wall, with framed pictures of our alma maters. Newspaper features about my father, recounting his humble beginnings before starting Real Time Delivery and his life afterward were also displayed on one of the walls for all to see.

Rare antiques were scattered about the house, though there were a few modern designs woven into the decor, designs that Julia had picked out. The place was totally different from the loving household my mother had made for us when we first moved in here. My childhood home now looked more like a chic museum than a place where a family resided. But like I said, cold and isolated were the feelings I got about the place whenever I came to visit nowadays.

When I stepped into the formal dining room, my stepmother, Julia's irritating laugh was the first thing I heard.

"Richard, darling, we should make a trip to the Summerland house sometime soon. We haven't been there in a minute. The weather has been warming up, and I want to wake up to the beautiful ocean view and breeze for a week or two."

My father cleared his throat and dropped the newspaper in his hands down a little to make eye contact with his wife. "Whatever you want, Julia. Have Helga get everything set up, and we can head out that way whenever you like."

Julia's eyes were beaming with happiness. "You spoil me so much, honey. What will I ever do without you?"

"Let's hope you never have to find out," he said, then bent forward and gave her a kiss.

She smiled at my father's response after he kissed her, but the smile didn't quite reach her eyes.

"Good morning," I said, making my presence known and interrupting the awkward moment between them.

"Good morning, Roman," Julia replied. "This is a surprise, seeing as we weren't expecting to see you anytime soon. I mean, with everything that has been going on and the way you stormed out of here last week, I thought you would still be in hiding or trying to lay low."

The day that I got back from Russia, I had had Marques bring me straight to my parents' home first so that I could see what was really going on with the moral clause and my father giving Benji my position without telling me what the hell was going on. What should have been a simple conversation between me and my father, Richard Black, had turned into a shouting match that became really heated. Julia adding her two cents in whenever she felt like it hadn't helped the situation, either. Needless to say, my words had fallen on deaf ears, and the support I thought that I would get from my father with what I had going on had been nowhere to be found.

I cut my eyes at Julia. "I'm not hiding from shit. Hiding would mean that I was ashamed of something that I did. Like I told you both last week, I didn't do anything. And this stuff with the IRS, it's like that shit just fell out of thin air. I've always paid my taxes, and I've always made sure RTD's taxes were taken care of."

"Well, you missed the ball somewhere," Benji said, walking into the dining room with the same big-eyed, blond-haired, ditzy chick he'd had with him the last time we all had brunch together. With nothing but some swim trunks on, he took a seat at the table and started filling his plate up with the continental spread in front of him, while his guest stood behind him in the skimpiest bathing suit, looking out of place. "But like always, little bro, big bro is here to save the day. Or in this case, the family business."

"Benjamin, honey, why is she standing up like that? Have your guest take a seat." The disgust in Julia's words could not be missed.

"Aye, are you going to eat something? If you are, take a seat. If not, go back to my house, and I'll be there in about forty-five minutes." His eyes roamed her petite body. "I don't know, Mandy, with the way you look in that bathing suit, make that about thirty minutes."

Benji's little friend started giggling uncontrollably. When she snorted, all eyes went to her, and she stopped laughing. Her cheeks turned a deep red from embarrassment. "Um . . . I . . . I'll go wait for you at your spot. And stop calling me Mandy, silly. My name is Sammy," she said sheepishly.

Benji threw her an apple. "Well, *Sammy*, take this and eat it while you're chilling at my spot. Get your energy up and be ready for me when I get back." He smacked her on her ass and then sent her on her way.

I shook my head, and Benji turned his attention to me. "What was that head shake for, Ro? I know me hitting her ass didn't offend you in any way. I mean, with the way you nearly beat poor Melonee Reid to death, that light tap I just gave Sammy should've made your dick twitch a little bit, right?"

Before his laugh slipped from the back of his throat, I lunged at Benji, knocked his chair down on the floor, and landed right on top of him.

Glasses breaking, silverware falling, and plates clanking together were the only things I heard as I began to pound my fists into his face, adding to the scratch marks that were already there. I felt a pair of hands pulling at my shirt and then my shoulders, but whoever it was wasn't strong enough to pull me off him.

Since I'd been back from Russia, Benji had been making little remarks like the one he had just delivered every chance he got. The muthafucka had gone as far as holding a press conference after being named the new CEO of Real Time Delivery and telling the world that I was guilty when one of the reporters asked him what he thought about the situation.

"It's very upsetting for me and the rest of the Black family that one of our own committed such an inhumane and heinous crime," he'd answered. "It saddens me more that the young woman that was attacked is lying in the hospital, in a coma, because of Roman's inability to accept when someone tells him no. Please understand that his actions do not reflect the ethics of, nor should ever be associated with, the Black name or Real Time Delivery. And to show that we are deeply sorry for what Roman has done, we, myself, as well as my mother and father, Mr. and Mrs. Richard Black, would like to take care of all of Ms. Reid's medical bills. Also, on behalf of Ms. Reid, a sizeable donation will go to the Women and Children's Shelter of Greater Los Angeles."

While some people were praising Benji for being this fraud-ass saint, the rest were denouncing me and invading my privacy for a crime that I didn't even commit. Paparazzi now followed me any and everywhere, bombarding me with questions about my guilt or innocence and asking how I felt about Benji being appointed the new CEO of RTD. It had been a total shit storm since all this shit went down, and instead of my family coming together to support me and prove my innocence, it seemed like they were all against me, my father included. Because of that, all this aggression had built up within me, and now I was taking my anger out on Benji, who laughed after every punch I landed on his face. A blood vessel in his eye had just popped from a powerful blow I sent to his temple when I felt something heavy hit the back of my head, causing me to fall over in pain.

"Get off my son, you animal!" Julia yelled as she hit me again with the crystal vase that, I remembered, had been on top of the table a few minutes ago. Purple Cattleya orchids and the water that they were in fell all over me. "Richard, don't just sit there! Do something."

My father stood from his chair and rounded the table until he was standing next to me. Bacon, sausage, eggs, scones, croissants, and all kinds of fruit now decorated the floor. The smell of coffee filled the room, as the pot that held the hot liquid had been tipped over and had spilled its content on the white tablecloth. Winded and trying to catch my breath, I looked at my fist, which was covered in blood, and wiped it on the carpet. Didn't know who the blood belonged to, but I was pretty sure it wasn't mine. My father's disapproving huff caused me to look up at him. He had a stern look on his face, but I could tell he had conflicting thoughts on his mind.

My mother's laugh started to echo in my head and had me wondering. Would my life be this chaotic if she were here? Would our family be this torn apart right now if she were still alive? Would my father be standing over me, about to kick me out of the house that I grew up in, if my mother were sitting at his side instead of Julia?

Benji's moan brought me back to the current moment and away from my thoughts. As Julia and some of the house staff worked to pull him up and place an ice pack on his knotted forehead, I looked at my father and waited to hear what he was going to say. We stared at each other for what seemed like forever. Not breaking eye contact once, saying so much through our glares. It wasn't until Julia continued on with her ranting that my father broke our silent conversation and turned his attention to her.

"Richard, you need to do something about that son of yours. He almost beat my poor Benjamin to death," she yelled.

My father remained silent.

"Richard!" she yelled again. "Get him out of here before I call the police and have him arrested. I'm sure he's violating some kind of law, putting his hands on someone like that again."

"Julia—" my father began, but he was cut off by his yapping wife.

"Julia, nothing. Get that piece of trash you did a terrible job of raising out of my house or else!"

"Or else what?" I asked as I slowly got up off the floor. It seemed like my father was conflicted about what he wanted to do, so I chose to make the decision for him. "What the fuck are you going to do, Julia, if he doesn't tell me leave?"

Her eyes turned into slits as she glared at me, but her Botoxed face was not able to move an inch. Had I not been looking at her, I probably would've missed the small smirk that played on her lips before she replaced it with a frown.

Gone was the bougie facade she seemed to sport for most of the day. Julia's appearance was now one I had never seen before. "You don't want any problems with me, Roman. Trust me. Now get the fuck out of my house before your father ends up with no children at all—"

"Roman," my dad finally interrupted. "I think you should leave and not come back until you figure out what's going on with your case. Maybe go to your lawyer and see if you can try to come to some type of agreement with the DA or something, son. Right now, I think it would be best for you to distance yourself from us until this thing blows over."

My face fell at my father's words. Just that fast, I was back to being Roman the rapist to him, and not Roman, his son. Just that fast, the silent conversation we had had with our eyes was null and void. Just that fast, any type of relationship with each other I had thought my father and I could salvage was gone. If he didn't want to stand by me in my time of need, well, then, fuck him.

As long as I had the memory of my mother, Chasin, Marques, Uncle Kazi, and soon Melonee, I didn't need Richard Black or his new family.

Melonee

A few weeks later ...

"So, Ms. Reid, you told my partner that you remembered something from the night of your attack," said the stubby man I'd come to know as Detective Warryn Lewis as he circled the small metal desk at which I sat. He dropped a manila folder down in front of me once he reached the chair on the other side of the desk and opened it up. "Now, I want you to be sure of what you are about to tell me. The doctor told us that you were going to experience some short-term memory loss and that you would periodically start to remember things as time went on." His beady eyes stared directly at my face. "With that being said, are you sure Roman Black was not the person who did this to you?"

When I looked down at the open folder, I saw pictures of myself beaten to a pulp and lying naked in a bed. The pictures were spread out on top of each other. I gathered them into a pile and then slowly started to sift through them. Each one looked worse than the one before. My face was unrecognizable. Deep purple and blue bruises decorated damn near every inch of my body. My lips looked as if they had been injected with a gallon of collagen and were in desperate need of some ChapStick. The knots on my forehead, shoulders, arms, and legs were the size of golf balls. There was blood pouring from the many lacerations on my thighs, back, and chest. I squinted my eyes to try to stop the tears that I knew were about to fall, but to no avail. Pulling my lips into my mouth, I wiped the tears away with my free hand and then placed the pictures of myself back in the folder. I felt a warm hand squeeze my shoulder. When I turned around, Aunt Bree was there, with a sad look on her face and tears in her eyes.

"If this is too much for you, Mel, we can always come back," she said as she handed me a piece of tissue.

I swallowed the lump in my throat and shook my head. "No . . . we can do this now, while it's fresh in my mind."

Aunt Bree looked at Detective Lewis, whose eyes were focused on me. "Can we get this interview going?"

He pulled at his beard, in deep thought, as his focus lingered on my face. The phone on his hip constantly went off, but he continued to ignore it. The wrinkled blue suit that he had on was your typical detective wear, nothing special. More than likely, it was one he had picked from the clearance rack at the Suit Depot. Small coffee stains were on his white shirt and on the top part of his tie. You could tell that he had tried to wipe all the coffee off with a napkin but hadn't been successful. His light skin was a little ashy and in desperate need of some moisturizing, just like the short, tapered 'fro on top of his head. Acne scars were very evident on his skin, from years of picking at his face. He furrowed his bushy eyebrows and looked toward Aunt Bree.

"I'm sorry, ma'am. What did you say?" he said, eyes back on me.

I heard Aunt Bree's lips smack. "I asked if we can get this interview going. It's been a long day, and Melonee needs to go home and get some rest."

"We could've easily come to you," he responded, eyes now on my protruding belly. "If it's too much for you right now, Ms. Reid, my partner and I can come by your home sometime tomorrow to get your statement."

"I'm not staying at my home right now, so that wouldn't be necessary. I'd like to continue here. Like I said, let's do it now, while some things are still fresh in my mind."

He looked at Aunt Bree, then back at me. "Okay then. Let's start with what you remember about the attack. I know you were in a little accident a couple of weeks ago, while you were on your way home from the hospital, and you said that you remember some things. Do you know who it was that attacked you, or can you remember anything about the person who did it?"

I closed my eyes and took a few deep breaths as I tried to remember some of things that had happened that night.

"I don't remember the person's face, because it was covered. But I do remember his eyes and that his lips were real dark."

"What do you remember about his eyes?" the detective asked.

"They weren't Roman's."

He cocked his head to the side, taking in what I'd just said. "Okay . . . And what about his lips? They were . . . real dark?" he asked, an eyebrow raised.

I nodded my head. "Yes, real dark, as in whoever it was had been smoking weed for a long time. He had those dark spots in the middle of his lips that only smokers get, and his breath smelled like a damn ashtray."

"So dark lips, eyes not like Mr. Black's, and his breath smelled like cigarette smoke. Is there anything else you can remember about this guy? Was he black or white? Tall or short? Skinny or fat?"

I closed my eyes again and tried to go back to that night. "He had on all black, so he blended into the darkness of the room real good. I remember at one point my body feeling as if it was being tugged and pulled over something that was burning my back. I opened my eyes when I came to at some point and saw a large figure standing over me. I don't remember if he was tall or short, fat or skinny, but I do remember him raising his hand to hit me, but I blacked out before he did it." My throat became dry, and when I tried to swallow, I didn't have an ounce of spit in my mouth. I began to cough. Aunt Bree handed me the water bottle from my bag, and I took a sip. After wetting my throat, I took a deep breath and continued with what I could remember.

"The next time I came to, it felt as if my body had been ripped apart. Like my flesh was exposed to the cold air, and I could feel the breeze literally in my bones." My whole body began to shake, and tears began to fill my eyes again. "I tried to move but couldn't, because there was something heavy on top of me. It wasn't until I heard and felt his hot breath and heavy breathing against my neck that I knew what was happening. I could feel my body being pushed into forcefully, but with all the other pain going on, it all blended in." My hands covered my face, and I began to sob uncontrollably. I could feel Aunt Bree hovering over me. When she tried to embrace me, I pushed her away. "I'm okay. . . . I'm okay, Auntie." I looked at Detective Lewis. "Who do you think could've done this to me? Why do you think they did this to me?"

"Who and why are what we're trying to find out right now," Detective Lewis replied. "You seem pretty positive that Roman Black wasn't the attacker. Is there anyone you've had problems with in the past who may have held a grudge all these years and would want to harm you now?"

I thought about his question. If truth be told, my list of enemies would be pretty long if some of the family members of my deceased husbands knew what had really caused their deaths. But I doubted any of them were on the list. We were very careful when we did our "marry for money" scams. And with Cowboy on the team, we didn't worry about anyone finding out too much information about us. Especially when he would change shit up and delete certain things

when needed. Then again, the question of why
Riana had resurfaced after all these years had
been on my mind for the past few weeks. When
I received a bouquet of flowers in my room at
the hospital, with a card that read *I hope you
die*, I had assumed that they were from her. I
had shown Fiona the message and had told her
about the little run-in Riana and I had had at
Roman's charity ball, but she had just waved it
off and had promised to take care of it before
I was due to go home. I didn't know if Fee had
taken care of it or not, but I hadn't received a
bouquet like that since then.

I pulled at my red- and blue-striped maxi
dress and placed my hand on my stomach. I
knew when I first found out about the baby
that I'd sworn up and down that I was going to
give it away for adoption, but for some strange
reason, something inside me would not let that
thought occupy my mind anymore. I still wasn't
happy with how he or she had been conceived,
but I was starting to be okay with bringing an
innocent child into this world and showing it
love the best way that I could.

The door to the small room we were in opened,
and a short Asian chick, with glasses hanging
from her neck and a dress so tight that you could
see the lining of her panties and bra, walked in
and handed Detective Lewis another folder.

He looked up at her, and an instant blush washed over her face. When she turned around to head out, his eyes stayed on what I assumed was her ass until she shut the door. He took the folder she'd just handed to him, and looked through it.

Aunt Bree cleared her throat. "Did the crime-scene unit find any useful evidence? I know Mel's attacker had to leave something behind. I mean, I know I'm only a scientist, but I have watched enough *Law & Order*, *Forensic Files*, and *First 48* episodes to know that there's always some clue." She scooted her chair up beside mine and grabbed my hand. "Did you find out what was used to knock her out to the point where she didn't feel someone doing all that . . . damage to her body?"

Detective Lewis closed the folder and looked at Aunt Bree. "Well, reports did say that Ms. Reid had a large amount of Rohypnol in her system." He looked at me. "Do you remember what you had to drink that night?"

I thought about it for a moment and shook my head. "The only thing I remember is having some wine. I remember drinking a couple of glasses of that."

Detective Lewis shifted in his seat across from me and wrote something down on the back of one of the pictures from the first folder. "Do you remember drinking wine with someone other than Mr. Black?"

I opened my mouth to say something, then closed it. I did remember who I was drinking wine with, but it seemed as if they didn't want to believe it. Ever since I had told them that I didn't think it was Roman who had raped and beaten me, they have been trying to make me think otherwise.

"I was drinking wine only with Roman Black. I remember we were eating and enjoying some good conversation when he got a phone call. He excused himself from the table while I continued to eat and drink my wine. When he came back, he poured me another glass as well as one for himself." Roman's beautiful smile and amazing green eyes popped into my head. Him raising a tumbler to his lips with some brown liquor in it flashed across my mind. "No, wait . . ." I shook my head. "Roman was drinking something else. It wasn't the wine he poured for me. He was drinking some whiskey or scotch he'd gotten from someone earlier."

"Earlier?" His eyebrow quirked. "Do you remember who he said he got it from?"

"I . . . I don't. I just know he said that he wasn't a wine drinker and that he preferred a much stronger drink."

"Do you remember ever leaving your drink unattended while in Mr. Black's presence?"

I shook my head. "Not that I remember."
Another memory flashed through my mind. "I
remember after eating our food and drinking,
I started to become dizzy. A few times I grabbed
my head, but . . ." I trailed off, remembering
why I had ignored the dizzy spells I was having.
Memories of the way Roman kissed and handled
my body started to play through my mind. I could
feel his hands lightly caressing my skin as he wet
every inch of my body with his tongue and lips.
My throat hitched, and I clamped my legs shut
when my clit began to beat uncontrollably.

"But what, Ms. Reid?"

"Mel, are you okay?"

Detective Lewis and Aunt Bree asked their
questions at the same time. My body was starting
to do that thing it had been doing for the past few
weeks, even when I was in the hospital. Craving
Roman's touch. Whenever his face would flash
on the TV screen, I'd think about him, or I'd see
something about him in the blogs, and my body
would do this whole heating-up thing and yearn
for his touch. I wanted to tell Aunt Bree about
it, but I didn't want her to think I was weird for
wanting my alleged attacker to make my body
simmer down.

After I assured them both that I was okay, and
after I answered a few more questions about
what I remembered from the night of my attack,

Detective Lewis advised that he would visit me sometime later on in the week to see if I remembered anything else. He also promised to get back to us with any circumstantial evidence that we didn't know about, once the reports from the crime-scene unit were back. With the interview complete, Aunt Bree and I left the police precinct in downtown Los Angeles and headed on foot to one of the many restaurants that lined Seventh Street.

"So, what do you and my great-nephew have a taste for?" Aunt Bree asked, rubbing my belly. It was as if she was more excited about me having this baby than I was.

"What makes you think it's a boy?"

She shrugged her shoulders and folded her arm around mine. "I don't know. I'm just ready for there to be some kind of testosterone in this family. I mean, after Daddy died, it was only me, Mama, and Shaunie. Then you came along and, shortly after that, the munchkin. I'm tired of it being all women in the house. When you have this little boy, all will be right in the family."

We shared a laugh, which quieted down to a comfortable silence as we continued to walk down the street. Bree mentioning my mother's name had me thinking about her and how my life probably would be if she were still alive.

"Do you miss her, Aunt Bree?" I asked as we both stopped in front of Fogo de Chão, one of our favorite Brazilian steak houses.

Bree untangled her arm from mine and grabbed my hand. Her eyes were focused on the double glass doors in front of us before she reached out and pulled one open. I looked at her for some type of answer to my question and got nothing but a small smile and a head nod before we walked hand in hand into the restaurant and sat at the first available table she saw. The tantalizing smell of steak, lamb, chicken, and pork skewered on metal rods and seasoned to perfection had my mouth salivating and the little life inside me jumping in anticipation, or so it seemed.

"Welcome to Fogo de Chão. My name is Robbie, and I will be your waiter this evening. Can I get you started with one of our delicious house wines or some water?"

After placing our drink orders with Robbie, Aunt Bree and I headed to the full salad bar and went right to work. Imported cheeses, an array of greens, hearts of palm, and black candied bacon were just a few of the delicious treats for us to sample. Once our plates were piled high with everything we wanted, we headed back to our table and began to eat.

Robbie appeared seconds later with our drinks and a basket of Brazilian cheese bread and warm rolls. "Have you decided what you want for your sides this afternoon?"

I looked at Aunt Bree, whose mouth was full of Caesar salad, but I knew what she liked, so I ordered for us. "I think we will have the crispy fried polenta, the caramelized bananas, and the garlic mashed potatoes. Oh, and can we get some *farofa* please?" I said.

Robbie wrote our order down, smiled, and headed back to get our sides together. Aunt Bree took a sip of her mojito and wiped her mouth with her napkin. I looked at the blue crop top with cascading ruffles on the sleeves that she had on and noticed how it complemented the light makeup on her face. The yellow pencil skirt she had paired the top with helped to show off every dip of her curvy frame. I knew she had to have the men in New Jersey going crazy over her, because the locals out here in Los Angeles were practically drooling whenever she walked by. Case in point, the handsome guy dining alone next to the window hadn't taken his eyes off her since we walked in.

"Uh, Aunt Bree, I think you have an admirer."

She looked at me, and I nodded my head at the gentleman, who was now looking at a newspaper. When she turned her head to look in his direction, he looked up and their eyes connected. I heard the second Bree's breath escaped her lips in a low hum, but when she turned back to me, she rolled her eyes and acted as if this fine-ass man didn't affect her in any way.

"Girl." She shook her head. "He's all right. I think I know him from somewhere, but I can't remember where I've seen him before. Anyways, back to what you asked me earlier." Aunt Bree licked her lips and began to fan her face when her eyes became misty. "I do miss your mother. Honestly, I miss Shaunie every day. I mean, she was my older sister, and even though I hated how she treated me like a kid at times, and I wasn't cool with some of the things she was doing, it didn't change the fact that I loved her more than anything."

"Some of the things she was doing? What are you talking about, Aunt Bree? What was my mother into that I don't know about?"

She waved me off. "It was nothing. Forget that I even said anything."

"But . . ."

"But nothing, Mel. Like I said, it was nothing." A weird look crossed her face; then she changed the subject. "No more mushy stuff. Let's get back to my great-nephew and how much I'm going to spoil him." She picked up a roll and bit off a piece. "I take it you're coming to terms with having him now? I mean, after the way you found out how he was conceived, I thought for sure you were going to give him up for adoption, like you said."

A meat handler stopped at our table with a skewer filled with big chunks of filet mignon. After slicing us a few medium-well pieces, he moved on to the next table.

"I was adamant about the adoption thing because I didn't think that I would be able to look my baby in the face and completely love him, not knowing where fifty percent of his looks came from, but something inside me kept telling me that if I did make that choice, I would regret it for the rest of my life. I didn't know what it was, but I'd been feeling this really strong connection to this baby. I was connected to Madison while she was growing inside me, but something about this baby feels different."

I didn't know how to tell Aunt Bree that I was starting to feel like this baby was inside me for a reason and that I could feel an undeniable amount of love for him already.

Aunt Bree smiled. "So you're hoping it's a boy too, huh?"

I laughed. "As long as it's healthy and doesn't have any complications or mental problems, then I'm going to be okay with that."

"Mental problems?" she asked, placing a piece of the juicy, tender meat in her mouth.

"I don't know who raped me. And with this being their baby, it will have some of their DNA. . . . I just hope it isn't no crazy shit that's hereditary."

"What makes you think it's your attacker's baby?"

I stopped chewing the food in my mouth and looked at Aunt Bree like she was crazy. "Who else could possibly be the father, Aunt Bree?"

"Didn't you say that you remember you and Roman sharing the most erotic, butt-clenching sex you've ever had? That's one of the reasons why you don't think it was him that raped you in the first place. What were the words you used? *Earth shattering?* You don't remember telling me that the day after the accident?"

She was right. The earth-shattering moments he and I had had was one of the reasons why I believed Roman wasn't the one who raped me. I remembered giving my whole body, mind, and soul to him freely before I blacked out, so what reason would he have to violate me in the way that I had been violated?

Aunt Bree and I continued to enjoy our late lunch and talk about everything under the sun. We were finishing our meal when my phone vibrated in my purse. I retrieved my phone. My eyebrows furrowed when I read the text message from a number I didn't recognize.

"What's wrong?" Aunt Bree questioned, taking my phone from my hand. She looked down at the screen. "I need to see you," she read to herself before focusing her gaze on me, concern written all over her pretty face. "Do you know who sent this, Mel? Maybe we should show Detective Lewis the text message. Have him trace the number or something."

"No." I shook my head. "No police," I responded while rereading the text message. I need to see you. For some reason, something inside me was telling me who had sent this message. That crazy butterfly thing had started happening in my belly again. "I . . . I think I know who this is from."

"Who do you know with an eight-one-eight area code?"

I took a sip of my water, licked my lips, and rubbed my hand down my stomach to try to calm the wild kicks the baby was now doing. "I think this text is from Roman Black."

Fiona

My eyes scanned the small parking lot of my apartment complex as I sat in my car with my Desert Eagle steady on my lap, ready to pull the trigger, if need be. For the past week, I hadn't been able to shake the chill running up my spine whenever I stepped outside my house to handle my business or make sure shit was still going according to plan with the clique. Someone had been watching me, and I didn't have the slightest idea who it could be. Many possible names had run through my mind, but no one stood out more than anyone else. So I had been keeping a watchful eye over my surroundings, hoping whoever it was would show their face sooner rather than later.

I turned my gaze to my apartment building when the back door swung open and hit the wall. My neighbor Faizon walked out and dumped the two trash bags he had in his hands in the Dumpster. After making sure the coast was clear, he picked his nose for a few seconds and then

examined his finger before wiping whatever
he had pulled out on his dingy jeans. I shook
my head in disgust. To think I had let his nasty
ass eat my pussy a couple of times when I first
moved in. I was so glad I didn't fuck around with
him like that anymore.

I searched through the parking lot again for
anything that seemed out of the norm, and
came up with nothing. After sliding my gun back
under my seat, I grabbed my purse, keys, and the
few shopping bags I had from my trip to the mall
earlier and hopped out of my car. If someone
was watching me, they'd more than likely leave
me alone, what with a witness milling around.
At least I hoped they would. If not, Faizon's ass
would more than likely lose his life today, acting as a human body shield for me. After locking
my car door and making sure my hair and everything else was in place, I walked over toward my
neighbor with a big smile on my face, while still
keeping an eye on the surrounding area.

"Hey, neighbor," I cooed as I walked closer to
his space, causing him to jump.

The finger he had digging for more gold
quickly went behind his back, where I was sure
he was getting rid of whatever evidence he
pulled out. A big smile crossed his face as his
eyes roamed over my body and took in the knee-

length strapless dress I had on, which hugged my body like a glove. My hair was up in a messy ponytail, showing off the chunky necklace with jade stones around my neck and the three-carat studs in my ears. Light makeup on my face gave me that mid-afternoon glow. But the Tory Burch sandals I had just bought did nothing for my five-foot, eight-inch frame, making me feel like an ant next to his six-foot-six body.

"Hey to you too, sexy neighbor. Long time no see." He licked his lips. "Where have you been lately? I knocked on your door a few times in the past few weeks but never got an answer." He put his hand over his heart. "I'm feeling some kind of way about you ignoring me. I thought you enjoyed my company."

As I walked up closer to him, the smell of whatever cologne he seemed to bathe in assaulted my nose, and it felt as if the hairs inside my nostrils were being burned. "I've been around. If I'm not working or at the hospital, I'm here. You probably just stopped by whenever I was out or asleep. You know I'm dead to the world whenever I'm knocked out."

His eyebrows furrowed. "Hospital? Is everything okay?" I smirked when his lanky frame took a few steps back, though he acted nonchalant.

Nose and whole head would literally be in my pussy, but you want to step back because I said I've been at the hospital? I thought. Muthafuckas killed me.

"Everything's okay. My best friend was in an accident, so I was checking on her," I revealed.

Relief covered his handsome face as he stepped toward me. This time he got a little closer and rubbed his crotch against my arm. A look of genuine concern was evident on his face now, but I knew that shit was fake. Faizon and I had never had that type of relationship, so I didn't understand why he was trying to act like we did. He stuck his hand out and ran it over my bare shoulder, then brushed his knuckles against the side of my breast as he moved his hand down my arm. Then he enveloped my hand in his.

"Is she all right? If there's anything I can do to make you feel better about the situation, you know I got you," he said.

"She's good now, Faizon. The doctors discharged her, and she's at home, resting. Thank you for the offer, though."

Just then the sound of someone walking on the gravel behind me caught my attention. When I turned around to see who it was, there was no one in sight. I looked over the parking lot a few times before turning back to my neighbor, but I didn't see a soul. I admit, the shit had me a little paranoid, and maybe I was tripping. However, I needed to get my ass in the house before something popped off.

"It was nice catching up with you, Faizon. But I need to get these things in the house." I held up my bags.

"I can take those in for you, Fiona. It's been a minute since we kicked it." He licked his lips again and smiled.

Faizon was a handsome guy, no doubt. But he was totally not my type. I liked a man who was aggressive and cocky as hell. A man who wanted to own the world and would do anything to obtain that goal. A man who could make me feel like I was floating on air with his dick and his tongue. Faizon could lick the hell out of the box, but there wasn't no levitating shit anywhere in his oral skills. And the fact that he was content with making whatever high school basketball coaches made nowadays was a definite turnoff for me. I was attracted to money and power, and Faizon had neither in his wallet or his mouth.

Already over the flirty conversation and his weak attempt to get into my apartment, I just waved Faizon off and headed for the door. I walked up a flight of stairs and down a short hallway and was at my apartment door in no time. Since I already had my keys out, I easily opened my door, and then I dropped everything in my hands on the couch. I went straight to my refrigerator, grabbed a bottle of water, and cracked it open, but I froze when this tingly feeling started to creep up my spine. Someone was in my apartment and was standing behind me. Not taking any chances, I grabbed the .357 revolver I had stored on the top shelf of my fridge and swung around, ready to let off on whoever had broken into my house.

"Is that how you greet family, niece?" my uncle Dro said coolly as he leaned against the arch that led into my kitchen. He had his hands up in surrender, but I didn't miss the heated look in his eyes. "I should be the one pulling out on you, seeing as you're the one who owes me some money right now."

With my gun still pointed at my uncle and my eyes trained on him, I drank my water and then threw the bottle in the trash. "How the fuck did you get into my house?"

"Come on now, niecey poo. You know I'm a man of many talents. I learned to break into apartments like these when I was still sucking on my mama's titty. Who do you think taught me everything I know?" He laughed when I didn't answer. "I see your dad hasn't told you anything about his past life. I'm surprised he hasn't broken out of that jail yet. I know he could do it if he really wanted to."

"My dad isn't anything like you."

He smirked. "Nah, not anymore. I don't even recognize this Maxwell. After Shaunie was killed, the nigga became soft. It's like his savage side died with her. I never did like that bitch, anyway. She always thought she was better than everybody."

My mind drifted to Melonee and how she sometimes acted like she was better than me.

He went on. "You know, I always thought Max Sr. should've stayed with April. Your mom . . . now that was a down-ass bitch. Real crazy with her gun play too." He had a dreamy look in his eyes. "Yeah, that April was something else. You look just like her too. Body and everything." Uncle Dro's eyes lustfully gazed up and down my frame.

"Don't speak on my mom or my dad, Dro. You may not know this about me, because of your lack of 'uncle skills,' but I don't play when it comes to my parents. Besides, your slumming ass could never be my dad on your best day."

"Wouldn't want to be him. Your father and I are two different niggas. But you . . . you're just like that muthafucka and your scandalous-ass mama. The apple doesn't fall too far from the tree, I see. It's funny how people can't see shit in front of them when it's clear as day. You hold that nigga on a high-ass pedestal, when in actuality that nigga's a bottom-feeder, just like everyone else."

I watched my uncle pick up an apple from my fruit basket, wipe it on his shirt, and then bite into it. The crunching sound he made while biting into the crisp Granny Smith echoed throughout my apartment and my soul. He winked his eye at me and smiled before he slowly began to chew. After taking another bite, Uncle Dro stood up straight against my wall and then walked over to my couch and took a seat. After picking up the remote, he flipped my TV on and turned it to ESPN. With his arms spread wide, his dirty boots up on my suede ottoman, and his head resting against the back cushion, he made himself comfortable in my shit like he lived here. This nigga was already getting on my last nerve. He needed to leave soon, before shit got out of hand. I took a seat in the armchair across from the couch, gun still held high, and we sat in silence for a few minutes, before I finally had had enough.

"What do you want, Pedro?" I growled.

"Oh, so I'm Pedro now? What happened to Uncle Dro? You want to address me by my full first name now that I told you some real shit about your bitch-ass daddy." He laughed. "It's cool, though, *niece*. I see what time it is. And to answer your question, I'm here to collect on that favor I did for you."

I smacked my lips and kept holding my gun up. I didn't trust my uncle for shit, and I would most definitely try to kill him before he ever tried to kill me.

"Look, I don't have your money just yet. But I'll call you whenever I get it, okay?" I said.

"From the looks of this apartment, it doesn't look like you're hurting for money to me. Twenty-three hundred dollars a month in rent, the fridge and cabinets full of food, plus bills, a car note, and money to splurge on shit like this." He lifted one of the Gucci shirts I'd just purchased from one of the shopping bags. "Looks to me like you can afford to slide me my cut so I can be on my way."

I blew out a frustrated breath. "Uncle Dro, shit isn't moving as fast as I thought it would. Plus, Melonee acts like she doesn't want to—"

"I don't give a fuck about any of that shit you saying or what that bitch Melonee isn't doing," he yelled, cutting me off. "You called for my services, I gave them to you, and now I want my money. Which, I might add, you're going to give me today, oh, beautiful niece of mine. Family or not, I will put a bullet right between those pretty little eyes of yours if I don't get my shit. You've been dodging my calls ever since I told you that little favor you needed had been handled."

"That's because I've been at the hospital, playing my role," I snapped back, agitated from this conversation. "Had you stuck to the original plan, the money probably would've been in our hands already. Shit, you almost killed the poor girl. Then you raped her and got her pregnant, throwing all kinds of monkey wrenches into the shit. We can't blackmail a white man with a black baby that's one hundred percent black asshole. As soon as Melonee gives birth to that child, he will know it's not his."

Uncle Dro cut his eyes at me. "First of all, I don't have a baby on the way with anybody. Ain't no bitch on this earth worthy enough to carry my seed, in my opinion. Secondly, if Melonee is pregnant, it's not by me. All I did was fuck her up, like you asked. Maybe a little more than what you wanted, but you never specified how near death you wanted the bitch to be. Now, the nigga who was with me that night may have a different story. He stayed in the house for about thirty minutes after I left, doing whatever it was he was doing. So that baby might be his." He bit into his apple again. "Oh, and you might as well go on ahead and put your little gun down. I guarantee you'll drop dead to the floor before you even get a shot off."

I cocked my gun back and aimed it at him. "Oh yeah?"

Uncle Dro laughed and turned his attention back to ESPN, completely ignoring the loaded gun I had pointed toward him. I wanted to pull the trigger so bad right now and end his pathetic, begging life, but then I remembered I didn't have a silencer on my shit. I didn't need my nosy neighbors calling the police before I could have someone come get his worthless-ass body up off my couch. I stood up, intending to head back into the kitchen to put my gun back in its hiding space, but I stopped when I felt the cold steel of someone else's gun against the back of my head. The person behind me snatched my revolver from out of my hand, spun the chamber, and then emptied every bullet out onto the floor. When my eyes connected to my uncle Dro, he had that devilish smirk on his face.

"You ain't talkin' all that shit now, are you, niecey poo? What happened to big, bad Fiona? You look like you're about to piss on yourself."

He doubled over in laughter. "You see this shit. Niggas always got heart when they have a gun in their hand, but they turn pussy as soon as they have one pointed at their head."

I could feel the tears trying to fall from my eyes, but I refused to let them fall. Me begging for my life would not be the last thing this nigga heard coming from my mouth. My phone started to go off, and I silently thanked God. When Uncle Dro picked it up off the couch, he had a weird look on his face.

"Who is this Captain Kirk–looking muthafucka calling you?" he asked as he laughed and held up the screen for me to see.

Even with a gun pointed at the back of my head, I felt the jolt of electricity that bolted from my heart to my pussy every time I saw Meyers's face. Just seeing the sexy smirk on his face, combined with his tanned skin, dark brown eyes, and sculpted, half-naked body, in the photo that popped up whenever he called always did something to me. I reached out for my cell, but Uncle Dro held the phone back and ignored the call.

"Why did you do that?" I said.

"Nigga look like a police officer to me. You working with the law now, niece?" The threat in his low tone was not missed nor was the deep scowl on his face. The person behind me pushed the barrel of their gun harder against my skull and cocked back the hammer. When I tried to turn around to see who was behind me, they raised their other arm and nudged my jaw with a second gun, turning my face back to Uncle Dro. He raised his eyebrow, waiting for my answer to his question.

"That was the man who has your money."

"*You* supposed to have my money," he exclaimed as my phone started ringing again. "Come on now, niece. I'm trying really hard to spare your life, so stop fucking playing with me."

"I'm not playing with you, Uncle Dro. I swear he the dude I've been working with all this time. How you think I knew all that information about the beach house and how y'all got in without the alarm going off?"

He looked at the picture flashing across my screen. "But you called that nigga Meyers whenever you talked about him. This muthafucka look like ole boy that just got appointed to be the new CEO of Real Time Delivery. What's his name again? Brandon Black . . . or some shit like that?"

"Benjamin Black, you mean."

"Yeah, that's right. Benjamin Black." Dro looked at me as if he was trying to read every thought in my mind. "You call him Meyers, though. Why?"

I thought about giving him some bullshit-ass lie but decided to tell him the truth. "I call him Meyers because that's his biological last name. He became a Black after his mama married Richard Black and he adopted him. When he and I met some years ago, he told me that Meyers was his last name, so that's what I've called him, even after finding out who his stepfather and brother were."

Uncle Dro nodded his head and continued to stare at my phone as it began to ring again, going over everything I had just told him and probably putting some shit together. I didn't miss the pressure of the gun pressing against the side of my face when the person behind me removed the gun from my jaw and then stuck it against my back.

"So who has my money, Fiona? You or him? And before you answer that, make sure you're about to tell me the truth, because if not, both of you muthafuckas will end up dead."

"Like I told you before, we are still waiting on the big money to come in. But I'm pretty sure I can get what you need from him."

Putting the TV on mute, Uncle Dro rose up from his seat on the couch and accepted the call. "Speak to him," he mouthed to me and then pressed the speaker button. The person behind me pushed the guns harder against my back and my head and steered me closer to the couch.

"Hello," I said into the phone.

"What's up, baby? I haven't heard from you in a couple of days."

"And there's a good reason why, Benji."

"Come on, Fee. I know you aren't still upset with that shit."

Anger started to build up in my body at his disregard for my feelings. The nerve of this asshole to call me and act like everything was okay. Yeah, I got all giddy whenever he called, but that didn't stop me from being mad at the little shit that had popped off at his house not too long ago. It had been a few weeks since I'd last spoken to Benji. He'd been ignoring my calls ever since everything with Melonee went down. After spending countless hours at the hospital, trying to convince her to press charges against Roman, to no avail, all I had wanted to do was unwind and relieve some of the stress in my body when I got home. After having my phone calls ignored for a couple of days, I had asked Cowboy to find me Benji's address, as I had decided to show up at his house unannounced. I had figured with all the new shit going on in his life, our little rendezvous would become less frequent, but I had never envisioned that they would stop altogether.

So dressed in nothing but a trench coat and a pair of thigh-high boots, I'd shown up at his new penthouse home in downtown Los Angeles, ready to relieve him of the stress I knew he had too. Assuming he would welcome me in with open arms and a hard dick, I untied my coat, exposing my naked body, and knocked on the door. With hard nipples and a pussy that was already starting to get wet just from anticipating what was about to go down, I held my breath and became more and more excited with every clicking sound the locks made when being turned. The big smile on my face instantly turned into a frown when some large-eyed, blond-haired bitch answered the door. Thinking I was the other chick Benji had called over for the threesome they were about to have, she assessed my naked frame and nodded her head in approval before she stepped back and allowed me to walk in.

With no questions asked, I beat the shit out of that girl for being in Benji's house, then went in search of him. I found him lying in the middle of his king-size bed, smoking a cigarette, and I almost laughed at the scene before me. His room reeked of that bitch's stale-ass pussy, so I knew he had just fucked her. He heard me clear my throat, and his eyes connected with mine before he started choking on the smoke he had just inhaled. I could tell he was shocked by my presence in his bedroom; however, his smooth, conniving ass quickly got over that when his little fuck buddy walked into the room, crying and holding her bloody head.

Being the cocky son of a bitch he was, Benji got up from his bed and tended to the little sobbing ho. After getting her situated in the bathroom, he came back out to his bedroom and got in my face. We argued in hushed tones about me showing up at his house unannounced for a few minutes, before I punched him in his chest and slapped him on his face. I didn't know why I was acting like that, because I wasn't the type of girl who got into relationships, but something about seeing him with another girl after us spending so much time together and me doing all the shit I did for him had done something to me. I was so mad that I tried to slap him one more time. Catching my hand before it could connect with his face, Benji pulled me to his chest and crashed his lips against mine, taking away whatever fight I had left in me. The stress lifted from my body with every touch of his tongue.

Before I knew it, he had me bent over the small couch in front of his bed and was fucking the shit out of me. Ole girl came out of the bathroom with a towel over half her face and watched me work my pussy all over the man she was supposed to be spending this time with. Blood still leaking from her lips and nose, she continued to watch as Benji fucked me six ways from Sunday and emptied his entire soul into me. When he called my name and came, everything seemed to be all right with the world for me. That was until he patted me on my ass and pulled out, but not before thanking me for my services and promising to call me the next day. To say I was humiliated was an understatement. I left Benji's house ashamed and angry as fuck. Too many times I thought about turning around and killing him and his little bitch, but I couldn't. I needed Benji's ass to see the rest of this plan through to fruition.

"Fee, you still there?" Benji asked, breaking me from my thoughts.

Uncle Dro held the phone closer to my lips. "Yeah, I'm still here."

"Okay. Well, I wanted to stop by before I go to the board meeting. You're home, right?"

"I am, but I need a favor before you come by."

"What's up?"

"I need ten thousand dollars."

"Ten thousand dollars? For what?" he asked.

"I owe that to someone for their services."

"Someone like who?"

Uncle Dro had taken the phone away from my mouth and had put it up to his ear. "Someone who put in some work for you and my dear niece here," he answered. "And since I now know who I've been working for, that price I quoted before just went from ten Gs to fifty."

"Fifty thousand dollars! I can't get that type of money without being questioned," Benji yelled into the phone.

"Well, if you want this to stay between us, you better find a way to get that shit. You got an hour, Mr. Black, or I'ma find your ass."

Benji started to say something, but Uncle Dro hung up the phone before he could get it out.

"You might as well come have a seat, niece, and watch a little ESPN with me. An hour will go by in no time. I'll have my money and be out of your way as soon as my shit gets here."

"Well, can you at least tell your guard dog to take the guns off me? I'm not going to try anything," I said.

Uncle Dro looked at the person behind me and nodded his head. The guns were removed from my head and my back. I wanted to breathe a sigh of relief, but I didn't want to let this nigga know that he had me a little spooked. I turned back to look at the person behind me but couldn't see their face due to the ski mask they had on. My eyes scanned the small body, and I noticed the curvy frame covered in all black. Instantly, I knew my uncle's guard dog was a bitch.

"So you working with females now, Uncle Dro? Need a bitch to have your back now? I bet if she puts them guns down, she won't be so tough."

The guard dog placed her guns on my dining-room table and smirked. "You're more like your mama than you know," she said as she lifted the ski mask off her face.

"You have got to be kidding me," was the last thing I said before she punched me in my face, knocking me completely out.

Roman

I sat back in the plush chair in Chasin's office, waiting on a reply to the text I had just sent. Yeah, I knew that reaching out to Melonee right now, in the middle of the mess that was going on, could potentially hurt me in some way, but low key, I didn't really give a fuck. I needed to see her. Needed to be next to her, for some reason, and I couldn't explain why. All the shit that the media and some of the world were accusing me of didn't make sense at all. The night Melonee and I were together was nothing short of amazing. Well, that was how it felt until I woke up to the police surrounding my house and every news outlet on my grass, snapping pictures of me being arrested.

Steepling my fingers under my chin, I thought about my life and everything that had happened in the past few weeks. Not only had my CEO position at my family's company been given to my brother, Benji, because of some damn moral clause, but the rest of my life had been spiraling out of control too. All my accounts were frozen right now and were being picked through by the IRS due to some money-laundering investigation and supposed tax evasion. The company cars I used as transportation and the penthouse apartment I considered home had been confiscated since they were all in the company's name. The only things I had left to my name were my motorcycle collection, the beach house that I took Melonee to, and the few stacks of money that I was smart enough to keep in a safe at my old house. It wasn't enough for me to live the rest of my life off of, but I could live comfortably for the next few years, or until I somehow got my job back.

After picking up my phone, I looked at the screen. I deepened the scowl on my face when I noticed I had yet to receive a response.

"So you went ahead and texted her, anyway?" Chasin asked as he walked into his office. I didn't even turn around to acknowledge his response.

"You should've never sent me that picture of her in the restaurant," I told him.

"I was trying to send you a picture of the woman that she was with. I don't remember where I know her from, but I know her from somewhere." Chasin walked around the desk and sat in the chair next to me. "Maybe she went to school with us or something." He shrugged his shoulders. "I don't know. But I know I've seen her before."

"Did she seem happy?"

Chasin stared at me for a second before he spoke. "Roman, man, I need you to let this thing you have for Melonee go until we clear your name. Do you not understand how bad it would look if the judge found out that you were low key stalking the girl you *supposedly* did not attack?"

I cut my eyes to him and raised my chin. "*Supposedly?* So you think I did it or something, man?"

With his hands held up in surrender, he sighed. "As your friend, I don't think you did anything. But as your lawyer, I have to look at this situation both ways. Attacking a woman isn't even in your character. However, all the evidence that's being presented says otherwise. I mean, it's your word against hers, and neither one of you can fully remember what happened that night. A source of mine said that she was down at the police station, giving a statement to some detective about some of the things that she seems to remember, but I haven't heard anything yet in regard to what was said."

I nodded my head and started playing around with my phone. I scrolled through my apps with one hand while I scratched at the light beard on my face with the other. Thoughts of sending another text message kept going back and forth in my mind. Maybe if I told her who I was, she would respond. I had had to change my phone number a few times shortly after I got arrested. Somehow the media had kept getting ahold of my shit and would call my phone all night, wanting statements or offering a shitload of money for an exclusive. It had got so bad that I had to change carriers and get a phone under my uncle's account just to get a break from the constant harassment.

The only people who had my newest phone number were Chasin, Marques, my parents, Uncle Kazi, and now Melonee. Hopefully, she would open at least one of my text messages and would hit me back. Right about now, I'd take a simple "Fuck off" if that meant she would respond. I knew meeting up with me was probably the last thing on her mind right now, and in all honesty, it should be the last thing on mine too. But I had to see her. I had to make sure that she knew that I would never hurt a hair on her beautiful body or let whoever had done this to us get away with it.

I blew out a frustrated breath after checking my blank screen for the tenth time and rubbed my hand over my face. Laying my head back against the headrest, I closed my eyes and blew out a low breath. With all this shit coming down and happening to me, all I wanted to do was be in Melonee's arms again and between her thighs. My memory was a little foggy, but I did remember the way her smooth thighs felt wrapped around my head, and the way her pussy tasted and felt.

"Have you heard from your uncle yet? Wasn't he supposed to be out here sometime this week?" Chasin asked, walking back around his desk to answer the phone that was ringing.

I waited for him to get off the phone before responding to his questions. "I haven't talked to my uncle since the last time we spoke on the phone. Either he's on one of his *business* trips or he's still working on trying to see who would set me up like this."

"I already told you who I think it is."

"And I already told you that you are wrong. Marques is my boy, and he would never betray me like that. Besides, how would he benefit from taking everything away from me? Dude already has a golden ticket with his family's chain of luxury hotels. Marques was born into money and is going to die with even more money, if he takes his job seriously."

Chasin shook his head as he took a seat opposite me at his desk. "I still think he has a motive. I always thought he was a little jealous of you, for some reason. Maybe it was because you got the cuter girls or something. I don't know. But the brother moves kind of weird. When was the last time you heard from him?"

I thought about Chasin's question and honestly couldn't answer it. The last time I saw Marques was when he picked me up from the airport after I came back from Russia. Other than that, he'd been MIA. Our only method of communication over the past few weeks had been a text here and there. We hadn't spoken to one another.

Chasin's assistant, Renee, spoke over the intercom, interrupting my thoughts. "Hey, Chase. You have a call holding on line one from someone named Lindsey Holt and a call on line two from a Mr. Cairo Broussard."

Chasin cleared his throat. "Thanks, Renee. I'll handle both calls." I watched as he loosened the tie around his neck and sat back in his chair before he hit a button on the base of the phone. "Cai, my dude. What's good? How's that growing family of yours? Happy wife, happy life, right?"

"Happy wife, happy life indeed. Although she's been tripping for a minute now."

"Aw, shit. What you do now, man?" Chasin put the call on speakerphone.

"Nothing really. I'm just trying to get Audri pregnant again, but she ain't having it. Quiet as kept, though, I think I already knocked her up with another set of twins. Her ass been real moody lately, and she's been craving Mama Faye's oxtail soup for the past few weeks." He laughed, and I could hear the smile in his tone. "Then you should see how tough she's been on your boy lately. Man, I swear to God, I can't even walk up the stairs sometimes before she's whipping my shit out and pouncing on me. Taking me down any and everywhere she can get it. I ain't complaining or anything like that. Shit, if she isn't pregnant right now, she will be soon with the way we've been going at it."

We all shared a laugh.

"Aye, bruh, I didn't know you had a client with you," Cairo Broussard said. "I heard someone else laughing in the background, which means you must have me on speakerphone. If you're busy, call me back when you get a second."

Chasin looked at me and shook his head. "Naw, Cai, you good. It's just my boy Roman Black. I just got back to the office, and this fool was already sitting in here."

"Roman Black? Isn't that the cat who's been all over the news, accused of attacking some chick at his house?"

I cut my eyes to Chasin. We were boys and everything, but that didn't mean he could talk about my case with some outsider. That attorney-client privilege shit still applied to this situation. Friends or not.

"You know I can't get into that with you, bruh. But just know that my man is a great guy, and I'ma leave it at that," Chasin replied.

I nodded my head at his response and started playing with my phone again. I read through a few e-mails, but I still listened to their conversation.

"I wasn't expecting you to, Chase, man. You've always been by the books." He paused for a second and then continued. "And if you say your boy is a good dude, then I believe you. Enough said."

"Enough said," Chasin agreed. "So what's up, man? To what do I owe the pleasure of this call? Audri let your ass up for a breather?" As he spoke, Chasin got up from his seat and poured himself a shot of the Johnny Walker Black Label on the small bar in the corner of his office. When he offered me a glass, I shook my head and declined.

"I'm cool for a few minutes. My baby needed to get something to drink." He cleared his throat. "The reason I'm calling, though, is to see if you had a chance to look over that paperwork for the club thing Toby wants me to go in with him on. I told him I'd get back to him in a couple of days."

"You having second thoughts or something?"

"No. It's not that I'm having second thoughts or anything. It's just that . . . Yeah, he and I are twins, but that doesn't mean that I automatically trust his business dealings, you feel me? I mean, I literally became a millionaire overnight, and I want to at least keep that crazy amount of zeros in my accounts for a few years."

"I feel you on that, man." Chasin gulped down his shot and winced, but he manned back up when he caught me looking at him. "I got the contract the day you sent it to me, and looked over it a little bit. From the numbers I did skim over, the deal looks pretty legit and profitable. Especially with the upgrades y'all are talking about doing to the place. I'll look over it later tonight and then get back to you tomorrow, all right, Cai?"

Cairo was quiet on his end of the line for a minute before he returned. Giggling and a flirty voice, which I assumed belonged to his wife, could be heard in the background.

"Yo, Chase . . . um . . . *shit* . . . *damn, Audri.* I gotta go, bruh. *Fuck.* Yeah, yeah . . . Call me tomorrow, man. Good looking."

"I got you, man. And tell Audri I said what's up."

"Yeah, will do. Later."

After ending the call, Chasin looked at me. "If I ever get married, I need me a wife like that."

I smirked. "Me too."

After taking his second call, from Lindsey Holt, his inside at the precinct, Chasin filled me in on what he'd learned. He said that Holt had revealed that Melonee had told the detective who interviewed her down at the station that I wasn't the one who had raped her. Although her memory wasn't all that clear, she'd given the detective a vague description of the person who actually did attack her. Now if she could only remember the connection we shared, shit could start getting back to the way that it was, I thought. Chasin and I went over the details of my case, including what the district attorney and the IRS were trying to charge me with. None of these charges made sense to me, but I had faith that Chasin could get me out of this shit, especially after finding out what Melonee had just told the detective.

We were going over the strategy for my court date coming up when Chasin's office door slammed open and a frantic Renee ran in.

"I'm sorry, Chasin. I tried to tell him that you were in a meeting, but he wouldn't listen."

"Who wouldn't listen?" Chasin said.

As soon as the question slipped from Chasin's lips, a dark figure blocked the doorway and then walked into the room, followed by two more men, who were dressed like him in black suits. Kazimir Slutzky stepped into the room next, in a charcoal three-piece Italian suit and wing-tipped loafers, looking like the Russian boss that he was. A cigar hanging from his mouth, he looked around Chasin's office and admired his plaques and accolades.

I stood up from my seat and hugged my uncle. He kissed both my cheeks and then held his hand out to Chasin, who shook it. The look on his hard face already told me that this visit wasn't going to be a pleasant one. In his thick Russian accent, he told the men who had walked in before him to leave the room and wait down at the car for him. Turning his eyes to me, Uncle Kazi blew out a cloud of smoke and sat down.

"I assume you're doing everything you can to make these problems for my nephew go away?" he said, addressing Chasin, with his eyes still on me.

"We—" I began, but Uncle Kazi held his hand up, silencing me.

"I do not want to hear your answer, Roman. I asked your lawyer, Mr. Smith." He blew out another cloud of smoke and turned his attention to Chasin. "Again, have you been doing everything in your power to make sure my nephew never sees a day in any of your American prisons?"

"I, um . . . I've been . . . doing everything legally possible to make sure that happens," Chasin replied.

Uncle Kazimir shook his head. "That is not enough."

"Uncle Kazi," Chasin said, trying to reason with him.

"Mr. Slutzky to you."

"Mr. Slutzky, I assure you that I am going above and beyond to help Roman out. Not only is he my client, but he's also a good friend of mine, and I would never—"

"You would never what? Right now, I don't trust anyone who says they have my nephew's best interest at heart."

Chasin looked at me with raised eyebrows. Although I trusted my boy, Uncle Kazi did have a point: Someone was fucking with me and trying to take me down, and I didn't have the slightest idea who it was. How did you go from having the time of your life to basically having nothing in the blink of an eye? It would take a lot for someone on the outside to get that type of access to me. But it would take some-one close to me no time to throw me to the wolves and ruin my life. My mind went back to the conversation Chasin and I had had earlier about Marques. I didn't feel in my heart that he would do anything like this to me, but he had been missing in action lately, something that was totally not the norm for him. I made a mental note to drive by his place as soon as I had handled my business here.

Uncle Kazi got up from his seat and walked over to Chasin's bar. After pouring himself a glass of bourbon, he downed it and poured himself another one. I could tell that something was on my uncle's mind and that at any second, he was going to tell us what it was.

He cleared his throat after downing his third shot and then walked back over to the chair he had just been sitting in. He looked at Chasin first, then turned his attention to me. "I think you should have someone else represent you until we figure out who is behind the shit going on around you." His Russian accent was a little thicker after his three drinks. "No disrespect to your friend and his accomplishments, but I would much rather have one of our own looking into things."

"But your people don't have all the connections I have with the police department," Chasin argued.

Uncle Kazimir puffed on his cigar. "I have something even better than your little connections."

Chasin scoffed. "Like what?"

"Debts."

"Debts?" Chasin looked puzzled.

"I've killed a lot of people in my lifetime. Some under the Russian Mob's orders and others . . ." Uncle Kazi shrugged his shoulders. "Others were some freelance contracts here and there. Some of your big officials owe me, and I feel that now is the time to collect."

"Okay. Well, we can work together, then. Your favors from the people you know, and the connections I have with the people I know. I'm sure we'll be able to get Roman off the hook in no time."

There was a knock on the door.

"Come in," Uncle Kazi said in Russian.

Both Chasin and I turned toward the door and waited to see who would walk in. Before she even passed over the threshold, the Dior perfume Hypnotic Poison, which she'd been wearing ever since we were young, wafted into the room. When my cousin Viktoria Petrova walked into Chasin's office, gone was the little girl with pigtails who used to follow me around during the summers Marques and I spent in Russia. In front of me now stood my beautiful grown cousin, who was one of the top defense attorneys at Banker and Bob, an international law firm in Moscow.

"Mr. Smith, allow me to introduce you to my daughter Viktoria Petrova. She will be taking over Roman's case from this point on."

Chasin looked at me. "Is this who you want to represent you, Ro? I mean, I understand if you want to let your family do it. But if you want me to stay on the case, I don't have a problem doing so."

The room went completely quiet as everyone waited for my answer. All eyes were focused on me. Before I could offer my opinion about any switch in representation, my phone vibrated in my hand. I opened the text message.

Melonee: I know we are probably breaking some type of law by doing this, but where would you like to meet?

"I gotta go," was all they got from me as I responded to Melonee's text. "Uh, whatever you guys come up with is fine with me." I gave Viktoria a hug. "It's nice to see you, cousin. I'm pretty sure we will catch up in a day or so. I gotta go take care of something right quick." I turned and faced my uncle and my friend. "Uncle Kazi, Chasin, I'll call you both in a couple of hours, all right?"

After grabbing my jacket off the lounge chair next to the window, I put it on and then scooped up my keys from Chasin's desk. My phone vibrated again, and I read Melonee's second text, which contained some address in Montecito that I wasn't too familiar with. But I was pretty sure the navigation on my phone would lead me to it.

"Roman," Viktoria called out. "Be careful going to see that young lady. You don't want to make your case any worse than it is. As your previous lawyer, I'm assuming Mr. Smith here advised you to stay away, and as your new lawyer, I advise you to do the same until we've cleared your name. From what I've been told, she remembers a little bit of her attack, but not much. Her seeing you may trigger a good memory or something bad. I hope she's worth you potentially spending the rest of your life in jail if this goes south."

I thought about what my cousin had said as I trotted out the door. And although everything she had said might be right, I was still going to take my chances and see what happened. Melonee was most definitely worth me risking my freedom, and I had no problem trying to make her remember that too.

Melonee

I sat in the living room of Aunt Bree's rental home and shook my leg nervously. Sending those two text messages to Roman was a big mistake. I wanted to text him back and tell him never mind, but the conversation Aunt Bree and I had had earlier kept going through my head.

"I think you should meet up with him. It might jog your memory some more about what happened that night."

"But what if it doesn't work that way?" I said.

"What do you mean?"

"What if I do remember what happened, and it turns out that Roman actually did attack me?"

Aunt Bree looked at me for a few seconds and then grabbed my hand. "Melonee, do you feel in your heart that this man attacked you? Forget the little shit you remembered after you hit your head when Proof's dumb ass crashed the car. Do you honestly believe that this man hurt you?"

"In my head, I don't think so."

"I didn't ask you about your head. That's where the problem is. I asked you about your heart. What does it tell you?"

Just like last time, the little life inside me started going crazy whenever I spoke about Roman, causing my heart to flutter.

"In my heart, I don't believe that Roman did it. Honestly, I believe he would never do anything to harm me. I know that may seem crazy, since I don't remember everything, but there's something about him that keeps pulling me his way. It's like the same connection I feel with this baby, I feel with him whenever I see him or talk about him."

"Even more reason to meet up and see what happens," Aunt Bree said as we walked to her car. "And just so you feel safe, text him back and give him the address to the house I'm renting in Montecito. The munchkin is with Proof for a few days, and instead of giving him your home address or Mama's address, just give him mine. That way he doesn't know where you actually live, and I'll finally get to meet my future nephew."

Rubbing my hand over my swollen belly, I tried to calm my nerves down a little more, but I failed miserably when I felt the baby kick my stomach.

"You must know that your dad is on the way, huh, li'l Black?" I cooed to my round belly.

"So you're finally admitting that it was Roman Black who raped you and got you pregnant?" Fiona asked as she walked into Aunt Bree's living room like she lived in this house.

"How did you get in here? I know Aunt Bree didn't let you in."

"She didn't. You guys left the door unlocked, like the rest of these siddity white people who live out here do, and I just walked in. I'm pretty sure when her chubby ass sees me, she'll have something smart to say."

"Don't do my aunt like that. It's not her fault that she calls you out on your bullshit and doesn't give a fuck," I replied. I laughed, but Fiona didn't.

Rolling her eyes at my comment, Fiona walked farther into the living room, until she reached the couch across from the one I was sitting on and sat down. The colorful maxi dress she wore had purple hues in it that matched her hair, and the gold sandals on her feet went with the hobo bag, her bracelet, her earrings, and the necklace around her neck. After opening her purse, she pulled out a McDonald's bag and threw it across the coffee table at me.

I took in her appearance and tried to figure out what was different about my best friend. She'd gained a little bit of weight since I came out of my coma, but there was something else that was different about Fee that I couldn't quite put my finger on. The heavy makeup on her face was typical for her whenever her skin was breaking out, and the new purple weave wasn't a surprise to me, seeing as that was her signature hair color. Maybe it was her eyes that were different. Yes, there was something in Fiona's eyes that didn't look familiar to me, and this had me questioning a lot of things. But until I figured out what was really going on, I would just keep my mouth closed.

"I knew your ass was probably hungry, so I bought you a Filet-O-Fish when I stopped to get me some McNuggets. They didn't have oatmeal-raisin cookies, so I got you the sugar ones instead."

I picked the bag up and inhaled the smell of my favorite thing to eat from Mickey D's, the Filet-O-Fish. "Did you get extra tartar sauce on it?"

She scoffed. "Yeah, I told them to put an extra dollop of that nasty shit on there."

After taking the sandwich out of the bag, I wasted no time taking a bite out of it and then another. With tartar sauce dripping from the side of my mouth, I continued the conversation with Fiona. "How did you know I was here? When I texted you earlier, I told you that I was going home."

"Me, Proof, and some of the fellas met up today to discuss this new mark, and Proof told me where you were."

"New mark? I thought y'all was taking a break."

"*We* aren't taking any type of break. There's no time for that. Since you don't want to go along with the plan to blackmail Roman, I figured we'd do one more hit, and then we can talk about going our separate ways."

"I already told you that I don't want to do this anymore, Fiona. My mind hasn't changed since I've been out of the hospital. I'm good on the Black Widow Clique. Love y'all, but I'm good." I took another bite of my sandwich and shook my head. "Even before everything that happened, I told you I was out, and I meant that shit. It's time for me to be a full-time mother to Madison, and when I have this baby, I want to be a hands-on mother with him. My granny is too old to be watching over my kids when I'm able to do it myself. Besides, I have enough money to live off of for a minute, so it ain't like me and mine will be hurting for anything."

Fiona shifted in her seat, with a scowl on her face. "You and yours? What about the rest of us who need these jobs to provide for our families?"

I wiped my mouth with a napkin I pulled out of the bag and took a sip of the water I had sitting on a coaster in front of me. "Fiona, we've been scheming and scamming since we were sixteen. You should have more than enough money saved up."

"Well, I don't. And even if I did, it still wouldn't be enough. And I know that little bit of change you are so-called sitting on won't be, either. What? You probably only have enough to live comfortably for a year maybe? Douglas's insurance policy didn't leave you with that much money once everyone got their cut. What will you do after that shit runs out? Come crying back to me and the BWC to let you in on one of our jobs?" She snorted. "Good luck with that. The clique ain't feeling the way you fucked up this last job. Which, I might add, has us questioning your loyalty with future endeavors."

"How did I fuck up the last job? And who the fuck are y'all to question my loyalty? I've been down since the beginning," I snapped. "The fucking beginning. So my loyalty should never be in question. But there comes a time in people's lives, Fiona, where other shit starts to become more important than money."

She laughed. "What? Like love? You really think you and Roman had some type of love connection, huh? When you were in the hospital, talking that crazy mess, I thought it was the meds, but now I can see that you really believe that shit. How dumb can you be, Melonee? The man damn near beat you to death and, as a bonus, raped you and put a little bastard baby in your belly. You should be angry right now. Instead, you wanna run around here like a dummy, acting like that child was made out of love and like that white man would ever take you seriously."

I was really taken back by the way Fiona was coming at me. Was she really blaming me for the shit that had gone down with Roman? Or was she just in her feelings due to the fact that I didn't want to go along with that blackmailing plan? How could I blackmail the father of my child? Especially when I could feel that we shared more than just this baby growing inside me. I rubbed my chest, trying to ease the heartburn that had crept up on me, while Fiona sat on the couch on the other side of the coffee table and typed away on her phone. I picked mine up and noticed that I had a missed text message from the number I'd come to know as Roman's.

Roman: I was wondering if we can meet up tomorrow or later on this week. I got a family emergency that I have to tend to, and I won't be able to make it today.

I read the message over a few times before I responded.

Me: No problem. Just let me know when you're available.

Fiona was still looking down at her phone and texting when she spoke to me again. "Muthafucka canceled on you, huh?"

"What?"

"Roman Black? That's who you were waiting for, right?"

"How did you . . ." I trailed off, but then realization hit me. "Fucking Cowboy." He had tapped into my phone again and must have sent Fiona my text message history.

"Fucking Cowboy is right. What the fuck are you doing, Melonee, inviting the enemy over here? Are you trying to blackmail him on your own and keep the money for yourself?"

"Like I have to do that."

"What the fuck does that mean?"

I debated in my head whether to tell Fiona my business but figured I might as well. It was the only way she would probably understand why I wasn't tripping on being a part of the BWC like that anymore.

"It means that I don't need to blackmail anyone for money when I have enough already."

She had a confused look on her face. "How much is 'enough already'?"

I licked my lips and looked Fiona dead in her eyes. "Around three mill."

"Three million dollars, Melonee? Where the fuck did you get that kind of money?"

I went on and told Fiona about the insurance policy my mother had left behind for me that was worth five hundred K and that I'd known nothing about until a year after Madison was born. I had received a letter in the mail advising me about the money, with a check attached to the bottom. Because I wasn't so sure how long the BWC would be together, I had taken that money and put it in an account under my child's name, just in case anything ever happened to me. My granny would have enough money to buy Madison her first car, her first home, as well as send her to any college she wanted to go to. The lifestyle we lived wasn't as dangerous as some, but if we were to get caught up, I would probably never see the light of day again.

"Okay, that's only half a million. What about that other two and a half?"

I knew the next thing I said was going to have Fiona feeling some type of way, but I didn't care

right about now. I was officially done with the
BWC and wished them nothing but the best.

"The other part of the money is from me saving
from previous jobs and the things I got from the
will Douglas left."

"The will Douglas left?"

I nodded my head. "The reason why I was
going to court all that time was Doug's will.
Doug's daughter Riana kept contesting it, saying
that the changes he had made to it weren't legit.
She tried to make the judge believe that I had
somehow brainwashed her father and had made
him add me to it."

Fiona sat back in her seat, taking in everything
I had just told her. Yeah, it may seem a little
shady that I didn't tell her, but this money from
the will was different from the insurance shit. As
soon as I got that insurance check, we split that
shit evenly. Anything else, I honestly felt was all
mine.

"Mel, you okay?" Aunt Bree asked as she
walked into the room and saw the look on
Fiona's face.

I couldn't help but laugh at the outfit my aunt
had chosen. Some yoga pants and a matching
jacket with some Timberland boots. And she had
her hair wrapped up in a scarf. The kicker was
the three layers of Vaseline she had spread over

her face. Aunt Bree looked like she was more ready to whip ass than to lounge around her house and relax.

"What's good, Mel? When did she get here?" she asked, raising her chin in Fee's direction.

"We good, Auntie. Just having a friendly little conversation," I said.

Fiona cut her eyes at me.

"Didn't sound like it from where I was in the back. What's going on out here? What happened to your other company?" Aunt Bree said.

"The muthafucka canceled on her," she replied, answering for me, her tone laced with attitude. She looked at me. "I see you ain't had no problem telling someone who isn't even a part of the clique what's going on with you."

"Listen, Fee—" I began, but Fiona cut me off.

"'Listen, Fee,' my ass. When were you going to tell us any of this shit? Does Proof know? Do any of the niggas that's been killing muthafuckas for you for the past damn near ten years know?"

I reached across the coffee table and tried to grab Fiona's arm and pull her to me so that she would come sit next to me, but she pulled away. Her eyes stayed on me, and she ignored Aunt Bree, who was now standing behind her, ready to fuck Fiona up if she tried to jump on me. My aunt knew I wouldn't do anything physical while carrying this baby, but my best friend was a different story.

"Well? Do they know?" Fiona questioned.

I shook my head. "No, Fee. No one from the clique knows, not even Proof. The only people who know now are you and Aunt Bree. I told her earlier, when I was contemplating how to separate myself from the BWC."

Fiona turned her attention to Aunt Bree and then back to me. "Let me guess. She was all for you leaving us hanging, huh?"

"I've been against this shit from the beginning. I didn't want my niece living this type of life, and I know her mother wouldn't have wanted it, either. She especially wouldn't have wanted it, seeing as the same lifestyle is what got her killed."

I looked at my aunt. "What are you talking about, Aunt Bree? What type of lifestyle did my mother have that caused her to die? Dezmond didn't have any money, so I know she didn't marry him because of that."

Aunt Bree walked from behind Fiona and sat down on the couch I occupied. Her eyes were tearing up. I'd never seen my aunt get emotional like this. Come to think of it, I had never seen Aunt Bree cry. She'd always been the strong one in the family, the one who made sure we were all good and cried out, especially after my mother died.

"I don't know if any of this is true, but back in the day, your mama and Fiona's mom used to do the type of shit y'all out here doing. Get with the ballers around the way or those wealthy men and take their money," my aunt revealed. "I don't know who all was involved, but I used to hear Shaunie on the phone, talking about new licks and all that shit. I wasn't really paying attention back then, because I always had my nose in the books. Me and my sister were as different as night and day. She loved that street life, and I was all about school." Aunt Bree smiled at the memory and wiped the single tear that was falling down her face. "And Max was crazy about her." Aunt Bree looked at Fiona, who was texting on her phone. "Your daddy is the reason why Shaunie and your mama stopped being friends."

"What are you talking about, Bree? My mama left when me and Cowboy were young. Way before Shaunie and Melonee came into the picture," Fiona snapped.

"She did. But Max, Shaunie, and April used to run together. They were thick as thieves."

"What happened?" I asked.

"Well, from what I took from the situation, April found out that Max and Shaunie were messing around behind her back and went to confront them. Max told her that it was true, and that's when she left."

Fiona started laughing. "You are a lying-ass bitch, Bree. My daddy never mentioned no shit like this to me or Cowboy. The story we were told was that he met Shaunie at some party, got the pussy on the first night, and couldn't shake her after that. My daddy was so heartbroken over my mama leaving that he latched onto the first pair of perky titties and fat ass that he ran into. The fact that she had a child already was a bonus, because that meant that she could help with his two kids."

"Do you really believe that bullshit?" Aunt Bree retorted.

"Yep, and you can't tell me shit differently." Fiona stood and picked up her purse from the couch. "Let me get out of here before you start spitting more lies and I end up beating your ass, Bree." She turned to me. "You real foul for keeping that money shit from us, Melonee. I already called a meeting with the clique to discuss this bullshit. You better hope they don't feel some type of way about this. Then you wonder why they questioning your loyalty."

"And they can keep on questioning it. I don't owe anything to anyone but Madison and this new baby I'm carrying," I told Fiona.

Fiona smiled and nodded her head and then turned and left Aunt Bree's home.

My back and my head were starting to hurt from this baby and from finding out all the shit that Aunt Bree had just laid on me. My mother used to rob niggas for their money too? I knew she hadn't worked and would be gone from home for a day or two, but I was sure it had never been anything by comparison to what we were doing with the BWC. My mind drifted to Roman. I wondered if my mother and Fiona's father had had the same kind of connection with each other that I felt with him. I was not even going to lie. I was a little disappointed that he had canceled on me. I had a good feeling that us meeting up would trigger some sort of memory from that night, so that I could finally figure out who was behind my attack, but I guessed I'd have to wait until he dealt with whatever family emergency had come up.

"You good, Mel? I didn't mean to drop all of that on you right now, but I felt it was time you knew the little that I do know about your mama and Fiona's."

"I appreciate it, Auntie. But can I ask you a question?"

Aunt Bree smiled and placed her hand on my belly and rubbed it. "What's up?"

"You said the same lifestyle killed my mama. Do you think one of the men she robbed killed her, and not Dezmond, like the police report said?"

Aunt Bree rubbed my belly and talked to my unborn child for a few minutes before she looked at me and shook her head. "Honestly, I never thought that it was Dezmond who killed your mother. He was a little jealous of the love that Shaunie still had for Max, but he was trying to do everything in his power to make sure she saw him as the man for her."

I winced as a small contraction shot through my body. "Then who do you think killed her if it wasn't Dezmond?" I winced again.

"What's wrong, Mel? Is the baby okay?" Aunt Bree asked, panic all over her face.

"Um, something doesn't feel right. I think I need to go to the hospital." Another contraction hit and had me damn near falling to the floor.

"Is that blood?" Aunt Bree screamed. I looked down at the white tights I had on and saw a growing red spot between my legs.

"Oh my God! Call nine-one-one! Something isn't right," I cried out as another contraction hit me, this time harder than the last.

Bree picked up my cell phone and dialed the police. Because we were in Montecito, it didn't take any time for an ambulance and a fire truck to show up and rush me to the hospital. The only thing going through my mind was the safety of my child. I prayed that the Lord would see fit that everything was all right and that my baby was okay. If anything happened to me, I would be all right with that. Like I said, mine were gonna be all right, whether I was here or not.

Roman

I swerved in and out of traffic as I flew down the 101 freeway on my motorcycle, headed toward Santa Barbara Cottage Hospital. I'd just pulled up at the Montecito address Melonee sent me when my stepmother, Julia, called to tell me that my father had had a heart attack and had been rushed to the hospital. Julia had been so distraught during the call that one of the nurses had had to take the phone from her and tell me which hospital they were at.

After getting directions to the hospital, I had tried calling Benji's phone a few times to see if he had any information about what had happened, but all it had done was ring. Marques was still missing in action, and Chasin was still working on my case with Viktoria. I had then called my uncle to tell him what was going on, but he hadn't seemed to be affected by it much at all. Uncle Kazi and my father had never really gotten along, so I doubted he'd shed a tear for my father if he didn't make it through this. Finally, I had sent Melonee a text to see if we could meet some other time, and then I'd headed in the direction of my father. Hopefully, Melonee didn't feel some type of way or think that I had come up with something else to do. Once I checked things out at the hospital, I'd call and invite her over to the beach house or see if she would rather meet somewhere of her choice.

The strong afternoon wind whipped over my exposed arms, causing goose bumps to cover my body. The loud hum of my motorcycle was the only thing I could hear aside from the occasional honk from the impatient drivers going ten miles per hour. While I focused on the road, looking out for cars switching lanes at the last minute, I allowed my mind to drift to my father. *A heart attack?* Richard Black had been the picture of health the last time I saw him.

After taking my exit off the freeway, I sped past the line of cars waiting to make a right turn and merged with the flow of traffic on the equally busy street. Two minutes later, I was pulling up to the ER doors of the large hospital and parking my bike illegally in the red painted section, not worried about getting towed or issued a ticket. Following the instructions from the nurse I had spoken with earlier, I skipped the crowded hall with the elevators and ran up three flights of stairs to the ICU. As soon as I rushed through the doors, I found Julia standing there, being comforted by an obviously drunk Benji.

"What's going on? How is he?" I asked as I walked up to the two of them as they talked in hushed tones. As soon as Julia's eyes landed on me, she began to sob uncontrollably and hug my neck.

"Oh, Roman, I'm so glad you made it. Your father and I were at the Summerland house for a few days just to get out of the city. Everything was going fine until today. He woke up this morning complaining about pains in his chest. I just thought it was heartburn from that spicy Italian food the cook served us for dinner last night. I gave him a couple of Tums and put him in bed, then went to take a swim. The next thing I know, he's holding his chest and stumbling down the stairs. I didn't know what to do, so I just called nine-one-one. When we got here, they took him straight to emergency." Her sobs became louder. "They just brought him to this room a few minutes ago. Roman, I can't lose my husband. What will I do without my husband?"

After removing Julia's hands from around my neck, I walked over to the double glass doors to my father's room and watched as he lay motionless in the small hospital bed. The face mask over his mouth, which was giving him oxygen, would fog up every time he took a short breath and his eyes would crinkle at the corners, as if he were trying to open them up but couldn't. All types of monitors were beeping as they kept track of his vitals, and wires were hanging every which way. The green hospital sheet covered half his body, and his exposed chest and arms had all kinds of tubes and IVs attached to them.

My throat went completely dry; and my mind, blank. Seeing my father this way was truly agonizing. I wasn't ready to see him like this. Right now he looked helpless, weak, and tired. He was not the strong, pompous, arrogant, and on-the-go man that he normally was. Lately, our relationship hadn't been the best because of all the shit that had gone down with the moral clause stuff, but that didn't stop me from feeling some kind of way when I saw him like this. My father was the only parent that I had left. Not to criticize Julia or anything like that, but she could never take my mother's place.

Walking even closer to the double glass doors, I watched as a nurse took my father's blood pressure and wrote some things down on the clipboard next to his bed. When she came out, I walked up to her and introduced myself.

"Nice to meet you, Mr. Black. Your father is doing okay right now. For a minute there, we thought he wasn't going to make it, but at the last minute, he pulled through."

My eyes were still focused on my father as I spoke to her. "Do you know what could have caused this? I mean, my father has never had any issues with his heart. He still works out, eats right, and takes his vitamins. He was okay the last time we spoke. Didn't look sick at all."

"Well, Mr. Black . . ."

"Call me Roman . . . please."

"Well, okay, Roman. And you can call me Tran."

I finally broke my gaze on my father and looked at his nurse. When her eyes connected with mine, I instantly knew that she was attracted to me. The way she licked her small lips and batted her eyelashes told me she was flirting with me, while trying to be subtle and professional at the same time. I could tell Tran wanted me to give her some kind of sign that I was interested in what she was offering, but when I continued to stare at her with questioning eyes, waiting on some more insight into my father's condition, she cleared her throat, embarrassed, and began to speak again.

"Um, I'm sorry. Uh, we . . . we initially didn't know what brought the heart attack on," she stammered, her cheeks flushing a bright red. "Um, but then we performed some tests and were able to determine that a blood clot outside the heart blocked an artery, which caused the attack."

"Outside the heart? Is he going to be okay, though?"

"Right now, it's touch and go, Mr. Black . . . I mean Roman. The first twenty-four hours after a myocardial infarction are the most important. I and the rest of the skilled staff will keep a close eye on his heart and will perform a series of electrocardiograms and blood tests. If he's stable after these twenty-four hours, we will send him to the telemetry floor, where a cardiac-care team will continue to watch over him. Because the heart attack was pretty severe, he may be here for about three or four days before he's released."

I nodded my head in understanding of what Tran had just told me. "Can I go in and see him?"

She shook her head and tucked the hair that had fallen in her face behind her ear. "Not right now. Maybe in a few hours. We still need to monitor your father closely, and we don't want to risk any kind of stress or anything that would cause his heart to react." Her eyes traveled over to Julia. "If possible, do you think you or your brother can take your mother down to the cafeteria for some coffee or something? The doctor told her the same thing I'm telling you about thirty minutes ago, and she started going crazy. We almost had to call security to come and get her out of the room, but your brother got here and was able to calm her down."

When I looked over at Julia, she was standing next to Benji, watching me and Tran. Her eyes weren't filled with tears, like they were a few minutes ago. The smeared makeup on her face had been wiped away and replaced with a brand-new coat. She looked as if she was camera ready, with her red designer dress, nude heels, and perfectly coiffed hair. The handkerchief in her hand covered her lips as she whispered something to Benji, who looked at me, then back at her.

"I'm sure Benji will keep an eye on her." I reached in my pocket, pulled out one of my cards, and handed it to Tran. "If anything happens or changes with my father, please have someone call me directly. And if possible, please make sure the media is prohibited from entering this area. Our family already has enough going on in the tabloids. I don't want this to get out and be on the ten o'clock news."

"We will make sure no one other than immediate family is allowed back here. Are you leaving right now?"

"I left my bike parked in the no parking section, so I'm going to go move it before someone else does. Then I'll go to the cafeteria for a bite to eat."

Nodding her head, Tran tucked my card in her breast pocket and then went back into my father's room to check his vitals again. Without a word to Benji or Julia, I headed back toward the stairs and took them all the way down to the floor with the emergency room exit. Luckily, my bike was in the same spot that I had left it in and had not been towed away. However, I grabbed the fat-ass ticket that had been placed on it, and made a mental note to take care of it as soon as I got home later that night.

After finding a parking spot near the front of the ER, I sat on a small bench in the outdoor smoking area and pulled out my phone to try to reach Mel. Not wanting to leave a message after the third unanswered call, I shot her a quick text and told her to call me back whenever she got a chance. Once I went through a few e-mails and checked in with Viktoria, I decided to head back inside the hospital to see if there was any improvement in my father's condition and to grab something to eat.

Just as I stepped into the street to take a shortcut to the ER, that crazy feeling I seemed to get whenever Melonee was nearby shot through my entire body. With the hairs standing on the back of my neck and my phone getting wet from the sweat of my palms, I searched the surrounding area but didn't see her anywhere. If that wasn't weird enough, a second later, a strong force that felt like a quick punch to my stomach had me crouched over in the middle of the street and gasping for air.

"Are you okay, sir?" asked a nurse who was smoking a cigarette near a tall bush. He put the cigarette out with the bottom of his shoe and then walked over to me.

"Yeah, I'm okay. I don't really know what that was. Felt like someone hit me in my gut."

"You're sure you don't need any medical help, right?"

I stood up to my full height and shook off whatever that was. "I'm good. Thanks for asking."

He stared at me for a second, as if he was trying to remember me from somewhere. "You're Roman Black, aren't you?" When I didn't answer, he nodded his head. "Yeah, you are. Those green eyes and your face are embedded in my mind. My girlfriend Googled you after that shit about you being a rapist and shit hit the news." He stuck out his hand. "I'm Joc, by the way. Nice to meet you."

"Nice to meet you too, Joc." I shook his hand.

"For the record, I don't think you did it."

"No?"

He shook his head. "Nope. And I'm not saying this only because I applied to be a delivery driver at RTD, either."

I looked at him with raised brows and laughed. "Your vote of confidence is duly noted, Joc, and I thank you for it. I'll have someone look into the application you filled out and get back to you, but I gotta go now."

As I walked away, I thought the short conversation Joc and I had had was over; however, I wasn't surprised to find Joc following behind me.

"Do you want to know why I don't think you did it?" he called.

"I'm pretty sure you're going to tell me whether I want you to or . . . ," I began as I walked through the ER doors, but I trailed off when I noticed the woman from the picture Chasin had sent me pacing the emergency room floor with a scowl on her face. She had her cell phone glued to her ear and was talking a mile a minute and waving her hands in the air. It seemed that whoever she was talking to was asking a lot of questions and making her more irritated by the second. "Hey, Joc, hold that thought for a second. I see someone I need to speak to."

Before he could respond, I was across the lobby and was standing in front of the plus-size beauty who I was sure had Chasin's attention. When she noticed my presence, she looked at me and then shook her head. And then she just went on talking.

"Look, Fiona, don't call my phone anymore, asking me all these damn questions," she said into the phone. "If you're so worried about Melonee, hop your ass off whoever's dick I hear in the background and come up here. . . . Bitch, I don't give a fuck. I told Mel to drop your trifling ass as a friend a long time ago. . . . On a scale of one to ten? Bitch, are you kidding me? It don't matter how much pain she's in! You, as her 'best friend,' should be up here to check on her regardless. . . . Proof is on his way. He had to drop off the munchkin. Wait, why am I explaining shit to you? Bring your ass up here, because Melonee wants you here. If not, trust and believe the next time I see you, I'ma slap the shit out of you." She ended the call abruptly.

Once her call was done, she turned her attention to me and held her hand up to keep me silent. "I already know who you are and why you walked up to me, Roman. I'm Melonee's aunt Brenae, but you can call me Bree. They just took her to the back, so I don't know how she or the baby is doing right now."

"Baby?" I gasped. That single word knocked the hell out of me. "Melonee's pregnant?"

Chasin's future wife hung her head down. "Shit . . . I forgot you didn't know. Um, I'm not one to bullshit or beat around the bush—plus, I'm hungry as hell right now, and my attitude is on ten—so I'ma tell you like this. The night you and Melonee 'made love,' as she put it, y'all created a baby. At first, she thought that the baby belonged to the person who attacked her, but now she believes that the baby belongs to you. She was going to tell you when you came to my house tonight, but you canceled on her. All this shit is crazy as fuck to me, but if my niece believes the baby is yours, so do I. I don't know what's going on now. All I can tell you is that she started having contractions and then started bleeding. Hopefully, everything is okay and you two will be parents in a few months. . . ." She shook her head. "If not, this might destroy my poor niece."

My head was swimming with the news that had just been told to me. Melonee was pregnant . . . and by me, at that. I closed my eyes and thought back to the one night that she and I had had sex. My memory was a little fuzzy about everything that had gone down, but I did remember emptying my entire soul and existence into her as I came. There had been no barrier between us that night, and I didn't regret it at all. Just that fast, my day had gone from being one of the scariest in my life to one of the best. When I had first laid eyes on Mel at Decadence, I knew that she would one day carry my child and wear my last name. I just hadn't thought it would happen this soon. While I was still marveling at the news that I was about to become a father, I felt a light tap on my shoulder. It was Joc.

"Hey, I heard everything she just said. If you want, I can go back and see what's going on with the baby and it's mother," he said in a low voice.

I nodded my head at Joc and then sat down in one of the vacant seats behind me. Bree walked over and sat next to me.

"It's a lot to soak in, huh?" she asked, eyes focused on me.

"It is, especially when she doesn't really remember what happened that night."

Bree crossed her legs and then leaned back in the chair. "Mel remembers some things, just not everything. One of the memories she's real adamant about is that you are not the one who attacked her. She's always said that to me, even after her trifling-ass friend Fiona kept trying to tell her that you did attack her." Bree laughed. "You don't know how many nights I have had to listen to Melonee talk about Roman Black.

About how sweet you are, how gentle you are . . . and those sexy green eyes of yours."

We sat in silence for a few minutes before she continued. "Can I ask you something, Roman?"

I nodded my head and looked directly into her eyes. Sitting this close to Bree, I could honestly see why Chasin was interested in finding out who she was. Her hazel eyes, cute round face, full lips, high cheekbones, and almond-shaped eyes would have any man drooling at her feet.

"Do you love my niece?" she asked, totally catching me off guard.

"Excuse me?"

"I said, do you love my niece?"

I cleared my throat. "I . . . um . . ."

"Don't give me that bullshit, Mr. Black." Bree laughed. "The way Melonee talks about the connection you two share, I'm pretty sure you feel the same way about her as she does about you."

I could hear people start to whisper around us at the mention of my name. From the looks on some of their faces, Bree saying my last name had confirmed who I was. While many continued to mind their business, there were some who pulled their phones out and started snapping pictures. I didn't know what they were expecting to see, but my reaction to their cameras now being in my face wasn't on their list.

My phone began to ring in my pocket, but I ignored it, as I already knew who it was.

I blew out a breath and wiped my hand over my face. Leaning back in my seat, I tilted my head back as far as it would go and closed my eyes. The conversation Uncle Kazi and I had had on this same topic back in Russia a few months ago invaded my thoughts.

"You love this girl, no?" he asked with his thick Russian accent.

I looked out the window at my uncle's beautiful garden that had been planted in memory of my mother, and thought about lying to him. Would he think I was crazy for falling in love with Melonee after being with her for only one night? Was it wrong that I craved her very being, that I longed to have her in my arms right now, even though I'd been ordered to stay away from her? In my heart, I believed that this thing between us was meant to be, regardless of what was going on around us, but my mind still had its doubts.

Uncle Kazi placed his hand on my shoulder and handed me the shot of vodka that he had poured for himself.

"Do you think I'm crazy for falling in love with her?" I asked.

"Depends on what your definition of crazy is. I've seen and heard a lot of craziness in my lifetime."

"Anything similar to my situation?"

I noticed a look of longing cross over his face. "When it comes to love, we're all crazy in some way, Roman."

"Why do you say that?"

He looked at me, then out at his garden. Standing tall, with his hands folded behind his back, dark eyes focused on something in the distance, he said, "If I told you that I fell in love and started a relationship with a woman I was given a contract to kill, would you think I was crazy?"

I slowly shook my head. "Not really."

"What if I told you that I put a bullet between her eyes the day after she gave birth to my child? Would that still be your answer?"

When I didn't respond, Uncle Kazi turned his hard gaze on me and smirked. "Like I said, nephew, when it comes to love, we're all a little crazy."

"So are you going to sit there and ignore me or answer my question?" Bree's voice floated to my ear, causing me to open my eyes and sit up.

Without hesitation, I replied, "I do."

A small smile played on her lips before she nodded her head in approval. "Well, I hope you're ready—" Bree began, but she was cut off when Joc came running up to us.

"Something was wrong. I don't know all the details, but they are about to perform an emergency C-section right now on your friend," Joc announced. He turned to walk away but stopped in his tracks when he noticed we were not following behind him. "You are the father, right?"

I looked at Bree, then back at him, and nodded my head.

"Well, come on, then. Don't you want to see the birth of your baby?" he said.

Without any further hesitation, I followed behind Joc. He led me to the room where they were about to remove my child from Melonee's body. Another nurse verified that I was the father, and let me in the delivery room. Melonee's screams and cries echoed throughout the room until her eyes connected with mine. At that second, it felt like everything around us stopped and only we were in the delivery room. A small smile formed on her lips as tears started falling from those beautiful gray eyes.

"Roman . . . ," she cried with a small laugh before her eyes rolled to the back of her head and she passed out.

Fiona

"Dreams," by the Game, was knocking hard in my car as I sped down the freeway toward the valley. So much stuff was going through my mind that I really didn't want to think about, one being the phone call I had just got from my uncle Dro a few minutes ago, in which he requested another fifty K payment. That nigga was crazy if he thought he was going to get anything else out of me. He had done his job and had already got compensated for it. I'd be damned if I'd pay him again for some shit I could've found a muthafucka off the street to do for two Gs. The only reason he had got that first fifty K was that I knew Benji would give it up to make sure his involvement in Melonee's attack would stay on the low. Uncle Dro really had the game fucked up if he thought we would keep breaking him off to keep his lips sealed. I'd kill that bitch-ass nigga myself before that happened.

While I took a puff from the Black & Mild I had just lit, my mind drifted to Melonee and the last conversation we had had. My so-called best friend was a sneaky, selfish bitch, and I had honestly underestimated her. I had called Cowboy and had told him to check into her finances to see if he could find out where all this money was sitting at, but the nigga hadn't returned any of my calls yet. I made a mental note to stop by his place after I left here to check on him and to see where the fuck his ass had been.

Blowing out a thick cloud of smoke, I smiled to myself at the new plan I had for Melonee's ass. The bitch still seemed to be living a happy life, even after the shit that had happened to her, and I couldn't stand it. When she vowed to be a part of the BWC, she had promised to break bread with us, ride till the end with us, and to always make getting this money her number one priority. But somewhere along the way, the bitch had stopped being about the BWC and had turned to looking out for herself. She had me all the way fucked up if she thought that she wasn't about to hand over some of that other money she got from the marriage she had with Doug. I deserved my cut of that, just like everyone else. Best friend or not, Melonee's ass was about to come up off that money; she just didn't know it yet.

My "no fucks given" attitude was at an all-time high right now, and no one was excluded. Especially Bree's fat ass. The way she had come at me on the phone the other day was super disrespectful. When she called to tell me that Mel had been rushed to the hospital because she had started having contractions and bleeding out, I had acted like I was really concerned, but in actuality, I really didn't give a fuck. Low key, I prayed to God that she would lose the damn baby so that she could feel some sort of hurt in her heart like I did, because obviously, she was doing just fine after getting the shit beat out of her.

I pulled up to the new house Benji had just purchased for himself in Santa Barbara, and shook my head. The private and secluded Mediterranean estate was a beautiful sight, but in my opinion, it was not worth the 5.7 million dollars he had paid for it. The twenty-three-thousand-dollar monthly mortgage alone would've turned me away, but I guessed when you were the new CEO of a multimillion-dollar company that had just closed two-billion-dollar international deals, money wasn't a thing. The view overlooking the ocean, a bird refuge, the harbor, and the city was indeed a fantastic one, but the place was still not worth that 5.7 million.

I walked up the pathway that was paved with red flagstone to the front door and rang the bell. A short Hispanic chick with a French maid's outfit, fishnet stockings, and some sky-high stilettos answered the door and smiled.

"Hola. Cómo puedo ayudarte?"

"Where's Benji?"

"Qué?"

"I know you speak English, little Spanish fly. Where's your boss?" I snapped as I sized her up. Benji had told me that he hired some staff for the house, but I hadn't expected a knockoff Jennifer Lopez to be among the new help.

She stared at me for a moment before shifting all her weight to her left foot and placing her hands on her wide hips. "You must be Fiona."

"If you know who I am already, that means you knew I was coming. Be a good little worker now and take me to my man." I didn't know why I had said that. Benji and I were nowhere near a couple, even though I kind of wanted us to be. Where that feeling had come from, I didn't know. I guessed you could blame it on the mind-blowing sex, the out-of-this-world head, and the fact that he was worth so much money right now. Just thinking about his net worth had my pussy wet as hell.

A small smirk played on this bitch's full lips as she looked over her shoulder at the empty foyer, then back at me. "Your man, huh?" She crossed her arms over her silicone-filled titties. "Benji told me that you had a smart-ass mouth. You're a rude little bitch, I see."

"He also should've told you that I have no problem beating a ho's ass. Stay in your place and your lane before you find your fake ass on the corner with the rest of your *familia*, selling fruit cups and pillows," I said, pushing past her and into the house. "Benji . . . ," I yelled. If she didn't want to take me to him, I was going to make him come to me. "Benji."

"And you have no home training, either. Oh, *Dios mío*. Benji sure does know how to pick 'em," said the wannabe Sofia Vergara as she closed the door and locked it.

Her eyes scanned my body from head to toe as she slowly walked around me. Although my titties weren't as big as hers, I knew my curvy frame still looked good in the tight jeans and the BOSS BITCH tank top that I had on. The thigh-high boots matched the black fedora hat on top of my head, while the light makeup on my face complemented the purple spiral curls in my hair.

"Never knew he had a taste for ghetto bitches, but you never know with him. His dick seems not to discriminate nowadays, I see," she mumbled to herself.

"What the fuck did you say?" I growled at her, but then I quickly turned my gaze in the direction of the wall from behind which Benji had just appeared.

"What the fuck you yelling for, Fiona?" he asked as his ass strolled to the front of his house. He was dressed in a big black robe and some silk pajama pants that were hanging low on his hips, that sexy washboard stomach and his V shape on full display. With a cigar hanging from his mouth, and a glass of some brown liquor in his hand, Benji was looking like the rich playboy that he was. No lie, he looked sexy as fuck too, with the light five o'clock shadow on his face and those dark eyes dripping with nothing but pure lust. I had to squeeze my thighs together to stop my clit from thumping so hard. Although I would rather enjoy christening every part of this small mansion with him right now, my reason for being here at this moment was strictly business.

The shit going on with Mel, this baby, and Roman had me really feeling some type of way. Not only that, but to know that this bitch had that huge amount of money sitting somewhere, untouched, had my left palm itching, and I knew that I would need Benji's help again to take it from her.

After walking up to me, my sexy partner in crime wrapped me in his arms and pulled me close. After kissing my cheek a couple of times, he lightly brushed his lips against mine before burying his nose in my neck and inhaling. "You always smell so good. Let's go to my room for a few minutes. I wanna show you the bed I just had flown in from Italy."

I pushed him off me. "Stop, Benji. I'm not here to see your pussy dungeon right now. We need to talk." I looked back at J Ho and noticed how she was pretending to clean up while ear hustling. "In private."

"Let's go to my bedroom, then. We can talk in private there," he suggested while grabbing my hand.

"No, Benji, I already told you. If we go to your bedroom, you and I both know we won't get any talking done. Let's go in the living room or in one of the other ten rooms I know you got in this muthafucka."

"We can't go in the living room."

"Why?"

He took a sip of his drink and hissed, "Because my mother's in there."

"Julia's here?"

"She is. Been here since Richard was admitted to the hospital."

Benji took a pull of his cigar before turning around and leading me into a room that was lined with panoramic windows that afforded a view of the city and was furnished with all-white furniture. Everything, from the fireplace to the big fur animal rug that was laid out on the floor in front of the couch, was white. Whoever had decorated the house for him was worth every penny he or she must've charged.

"Take your shoes off before going any farther," he said over his shoulder as he let my hand go and dumped the ashes from his cigar in a crystal ashtray. Molly the maid fluffed a few pillows on the couch before refilling Benji's glass with some more of whatever liquor he was drinking. "What did you want to talk about?"

"Didn't I say in private, Benji?"

"Carmen isn't going to repeat anything we talk about in here, so go ahead and say what you need to say."

The bitch had the nerve to smirk at me as she began dusting off the white baby grand piano, which I was sure was in here only for show.

"I don't know her, which means I don't trust her," I countered as I sat down on the couch.

"Your trust in people is up in the air with me right now."

"What the fuck does that mean?"

"Am I or am I not out of fifty K because of the uncle you trusted to do a job and then disappear?"

"But that's—" I began, but Benji held up his hand to cut me off.

"That the same uncle who called me early this morning, requesting another fifty K to keep his mouth shut," he growled.

I silently cursed myself for not listening to my father and leaving Pedro's money-hungry ass alone. Seemed like I was more like him than I was like my own daddy.

"Don't worry about my uncle Dro. I'll take care of him," I said. "What I want to talk to you about is Melonee and how I need your help with what I have planned for her."

Benji shook his head and laughed. "What's up with you and this revenge shit against Melonee? At first, I thought it was kind of hot that we both bonded behind wanting to fuck up the lives of people we considered family, but now it seems like your taste for revenge is on a whole other level. You have to know when to stop and leave well enough alone, babe, before the shit starts to blow up in your face. What have I always told you? Come up with a plan, execute it, and then get out. Three things to live by when you're doing 'white-collar' crime. The little shit you had going with the Black Widow Clique, or whatever y'all call it, was cool when you were getting money from those cheap-ass insurance policies. But you're in the big leagues now."

He went on. "You see me. I got what the fuck I wanted and haven't thought about my poor stepbrother since. Roman's position, his money, and basically his life are all mine, like they should've been from the beginning. When he goes to jail behind those rape charges or that IRS bullshit, I will call a press conference to express the hurt my family has suffered from Roman's bad choices in life. Then, after that . . ." He shrugged his shoulders.

I heard everything Benji was saying, but I wasn't trying to hear that shit. It was because of Melonee and her ho-ass mama that I had to grow up without my father or my mother. It was because of them same two bitches that I had to do things no fifteen-year-old should have to do, and I wouldn't have been subjected to this had my parents been around. It was because of Melonee that my life had been pure hell since the day she came into it. When we were young, I noticed the way my father would coddle her and give her more attention whenever she and Shaunie came around. I also noticed how whenever my father bought me something, he would make sure

Melonee got the same thing. And as if her robbing my childhood wasn't enough, the bitch was about to try to stop my cash flow with the BWC, something I wasn't seeing eye to eye with her about. Before that shit went down, though, I was going to make Melonee's life a living hell.

"Well, well. Who do we have here?" Benji's mother said as she sashayed into the room like the ice queen that she was. "Fiona dear, Benjamin didn't mention that you were coming over today. What brought this visit about?"

I got up from my seat on the couch to hug Julia and continued to stand. I didn't trust her old ass for shit. "I wanted to talk to Benji about some shit."

"Carmen, will you please do me a favor and go to the parlor and make me a White Russian?" Julia said. Then she turned back around to me. "Would you like something to drink, Fiona dear?" The expression on Carmen's face was hard.

"Naw, I'm good. If I can't watch her make my shit, then I don't want it."

Julia smiled. "Good girl. I don't know why my Benjamin has to have all these exotic pets around when he has the perfect woman in you. Cunning, manipulative, cutthroat, and loves money. Reminds me of someone else I know." She winked her eye at me and went and sat on the couch. Patting the spot next to her, Julia summoned me to sit back down. I did. "Now, what is it that you needed to talk to Benjamin about?"

By the time I finished telling them everything that was on my mind, from the money that Mel had told me about to the fact that she thought the baby she was carrying actually belonged to Roman, Carmen had returned with Julia's drink—and with the last person I expected to see.

"I see the party is all here and is making plans without me," the newcomer said.

"April, you know we never make a move without everyone in the group being privy to what's going on," Julia replied before she took a sip of her White Russian. "Now play nice and say hello to your daughter."

April looked at me and smirked. "How's your jaw doing, baby girl? I didn't mean to hit you that hard, but you were giving my man so much lip."

If you haven't figured it out already, the person who was there with Uncle Dro the day he broke into my house was my long-lost mother. The same woman who had knocked me out and had had one gun pointed at the back of my head and one at my back, ready to kill me if Uncle Dro gave the word.

The second I laid eyes on her now, I knew who she was. She was somewhat identical to me: my mother and I shared the same height, the same dark brown eye color, the same petite body frame and, apparently, the same attitude.

The only thing that I had got from my father was his skin tone and his hair. Everything else I had inherited from April. Despite the fact that ours was a dysfunctional relationship, you would have thought that our little reunion would be all emotional and shit, but April was more interested in the fifty K Benji had dropped off than any of the questions I had for her. Her intention was to talk about money, then bounce.

Looking at my mother, I couldn't help it when my eyes became a little misty. But I regretted this after she noticed and laughed.

"Come on now, Fiona," she said with a smug look on her face. "I know you're not about to get sentimental on me again. Like I told you before, street bitches don't have emotions. It's the law of the land. Money is the motive, and money is what makes you cum. You know that. I used to whisper that shit to you every night, before I put you to bed."

"April, don't be so hard on the girl. I mean, you just popped back up in her life, with no explanation about where you've been for the past twenty years. How do you think she's supposed to feel?" Julia interjected, coming to my defense.

"Honestly, I don't give a fuck how she feels. Maxwell raised her right, and she didn't end up in no foster-care system when his dumb ass ended up in jail, so what is she feeling some type of way about? Yeah, money was scarce in the beginning, but she got her shit together. And she obviously isn't hurting for nothing, with those Gianvito Rossi boots on her feet and that presidential Rolex hanging from her wrist."

Julia laughed. "You've always had an eye for fashion. Between you and Shaunie, I don't know who stayed in the mall more, boosting that expensive shit from Neiman Marcus, Saks, and Barneys."

"Shaunie?" I asked, assuming they were talking about Melonee's mom. "You all were friends?"

"Friends?" Julia scoffed, as if I had offended her. "Who do you think started the original Black Widow Clique in the first place? I know when you met Benji all those years ago, you didn't think the little seed he planted in your ear about setting men up for money came from him, right?" Her boisterous laughter filled the room. "Oh no, no, no, honey. Your mother, myself, and Shaunie started it all. And if I might say, we were quite the crew back in the day."

My eyes traveled over to Benji for some type of confirmation, but he was too busy whispering something in Carmen's ear while she sat on his lap and rubbed his chest.

"See? That's your problem right there. Opening up your heart to emotions when it should only open for money," my mother said as she walked over to the two lovebirds. Before Carmen had a chance to place her lips on Benji's, April grabbed a handful of her hair and threw the Mexican ho down on the white-carpeted floor. Her body hit the floor with the same thud that a sack of potatoes might make when thrown. A loud yelp tore from Carmen's lips.

"Really, April?" Julia snarled. "Now the bitch's blood will be on my son's carpet. Do you know how long it took me to find this? How much it cost per square foot?"

April shrugged her shoulder, leaned over the piano, and pressed a few keys like she knew what she was doing. An all-black outfit hugged her body, the same way one had the last time I saw her. "I told you that I didn't like the bitch when I first met her. Fiona having a problem with her only gave me the okay to do something about it."

"I told you that your motherly instinct would hit you once you started to be around her," Julia commented. She finished her drink and sat the cup on the glass end table, then looked at me. "Now, I like the little idea you just told us about, Fiona dear, but I think I have one that is much better. Especially if this DNA test comes back and shows that Roman is indeed the father of this baby Melonee just gave birth to."

Carmen groaned and tried to rise up from the floor, but she fell back down when my mother accidentally bumped her as she passed by her.

"What's on your mind, Julia? You know you've always been the brains behind this operation," April said.

"Benjamin, honey, help Carmen up and do something with her. I don't want her around when we start talking official widows' business," Julia said.

April laughed. "Widows' business? Your husband isn't dead."

"You forgot to add *yet* to the end of your statement." Julia smiled as she looked at me.

"Hold up. Wait one minute. What makes you think I want to do anything with the two of you or cut you in on any of this money?" I said. My eyes went over to my mother, who was smirking and shaking her head, as always. She moved from her spot at the piano and sat on the couch across from me and Julia.

"You don't have no other choice, Fiona, because you're already in too deep, baby girl. I know I'm your mother and all, but I will kill you if you come between me and this money. So shut up, listen up, and take some fucking notes."

Melonee

"So it was all a setup, huh?" Roman said as he sat in the chair near my hospital bed.

I looked at the flowers and balloons, tokens of well wishes and congratulations, that filled my room, trying to avoid eye contact with Roman, which was kind of hard to do. For the past few days, ever since my surgery, we had been in my hospital room, getting to know each other on a personal, emotional, and at times spiritual level. In between his visits to see his father, who was still in bad shape after his heart attack, and his visits to see my son in NICU, we'd had some very interesting conversations with each other. And the connection that we'd shared since the first time I laid eyes on him seemed to be getting stronger every day.

Spending time with Roman had been great. Not only did I know pretty much everything about him and his family now, but I'd also had the pleasure of meeting some very important people in his life, like his best friend, Marques; his lawyer and good friend, Chasin, who, by the way, had been sniffing behind Aunt Bree like a love-struck puppy; and his strikingly beautiful and very smart cousin Viktoria. The half-Russian and half-black siren had an attitude that was out of this world. She'd been a little stand-offish when we first met, but once she'd realized that I didn't have a problem with having a DNA test performed on my baby, and that my feelings for Roman were genuine, she kind of opened up to me. Her ass was here just as much as Roman was, when she wasn't working on his case. We had kind of developed a little friendship, and in all honesty, I liked it.

Although I was celebrating the birth of my second child with my new set of friends, I still felt some type of way about Fiona not showing up at the hospital at all. She was a straight no-call, no-show. Even though I'd called her phone over a dozen times, I still hadn't heard anything back from her. I'd even sent pictures of my baby in his little incubator and all, and still no response. Bree had told me to let sleeping dogs lie and to take this as a sign that Fiona and I had finally reached the point in our friendship where it was best for us to part ways, but I couldn't let it end like this. At least not without an explanation.

I mean, Fiona had been there for my whole pregnancy and for the birth of Madison, so I had assumed she would be here for this one as well, regardless of how he was conceived. But I guessed I was wrong. The last time we spoke to each other at Bree's house, the conversation had got a little heated, but that wasn't out of the norm for us. Looking at my phone, which was on the makeshift nightstand, I thought about sending her another text message but did not. Maybe I should just take Bree's advice, seeing as she'd been right about Mr. Black here.

The atmosphere in the room had shifted a little, owing to the conversation we had been having for the past hour or so, and I could feel it. There was a little tension now, and I didn't like it. But when Roman had asked me what I did for a living, I didn't know why, but I had told him the truth. I had told him about everything I'd done since the day my mother died up until now. Told him about the Black Widow Clique, what we were about, and how we got our money. Told him how he had been our newest mark, and how he was supposed to be the wealthy bachelor that Fiona snagged and everything.

I knew telling him the truth was probably the dumbest thing on my part, but if we were going to have any chance to raise a baby and be a family together, he had to know the truth. I didn't want any secrets between us. Besides, I would rather he hear it from me than from somebody else. That someone else mainly being Fiona. She'd threatened to expose what I'd done a few times when I wouldn't agree to lie about Roman being my attacker and when I first told her that I wanted out of the BWC. The fact that our friendship was dissolving would probably give her the jump to do it now.

I looked at Roman, and those green eyes that mirrored my son's stared back at me. After an emergency C-section, I was now the proud mother of a bouncing baby boy. At twenty-nine weeks, he was what the hospital considered a very premature baby, so he had a few complications right now. I wished like hell I could have carried him to full term, but I guessed this was a bit of karma for me. My heart broke every time I went to the NICU to visit him. All the IVs stuck in his little body, helping with his digestive system; the big tube going through his nose to help him breath; and all the stickers on his chest, wrists, and feet, monitoring his heart rate, breathing rate, and oxygen saturation, always had my eyes filling with tears and me praying that my little boy would be okay.

The daily progress he was making was the only thing that kept me from breaking down completely. Like this morning, when I got the opportunity to feed him with a bottle instead of through a tube, my heart damn near exploded. When I looked up and saw Roman watching us from behind the large window that looked onto the nursery, with this prideful look on his face, I fell in love with both of these Black men all over again. But after admitting to him what I'd done in my life, I just hoped that Roman found some way in his heart to forgive me.

An awkward yet comfortable silence passed between us before he spoke again.

"The waitress at Decadence, the one who was in our VIP section that night, trying to get my attention, she was in on it too?"

I slowly nodded my head. "Fiona is actually the brains behind everything. She finds the men we target, does the research, then gives us the information."

"And your daughter's father? He's a part of this clique thing as well?"

I nodded my head again, and Roman shook his head in disbelief.

He and Proof had met briefly the night that I was brought to the hospital. I hadn't been out there to see everything that went down, but

Bree had told me that shit went way left the second Proof walked into the nursery and saw Roman standing there, looking at the baby. What started out as a shouting match in the hallway turned into a full-out brawl by the time they got to the lobby. Proof didn't understand why Roman was there, and Roman was simply trying to defend himself from Proof. Some dumb shit, if you asked me. Especially since Madison was out there with them. Too tired to deal with everything that was going on, and not in the mood to explain my reasons for wanting Roman to be here with me, I asked Proof to leave. Aunt Bree ended up taking the munchkin for the night, giving her father some time to cool off and me some time to spend with Roman alone for the first time since the night we last saw each other.

Somewhere down the line, though, paparazzi had got word of the birth of my child and had started doing any and everything they could do to get a shot of Roman and me together or of my baby. The foot traffic in and out of the hospital had got so bad that I was moved to a more private room, one normally reserved for celebrity patients.

Newspapers as well as blogs had been reporting all types of crazy things. One newspaper had gone so far as to say that Roman's presence at the same hospital I was in was in no way a coincidence. According to the paper, he was here to finish the job he had started—and that meant getting rid of the baby in order to stop any DNA test from being performed and proving his guilt—so that he wouldn't spend one single night in jail. The sleezy tabloid stories were geared toward me a bit more, saying that I was suffering from some type of psychological trauma that had me confusing the hatred I should have for my attacker with lust. It was crazy, because even after I had the DA drop the charges against Roman, people were still speculating that he was engineering some type of foul play.

I smoothed back my hair, which was in a high bun on top of my head, and pulled at the ugly hospital gown, which was falling off my shoulder. After throwing the sheets off my legs, I carefully got out of the uncomfortable bed, pulled the IV pole alongside me, and went to the bathroom. Still a little sore from the big-ass gash across the lower part of my belly, I handled my business. As I washed my hands, I finally answered Roman's question.

"Yes, Proof . . . I mean Jaylen, is a part of it too. His position is what we like to call the enforcer.

Pretty much the muscle we need just in case some shit doesn't go right." I slowly walked back to the bed and sat on the edge of it and looked at Roman.

His eyes were a little misty, and he looked away when he noticed me staring at him. Sitting back in his chair, he ran his hand down his handsome face, and I couldn't help the tingle that shot through me just by my looking at the sexy sight in front of me. The five o'clock shadow covering almost half his profile did nothing but enhance his strong jawline. His curly caramel-blond locks were a little longer than they were when I first met him. His skin was a little pale today, despite his tan, but it didn't take away from his sexiness. I wanted to grab him by his ears and kiss away any doubt he had about my love for him, but I waited for him to get off whatever else he had on his chest.

The silence was killing me.

"Will you say something?" I urged.

Roman flexed the muscles in his jaw. "What do you want me to say, Melonee? What could you possibly want to hear me say?"

"I don't know. Something. I'm—" I began, but he cut me off.

"You just told me that you and your friends were planning to kill me," he said, his voice a little louder now. "I'm still trying to figure out how exactly am I supposed to respond to that. Or even try to understand that in my mind without feeling some type of way. The woman who has literally invaded every waking thought I've had since the day I met her, the woman whom I've craved since the night you let me inside you, the woman who just gave birth to my son wanted to *kill* me. And for some shit that I would've traded for you, had you given me the chance."

"The DNA test hasn't come back yet, Roman." Despite everything he had just said, this was the only thing I could think of to say in response. I was feeling guilty and ashamed, and all I wanted to do was make everything right—if I could.

"*DNA test?* Melonee, I don't need a test to tell me that that's my son out there. From the top of his tiny head to the bottom of his small feet, all three pounds and three ounces of him is me. You don't think I've noticed the color of his eyes whenever he opens them? Or the blond hairs on his tiny body, which seem to sprout from somewhere new every day? You don't see the way our son responds to me whenever I hold his small body in my hands? If the Black characteristics weren't a sign for me, that feeling I get in my chest whenever I hear his little cries or am simply in his presence, period, lets me know that I am his father. I didn't need a test. It was you and Viktoria who wanted one done."

Roman stood up from his seat, walked to the edge of the bed where I was sitting, and stood between my legs. After placing his fingers under my chin, he raised my face up toward him, and wiped away the few tears that had fallen from my eyes.

"I understand if you don't want anything to do with me after everything I've just told you. Us trying to be together would probably be crazy, right?" I said.

"It might be, but like my uncle Kazimir told me, *crazy* is how you define it." He laughed and placed his forehead against mine as his hands palmed both sides of my face. "If *crazy* means I fell in love with a blackmailing stripper, whom I unknowingly got pregnant on the night that she gave me some of the best sex in my life, then I guess I'm crazy. What's even crazier is that after telling me that she was in on a scheme to set me up and kill me for my money, I still can't help the way my heart skips a beat whenever she smiles." He paused and licked his lips. "Or the way my dick gets hard whenever she pouts her full lips or flashes me that thick, sexy ass whenever she walks to the bathroom."

Roman kissed my lips, and the taste of him sent those electric jolts down my spine. I could feel my nipples pressing against the hospital gown, screaming to be touched. My lips parted slightly, and his tongue swept inside my mouth, causing a low moan to escape from the back of my throat. I'd been waiting all week for us to connect like this, and finally it was happening. Pulling him closer, I deepened the kiss, hoping he could feel the love behind it. A cool chill swept across my chest when Roman pulled the hospital gown down and exposed my breasts. His fingers lightly trailed down my skin until they found my nipples and tenderly squeezed, causing a little of my breast milk to trickle out.

"You are absolutely breathtaking. I hate that I wasn't able to experience the changes in your body when you were carrying my child. You don't know how bad I want you right now, Melonee," he breathlessly whispered in my ear. "How hard you got my dick right now."

My eyes immediately focused on the bulge between his legs. The blue sweatpants he had on gave me the perfect view. "I . . . I'm ready right now," I responded, lips already missing the softness of his. Small lump was stuck in my throat from it being so dry. "I want you just as bad, Roman. . . ."

He drew his bottom lip into his mouth, and I swear I felt the walls in my pussy collapse from the tidal wave of juices that just came flooding out. When he brushed his lips faintly against mine, I couldn't stop my short intake of breath before he pressed his mouth to mine again.

"Well, well, well, I see baby number two is in the works," Aunt Bree announced as she walked into my room. The overnight bag I had asked her to pick up from my house was on her shoulder, a bag containing her food and my Jeanne Jones Omelette and side waffle from Roscoe's House of Chicken and Waffles was in one hand, and my big-ass pile of mail was in the other. "You got me out here running your errands when your baby daddy looks well enough to do them for you."

Roman laughed and buried his face in the crook of my neck. The stubble on his face tickled my skin as he inhaled my scent.

"Hey, Bree. How are you?" he said, his voice muffled. The smile that I could feel on his lips as he kissed my shoulder caused me to smile.

"Like you really care," Aunt Bree joked and placed my things on the chair next to my bed and my food on my nightstand. "What have you guys been up to, besides dry humping in the hospital? Have you come up with a name for my nephew yet?"

"Yes and no, because we haven't made it official yet, but I want to name him Mason since that's the name that Madison likes," I replied.

"And I wanted to name him Kazimir, after my uncle," Roman added.

"So to compromise, we came up with the name Kason Zamir Black. What do you think?" I said.

Aunt Bree sat in the chair Roman was in earlier and opened the Styrofoam container with her food in it. The smell of fried chicken and syrup filled the air. After taking the lid off her souffle cup, she drizzled melted butter over her waffles and then two packs of syrup.

"I like the name Kason. What did Mama say?"

"She likes it too. Said he looks like a Kason Black." I laughed, thinking about the conversation I had had yesterday with my granny, when I told her about the baby's name. "Where's Madison? She's the only one who doesn't know her new brother's name."

Aunt Bree had just taken a bite of her chicken but still answered my question. "Proof came and got her before I came back here. Said he wanted to spend some time with her before he went to meet up with y'all's little crew. He said he'll drop her off at Mama's and I can pick her up there."

Fiona sure hadn't wasted any time in finding a new mark. If the clique had a meeting today, that meant information on the next lick was about to get passed around. Although I wasn't a part of the crew anymore, I was still in my feelings a little, knowing Fee had called a meeting but had yet to call me or come see me. Wiz, Mouse, and Banks had all stopped by this week, with gifts and everything, but not Fiona.

"I'm about to go check on my dad real quick, and then I'll go by the house to change. I'll be back in a few hours," Roman said, breaking me from my thoughts. He kissed my cheek. "You need me to bring you back anything?"

I shook my head no, got up from the edge of the bed, walked over to the opposite side, where my phone was, and picked it up. "I'll see you when you get back."

He nodded. "All right then. See you later, Bree."

"Bye, Roman," she said and then watched him leave. "With your fine ass," she mumbled after he was out of the room. "That man knows he sexy as hell for a white boy. I don't see how you do it. Especially with him being here damn near every day, looking like that. I would've fucked the shit out of his ass the minute I could start walking again. Popped a few extra pain pills just in case and would've been popping my ass on a handstand." Aunt Bree shook her head and stuffed a forkful of waffles in her mouth. "What you doing on your phone?"

I found Proof's name in my contacts and sent him a text.

Me: What's up? There's a BWC meeting today?

"Texting Proof."

Proof: About to drop my baby off at your granny's, then head out to meet up with the crew. Why?

"What you texting him for?" Aunt Bree asked.

Me: I wasn't informed about the meeting.

Proof: Didn't you quit?

Me: Yeah, but still. I guess I'm just in my feelings, because it seems like Fee is talking to everyone but me.

"I just had a question about Madison," I lied to Aunt Bree.

Proof: You know how your girl is. She's probably still mad that you don't want to fuck around with us anymore. To be honest, I've been thinking about falling back too. Getting into some legit shit. Don't want my baby growing up without me if something happens.

"Have you decided if you are coming to my house after you get discharged or going to your place?"

Me: If something happens? What's going on, Jaylen?

Proof: Nothing, Mel. Stop tripping. I just know we can't keep doing this shit forever. Someday the shit might catch up with us, and I'd rather get out before it does.

"Mel?" Aunt Bree called, touching my shoulder as she stood over me. "Is everything okay? Your whole attitude has changed. Are Proof and Madison okay?"

I licked my lips and looked up at my aunt, a forced smile on my face. "Yeah, everything is okay. He and Madison are all right. I was just thinking about something, that's all."

By the look on her face, I could tell that she didn't believe what I'd said, but instead of pushing the subject, she changed it. "So have you decided where you're going to stay after you leave the hospital? You know my house is always open. I love having you and the munchkin there."

I sent Proof one last text before responding to Aunt Bree's question.

Me: Well, be careful, Jaylen. And if shit doesn't seem right, you need to walk away. Madison and I both need you.

"Um . . . I think I'ma stay at your place until Kason is able to come home, since your place is closer to the hospital than mine. Once he's well enough to leave here, then I'll go to my house."

"So you're not going to take Roman up on his offer to stay at the beach house with him? His house is close to the hospital as well."

Roman had asked me to come stay with him, but I felt like it was too early. And although

I knew that he wasn't the one who had attacked me, just being in the place where it had happened might be a little too much for me. Memories of that night had been flashing in my mind a lot in the past couple of weeks. To the point that I had got a few glimpses of the man who actually beat me up. The man's identity was still fuzzy to me, but something about the way he moved was familiar. And the way he caressed my hair a couple of times while he was on top of me. I could taste his scent in my mouth sometimes, and I would know that smell from anywhere if I smelled it again.

"I don't think that would be a good idea right now. Plus, Roman hasn't officially been introduced to Madison yet. I can't move her into his house if she doesn't have some type of relationship with him."

Just then my phone pinged. Another text from Proof.

Proof: Didn't think you did, what with your Russian-mafia lover now in the picture

I laughed at Proof's hating ass.

"I can understand that. Well, the guest rooms are yours whenever you need them."

I thanked my aunt, then texted Proof.

Me: Regardless of who's in my life, Jaylen, you will always be the father of my firstborn. And for that, I will always love you.

"Will I run into Chasin while I'm staying in your guest quarters, Your Highness?" I asked with my fake British accent.

Aunt Bree blushed and shook her head. "No, you will not. Chasin and I are just friends right now, that's all."

"Friends who seem to be together damn near every day."

"Like you're one to talk. Roman hasn't left your side since Joc took us to the delivery room when you were in labor."

It was my turn to blush. "And I thank Joc for that every time he drops by to say hello."

My phone pinged. It was Proof again.

Proof: I love you too. Just pulled up to your granny's. I'll hit you after the meeting.

Proof: And keep my baby away from that white muthafucka. The only man she needs in her life is me.

Me: LOL. Bye, Proof.

I shook my head and placed my phone down on the nightstand. While my Aunt Bree finished her fried chicken and waffles, I opened my Styrofoam container from Roscoe's and dug in. After I had eaten all my omelette and waffle, my aunt headed out of the hospital, and I went to visit Kason in the nursery, where I got to hold him and feed him again. When my baby was finished with his meal, burped, and then changed,

I stayed in the nursery and just watched him, with happy tears in my eyes. I thanked God for allowing him to get better and better with each day.

I must've been tired, just like Kason was after filling his belly, because I ended up dozing off in my wheelchair at the same time he did in his bassinet. It wasn't until Roman gently shook my shoulder and rolled me back to my room that I woke up. But my eyes were still heavy, and my body was still in need of sleep, so Roman picked me up from the wheelchair and tucked me into my hospital bed. After taking his jacket off, he pulled the covers back a little and slid into bed with me. He pulled me closer to his chest and kissed me on my forehead before closing his eyes and joining me in the first comfortable sleep I'd had in a long time.

Fiona

My mind was going a mile a minute right now as I tried to figure out what my next move with this Melonee shit was going to be. The plan that Julia and April had come up with was sure to get us a boatload of money, but once we split it between the three of us and then gave some to the new heads that April was bringing in to help with this shit, I didn't see the point. Doing everything by myself seemed like a much better idea to me, since I would get a fat nest egg, but with this bitch clocking my every move now, it was kind of hard for me to put my plan into motion.

"You talk to your brother yet?" April asked me as she sat on the passenger side of my car, playing on her phone. We were on our way to the small warehouse out in Rancho Dominguez that we used whenever the clique met up to go over the details of this plan.

"Nah, I haven't seen or spoken to Cowboy in weeks. The last time we went to see Daddy was the last time I saw him."

"And that doesn't seem weird to you?"

I cut my eyes at her. "Why would it be weird? Cowboy does this sort of shit every now and then. Cuts himself off from the world and resurfaces after some time. But you would know this had you been around us when we were younger."

"What does me being around have to do with knowing when a nigga is moving funny?"

"Nigga? You talk about your own son like he some regular Joe Blow off the street. Like you didn't give birth to him. Like he's not family."

"Family is who you make it, baby girl. I may have pushed that *nigga* from my pussy, but that doesn't mean we have any sort of ties to one another."

I stared at this coldhearted bitch for a minute. Although I hated to admit it, she did kind of sound like me. I didn't use the word *family* lightly, but when I did, it meant something to me. Her talking about Cowboy the way she just did further let me know that she really wouldn't have a problem putting a bullet in my head if it came down to that. Regardless of whether I'd come out of her pussy or not. Uncle Dro wasn't lying when he said the apple didn't fall too far from the tree. Now I could see where I had got some of my vindictive ways from, but I would never tell her that. We sat in silence for a few minutes before April placed her phone in her pocket and then turned her attention to me.

"I see that your brother is a sensitive topic for you. What about your dad? How is he doing?" she said.

I looked out the window at the traffic surrounding us and shook my head. I hated the fact that I had to sit in the car with her for this long. Now she wanted to ask questions about my father, knowing damn well she didn't really give a fuck. She was probably just trying to get in my head to see if I had any weak spots. Funny thing was, I had only one, and she would never figure out what it was. I turned the radio up, hoping she would see that I wasn't really in the mood to talk, but she just turned it right back down and waited for me to answer her questions.

"Why don't you go and see for yourself? I'm sure he would be delighted to hear from you," I snapped.

"Because I'm asking you."

"That doesn't mean I have to tell you shit," I groaned and licked my lips, aggravated at this whole conversation. After looking over my shoulders to switch lanes, I cut off the car next to me and pressed my foot down on the gas, trying to hurry up and get to our destination.

I continued. "Look, April, why don't we go back to acting like we don't know shit about each other? Like you're not my mother and I'm not your daughter. We are coworkers, with one objective right now, and that's to get this money. Don't ask me about my father. Don't speak on my brother, and definitely stop trying to get in my head. You don't care for me, and I'm starting not to give a fuck about you. Because my father did teach me to be respectful, I won't disrespect you as my mother, but don't get shit fucked up. Now that I know all bets are off with any type of mother-daughter relationship with you, please know that I won't hesitate to put a bullet in your shit, either."

She laughed. "Oh, someone grew a pair, I see. But if that's the way you want it, Fiona, you got it, baby girl."

"And please stop calling me baby girl. You lost that privilege."

"Didn't really want it," she said before pulling her ringing phone out of her pocket and answering it.

Ten minutes later, we pulled up to the warehouse and were greeted by my crew— with the exception of Melonee and Cowboy—and the six niggas April had called in to come help out. Didn't think we really needed all these bodies, but we would see. I was going to be making cuts during this briefing session, and if I felt like they didn't fit the bill, then they were out. Fuck what April had to say. After making sure my gun was tucked in the back of my jeans, I grabbed my purse, keys, cranberry juice, and went inside.

"Aye, Fee, you know I'm down to ride with the clique and shit, but what you talking about right now, I'm not down with that at all. Mel ain't been nothing but loyal to us. How the fuck we gon' sit here and turn on our own?" Wiz said as he stood up from his seat. "Then you got these new niggas in here, like they a part of the fam. Where these gorilla-looking muthafuckas come from, anyway? You really tripping, Ma . . . hard."

"Sit your ass down and shut the fuck up, son," said one of April's men, who was introduced to me as Rocko. He laughed.

"What the fuck you gon' do if I don't, goofy-ass nigga?" Wiz lifted his shirt to show his gun. Banks, Mouse, and Proof all sat up in their chairs, ready for whatever.

"Yo, Fiona, you really work with these clowns? No wonder y'all ain't getting money like y'all should. Muthafuckas all in they feelings and shit," Rocko commented, then turned his attention to Wiz. "Y'all ain't the only niggas with guns in here, B. Understand that. And if you pull that shit out on me, make sure you aim right here." He pointed between his eyes. "Make sure a nigga really dead."

"Don't temp me, nigga," Wiz growled. Proof touched Wiz's shoulder and said something in his ear, causing Wiz to sit down in his seat.

"Do y'all still need a few more minutes to see whose dick is bigger?" April asked. "Or can we get back to the business at hand?"

"And who the fuck are you?" Proof wanted to know. His gemstone-green eyes were now a dark emerald color as his focus stayed on April. I could tell by the expression on his face that he wasn't feeling the plan, either, but was trying to gather a little more information before he expressed how he felt. With his hat turned backward, his arms folded across his chest, and a scowl on his face, I couldn't help but appreciate how fine Proof's ass really was. His walnut complexion, pouty pink lips, and athletic build were sexy as hell.

"Who I am shouldn't be a concern of yours right now," April said coolly.

"Anyone who has intent to harm my child or the mother of my child is a concern to me," Proof retorted.

April stared at him. "Did someone say anything about your child being touched? I coulda
swore it was the other man's child we were
talking about taking."

"Anything that affects Melonee will ultimately
affect my child, and I'm not about to put her
through that." Proof turned his cold gaze toward
me, and my pussy thumped. "I can't believe you
really down with this shit, either, Fiona. What
happened to loyalty? What happened to our
Black Widow Clique family? We've been eating
together for years, and now, because Mel wants
to do something better with her life, you mad?
You really about to kidnap your best friend's
child just because you're jealous she didn't give
you a piece of the money the nigga she married
left for her? Has it really come down to this?" He
pointed at April. "Are you that money hungry
that you would let this bitch and these fuck-ass
niggas talk you into doing the one person that's
had your back since y'all was younger like this?"

I shook my head. "Proof—"

"Proof, my ass," he snapped, cutting me off.
"You moving real grimy right now, Fee, and that
shit's not cool at all. I'm with my nigga Wiz
on this right here. Dead this shit and find us
another target, or I'm out, like Mel, too. These
new muthafuckas you brought up in here got

your thought process way off. Got you turning on the only family you've had since your pops went to jail."

"Why are y'all so quick to throw that damn word around in this bitch? You and I both know that there's no *family* unit in here," April said, a smirk on her face. "Where was all that family talk when you were fucking your baby's mama's best friend the night she was rushed to the hospital a couple of weeks ago?"

Proof's eyes shot toward me, and the scowl on his face deepened.

"Aw, nah, bruh. Please tell me you were not busting Fiona down while Mel was in the hospital," Banks said to Proof, turning his attention to him. "Don't tell me you did my girl like that!"

Banks's sympathy for Melonee had my blood boiling. "He didn't do Mel's ass like nothing, Banks. Her ass was in the hospital, having a baby by another muthafucka, or did you forget that? The same muthafucka she refused to help us blackmail after she woke up from her damn coma. Another way she was taking food from us and wanting to keep it all for herself. But y'all refuse to see it that way. Y'all sit in here and applaud Melonee's ass like she's the only one who was putting in work out here. Like she was the only one breaking bread with y'all."

My body started to shake, I was so mad. Hearing them defend or praise Mel was nothing new. But after seeing how selfish this bitch really was, I couldn't take it anymore. "What about me and my sacrifices? Huh? Do my feelings not matter as much as hers? You know what? Don't even answer that, because I can already see that they don't. So you know what? Fuck Melonee and whatever bullshit sympathy y'all have for her. She's not the only person who lost a parent back then. She's not the only person who had to come up with some kind of hustle to get this money. A hustle, I might add, that was working just fine for us until she fell in love with the nigga we were supposed to be setting up. A hustle that was feeding us crumbs and would've been one of our biggest come ups, had she stuck to the plan. Instead of feeling sorry for her, y'all asses need to be feeling anger toward her."

My blood was boiling harder now. "Did y'all know she had three houses?" I shook my head at the stuck expressions on their faces. "Nah, I bet y'all didn't know that. And they all paid for too. What about that five hundred K she got from her mama's insurance policy? Huh? Didn't tell y'all about that, either, right? From the look on your face, Proof, I'm assuming you didn't know about any of that." I threw my head back and laughed.

"Everything that has happened to Melonee since she deviated from the plan is exactly what she deserved. From her getting beat to within an inch of her life to the premature labor she went into. The bitch deserved all of that for what she's done."

"Damn, Ma. You really feel some type of way about this bitch, huh? If I didn't know any better, I would think that you were the one behind the attack you just mentioned and the cause of her going into premature labor," Rocko said as he typed away at some shit on his computer. He reminded me of Cowboy but was more thuggish. He was a little cutie with his chocolate skin and looked like a bearded Lamman Rucker. Dimple and all.

"Wait. Hold up. *Did* you have something to do with Melonee's attack, Fiona?" Mouse asked. "Because if so, that's some fucked-up shit, man," he added, looking like the rat-faced mutha-fucka he was.

Everybody in the room turned their attention toward me and waited for an answer. Proof especially. The way his nose was flaring and his chest was heaving up and down told me that he was ready to fuck me up if my answer wasn't the one he wanted to hear.

"Well . . . ?" April said, trying to instigate something, when I remained silent. "Are you going to tell them the truth, or are you going to continue to skate around it just so this cozy little *family* y'all started doesn't become a dysfunctional one?"

"Bitch, ain't nobody talking to you. We talking to Fiona. Now shut the fuck up, before your fate ends up the same as hers if she doesn't answer this question the right way," Proof said through gritted teeth. His dark eyes were burning holes into mine.

Obviously finding the threat Proof had just issued funny, April laughed and hopped down from her seat on top of some stacked-up boxes and walked over to where he was sitting. Standing in front of him, with one hip poking out and one arm behind her back, she tried to kiss Proof on his cheek, but she missed when he moved his face out of the way. After grabbing his head forcefully with her free hand, she stuck her tongue out of her mouth and licked his top and bottom lip before pulling her gun out and shooting him in the spot right behind his ear.

The loud sound of the shot from her gun ricocheted off the walls and through my body.

Blinking my eyes a few times, I tried to focus on the loud commotion that had started up as soon as Proof's lifeless body slumped over in his chair and fell to the floor. Before I had any time to react to what was going on, there was four more gunshots and four more loud thuds from bodies hitting the floor. Finally able to focus my eyes, I scanned the warehouse floor and saw Wiz, Banks, and Mouse lying lifeless a few feet from Proof.

April stood in the middle of the bodies, with a satisfied grin on her face and the smoking gun still in her hand. Bloodstains and small pieces of brain matter decorated her face and shirt. Licking her lips, she pulled a pack of Newport 100s from her back pocket and patted them down on the back of her hand. After opening the fresh pack, she pulled one of the longs out, placed it in her mouth, and lit it with the lighter one of her crew members handed to her. After taking a deep pull, she blew out a thick cloud of smoke and looked at me.

"What?" she said when she saw my questioning glare. "You and I both know that they were going to leave here and go straight to Melonee and tell her everything. And you know I don't play about my money."

She turned to those in her crew who were still alive. That did not include Rocko. His sexy ass was dead. He was slumped over his laptop, a bullet through his head. "Y'all clean this shit up, and then let's get back to work. Grab Rocko's laptop and try to see if he was able to find out anything about the hospital's security in the NICU and shit." April looked back at me. "Fiona, you try to get ahold of that brother of yours and see if he's done doing whatever the fuck it is he's doing. We're going to need another tech guy since Roc is gone."

I felt a small pain in my chest as I looked down at the bodies of the four men I had considered friends to some degree. Shit was most definitely about to hit the fan now that Proof was gone.

Roman

"Your Honor, my client has never been convicted. What he has been is maligned, targeted, and accused of a crime that he did not commit."

The judge, who ironically looked similar to that Mills Lane dude who did a reality court show on TV, flipped through a few sheets of paper in a manila folder that had been placed in front of him by the bailiff. More than likely the lack of evidence the DA had against me. "Mr. Channing, do the people have any witnesses at this time who can corroborate the charges filed against Mr. Black?"

"At this time, Your Honor, the people do not. The victim in this case recently dropped all charges against Mr. Black."

The judge pulled his glasses down his nose and looked over them. "For what reason, Mr. Channing?"

"Unfortunately, we don't know."

"Objection, Your Honor," Viktoria said. "The prosecution is lying. The victim, Melonee Reid, who was their star witness, has dropped all charges against my client because she has stated that it was not Mr. Black who attacked her on the night in question. In fact, Ms. Reid remembers in detail what happened. She has given a statement to the police department, which I am sure the DA has received a copy of. The rape kit that was done on Ms. Reid showed that there was not one, but two different spermicides found. One from Mr. Black, who she remembers having a consensual intimate night with, and one from a suspect the police department has yet to find." She leaned toward Chasin and whispered something in his ear.

Judge Lawrence closed the folder in front of him and sat back in his chair. His eyes zeroed in on the nervous DA, who was probably wasting his time with this motion hearing. "Is there any truth to the evidence that the defendant has provided today, Mr. Channing?"

"Yes . . . and no, Your Honor. The state thinks that Ms. Reid dropped the charges only because she recently gave birth to a baby who might in fact belong to the defendant."

"What does a baby have to do with a rape charge, Mr. Channing?"

"We believe Mr. Black possibly paid Ms. Reid to drop the charges."

"Your Honor," Viktoria said, with irritation in her voice, "it's obvious that the prosecution is trying to find any and everything to build a case against my client since the first one didn't work. Up until a few days ago, all of Mr. Black's assets were frozen. He did not have access to any of his bank accounts, his 401(k), pensions, IRA, stocks, bonds, or his trust fund. There is no way that he was able to pay Ms. Reid anything to change her story. And in light of the new evidence, the statement we were able to obtain from the police department, and the fact that the DA's charges against Mr. Black have been dropped, I move that the case be dismissed and my client hereby freed of all charges."

I looked over my shoulder at Marques, who was present in court with me today. He had been MIA for a minute but had shown up when I really needed him to. Melonee wanted to come and support me, but Chasin had thought it was a good idea for her to sit this one out. Although her memory was the saving grace behind these charges being dropped, he felt that her being here today would start a media frenzy, which neither one of us wanted right now.

The judge's deep baritone voice as he rendered his verdict brought me back from my thoughts.

"Mr. Black, in light of the lack of evidence the DA has against you and the fact that their star witness has recanted her story, I have no other choice but to free you of all charges." He banged his gavel. "You are free to go."

I stood up from my seat and released the breath I'd been holding for the past two minutes and pulled Viktoria into a hug. "Thank you, Vik. I really owe you and Chasin one." I clasped Chasin's outstretched hand, tugged on it, and brought him in for a brotherly hug. "Thank you, man."

"No problem, bro. I told you, and your uncle, too, y'all could trust me. All you had to do was let me handle it, and I'd get you off clear and free," Chasin told me.

"Mel's memory coming back wasn't a bad look, either," I whispered in his ear as we released each other from our embrace.

Marques walked up behind Viktoria and wrapped his hand around her waist. "Don't go taking all the credit, man. My girl put in just as much work as you and in a shorter time frame. I don't know how many nights I had to go without—"

Viktoria elbowed Marques in his stomach.

"What was that for, babe? All I was going to say was, 'I don't know how many nights I had to go without her sleeping next to me.'" Marques furrowed his brows. "That's all."

"Marques, shut your lying ass up," Viktoria told him. She laughed and then turned to me. "How about we all go to the bar down the street and have some celebratory drinks? I think this calls for a few rounds of vodka."

"Vodka?" Marques scrunched up his face. "Just like your crazy-ass daddy."

"What about my father?"

"I love the man. . . . That's all. So what do you say, Ro? First round's on me," Marques said.

As much as I would love to celebrate finally getting my life back in order, I had other things to take care of right now. "How about we meet up later on in the week? I gotta go make sure everything at my new spot is set up for Melonee, Madison, and Kason."

"So you finally found a place, huh?" Chasin asked.

Marques rolled his eyes. "You would know that if you came up for a breather every now and then. I understand, though, that Bree's ass is fine as—" He frowned. "Ouch, Vik. What was that for?"

"Because you don't ever know when to shut up, Marques," Viktoria snapped. "What if Chasin was describing me in that way to one of your other friends?"

"Shit. Let him. I know my baby is fine as fuck. I'm a secure man, and I don't have a problem with these other fools seeing that, either." Marques kissed Viktoria on her lips, and she blushed. Even with her dark skin, you could see the tint in her cheeks.

"I'm still trying to figure out how the two of you got together," Chasin mused. "Marques isn't the type of dude I would have ever imagined you with, Viktoria. You have your own money, so I know you don't need his. Plus, you live, like, on the other side of the world. And if Marques isn't running behind Roman, he's in your nearest strip club, harassing the strippers. When did he have time to get his passport stamped?"

"You sound like you're hating, bruh," Marques said as he stepped toward Chasin. "What? You mad because she's with me? What? You want my girl too, Mr. *GQ*? I thought Bree had your nose wide open."

"Would you guys stop! We are still inside the courthouse," Viktoria hissed, looking around at the eyes that were now focused on us. Paparazzi stood waiting, with their cameras out, ready to snap some good shots.

Chasin laughed and handed his business card to some dude being escorted out of the courthouse in cuffs.

I shook my head. *Always the working man.*

"I would never hate on you, Marques," Chasin said, a grin on his face. "You're a trust-fund baby with no sense of what you really want to do with yourself. Never had to do a day's worth of hard work in your life. Always had that silver spoon in your ass and mouth. Believe me, bro, I would never hate on you. I was just curious to know how you pulled Viktoria, that's all."

That was a question that had gone through my mind, until Marques told me that he and Vik had been messing around since we were younger. During the summers when we would visit Russia, he and my cousin would sneak into each other's rooms whenever my uncle and the staff had retired for the night. It was weird that I had never noticed, seeing as my room was between theirs. He'd told me that they tried to do the long-distance thing once we got older, and would travel back and forth to see each other. But once Viktoria got into law school and the trips to see each other became less frequent, they decided to chill for a minute and to pick back up if the opportunity ever presented itself again. Now that Viktoria was back in the States and was thinking about staying out this way, I guessed they were trying to pick back up.

When I asked him where he'd been during the past month or so, while I was going through all my bullshit, Marques told me that his parents and lawyers thought it would be a good idea if he distanced himself from me so that none of the negative press about me that was going around would be associated with King Palace Resorts and their brand. From a business perspective, I understood what they'd been trying to do, but from a best friend perspective, I had a hard time wrapping my head around this. Needless to say, we'd talked it out and thrown that shit under the bridge. Q and I had been rocking with each other for far too long to let this little hiccup cause a rift in our friendship. Especially when good friends were hard to come by nowadays.

"Look, y'all, I'm about to get out of here. Like I said, I got some things to do before Mel gets to my house. Chasin, call me tomorrow. Vik, I'll see you later on in the week, and, Q, don't let what Chasin said bother you. I think you and my cousin being together is a good look. She already got you to cut off that mop on top of your head, and your jeans are actually a good fit, and not those nut-hugging things you used to wear. Shit, you even talk a little different. Haven't heard a woman's body part or a curse word fly out of your mouth while we've been standing here."

"Fuck you, pussy." Marques laughed. "And for your information, the change in the way I look was all me. If I want people to take me seriously as a businessman when my father passes the shit down to me, I have to look the part, right?"

"My man," I said, pulling him in for a hug.

"Tell my girl Mel I said hey, and kiss my baby Kason for me," Viktoria cooed.

I nodded my head and waved good-bye before I walked out of the courthouse lobby. I had called a car service, and the driver was waiting at the curb to pick me up. Surprisingly, there were only a few print and broadcast media outlets in front of the building to take my picture and push their microphones in my face as I walked down the small flight of steps outside the courthouse doors. I guessed with me no longer being front-page news, my life wasn't as interesting to them as it had been. Pushing my way through the small crowd, I made it to the tinted-out SUV and nodded my head at the driver, who already had the back door open for me. As soon as I slid into the backseat of the car, I loosened the tie around my neck and pulled it off. Next to go was my jacket. I rolled both sleeves of my shirt up and laid my head back on the seat. I couldn't wait to get home so that I could pull the rest of this shit off and get into a pair of shorts and a T-shirt. I also couldn't wait to see Melonee and the kids.

It was crazy how the night we took a chance on each other had turned into a conundrum. I often wondered if whoever was really behind the attack would ever reveal themselves or slip up and get caught. I mean, I'd gone over everything I remembered from that night, as well as some of the things Melonee remembered, and I hadn't been able to link anything together. For instance, Melonee didn't know Benji from anywhere, and I sure as hell didn't know Fiona or Proof. I didn't have any enemies out there, to my knowledge, and neither did she. Of course, there was the daughter of her ex-husband, who, Melonee had said, unexpectedly appeared at my benefit banquet and tried to cause a scene, but when I had Uncle Kazi look her up, he said that she had died in a car crash.

I had asked Mel if she thought her Black Widow Clique could've been behind the attack, since I was the intended target, anyway, but she doubted they would make a move like that and harm her in any way. All in all, I was pretty stoked that the shit was now behind us and that we could start to live our lives without having to watch our backs constantly.

I pulled my phone out of my pocket and turned it back on. I knew I would have a ton of e-mails and text messages waiting for me when I did. Sorting through those, I responded to the ones that needed my immediate attention and saved the rest for tomorrow. It seemed like ever since Benji took over as CEO for Real Time Delivery, things had been going okay but could've been better. He had closed a few more international deals but hadn't been able to come to an agreement to buy out FedEx or a few courier businesses that I was ready to sign the contracts for when I was CEO. And a lot of the employees had either quit or were out on disability, draining the funds in that pool. My ex-assistant, who still sent me daily reports, had said that she was about to put in her two weeks' notice and resign because being Benji's "ho wrangler" was not in her job description. Now that I was free and clear of the rape and IRS charges, I was going to talk to my father and see if there was any way I could get my job back. RTD was a family business, and although Benji's last name was Black, his veins didn't have the same blood pumping through them as mine. But more importantly, Benji hasn't been doing a stellar job.

After sending a text to Bree, I made a few phone calls, the last one to the in-home nurse I had hired to watch over my father, since Julia's ass was too busy doing other things. If she wasn't at Benji's new house, lounging by the pool, she was in someone's high-end store, running up the company credit card, which she wasn't supposed to have, or splurging on surgical procedures for herself and her friends. The day that my father was released from the hospital, she hadn't even shown up. She'd left a note on the refrigerator that said she was on her way to Hawaii for a weeklong vacation to relieve some of the stress that I'd caused her and our family over the past few months. I had snatched the note down before my father could see it and had reached out to Joc to see if he would be interested in this nurse position for the next few months. At first he had declined the offer, but once I offered to pay him twenty-five hundred dollars a week, he was at my father's house the next day, bright and early.

My phone vibrated, and I read the message Bree had just sent, telling me that everything was in place and that she would be at my house by the time I got there. Melonee had no idea what I had planned for her tonight. I just hoped everything went according to plan.

Girl, I know you're scared of love, but you never had a love like this. I know you been hurt before, but you never had a love like this

"Roman . . ." Mel laughed. "What's going on?"

With a scarf covering her eyes and my hands gripping her hips, I guided Melonee through the living room of my new loft and into the dining area, where I had something special set up for her. In our talks at that hospital, I had found out that she was a big fan of Donell Jones, so I had a mix of some of his greatest hits playing in the background. One of my favorites, "Love Like This," was now coming through the surround-sound speakers, and I hoped Mel was taking every word of this song to heart.

"We almost there. Just a few more steps, and then I'll take the blindfold off."

"If you let me fall, I'm going to kick your ass."

"You know I got you, baby. Now stand right here for a minute, and I'll be right back."

"Roman," she called, but I was already on my way into the kitchen to grab a lighter to light the rest of the candles, the ones that Bree hadn't got a chance to.

After making sure everything was perfect and in its right place, I stood in the dining area, across from Melonee, and stared at her. The way her body filled out the jeans and low-cut top she had on was nothing short of amazing. And just after giving birth to my son. Her breasts were full and round. Her hips and ass, man . . . I shook my head. Damn, she was beautiful. Wrapping her arms around her body, Melonee moved nervously to the left, then back to the right. A slight crackle from one of the flames beside me caused her head to turn in my direction.

"I know you're there, Roman."

"How do you know that? You can't see me, can you?"

She shook her head. "No. But I can feel you. The same way I always have."

I could feel her too. Her presence still affected my body and had it reacting in that belly-fluttering, hair-raising, sweaty-palm crazy way. After walking back over to Melonee, I undid the loose knot of the scarf at the back of her head and removed it from her eyes. Once they adjusted to the light, she looked around the room in amazement.

"What's this?" she asked.

"Our do-over date."

I looked over my shoulder at the romantic scene behind me, now that everything was in place, and made a mental note to thank Bree for executing my vision. Chilled champagne, a picnic basket with a three-course meal for two, chocolate-covered strawberries, and rose petals were spread out over a white shag rug, with vases of flowers and candles surrounding it. The setting was real intimate, as the lights were off and the candles gave the space a warm glow. After grabbing Melonee's hand, I carefully stepped onto the rug, took a seat, then pulled her down to sit between my legs.

"This is beautiful, Roman. How did you . . . When did you do this?"

"I'm not gonna lie. I had a little help, but the vision was all mine. I wanted to make our do-over date one to remember."

Melonee turned in my arms and looked at me. The way her eyelashes kissed the top of her cheeks every time she blinked, and the way they curled upward when she looked at me, drew me in. Captivated me. My heart started to beat faster. Those gray irises were pulling me in deeper and deeper. And despite looking directly into her eyes, I couldn't help the way my peripherals took in her breasts, rising and falling, and the curved shadows under her collarbones.

I swallowed hard to relieve the lump that had grown in my throat. For some reason, I was nervous as hell, and I knew Melonee could tell. Her eyes softened as our eyes connected again, and a cute but sexy smirk played on her lips before she raised her head up and pressed her mouth to mine. When she wrapped her arms around my neck, her breasts pressed intimately against my chest. Her legs straddled my lap, and she opened her mouth and licked my bottom lip tenderly, eliciting a low growl from me. After moving my hands from her waist up to her face, I pulled Melonee into me as much as I could and deepened the kiss.

Melonee had me in a daze as she slowly rocked her hips from side to side. My dick was already hard as a rock, but with the way she was moving, I could feel it trying to bust through my pants. I wanted—no, I needed—to feel the inside of her. And I needed that feeling now. After removing her jeans and panties in one swift move, I slid my hand between her thighs, where her essence was already spilling over. As I gently massaged her swollen clit and she moved in rhythm with my fingers, I could feel her orgasm building. Melonee bit her bottom lip as she tried to fight the pleasure I was giving her, though small whimpers kept slipping from her throat.

"Let it go, baby. It's mine, isn't it?"

She nodded and laid her head on my shoulder, giving in and opening herself up fully to me. After unbuttoning my jeans, I placed my hands under her ass and raised her up in the air slightly, then positioned myself at her entrance. The warmth and wetness that enveloped my dick as our bodies connected had me closing my eyes and sucking in a deep breath.

"Fuck!" we both exclaimed at the same time.

I threw my head back, gasping for air, as the tightness of her pussy and the remains of her last orgasm enveloped me whole.

"Roman," Melonee moaned, her body adjusting to my size. "Oh my God, baby. Oh, my God."

I started to move, withdrawing until just the tip of my head was in and then pushing all the way back in. I set a punitive pace as my dick stroked her G-spot over and over again. Melonee wrapped her legs around my waist and wasted no time matching me thrust for thrust. It was like we were trying to convey any and every emotion we were feeling right now, and I gladly accepted all the love she was giving me. Our lips were like magnets, unable to break contact as our souls became intertwined.

A slow tingle started to build up in my toes, and it traveled all the way up to my belly. I wanted to hold out for a little while longer, enjoying the feel of this woman, who had completely stolen my heart, but I couldn't. My body tightened as she panted with each lift of her hips, each grind of her wet, cushioned walls against me. Melonee's breathing became faster as she wrapped her arms around my neck tighter, helping her with the up-and-down motion that was driving me crazy.

"I . . . I . . . can't hold it any longer, Mel," I said breathlessly into her ear, then bit down on her neck, trying to gain some kind of control.

"Cum with me, then, Roman. Shit! Cum with me, baby. Aw."

No other word was uttered as I gripped Melonee's hips and pushed my dick in as far as it could go, then pounded into her, never letting up on the speed or power of my strokes. Even before the contractions in her had completely subsided, my fingers massaging her swollen clit had her cumming again. This time, my own release was near. With a loud groan and one final push, which sent her over the edge for the third time, I came too. Decorating every inch of her insides with my name and seed. Secretly hoping another baby would be conceived.

Melonee's body collapsed on top of mine, causing me to fall back on the rug. After wrapping my arms around her and pulling her closer to my chest, I tucked the loose strands of hair that had fallen into her face behind her ear and kissed her forehead and basked in the intense connection that just happened between us.

"Mel . . . ," I called but got no answer. "Mel . . ."

She licked her lips, and the soft touch of her tongue as it lightly brushed against my chest sent a shiver down my spine. She cleared her throat. "Yeah?"

"Your phone is going off again."

"I know, but I don't care."

I smiled. "As flattering as it is to know that I have this 'drunk in love' effect on you, I think you should get that. It might be Bree calling."

If the circumstances were different, I probably would've said, "Fuck the call," too. But Bree was watching Madison and Kason tonight, and although my son had been cleared by the hospital to come home, we had been advised that some complications from his premature birth might still arise. I sat up, with Melonee still clinging to my chest like a newborn child. The warmth from between her legs was waking my dick up, and I could feel it stretching her out again.

"Mmm," she moaned and began kissing my neck. I closed my eyes, savoring every touch, feel, and taste of this woman. Her arousal turned me down even more. When she wrapped her chocolate limbs around my waist a little tighter and pulled my dick deeper into her wetness, I forgot all thoughts of her phone going off again.

"You sure you're ready for round two?" I asked as I flipped her onto her back, knocking over the picnic basket and the champagne. I grabbed one of the chocolate-covered strawberries and fed it to her. Licking the sweet berry taste from her lips, I pushed into her and was taken to paradise again.

Two hours later, we were lying comfortably in the same spot we'd just made love in, and were dozing off when there was a loud bang on my front door. Melonee, who had been asleep for the past thirty minutes, shot up, with a worried look on her face.

"Who could that be this late?" she asked, reaching for her phone to check the time. "What the fuck?"

I stopped pulling my pants up and turned my attention to her. "What's wrong?"

"My granny and Bree have been calling my phone all night. Oh my God, something's wrong! My babies. Shit, shit, shit, shit, shit," she cried as she frantically searched around the room for her top, her cell phone nestled between the side of her face and her shoulder.

Someone banging on the door again caused both of us to look in that direction.

"Roman, maybe you should go answer the door while I try to call Bree."

I nodded my head, pulled my pants up all the way, grabbed my shirt, then walked to the front of the house, turning on a few lights along the way. A little déjà vu pegged me for a second, but I doubted whoever was banging on the door was the police. After pulling my shirt on over my head, I unlocked the dead bolts and swung the door open, just as the person standing there was about to knock again.

"Bree . . . is everything all right?" The look on her face caused my heart to drop. "Where's my son? Is everything all right?"

"The kids are good. They're at my mom's house. . . ." Her wet eyes looked up at me. "Where's Mel?"

I looked over my shoulder. "She's in the back, throwing some clothes on and trying to call you. If the kids are okay, what's going on, Bree?"

"Auntie!" Melonee yelled as she pushed past me. "Where's my babies? Are they okay? Tell me my babies are okay!"

"They're good, Mel. I just dropped them off at Mama's so I could come over here. We've been calling you all night."

Melonee's eyes turned to me. A look of embarrassment was on her face. "We . . . we were a little busy. But that's a topic we can discuss later. Why are you here? Why do you look like you've been crying?"

Bree nervously licked her lips. "I think you should let me come in so we can talk. You might want to have a seat when I tell you this."

I looked around my bare townhome. The only piece of furniture I had in it right now was the coffee table that had belonged to my mother. I was going to leave the task of decorating this place to Melonee, when and if she and the kids decided to move in with me permanently.

"Auntie, just tell me what's going on please. My nerves are already on edge."

Blowing out a breath, Bree looked up, trying to stop the tears from falling down her face. "Proof . . ." She shook her head. "Proof's mother called Mama and told her that they just found his body in a Dumpster behind some shitty motel."

Melonee looked bewildered. "What?"

"Proof's dead, Mel. Someone shot him in the back of the head and just threw his body away like trash."

"No, no, no, no! Don't tell me that, Aunt Bree. Please don't tell me that. My baby . . . What about my baby? She loves her daddy. What do I tell my baby, Aunt Bree? Jaylen. No," Melonee cried. She began to sob loudly. "What about my baby?"

Melonee fell back against my chest, and I wrapped my arms tightly around her. She began shaking and fell to the floor, her cries ringing loud in my ear. I wanted to take the pain away, but I knew that I couldn't at the moment, so I just held her tighter. Proof and I hadn't been the best of friends, but I did care for their daughter and would never want a child to experience the loss of a parent. My heart went out to Madison, and I prayed that in time, I could replace that missing part in her heart.

Fiona

Ever since April had killed Proof, it seemed like everything going on around me was all out of whack. I had never believed in karma or anything like that, but I was starting to become a believer, as I felt that was indeed reaping what I sowed. Not only had I been demoted from my position as the head of the Black Widow Clique by April's ass, but I had also found out last night that I was carrying Proof's baby. For a second I had thought it was Benji's, but after confirming with the doctor that I was a little over ten weeks, I had to have gotten pregnant the night Proof and I had sex when Melonee was in the hospital. A drunken night that honestly never should've happened, but had. I had never been one to regret anything that I did, but this shit right here . . . I shook my head. I didn't deserve to be a mother. Didn't deserve to bring a child into this world, one whose father had been killed by his or her grandmother.

Wiping away the tear that slid down my cheek, I took a deep breath and quickly got myself together. I needed to see what the fuck was going on with my brother and why he'd been missing in action for so long. Furthermore, his phone number had been changed, his e-mail had been deleted, and all his social media had been deactivated. Cowboy had gone completely off the grid, and I wanted to know why. Everybody I had ever cared about was gone, and he was the only family I had left. That was why, at the present moment, I was sitting in my car, which was parked in Cowboy's driveway, and watching as the curtain in his living room moved every ten minutes or so, letting me know that someone was in there. I'd been coming by his house for the past week but could never get an answer when I knocked. Today I had decided to park my ass right here and wait until he pulled up or came out to dump the trash or something.

When I looked over, the time on my dashboard read 8:45 p.m., which meant I had been sitting in this spot for six hours now. My stomach was growling, I was thirsty, and I needed to pee bad. Cowboy was going to let me in this house today, or I was going to shoot the hinges off the door and let myself in. I responded to a text from April, placed my phone in the cup holder, took my keys out of the ignition, and got out of my car.

The cool evening breeze hit my face the minute I stepped out and closed the car door behind me. Autumn leaves in orange, yellow, and red hues decorated the ground. Kids rode down the street on their scooters and bikes, laughing and having fun before their parents called them in for the night. I loved the residential area Cowboy lived in, but I had always wondered why he moved out here. For someone who was so low key and was such a stickler about his privacy, you would think he'd have moved to a kid-free and secluded area.

After walking up the two steps that lead to his screen door, I rang the doorbell and waited to see if I would get an answer. Five minutes passed, with me just standing out there, before I began to bang on the door, the mail slot, and the adjacent window. The loud noise I was making did draw a bit of attention from Cowboy's neighbors, but I didn't give a fuck. Like I said, he was going to let me in today, or I was going to let myself in.

"Excuse me, honey. Are you related to the young man who lives here or something?" his old-ass neighbor asked as she walked across her lawn to the fence that separated her and Cowboy's houses.

"Why do you want to know?" I wasn't trying to be mean to her, but I hated nosy muthafuckas.

"Oh, honey. I meant no harm. I just wanted to make sure he was okay. Max normally pulls my trash bins to the front on trash day, but he hasn't done it in weeks. I had to pay one of these little bad fuckers around here to do it. Do you think he's okay? I haven't seen any type of movement or lights on in a while. So unlike him."

"I'm sorry, ma'am, but what goes on over here shouldn't be your concern. But thanks for the information. Now, take your nosy ass back in your house and go knit a sweater or something."

She grabbed her chest as if she were clutching some pearls. "I was just trying to help you, little bitch, but you don't have to worry about me bothering you anymore. I will tell you this, though. I'm in charge of the neighborhood watch in this here neighborhood, and if he doesn't answer the door for you in the next couple of minutes, I'ma make sure the police know a suspicious figure is lurking around." She turned on her heels and marched away from the fence. "Tell me to go knit no damn sweater. I ain't even that old," her ass mumbled before she walked back into her house.

After waving her off, I went to knock on the door again when I saw the same curtain next to the door move.

"Cowboy, I know you see me out here. About to get arrested and shit. Open the fucking door before I have to kill your police-calling neighbor next door." I waited for a few seconds for some kind of response but didn't get one. "Cowboy, I know you hear me out here. Open the door, damn it."

I stood there for another two minutes before I went back to my car and pulled my gun out from under my seat. After making sure no one was paying attention to me, I screwed the silencer on the gun and walked around the side of his house to the back door. Before I used any type of force, I checked the knob to see if the door was unlocked, but it wasn't. Standing a few inches back, I raised my gun and shot three bullets in each hinge and one in the lock. A small push had the door falling straight back to the ground with a loud thud. I walked over the broken glass and entered the kitchen of Cowboy's house and had to hold my mouth to keep from throwing up. The smell of week-old garbage, rotten food, and cigarette smoke lingered in the air. The dishes were piled high in the sink and on the counters. Maggots were feasting on old Chinese food and half-eaten burger meals. Empty alcohol bottles were everywhere. My stomach turned even more at the sight, and I couldn't help the vomit that spewed from my mouth and onto the floor. After what felt like puking my entire soul out, I walked farther into Cowboy's house, looking for him.

If I thought the kitchen was bad, the living room was even worse. Clothes were everywhere, along with half-empty take-out and pizza boxes. All of Cowboy's electronic shit had been thrown all over the place and was in pieces. I picked up one of his laptops and dropped it just as fast when a family of roaches ran across it.

"What are you doing here, Fee?" Cowboy asked from somewhere, but I didn't see him. I cursed myself for leaving my phone in the car and wished like hell that I hadn't. Squinting my eyes, I tried to find him somewhere in this mess but couldn't.

"Can you turn on a light or something? I can't see shit in here, and I don't wanna fall," I said.

"Then get the fuck out."

"Not until you tell me where you've been. I've been calling you for weeks now. So much shit has happened, and I needed your help, but you've been nowhere to be found. April's ass decided to resurface and has been causing all kinds of havoc. Then you will never believe the shit I found out about her, Shaunie, and Benji's mother, Julia. Shit is crazy. Where are you? I can't see you."

"Fee, just leave please. I'm not ready to be around anybody right now."

"Why, Maxwell? What the fuck happened that you are hiding and shit? I mean, I know you used to have these little episodes when we were younger, but I thought you got over that shit."

The room became quiet and stayed that way for what felt like thirty minutes. Finally, I decided to speak again.

"Cowboy, what the fuck, man? Get up and come to my house, and we can talk. I'm not about to stay another second in this dirty-ass shit. I'm surprised your nosy-ass, police-calling neighbor hasn't called code enforcement on you. This shit looks worse than them crazy muthafuckas on that hoarders show." As I inched my way farther into the living room, I tripped over something wet on the floor and screamed. "What the fuck, Cowboy! Let's go now."

I didn't know if it was instinct or not, but the second I heard a whooshing sound in the air, I ducked my head, just in time for the glass that Cowboy had thrown at my head to crash into the wall and shatter. I raised my gun and pointed at nothing.

"I can't see your ass, but I have half a clip and another full one ready to shoot this bitch up until I hit your ass. Throw something else at me,

Maxwell, and brother or not, I will put a hot one in you."

I could hear Cowboy moving around somewhere and swung my arm in the direction the noise was coming from. After I heard a few clicks—which was him turning something on—a small house lamp went on and illuminated the area he was sitting in. My eyebrows furrowed from confusion as the sight of my brother registered in my brain. Cowboy looked bad. His hair had grown out and was matted as hell. The thick beard on his face was no better. There had to be bugs in that shit. He had old noodles and everything hanging from it. His eyes were bloodshot, and his lips were as white as snow. My brother had always been a stocky guy, built like a pro football player, but now his body was as thin as a string bean. I tried to blink back the tears that were trying to fall, but I couldn't. I didn't recognize my own brother, and my heart broke.

"Maxwell . . ." My voice was barely above a whisper. "What's wrong, brother? Why are you living like this?"

He took a swig from the bottle in his hand. "Fee, you've seen me now. I'm okay. So please . . . leave."

"Why? So you can sit here and continue to kill yourself? I'm not going to let you do that to yourself . . . to me. You're the only family I have."

"I'm sure Proof, Mel, and the rest of the clique will be there for you."

I bit my bottom lip. Cowboy and Proof had their differences when it came to Melonee, but they were just as close as we were. "Um, I don't know about that."

"Why? Mel found out what you did?"

"No," I snapped. "And she's not going to find out, because I got plans for that bitch."

Cowboy laughed. "When will you ever get over that, Fiona? Melonee did not cause our father to go to jail. Nor did she steal from you any type of silver-spoon childhood, which you wouldn't have had, anyway."

"She stole everything from me, and you know it," I said, my voice cracking as it rose. "The bitch deserves everything that has happened to her and is about to happen to her. Believe that."

Cowboy stared at me for a minute before shaking his head and taking another swig of his drink. "You need to get over it. You know if Proof finds out before she does, he will kill you. He's still in love with Mel. Always has been, always will be."

"Well, I doubt Proof will be killing me anytime soon."

He raised his eyebrow. "Why you say that?"

"Because he's already dead."

"Wait . . . what?"

"Him, Mouse, Wiz, and Banks. They're all dead."

"What?" Cowboy's eyes squinted, and he licked his dry-ass lips. "How?"

I tucked my gun in the back of my sweatpants and pulled my jacket down over it. Pulling my hair back in a ponytail, I carefully walked over to the ottoman in front of Cowboy and sat down.

"April. I called a meeting to tell everybody about the new target, and things got a little heated when they found out it was Melonee."

Cowboy opened his mouth to say something, but I held my hand up, stopping him.

"Before you say anything, let me tell you what this bitch did," I said.

After I explained to Cowboy my reason for picking Melonee as the next target, he didn't say anything. Just shook his head. I then told him about the plan that Julia and April had come up with and everything I had found out about them. I wasn't surprised when Cowboy admitted to me that he already knew a little bit about what our mothers had done back in the day. Said that was one of the reasons why he had started to get into that computer geek shit. Our mother had planted that seed in his head.

"So now the BWC are kidnappers?" Cowboy asked and laughed. "You got me fucked up, Fee, if you think I'ma let y'all harm my seed."

"Your seed?" I muttered. "Max, what the fuck are you talking about? Melonee's baby doesn't belong to you."

The minute the scowl appeared on his face and his eyes darkened, I knew I wasn't talking to my brother anymore. "Who the fuck you think got her pregnant that night?" he yelled.

"They did a DNA test on—"

Before I could get the words out of my mouth, Cowboy slapped the shit out of me, causing me to fall off the ottoman and onto the dirty-ass floor. I tried to pull my gun from the back of my pants but couldn't when Cowboy grabbed me by the throat and slammed me against the wall, knocking down the picture hanging from it and exposing the hiding space of another family of roaches.

"Let . . . me . . . go . . . Maxwell," I barely got out. He was crushing the fuck out of my windpipe.

"Who do you think went with Uncle Dro that night to the beach house? Wasn't no way I was going to let him and that white muthafucka get what belonged to me."

"Wh-wh-what?"

Cowboy yanked my body forward and then slammed it back against the wall. My head took the brunt of the hard blow. I tried to focus my eyes on him, but all I saw was stars.

"Melonee always has and always will belong to me. Now that, that bitch-ass nigga Proof is gone, we can live happily together with our little family. Me, Melonee, Madison, and li'l Max. Have you seen your nephew, Fee? Huh? Isn't he the cutest thing you've ever seen?"

"You . . . you . . . seen the baby?" My vision was a little clearer, and I could see this deranged look in Cowboy's eyes.

After taking the last swig from his drink, he threw the empty bottle on the floor, next to the others. His eyes had become a little misty. "My son was so small, Fee. Barely hanging on to life. I had to go see him and make sure everything was all right. I saw that cracker asshole there a few times and wanted to murk his bitch ass, but I couldn't without being seen. I thought me tapping into his business accounts and doing that shit with the IRS was going to send him away, but I guess I didn't do a good enough job." His voice cracked, and he shook his head. "That bitch-ass nurse wouldn't even let me hold my son. I had to sneak in between feedings and when I knew Melonee or bitch boy wasn't stopping by for a visit. Seeing him in that little incubator damn near broke my heart."

As if he had just thought about something, Cowboy's eyes cut toward me, and his grip around my neck became tighter. "Fiona, I better not find out that it was you or your fucking mama that caused Mel to go into labor with my baby so early."

I shook my head no, honestly not knowing if it was I who had caused it or not. I mean, I had put a couple of crushed-up Plan B pills in all that extra tartar sauce she had on her fish sandwich, but I hadn't thought it would work that fast. "I would never kill a kid . . . not even the one in my belly."

At that admission, Cowboy released the hold he had on my neck and stepped back. "You're pregnant? By who?"

Rubbing my neck, I took a few moments to get my breathing together before I answered his question. "The baby is Proof's."

"You gotta fucking be kidding me." Cowboy laughed. "For someone who hates Mel so much, you sure do want to be like her so bad." After walking over to the spot on the couch that he'd obviously been sitting in a lot lately, Cowboy picked up a new bottle of Jack, opened it, and gulped some down. "Fiona, get the fuck out of my house, and I mean that shit this time. Come back, and I'm going to feel the same way you do about me. Sister or no sister, I will kill you."

Walking backward, with my gun now aimed at him, I used the wall as a guide back to Cowboy's kitchen, and then I turned and trotted out his back door. I guessed April was right. Family was what you made it. Because right about now, the only family that I had thought I had was dead to me.

"So do you think he'll be a problem?" April asked.

"Nah. I don't think so," I said into the phone. "He's too busy self-medicating with alcohol and drugs to do anything. All his equipment is broken, and he seems pretty satisfied wallowing in his self-pity on that dirty-ass couch of his."

"But still . . ."

"But *still* nothing. Even though Cowboy is dead to me right now, he's still my brother, and my father told us to always look out for each other."

"Maxwell was always one of those muthafuckas who didn't like to practice what he preached."

"Bye, April." I didn't even give her time to respond before I hung up in her face.

Telling her about Cowboy seemed like the right thing to do, seeing as he thought Mel's baby belonged to him. I didn't think he would interfere in this plan, but with him, you never knew. A week had passed since the day I went to Cowboy's house, and I couldn't lie and say that I didn't still miss my brother, but we needed some space right now. After we got this money, maybe I'd try to reach out to him again.

For now, I needed to get my head in the game and find out some info on Mel and where she'd been hiding out. When April had a few members of her crew break into Melonee's houses, they said it had seemed as if no one had lived in them in months. Furniture, clothes, toys, and basic household things were there, but the fridge and cabinets were bare, and the mail was piling up at both addresses. I had tried calling her old phone number, but that had been changed; and I had even stopped by Ms. Regina's house, but she had tried to act like she didn't know where Mel was staying. The only option that was left for me was to try Bree's house. The last time she and I had talked was at her place, and I was pretty sure that was where she was going to be. This was the type of shit Cowboy and Rocko were useful for, but with both of them out of commission, we had to do this shit old school.

***

I pulled up into Bree's driveway and noticed the fly-ass CL65 Benz parked next to her rented shit. Wasn't the type of family car I would've copped, but Mel and I had always had different taste. Checking myself in the mirror, I made sure that my makeup was on point and my bone-straight purple weave was still in place. The white-on-white J's on my feet went perfect with my Pink by Victoria sweat suit, while my MCM backpack did what it was supposed to do. Let these bitches know that I was out here, gettin' it.

After zipping my jacket up all the way to try to hide the hand marks that were still on my neck, I walked up to Bree's door and rang the doorbell. A minute or so passed before I could hear the locks start to turn. Expecting Bree's mean ass to be the one answering the door, I mustered up the most remorseful look I could get on my face and even had a tear ready to drop, if need be. But when I turned around, I came face-to-face with one of the finest men I had ever seen. Since he had nothing but a towel around his waist and a phone at his ear, I quickly took in his muscular frame and rich cinnamon-brown skin.

The water droplets still trickling down his chest and shoulders told me that he must've just hopped out of the shower and come straight to the door, while the bulge poking through the thickness of the fluffy towel told me that he was packing something serious between those muscled thighs. His dark eyes scanned me from head to toe before he cocked his head to the side. A sly smile played on his full lips as he continued to stare me down. The cocky asshole knew that I was checking him out, but I didn't care. Whoever he was could definitely get it. Especially if his pockets were as fat as his dick seemed to be.

"Aye, Cai, man, let me call you right back," he said to whomever he was talking to on the phone. Voice deep and raw like honey. He licked his lips, and I damn near fainted. "Can I help you?"

I opened my mouth to say something but couldn't.

He laughed and thumbed his nose, then crossed his arms over his chest, his legs sliding farther apart. "I guess we should try this again. Can I help you?"

I swallowed hard. "Um, I . . . I was wondering if my friend Melonee still lives here."

"Melonee? Who are you?"

"I'm her best friend, Fee." I shook my head. "I mean Fiona."

He stared at me for a second. "Fiona? What do you want with Melonee? From what I hear, y'all haven't spoken in a while."

I furrowed my brows. "So you know who I am?"

"Nah. I don't know who you are. But I've heard plenty about you."

I bit my bottom lip. "I hope all good things."

He chuckled. "What can I help you with, Fiona?"

"I doubt you can help me with what I really want," I said, flirting. "But I'll settle for an address or phone number for Mel." I knew asking for the shit was a stretch, but he didn't really know who I was.

"Babe, who's at the door?" I heard Bree call from behind. When she walked up behind him and looked over his shoulder, she laughed. "Bitch, you got some nerve showing your face at my house again."

I rolled my eyes and wanted to snap back at this bitch, but I knew I needed to play nice if I was hoping to get any type of information on Melonee's whereabouts. "Hello to you too, Bree. All I want is a way to reach Mel. That's all. I heard about Proof and wanted to see how she and Madison were doing."

"So now you're concerned?" she said as she moved in front of the dude who had answered the door, and pushed him back a little with her ass. When he smacked her on it, she waved him off but never took her eyes off me. "Why are you really here, Fiona? Didn't I tell you the next time you showed up at my house unannounced that I was going to beat your ass?"

I held my hands up in surrender. "I don't want any trouble, Bree. I just . . . I just wanna speak with Mel. You know, I miss her. I miss our friendship. If Proof dying showed me anything, it showed me that life is too short and the bullshit we got going on is just what it is—bullshit." When the fat tear I had ready slid from my eye, I thought I almost had her, but knowing Bree, she saw right through that shit.

"Bitch, cut the act. You really have me and life fucked up if you think I believe those fake-ass tears and that fake-ass speech you just gave. Now, I'm going to be nice only this one time and give you ten seconds to get off my property. After that, I'ma bless you with that ass whipping I promised."

I looked at Bree, who was dressed in some booty shorts, a spaghetti-strap top, and ankle socks and had a bonnet on her head. Cellulite, stretch marks, and sagging titties on full display. If ole boy was really here for her, even though she looked like that, his mentals really needed to be examined. Yeah, Bree had a cute face, but there was too much fat around her waist, thighs, arms, and everywhere else.

"Look, Bree, like I said . . . ," were the last words that left my mouth before this crazy bitch grabbed my hair and swung me from her porch. I landed hard on the ground.

"Baby, wait," yelled the dude who had answered the door. I smiled. I knew he was feeling me in some type of way. Bree knew he wasn't for her. "You don't want to put your Tims on before you get down?"

Wait. What?

"Chasin, shut your ass up and go put some clothes on before I beat your ass. You know I'ma need a lawyer once they take me to jail," Bree told him.

I tried to get up and rush her from behind while she had her back turned, but I was rewarded with a punch in my face.

"Bitch, you thought I was lying." *Whap.* "I told you I was gon' beat that ass, didn't I?" *Whap.* She smacked me in my face again. "Yeah, all that slick shit you was talking at the hospital and the last time you came here." *Whap.* "I remember all that shit." *Whap. Whap.* "Then your ho ass just tried to push up on my man like that shit is cool!"

I felt the blood gush from my busted lip with this last hit. I was trying my hardest to get up, but with Bree's fat ass sitting on top of me, that shit was damn near impossible.

"I never did like your ho ass," she grumbled. "Always told Mel to watch her back around you." *Whap*. "So glad she sees you for the sneaky bitch you really are." *Whap*. "Now, get your ass off the ground so you can fight me heads up. I don't want you walking around, lying, talking about I didn't give you a chance for a fair one."

After scrambling to my feet, I swung at Bree. My fist connected with her jaw, and her head snapped back. When she turned around, I could see blood all over her teeth.

"Damn, babe! You let her draw a little blood? What the fuck! And why you let her up? Ain't no muthafuckin' rules in fighting," said Chasin, clothed now, from his seat on the steps. He looked at his watch. "Now you got about two minutes to put some work in. After that, I will have to intervene, being an officer of the law."

"Chasin . . . ," Bree snapped.

"Don't 'Chasin' me. What you need to do is Donkey Kong Jr. that bitch before the police show up."

I guessed Chasin telling her that was the green light for Bree to finish the ass whipping she had promised me. By the time he actually did break up the fight, Bree had dragged me all over her yard and had even managed to fracture two of my fingers. When the police did show up, Chasin's ass shifted into lawyer mode real quick and told them that I had trespassed and had come with the intent to harm Bree. Asshole even told them that it was me who had swung first. They asked Bree if she wanted to press charges, and surprisingly, she said no. The police uncuffed me and let me go, but not before giving me a warning to stay away from Bree's house and anywhere else she might be. Because I didn't need the law or anyone else sniffing around me, I picked up my shit, got in my car, and left. Bree had beaten my ass, like she'd promised, but I had something for that bitch right after I fucked over her niece.

Melonee

"Ladies and gentlemen, if you are here for visitation, please have your IDs out and ready when you get in line over here. Any personal items, such as purses, backpacks, diaper bags, and so on, will not be allowed beyond this point. The only things that will be allowed are the preapproved items on the list that you saw on the Web site or read in the letter that was sent to you. If your items are not in an approved clear ziplock plastic bag, they will not be allowed in. Also, if you did not receive a notice in the mail stating that you were approved to visit the inmate whom you are here to see, you will not be allowed inside, regardless of what type of relationship you have. We don't care if you are the mother, father, brother, sister, baby mama, or any other relative. You will not be allowed in. Please make sure no cell phones or electronic devices are in your possession, for those are not permitted beyond this point, either. Thank you."

Cries and questions were all I could hear as people crowded around the correctional officer who had just run down the list of rules as I stood in line at Corcoran State Prison, waiting to go in for my visit. Babies with snotty noses were hollering at the top of their lungs, while their gum-popping, gold-plated jewelry–wearing mamas ignored them and applied more makeup on top of the boatload that was already on their faces. Those women wore outfits that more than likely violated the approved dress code, but they were still trying to get in. Then there were the grandmothers who had *tired* written all over their face but still made these monthly trips to bring their grandkids to see their father. And last but not least, there were those women who had come to see their man, unaware that another woman was here for the same visit. So far five chicks had been kicked out for fighting, and I was sure there would be more before the day was out.

While I was in the hospital, I had received a letter from Fiona and Cowboy's father, asking me to come see him as soon as I could. The request wasn't odd to me, because Max had asked me to come visit a few times over the years, but I had always declined. I sent birthday cards and shit like that and even dropped a few dollars on his books every now and then. Max had been like a father figure to me when I was younger, and I loved him, so it was only right that I looked out for him in some type of way. If my mother was here, I knew she would do the same thing.

After picking up some counseling pamphlets off the table, I fanned my face, trying to get some cool air in this stuffy, hot-ass lobby. The line was moving slow as hell, and I needed to use the bathroom. Maybe wearing this long-sleeve turtleneck dress and tights was the wrong thing to do. My edges were already starting to frizz up, and the light makeup I did have on my face was probably about to melt off. After walking up to the security checkpoint, I handed the security officer my keys and ID, then walked through the metal detector. After being checked in, I followed the rest of the crowd to another waiting room and waited to be further instructed on what to do.

Fifteen minutes later, I was sitting on a bench behind a table in the back of a cafeteria-like room, waiting on Max to come out. A loud buzzer went off, and a huge metal barred gate slid open. A couple of officers with batons and Taser guns on their hips walked through first, followed by a line of inmates. In light blue scrubs with bold lettering on the back, they filed out one by one, immediately spotting their family members or still searching for them. My eyes scanned the large group of men for Max, but I didn't see him at first. It wasn't until the last inmate had walked in and the gates had been closed that our eyes connected.

The smiles on our faces expanded at the same time, and when he finally reached me, I stood up and wrapped my arms around his waist. For a while we stood there and just held each other. It wasn't a surprise to me when tears began to fall down my face. Everything I'd been through in the past year had come rushing back to me, including the most recent traumatic event, Proof's death. My heart was still broken over that, and the way my daughter mourned her father didn't make it any better.

"Shhh, Mel." Max pulled back from our embrace and wiped the tears from my eyes and then kissed me on my forehead. "It's okay. It's okay. Let's sit down before these asshole COs come over here, trippin'." We took a seat next to each other on the same bench I'd occupied earlier.

"I'm sorry, Max. It's just that . . ." I shook my head. "You're, like, the only parent figure that I have besides my granny and my aunt Bree.

They've been there for me and shit. But that fatherly hug just . . ." I trailed off and shrugged my shoulders. "So how are you? Long time no see, huh?"

Max's handsome face lit up with a smile. "And whose fault is that? I've asked you to come visit me since I've been here, but you've never come, until today."

"Yeah, I know. I just didn't want to see you like this."

He nodded his head. "I understand. These jail visits aren't for everybody. I appreciate the cards and money, though. Thanks to you, Fiona, and Cowboy, I'm going to be a millionaire by the time I get out of here."

We shared a laugh.

He went on. "How is my grandbaby? She's as beautiful as you were at that age."

"Thank you, Max. Madison is, indeed, me in my former life, but she has a lot of her father in her as well." At my mention of Proof, I felt the tears building up in my eyes again. "I'm sorry. I can't help but cry every time I think of Jaylen and how I never would wish for my daughter to go through the same thing that I had to go through . . . losing a parent. And at her age. Telling her that her father was gone and wasn't coming back was the hardest thing I have ever had to do."

Maxwell grabbed my hands, which were on the table, and squeezed them. "It'll only get better with time, Mel. You got through it, right?"

I nodded my head, tears falling down my cheeks now.

"You gotta be strong for my grandbaby now," Maxwell told me. "If you falling apart, who will she have then? Just make sure she knows how much her daddy loved her, and that if circumstances were different, he would be here for her."

I thought about everything Max had just said. Although it was going to be hard, I knew what he'd said was nothing but the truth. "I will. . . ." Using one of my dress sleeves, I wiped my face dry. "So . . . tell me what you've been up to, old man."

For about an hour, Max and I just basically sat at our bench, shooting the shit. Reminiscing about old times and talking about any and everything we could think of. Topics ranged from our new president, who knew nothing about running a country, to what food places were still around or had closed down while he'd been gone. I was really enjoying our visit, and I realized I had really missed the bond that he and I used to have when I was younger.

Looking at Max, some would probably think that he was my real father if I was standing next to him. His skin wasn't as dark as mine, but it wasn't as light as Fiona's, either. Maybe a deep chestnut color. And the way his eyes twinkled when he laughed was something mine did whenever I laughed too. Whereas I had gray eyes, which I'd inherited from my granny, Max's were a warm brown mixed with specks of honey. Our eyelashes were similar, though. Long, thick, and curled at the end. And while my face was round like my mother's, his was more oblong, and he had a strong chin to match. However, our ears were strikingly similar: the tips were pointy, like an elf's. Max was a very handsome man, indeed, and even after all these years, I could see what had attracted my mother to him.

"Are you hungry, Mel? We don't have any Roscoe's or anything like that in here. But the food in that food machine over there is pretty good."

I looked over at the large vending machines, which had everything from bags of chips to prepackaged chicken wings that you warmed up in the microwave. As delectable as some of those snacks looked, I had to pass. After winning a bet Roman and I had on who would tap out first, I was rewarded with a big breakfast this morning, so I wasn't really that hungry. Thoughts of the fuck session we had had last night and early this

morning must've shown on my face, because
Max laughed when he noticed the dreamy look
in my eyes, and asked me what I was smiling
about.

"Nothing." I blushed. "Just thinking about . . .
some things."

"Must be the new man in your life."

"Something like that."

His face became serious. "Does he make you
happy?"

I thought about his question for a minute.
Since the day that I met Roman, I had always
felt this happiness whenever I was around him.
Without fully knowing who he really was, I had
always had a sense that he was a protector and
would do anything to make sure that the people
he loved were safe. He had been nothing but a
godsend since Kason was born. And then when
Proof died, I think I fell in love with him even
more. Many nights I had cried on his shoulder
for my baby's father and he had let me. He'd
exhibited no insecurities. Had just held me in his
arms until I stopped crying or fell asleep. He had
even cried with me when we both spoke about
our mothers and how their deaths affected us.
Roman was around the same age as Madison,
or maybe younger, when his mother passed, so
he knew exactly what she was going through

now. I, on the other hand, was a little older and had a better understanding of death when my mother passed, so while it hurt, I understood why. Everything about this man made me happy, so I told Max just that.

"You should bring him up here one day so that I can meet him. I'll add his name to the list. Him and the kids."

"Maybe . . . So what did you want to talk about, Max? In your letter you said that you needed to tell me something."

His face went blank, and his grin disappeared. The way his face changed had me feeling a little uncomfortable now. Whatever he needed to tell me must be serious.

"You know I met your mom when we were younger. Maybe in the third grade. She and I became the best of friends after she kicked some girl's ass for breaking my glasses." He smiled. "That was one of the best days of my life. I used to follow her around after that like I was her shadow. Developed a little crush on her and everything. It wasn't until we got to middle school that we actually tried to be boyfriend and girlfriend. Lasted all the way up until our junior year of high school. We were each other's first loves. I had the girl of my dreams at my side, but

I messed it all up when I fucked the chick who moved next door to me during that summer." He swallowed hard.

"Till this day, I don't know how your mother found out, but she did," he continued. "A mistake damn near cost me everything. We broke up, and she wouldn't talk to me for a long time. Me and April, the girl next door, started fucking around heavy during that time, and of course, she ended up getting pregnant. Shaunie was really mad when she found that out. I didn't regret having my son, but I did regret getting April pregnant. Somewhere down the line, your mom must've forgiven me, because after li'l Max was born, Shaunie and I started talking again. She even became friends with my baby mama. I would talk to your mama 'bout the shit April was doing out in the streets, and she would talk to me about whatever nigga she was fucking with at the time." He paused and took a deep breath.

"One night, things between us got a little heavy, and we ended up having sex," he admitted. "A few months later both April and Shaunie ended up pregnant. I always had a feeling that the baby April was pregnant with wasn't mine. But Shaunie . . . When I asked her if she was carrying my child, she denied it so bad.

Wouldn't tell me her due date or anything. One day I went to Ms. Regina's house to tell your mama that I wanted a DNA test done, but she was gone. According to your granny, she ran off with some dude and was never coming back. I was hurt. Tried looking for her but couldn't find her anywhere. A year and a half later, she shows up at my doorstep, with a beautiful little girl on her hip."

"Me?"

"Yeah, you. The minute I laid eyes on you, I knew you were mine. Even with those gray eyes and round face like your mother's, you still had some of my features."

My heart dropped, and my body started to shake. "Wait a minute, Max. I know you're not trying to tell me that you're my father, right?"

He lowered his chin to his chest and shook his head. "The crazy thing is, your mama knew that you were mine too. But she didn't want April to know, because they had become best friends."

I sat back on the bench, in disbelief. I mean, like I said, I knew that we had some similarities, but not enough to make me question whether he was my father or not. "So Fiona and I are sisters?"

He shook his head. "No."

"Wait. I'm confused. If I'm your daughter and she's your daughter, that means we're sisters."

"I told you I always felt that Fiona wasn't mine. The way April was moving back then, she and I barely had sex. She was always in the streets, getting money. Only thing she's ever loved more than herself." He blew out a breath and wiped his hand over his face. "I did a DNA test on the both of you. Yours came back positive, and Fiona's . . . Although she wasn't mine, her blood still had my family's DNA running through it."

"Your family's?"

"Yeah . . . family. I have a brother named Pedro, who only comes around when money is involved. Ruthless-ass muthafucka. Would kill his own mama if the price was right."

"So you're saying Fiona's dad is your brother? And you are my dad?"

Max just looked at me without saying anything, and we sat in an awkward silence for a minute. My emotions were flying all over the place, the strongest one being hurt. Hurt that my mother had never told me, despite all the years I had asked her, who my father was. Hurt that Maxwell had never said anything to me when he had the opportunity to do it. I could feel the tears forming in my eyes, but I was not about to let them fall. All this time I had thought I didn't have any parents left, when in fact I had one.

Maxwell reached out to touch my hand again, but I snatched it away. A remorseful look crossed his face, and I could tell that he regretted keeping this information from me for so long.

"Why now, Max?" I asked, my voice cracking, my tears at bay. "Why tell me this now?"

"Because . . . I needed you to know *that* backstory before I told you what I really called you up here for."

"What more is there for you to possibly tell me?"

His brow rose as he leaned forward on the bench, his fingers crossing in front of him. "You have no idea."

I drove like a bat out of hell from Corcoran, trying to make it back to L.A. in record time. The shit Maxwell had just told me had my blood boiling like crazy. And it wasn't the part about him being my father. That situation didn't have shit on what I had found out from Maxwell about that two-faced, jealous-ass, backstabbing bitch Fiona. All this time, I had thought that, that scum-bucket, bottom-feeding ho was my friend. Come to think of it, Aunt Bree had always tried to warn me about her, but I guessed when someone showed you only what they wanted you to see, you believed it. Best friends. When, in actuality, we were cousins. And to think that Cowboy, my own brother, had had more than just sisterly thoughts about me.

I pressed my foot down on the gas pedal and prayed that the highway patrol was already done with its quota for the day. I needed to get back to L.A. fast and take care of this bitch before she tried to bring any more harm my way. I tried calling Aunt Bree a few times, but her phone kept going to voice mail. And when I called Roman, Kason had just woken up and needed his diaper changed, so he told me that he would call me back. I thought about calling my granny and asking her about any of the things Max had said about being my father, but that was a conversation that she and I needed to have face-to-face. The only other person left with whom I could share my thoughts about this bitch Fiona was Viktoria. Hopefully, she wasn't in court and could pick up her shit. After pulling my phone out of the glove compartment, I dialed her number, and surprisingly, she picked up on the first ring.

"Hello."

"Hey, Vik. Sorry to be calling you like this, but are you busy?"

"Hey, Mel. I'm not too busy. Just looking over some case files and listening to Marques ramble on about something." She paused for a moment. "Are you okay? You sound like you're crying."

I looked in the rearview mirror at my red eyes and noticed the tears, which I hadn't even realized were falling down my face. "No, I'm not," I lied.

"Where are you? Do you need me to call Roman?"

"I'm on the freeway right now, headed back to L.A."

"From where?"

"Corcoran State Prison."

"What were you doing there?"

After blowing out a breath and licking my lips, I ran down everything that Maxwell had told me about Fiona, Cowboy, April, my mom, and some chick name Julia, whom my mom had met during that short time she skipped town while pregnant with me. According to Maxwell, while my mother was living up north, she met this Julia chick, who introduced her to scamming men for money. When my mother came back to town, she and Julia basically picked up where they had left off with their little jack girl schemes. It wasn't until they added April to the equation that they started killing men for larger amounts of money. For a while, they were doing good, until Maxwell and Mom started messing around again. When April found out, she disappeared, leaving Fiona and Cowboy with Maxwell, and Julia went off on her own.

The kicker to that whole story was that Fiona blamed me for everything. She blamed me for losing her father, for April walking out on her and Cowboy, for being homeless and broke, and for robbing her of her childhood. The funny thing was, we had been in the same boat. My granny hadn't been making any type of money to really take care of me, and with Bree away at college, Granny had basically robbed Peter to pay Paul in order to care for me, so it wasn't like my life was any better than Fiona's. And there had been many nights when I would let Fiona sleep at the other end of my twin-size bed, such as when she and Cowboy ran out of money to stay at a motel. And there had been times when I gave her my lunches at school, just so that she could fill her belly with something.

She and I had both lost a lot on the day that my mother died, but I hadn't blamed anyone for shit. Then I'd found out that she was behind the attack that had put me in the hospital. That she was the one who had set the whole thing up, just to get more money out of Roman. That bitch's time was up. Fuck loyalty, fuck friendship, fuck any type of love I had ever had in my heart for her. Fiona was dead to me now, and I had a bullet with her muthafucking name on it.

Viktoria blew out a breath. "Damn, Mel. I think you should call Roman before you do anything else. My cousin may be a businessman, but he's with the business, if you get what I'm saying."

"Girl, Roman wouldn't hurt a fly. That's what I love so much about him. Totally different from the men I used to date."

"You keep telling yourself that. I know my cousin, though, so you should just give him a call. Run it by him and then go from there."

After we hung up, I thought about what she had said, but this was some shit I needed to handle on my own. Fiona had the game fucked up if she thought shit was about to go down like this. Checking the clip of my Beretta 84 with the black-lace handle, a gift Proof had given me for my birthday a few years ago, I thought to myself that Fiona just didn't know who she was messing with. Her life was ending today, and anybody else who was in on this shit . . . I had a hot one for them too.

Fiona

Someone had been knocking on my front door for the past ten minutes, adding to the massive headache I had. I was hoping that whoever it was would eventually get the picture that I didn't want to be bothered and would leave me the fuck alone. So much shit had me stressing the hell out, and I didn't know where to start in terms of alleviating some of it. My mother was starting to become a real pain in my ass, making me regret ever wishing that she and I would reconnect one day. The shit with Melonee wasn't going as planned, but I was sure I'd be seeing her sooner than later.

Bree's ass was already dead in my book, and then Benji wasn't returning any of my calls or texts. I'd gone by the monstrosity he called his bachelor's pad after I came from the hospital, but he and that bitch Carmen had left for some kind of vacation, according to his housekeepers.

I had tried calling his phone a few more times after that and had kept getting sent to voice mail on the first ring. When I'd asked April if she had heard anything from Julia since the last time we met, she told me her results were the same as mine: no answer when she called Julia's phone. Something in the pit of my stomach was telling me that something was going on, but with my lust for money, I just wouldn't leave well enough alone.

I eased my sore body down into the bubbly water in my deluxe spa tub and was instantly relieved of the pain radiating through me. After laying my head back against the tiled wall, I closed my eyes and slowly sank deeper into the hot water. It had been a few days since the fight I had with Bree, and I was still feeling the effects of it. The splint I had to get for my two fractured fingers had taken a little getting used to, but I was handling it well. The doctor had said I had to wear it only for a few weeks, and then I'd be back to normal. The bruised skin on my arms, legs, back, and sides was healing much slower than I would have liked, but at least I could cover up the black eye I had with a much-heavier coat of foundation. I shook my head and smiled when the lyrics of Nipsey Hussle's song "Bullets Ain't Got No Name" started playing in my head.

Pull the trigger, shoot that nigga. Make sure that you get him, 'cause bullets ain't got no name.

The funny thing was, the bullet I had for Bree most definitely had her name on it and would be planted right between those pretty little hazel eyes of hers. Thinking about that song had my mind drifting to Proof for a second. I rubbed my hand over the small bulge in my belly, wondering how he would feel about my pregnancy if he were still alive. With the way Bree had stomped on my sides and my stomach, I had thought I would miscarry, but I didn't. The doctor had run a few tests while I was at the hospital, and it had turned out that the baby wasn't harmed.

In any normal situation, the expectant mother would've been overjoyed to receive such news, but with me, it had been a different story. When the nurse had tried to hand me the sonogram, after making sure everything was okay, I'd refused to take it. There was no need to look at a picture of a baby I wasn't going to keep. Having a child right now would slow me down tremendously, and quite frankly, I didn't think that being a mother was in the cards for me. With April as my example of what a mother should be, it was pretty safe to say that this baby was better off being sucked out and disposed of than being born to me.

I guessed with so much shit on my mind, combined with the soothing hot water and the couple of pain pills that I'd taken, I must've dozed off, totally forgetting about the insistent knocking at my front door. When I awoke and picked up my phone to look at the time, two hours had passed by, the water in the tub had turned cold, and my body had started to ache again. I positioned myself to get out of the tub but stopped when I felt a presence in my bathroom. When I pulled the shower curtain back, I wasn't surprised to see my uncle Dro sitting on my toilet, skimming through the latest copy of *Blackhair* magazine, which I had picked up from the store earlier. A toothpick was hanging from his mouth, and he was dressed in all black, like he normally was. The smell of whatever cigarette brand he smoked hovered in the air, making my stomach queasy. The nigga smelled just like an ashtray, the same way Cowboy's house had smelled when I last went over there.

He twirled his toothpick around in his mouth a few times before he laid the magazine down on the sink and turned his attention to me. Voice low and raspy, he said, "Your boy hasn't coughed up that additional fifty K I asked for. Where's my money?"

I rolled my eyes and remained in the cold water and tried to cover my body up as much as I could with the shower curtain. The lust in Uncle Dro's eyes was very apparent as he gazed at my feet, legs, and thighs, which were still exposed. "I don't know. I'll make sure to ask him about it whenever he answers one of my calls. Seems like you're not the only one he's been dodging."

"What does him dodging your calls got to do with my money? I told you that I wasn't playing about that shit the last time I was here, Fiona." He licked his lips and trained his eyes on my breasts, which were covered by my arms and a bit of the shower curtain. He squinted his eyes a little as he tried to get a glimpse of my bare breasts. "If you can't get my paper right now, I'm more than willing to take other forms of payment until you can."

"Nigga, are you serious? *Other forms of payment?* Like what?"

He pursed his lips and raised his eyebrows, as if to say, "You know what I'm talking about."

When it finally registered with me what he was actually hinting at, my anger level went up ten more notches. Was this bum-ass leech really propositioning me for sex as a form of payment? *The fuck?*

"Nigga, I'm your fucking niece."

"Whose pussy is just like any other bitch's in this world. You bleed once a month and give it up to any nigga who pays you any attention." He looked down at my belly. "And from the looks of things, you fucked around and let one of these bitch-ass muthafuckas nut in you. But I'm cool with that. Pregnant pussy is better, anyway."

I shook my head in disgust. This muthafucka really had me and life fucked up if he thought I was so desperate that I'd let him fuck me just to pay off a debt. My father's warning not to reach out to my uncle after I'd asked him for my uncle's phone number started playing in my head. That was one of the times I should've listened but hadn't.

"Dro, you need to get the fuck up out of my house with that bullshit, or else."

He smirked, an evil glint in his eyes. "Or else what?"

"Or ... or ... else ..." I fumbled with my words. "I'ma call the police." The second those words slipped from my lips, I knew that Uncle Dro didn't believe me by the smile that formed on his face. I couldn't threaten to kill him, because the gun I had hidden in my bathroom was underneath the sink, which he was sitting right next to. If I went to reach for my piece, he would most definitely see what I was going for.

"Call 'em," he taunted, voice low and threatening. Leaning over the tub, Dro snatched the shower curtain from my grasp and then wrapped his hand around my throat. "By the time they get here, I'll be gone. But not before doing you the same way me and that dumb-ass brother of yours did your friend."

"My brother? What the fuck are you talking about?"

Uncle Dro's grip tightened around my neck, and my hands automatically flew up, causing my breasts to fall from behind my arms. A low moan seeped from his lips as he watched my titties jiggle freely while my hands struggled to loosen his grip.

"Who do you think I took with me that night to do the job? How do you think I got in and out undetected? Past the security system and surveillance cameras? Who do you think raped your friend and got a piece of some of the sweetest pussy he ever had, according to him? I always thought the nigga was gay, but I was wrong." My uncle Dro laughed. "The boy is backward as fuck. He couldn't stand to watch me beat the fuck out of her, so he left out of the room, but he didn't have a problem sticking his dick in her bloody and bruised body. How ironic is that shit?"

Was that why Cowboy thought Mel's baby was his? So he was the other person Uncle Dro had taken with him that night. But why hadn't he told me? When I had told him about the plan to set Roman up, Cowboy had been with it, until I told him that Melonee was a part of it too. The nigga had actually nutted up on me and had threatened to fuck my whole life over if I went ahead with it. Nah, Dro's ass was lying.

"I don't believe you," I managed to say through gasps. "My brother thinks the world of that bitch. Even though he knows how I feel about her."

"Well, you don't have to believe me, and I don't give a shit about what he thinks. Especially when his thinking can't make my fifty K appear. Now, either give up some of that pussy, which I know is as good as your mama's, since the apple doesn't fall too far from the tree, or start asking God to forgive you for all the sins you've committed over the years. Only way he might let you into heaven, if you think about it."

Letting my uncle fuck me was not and would never be an option. And to just sit here and let him kill me wasn't going to work, either. Thinking quickly on my feet, I grabbed the Dove body wash I used and squirted it in his eyes. When he fell back, I jumped out of the tub and hopped over him, falling right on my ass in the process. I tried to get up but slipped again because of the wet tile floor, this time catching myself on the toilet.

"Bitch!" Uncle Dro yelled, wiping his eyes with the sleeve of his shirt. "I was giving you the chance to pay off some of your debt, but now I'ma take that pussy, and I want my money before the night is over."

Making sure I stepped on the bathroom rug this time when I got up, I was able to get a head start toward my kitchen, where I planned to grab the gun I knew was in the refrigerator. I had just reached for the handle of the fridge to open it when the hair on the back of my head was pulled with so much force that I felt my head hit the floor before the rest of my body. I was seeing stars, moons, and horseshoes when I tried to open my eyes, to no avail. The moisture I could feel slowly spreading beneath the back of my head had to be blood, but I was too dazed to reach back there with my hand and see. Uncle Dro's heavy body sliding on top of me was the only thing I could feel, and when I tried to push him off me, I was rewarded with a blow to my face.

God must've been looking out for me, though, because before Uncle Dro could even unzip his pants, there was a loud knock at my front door.

"Fiona!" Melonee yelled. "I know your bitch ass is in there. Come open the fucking door. You think Aunt Bree beat your ass the other day . . . ? Bitch, you already know I have hands, and I owe you this for all the bullshit you've been doing."

"Oh, Mel . . ." I slowly shook my head from side to side, trying to stop the constant ringing in my ears. "Melonee . . . help," I called out, not sure if she could hear me or not.

"Fiona, you got ten seconds to open this muthafucking door, or I'ma kick it down," she said, banging on the door again.

Uncle Dro, who had gotten up from on top of me and was now standing behind the front door, pulled his gun from his waist and waited for Melonee to make good on her threat. I tried to stand but was able only to lift myself up on my elbows. While I remained in that position, trying to at least get the strength to make it to my knees, the door came crashing in, slamming Uncle Dro right in the face. Blood instantly began to pour from his nose, but when Melonee walked through doorway and entered my home, he had his piece cocked and aimed at her head.

She spotted him instantly and then saw me lying in the kitchen doorway. "Whoever you are, I don't want any problems with you. I just came here for that bitch right there," she said through gritted teeth, eyes now trained on me. "Right about now, I don't give a fuck if you kill me after all this shit is said and done, just as long as I get to kill that bitch first."

Uncle Dro picked up one of my scarves that were lying across the top of my couch and put it up to his nose to try to stop the bleeding. The whole center of his face was covered in blood and was swelling up by the minute. He looked at me and then back at Melonee. "If I let you kill this bitch, I won't get my money. So either you pay her debt and I let you handle your business or you sit back and watch the show I was just about to put on. I'm sure it'll bring back a few fucked-up memories for you, but you shouldn't feel sorry for this bitch." Uncle Dro laughed and pointed the gun at me. "Seeing as she's the one who is responsible for everything that happened to you."

I looked up at Melonee to see the reaction on her face to the news Dro had just spilled, but surprisingly, she didn't have one. Her eyes were still focused on me, but the look in them told me that she already knew. Hence the reason for her visit, I assumed. But how did she find out? I was pretty sure Cowboy didn't tell her, and April . . . Well, that would just fuck up her whole kidnapping plan. Walking farther into my home, Melonee still had her eyes on me, obviously not caring about the gun Uncle Dro was still pointing at her head.

"Why?" she asked, a little emotion showing when her voice cracked. "Why would you do that to me, Fiona? I thought we were best friends."

I rose up onto my knees and slowly crawled over to my couch. Only thing on my mind was getting to one of my guns before the opportunity to kill this bitch passed me by. Just like her, I was willing to endure whatever Uncle Dro had in store for me, just as long as I was able to kill her ass.

After clearing my throat, I answered her question. "Because I've always hated how you stole my childhood away from me and didn't even apologize for it. You and your whore-ass mama played a part in one of the worst days of my life."

Her eye twitched. "You're going to stop disrespecting my mother, and I'm not gonna tell you again."

"Melonee . . ." I said and laughed as I pushed my hands beneath the soft cushions of my couch, feeling for my gun. When I didn't feel it, my eyes went directly to Uncle Dro, who winked and blew a kiss at me. The grimy muthafucka had already taken it. Hopefully, he hadn't found the one I kept taped to the underside of the coffee table. All I needed to do was distract Melonee's ass somehow and then get my shot off. The bitch would never see it coming. And I knew April's ass would be mad, but I didn't give a fuck. There was always Roman to send the ransom note to. "Whore, ho, slut. I don't see why you get so uptight when I call your mother by her rightful name. Anyone who deliberately fucks another woman's man and messes up their happy home is a slut by my books."

"Funny you feel that way when it was your mama who fucked her man's brother and got pregnant with you," Melonee countered.

My eyes went big as they flew over to Uncle Dro. The same shocked look was on his face that was on mine. Ain't no way in the world Pedro was my father. I didn't look shit like him. I looked like my father. Nose, ears, and all. The bitch had to be lying to get some type of reaction out of me, but I wasn't going to give her one.

"Stop lying to justify the actions of the tramp who gave birth you."

Melonee smirked and walked closer to me. "Well, seems to me like you need to take a visit to Corcoran and see your *uncle* Max. This little story you've been telling yourself all these years about me robbing you of your childhood is nowhere near the truth. As a matter of fact, you might want to speak to your mama and direct your anger toward her. Because, if I remember correctly the story Max told me, it was your mama who left, because she was out there running the streets and was more worried about money and dick than she was about taking care of you and Cowboy. It was your hating-ass mama who couldn't stand the fact that Max's heart belonged to my mom and would never be hers." She took a deep breath.

"They had a nice little setup going on. Robbing men and taking their money. Just like us, but on a smaller scale," she continued. "Your mother's jealousy is what tore their whole little crew apart. Just like what your jealousy did to the clique. Why don't you just admit it, Fiona? You are jealous of me. Always have been and always will be. The funny thing is, you never had to be. Everything that you went through, I went through. Not because I had to, but because I didn't want you to feel alone. Because I was your best friend. I lost my mother that day too. Did you ever once stop to think how I felt? I didn't even get a chance to mourn properly for her, because I was too busy making sure that you and Cowboy had a roof over y'all head after he fucked off all that money, that you had food in your belly when you sometimes didn't eat but once a day, and a shoulder to cry on whenever you wanted to know why your trifling-ass mama didn't love you enough to stay."

She now had tears in her eyes, but I wasn't fazed by that shit or any of this bullshit she was spitting. We would see how many of those same tears came pouring down her face when I hit her with a little secret I had found out myself. I felt under the table for my gun and jumped for joy when my hand hit the barrel. I knew once I said what I was about to say, the opportunity I'd been waiting for was going to present itself. Regardless of who my father really was, this bitch still had to die.

"Mel, I've never been jealous of you, and to prove that I'm not, I'm going to let you in on a little secret. It wasn't Dezmond who killed your mother that night. It was my mother. The same bitch who killed the father of our babies." Since I was already naked, I rose up to show her my little belly. "Sucks that he won't be here to see our kids grow up to be siblings, but his loyalty to you was a problem for us." I shrugged my shoulders. "Sorry . . . but not sorry."

The chain of events happened so fast that I didn't even have time to react. The way Melonee leapt across the couch and landed on top of me completely caught me off guard.

The gun she had tucked behind her back was at my head at the same time I pulled my gun from under the table and aimed it at hers. With murder on both of our minds and revenge in our hearts, we both pulled our triggers at the same time. The loud ringing of multiple gunshots going off echoed throughout my apartment. The smell of gun smoke filled the air.

Everything around me went black, and when I tried to open my eyes, I couldn't. My heart started beating at a slower pace, and I could feel my bladder releasing itself one last time. The only thing I remembered hearing before my final breath was Melonee wishing me a long, slow, and painful death in hell. The Black Widow Clique had been my life, and I had enjoyed all the money I made with the clique. But I guessed my web of lies, deception, and disloyalty had finally caught up with me, leaving everything I had hustled so hard for sitting in a safe underneath my bed.

Did I regret anything I'd done? No. Would I do it all over again? In a heartbeat. Except this time, I would make sure all my paper came right along with me.

Epilogue

Roman

One year later . . .

It was crazy how much my life had changed in the course of two years. Nothing could have prepared me for any of the shit I had gone through, but I would be lying if I said that if given the chance, I wouldn't do it all over again: from the night Benji and Marques talked me into taking those Japanese investors to Decadence for a round of celebratory drinks to a couple of days ago, when I asked Melonee to be my wife. I was, indeed, a happy man, despite all the bullshit my stepmother, Julia, and her son, Benji, had put me through. And with the love of a strong woman, and with a real family having my back, I was ready to take on the world and spend the rest of my days making my life and the people I held dear to my heart my number one priority.

As I watched Melonee play on the beach with our children, Madison and Kason, and as I contemplated the new life she was carrying, my heart was filled with a warmth I hadn't felt since my mother passed. It was with every beat of my heart that I would live for them, and I would do all I could for them, even die for them if it meant they would live.

There had been many nights in my life that had scared me, but all of those paled in comparison to the night Melonee tried to confront that bitch Fiona on her own and almost lost her life for a second time. Had it not been for the security detail my uncle Kazi had following her, I'd probably be raising Madison and Kason on my own.

When Peter and Yurik had called my uncle to inform him about Melonee's whereabouts and about the screaming match she was involved in, which could be heard from the street, I left the kids with Viktoria and made it to Ladera Heights in about ten minutes. I'd wanted to run in with guns blazing, but Uncle Kazi had thought it wise to hold off until we got an official head count of everybody in the apartment. Once the number, three, was confirmed, I walked through the

busted door just in time to see Mel and Fiona
pointing their guns at each other and some man
I'd never seen before walking up behind my
baby with his pistol aimed at her. The first bullet
from my gun went through his neck and out his
mouth. The second one went straight through
his heart.

When Mel slipped up for a second and turned
her head to see who else was in the house, shooting, that slick bitch Fiona tried to pull her trigger
but couldn't, as her gun had jammed. The look
on her face would have been funny had Mel not
blown her brains out a few seconds later . . . with
no remorse whatsoever. But I could tell that,
that was all a front, especially when Mel began
crying the minute we got home and cried in my
arms all night long.

As I watched her and the kids continue to
make castles in the sand, I made a promise
to always be there for her in any way that she
needed. Mel was the love of my life, even if we
did meet in the most unconventional way. We
were two people from two separate worlds but
with the same pain from suffering a loss. Losing
our parents might be what bonded our hearts,
but our love for each other was what connected
our souls.

Melonee

I blushed and could feel my cheeks heat up when I saw the look on Roman's handsome face as he watched me and our children play on the beach. It was Madison's seventh birthday, and she wanted to have a fun day in the sun with us and the rest of our family. Everyone whom we held close to our hearts was here to celebrate my baby turning a year older.

Viktoria and Marques, who had dubbed themselves the munchkins' godparents, were somewhere in the house, fucking like rabbits, trying to make the first of their tribe of kids. Granny was lounging in her beach chair, soaking up the sun and chatting with some man whom she had bumped into at the grocery store earlier. And Aunt Bree wasn't here yet, but Chasin was on his way to the airport to pick her up. Their long-distance relationship seemed to be working for right now, but I knew it was only a matter of time before Chasin made Aunt Bree move back out to California permanently. Yeah, they were racking up a gang of frequent flyer miles between the two of them, but there was nothing like waking up to your man or your woman every day and being able to spend time with him or her at the drop of a dime.

When the hairs on the back of my neck began to rise, when my palms started to sweat, and when my stomach did that fluttery thing it always did whenever Roman was around, I knew that he was behind me. His arms slid around my waist, and his hands palmed the roundness of my full belly. I was in my ninth month and couldn't wait to meet the newest addition to our family. When I first found out that I was pregnant again, I was a little worried about whether or not I'd carry this baby to full term. Although Kason hadn't suffered any major complications from being born at twenty-nine weeks, I wasn't too sure if this baby would thrive if he or she was born prematurely. All those worries were thrown out the window, though, once Roman got me to confess how thrilled I was to be carrying this baby. I swear, I hadn't smiled so much in my life.

Roman was making sure that his every waking minute was geared toward catering to me and making my life as stress free as possible.

Roman had even cut back on his hours at RTD. After Benji's body was found in Mexico, with his head nearly severed, Roman's father had reappointed Roman CEO of the company. With the negative press and legal charges now behind him, the moral clause that had got him fired was the same one that got Roman rehired. Especially after Papa Black had it removed from the new contract Roman had to sign.

And speaking of Papa Black, he was doing pretty good nowadays. He and Uncle Kazi's goddaughter Carmen had become real close in the past few months. Whenever she wasn't out of town, doing some work for Roman's fine-ass uncle, she was here at the Summerland house, working out with Papa Black and keeping him heart attack free.

When Roman's soft lips touched my neck and then my shoulder, a low moan escaped my lips. The tingly feeling that had started at the bottom of my feet easily traveled to my core and exploded. This man, with his dreamy green eyes, tanned olive skin, caramel-blond hair, and beautiful soul, was my everything. There wasn't anything about him that I didn't love or find interesting.

For instance, I liked the fact that he had exceptional marksmanship skills, courtesy of

that sexy-ass Uncle Kazi. While Viktoria and
Marques had been sneaking around during their
summer visits to Russia, Roman had sometimes
been found in the underground bunker his uncle
had, learning how to shoot. When I asked him if
he had killed anyone other than Fiona's bitch-
ass father, Dro, he had simply kissed me on my
forehead and had never answered the question.
And then, when I asked him about those four
days he and a few of Kazi's men had spent on a
crazy manhunt for April and her crew—whose
dead bodies turned up on the six o'clock news
the following week—mum was the word again.

My little CEO thug was all mine, and I'd kill
any bitch who tried to get in between us. Well,
after I had this baby, of course.

Kazimir

I sat beside the pool at the luxury resort in Turks and Caicos, watching the insanely beautiful woman I couldn't take my eyes off down her fifth dry martini. The small bikini she had on left very little to the imagination, as it showed off her newly bought breasts and ass. She wore one of those big floppy hats on her head, which covered half her face, and the view of her pink, pouty lips had my dick hard as fuck. When she looked up at me, our eyes connected for a brief second, before she turned her gaze away. I laughed at her failed attempt to play coy, but if this mouse-and-cat game was what I had to play to get her to my room, then so be it.

Tired of basking in the sun, I pulled my tank top over my head and dived into the coolness of the water. Holding my breath, I swam to the other end of the Olympic-sized pool, came back, and then stopped in front of the person whose attention I'd been trying to get for the past hour.

"You've been watching me since you took your seat over there. Do you know me from somewhere? Have we met before?" she asked.

I shook my head no.

"Are you sure?" she said.

She got the same answer from me.

"You're not much of a talker, though. I can tell," she noted.

"I talk when there's a need to."

She licked her lips and sat up in her seat, pushing her chest out a little more. "Your accent, it's very sexy. Where are you from?"

"The United States."

She slid her shades down her nose to the tip and smiled. "Not with bone structure like yours. What does that say on your chest?"

I looked down at my tattoo that read NO HONOR AMONG THIEVES in Russian. "It means you only live once."

Her smile widened. "Indeed you do. You come to vacation with family . . . friends . . . a wife . . . or girlfriend?"

"I'm vacationing alone. What about you?"

"The same."

"Would you like another drink, ma'am?" a young waitress asked, interrupting our conversation while her lust-filled eyes stayed on me.

The beautiful woman's lips tightened. "I'm not old enough to be a ma'am, suga. Remember that when it's time for your tip. And I'll take another dry martini, extra olives please. What about you, handsome?"

"I'll take two Coronas and the bill for what she's drinking from here on out," I told the waitress.

Needless to say, once the drinks started flowing, so did the chemistry between us. By the time the sun had gone down, she was way past drunk and more than willing to come up to my room.

The minute I closed the door to my room and dimmed the lights, we were on each other and ripping off the few clothes that we had on. After bending her over the couch, I drove right into her pussy and started to fuck the lining out of her. No gentleness, no names or lovemaking involved. Just straight fucking, without the slightest interruption. It wasn't the grade A shit I was used to, but it helped me get this nut off. By the time I finished flipping her around in every possible position I could think of, it was time to get to the real reason I had brought her up here.

"Julia, you've been a naughty, naughty girl."

Her body froze at the mention of her name. "My . . . my . . . name isn't Julia. It's . . . it's Daphne," she stuttered, pulling away from me.

The terrified look on her face almost made me laugh.

"We both know that, that isn't true. You've been hard to find after changing the way you look a couple of times, but I finally found you."

"Who are you? Wh-what . . . what do you want? If it's money you need, I can give you double or . . . or . . . or triple. Name your price, and you got it. I can call my son. . . ."

I raised an eyebrow. "Your son who's already dead?"

Her face dropped. "I meant to say my husband. Richard Black. Legally, we're still married, and I know he'd be willing to give me whatever amount you want. Just tell me a price."

I removed my gun from my bag that was next to the bed and screwed the silencer on. Her pleading became a bit more garbled as she started to talk and cry at the same time. I lifted my gun, aimed it right at her head, and then pressed it to her temple.

"Fucking you was never supposed to be a part of the plan, but I couldn't resist, with this new look of yours. It's no wonder Richard was cheating on you behind your back for all these years with those little waitresses down at Decadence. The pussy wasn't that great, and you don't know how to fuck."

Before she could say anything else, I pulled the trigger and shot her in the head. After making sure every trace of my having been here was gone, I walked out of the room. Then I pulled out my cell phone, dialed a number, and waited for an answer.

"Hello."

"It's done."

"Your money will be transferred to your account by the morning."

"No need. This one is on me."

The line became quiet. Then he said, "Thank you, Kazimir."

I nodded as if he could see my face.

"Will you be back in town for the baby shower?" he asked.

"I might be. If I can't make it, tell my nephew that I will see him when he brings the family to Russia for summer vacation."

"Will do."

I started to hang up the phone, but then I remembered I needed to relay a message. "Carmen will be back in a couple of days. She wanted me to tell you to have the coconut oil ready."

His rich laughter echoed through the phone.

"Should I even ask?" I said.

"Not unless you want to hear some things about your goddaughter that—"

"Enough," I said, cutting him off. "I'll see you soon."

"Will do. And, Kazimir . . ."

"I already know. I love my nephew and will do anything to make sure that my sister's son is happy too. I gotta go, though. Take care, Richard, and as always, nice doing business with you."

After hanging up the phone, I made my way to the car that I was driving and hopped in. My next target was some kid named Maxwell, who went by the nickname Cowboy. Another thread in that web of deceit that Melonee and her friends had built. He was a little hard to find after he disappeared from the place where he'd been staying. And because his information kept changing, my tracker had been having a hard time pinpointing his exact location. However, there was always a way to find someone who didn't want to be found: you just needed the right type of bait to catch them. Too bad for him, the kind of bait that I had cast out was already leading me in his direction.

All right, readers . . . I know this one took a minute, but I hope you enjoyed this little installment with Melonee and the crew. If not, I promise to do better with my next release. As always, I want to thank you for your continued support. You just don't know how much I appreciate each and every one of you. Now, there are a lot of you I want to give a shout-out to. However, I don't want to forget anyone's name. So just

(Insert Your Name Here)

Thank you for your e-mails, Facebook messages and, in some cases, phone calls.

I appreciate and adore each and every one of you!

Up next for me . . . I have a couple of stand-alones in the works.

The Wright Kind of Love: Toby & Niecey, which is a spinoff of my Black Love, White Lies series, is now available on Kindle.

Love, Lies, and Consequences 2, with my guy Blake Karrington, is in the works and should be out at the end of April 2018 (Keep those fingers crossed.)

And a couple of new characters that I'm working on will be introduced to you guys later on in the year, as will the last book I'm doing for ***The DuPont Sisters*** series.

Bear with me. You all know I try to drop a book as soon as I can.

For those of you who are new to Genesis Woods or have been with me awhile and would like to keep in contact, you can reach me via the following:

www.genesiswoods.com
www.facebook.com/thebeginning616
IG: @iamgenesiswoods
Twitter: thebeginning616
E-mail: thebeginning616@gmail.com

Again, THANK YOU for the continued support, and THANK YOU for rocking with your girl.
~Gen